ARCADIA

MARK LAGES

authorHOUSE®

AuthorHouse™
1663 Liberty Drive
Bloomington, IN 47403
www.authorhouse.com
Phone: 1 (800) 839-8640

Published by AuthorHouse 10/02/2019

ISBN: 978-1-7283-3022-8 (sc)
ISBN: 978-1-7283-3021-1 (e)

Library of Congress Control Number: 2019915461

Print information available on the last page.

This book is printed on acid-free paper.

Although commonly thought of as being in line with Utopian ideals, Arcadia differs from that tradition in that it is more often specifically regarded as unattainable.

CHAPTER 1

GOODBYE

———————— •◦• ————————

I knew right away that we had a problem on our hands—a very big problem. My heart was beating a million miles a minute, and I was— well, what the hell was I? I was terrified! It was all in the poem.

I look back now, and it all seems like such a long, long time ago. It's fair to say I knew as much about poetry back then as I knew about trigonometry, and just so you understand, I barely passed my trigonometry class in high school. The two times half the cosign of this equaled the square root of the cosign of that, or whatever—I had no idea what the fuck they were talking about. I would have no use for any of it as an adult, and I just didn't care. Please, please, just give me a passing grade in the class, right? I just wanted to move on with my life and get my high school diploma at the end of my senior year. And I felt the same way about poetry as I did about trigonometry. I never did get it. I never got why some poets were considered geniuses and why others were considered poor or average. To me, poems were just poems, and poets were just poets. Roses are red, and violets are blue. Or shouldn't violets be violet? I don't know what color violets actually are, since I don't recall ever having seen one in the petal-flesh, but if they're called violets, I would think they'd be violet and not blue.

No, I don't know much about poetry, but I'm not stupid either. I have a high IQ, and while I'll often feign a likeable degree of ignorance, I do understand most things that come my way. So I can read a poem and get its general meaning even though I'm not connecting with the mood. I might have to read it three or four times, but I will eventually figure out what the poet is trying to say. And I understood my youngest son's many poems—most of them, anyway. There were an awful lot of them to read and decipher. Christ, Jacob churned out poetry like the Hershey's chocolate company churns out foil-wrapped Kisses. Do you know how

1

many Kisses they churn out each year? Look it up on the internet when you have a free moment. It'll probably surprise you.

I just happened to be in Jacob's bedroom. I was looking for him. It was a Saturday, and I had asked him in the morning to mow the lawn. But it was now four o'clock in the afternoon, and he hadn't even taken the lawnmower out of the garage. This was unlike Jacob. I mean, he was an odd kid, and he lived to the clicks of an eccentric metronome to be sure. But he almost always did his chores, and he didn't argue about doing them. He just did them without a fuss. This is not to say he never argued about anything. Heck, we argued about all kinds of things—just not the chores. For some reason, he had no problem accepting the idea that he should pull his weight. All you had to do was ask for his help, and the next thing you know he'd be at it, quietly, pensively going about the business of doing his share of the work.

We had second son who was a year older than Jacob. We named this kid Zachary, and the two boys were as different as night and day. It wasn't a Cain and Abel thing, or a Steinbeck *East of Eden* storyline. No, not at all. I would never say one boy was especially bad and the other good; it was just that they were so different, as if they'd come from two different sets of parents. Although this story is really about Jacob, I'll begin by telling you about Zach, the honor roll student, the hockey player, and the boy who never met a girl or a high school party he didn't like.

Zach was a blonde, and he was as tall and handsome as they come. Seriously, the kid had a smile that would make you want to drop everything to be his friend. There are all kinds of smiles in the world, and I've often wondered—does a smile express one's inner self, or is it just a function of flesh, muscle, teeth, and bone? In other words, does the smile make the person, or does the person make the smile? Do good people have nice smiles because they're good, or is it just the luck of the draw? And does a nice smile *make* you good? You know, I had a friend in high school named Thomas Bake. He had the strangest smile, like that of a horse baring its teeth. I mean, it was really disconcerting. But he was a great kid, and we always got along well. But that was because I knew him. Other kids were wary of Thomas, and others (especially girls) didn't exactly go out of their way to befriend him, probably because of his queer smile. I lost track of Thomas after high school, but I've wondered what happened to him. Did his smile finally catch up to his personality and make him a stupid and bitter adult? What kind of girl did he finally marry, if he married at all? And what kind of girl would marry a man who smiled like a horse? Would it be a girl who also smiled like an animal? Or a cross-eyed girl? Or a girl with hairy arms? Or maybe I'm way off base here, and maybe Thomas is doing just fine, disconcerting smile and all.

It has always been my feeling that Zach's smile would take him far in life. He seemed like one of those kids who would grow up to succeed. He would do well in high school. He would go to a good college and excel in every class. He would marry a terrific girl, have a wonderful family, and get a good job and be a fantastic parent. Of course, my version of a person succeeding has changed. But I'll get to that. We all live and learn. We open our eyes. Or maybe I should say our eyes are opened for us.

This brings me to Jacob. As I said, Jacob performed to the clicks of an eccentric metronome. He was different from other kids his age, and one of those differences was his love of poetry. How many of the young boys you know love reading and writing poetry? I mean, that's kind of a girl thing, isn't it? Girls read and write poems, while boys play sports and ride bikes and look under rocks for disgusting little snakes and creepy, crawly six-legged creatures. But as far back as I can remember, Jacob wrote his poems, and I saved nearly every darn poem he wrote. Sometimes he would give the poems to April and me, asking us what we thought. By the way, April is my wife. Often Jacob would crumple his poems up after writing them and toss them in his wastebasket. I saved the poems he gave us as well as the ones he tossed. I saved all of them in a cardboard box which I kept in my study closet. They were the windows into my son's heart and soul, and I couldn't fathom throwing them away, even if I didn't understand half of them, and even if many rubbed me the wrong way.

I guess I should give you a physical description of Jacob before I proceed any further. He was not a blonde like his brother; instead, he took after me. He had thick brown hair, and his skin was semidark like mine. He had almond-shaped brown eyes; a small, innocuous nose; and a smile that tried to be like his brother's. It was a nice smile, but nothing to write home about. It was nothing near as compelling as his brother's. But Jacob was a good-looking kid. He wasn't a great-looking boy, but *good*-looking. He wrote a little poem titled "Mirror, Mirror" about his appearance when he was twelve years old that I rescued from his wastebasket, and I think it makes for an interested read. It not only tells you a little about what he looked like but, more importantly, how he felt about his looks. Here's the poem he wrote:

Mirror, Mirror

That's me in the bathroom mirror,
My hair all wet from the shower.
I want to grow my hair out long,
But Dad says I have it all wrong.

So right now, my hair is cut neat
Like I am on my way to meet
With the boss at Dad's company
To interview me and then see

If I'll have what it takes to sum
Figures and factors and to come
Home each night to the TV news
And take off my jacket and shoes.

Oh, face of mine, what do I see
In your future but just to be
Like every other robot man,
Almond eyes, small nose, and a tan,

Same, same, same as the guy next door.
Please tell me there is something more
In store for your poor, boring,
Wet young face!

It's pretty good for a twelve-year-old, don't you think? April and I finally gave in to the long hair thing. We told Jacob at the age of thirteen that we would no longer force him to get haircuts—that he was now a teenager and had the right to choose his own hairstyle. And if I was to put my finger on a time that coincided with the marked change in our son, I suppose this would be that time. The hair was only the beginning.

By the time Jacob reached the age of sixteen, he was a full-blown hippie. You heard me right. He had the long hair, love beads, Mexican leather sandals, tie-dyed shirts—the whole peace-and-love nine yards, as if he'd just stepped out of a time machine that had travelled forward from the 1960s.

But I'll get into this further later on. Just know for now that kids can have a way of blindsiding you. Who really knows what goes on in their inchoate little brains? Did I say "little"? I probably shouldn't describe Jacob's brain as little. He was a very smart kid. Seriously, this was a kid who could've been anything he wanted. He reminded me of me in many ways. Both of us had high IQs, and both of us had loving and nurturing moms and dads. I remember when I was a kid growing up in Anaheim, my parents were nothing short of wonderful. Sure, we had our minor disagreements, but my parents always encouraged me to pursue my dreams. This is so important, isn't it? I can't think of a more important thing for a parent to do.

When I was in grade school, I wanted to be a scientist, and Mom and Dad encouraged me by buying me all kinds of books about geography, astronomy, biology, and physics. Christ, I gobbled up all those books as if they were made of roast beef and chocolate. And I learned the most amazing things. Do you know, for example, how enormous the sun is? They say that over a million Earths can fit inside of it. And do you know how many cells make up the human body? Each human body is made up of about thirty-seven trillion cells. It boggles the mind, and to top it all off, these thirty-seven trillion cells all get together and organize themselves. Heck, I sometimes have trouble just organizing my work weeks. Science isn't just intriguing and amazing; it can be utterly beyond belief.

When I was in high school, I'd had enough of science and grew more interested in architecture. I can't remember what got me curious about the subject, but buildings suddenly fascinated me. I marveled at the enormous amount of creativity involved, and at all the complexities, and at the great genius of some of its more talented men and women. I came to be especially fond of Frank Lloyd Wright. There was no one quite like him. While the modern movement in architecture was stripping away all of its "superfluous" detail, Wright was designing buildings that were loaded with ornate personality. The man was an artistic force to be reckoned with, a genius who blazed his own trails, and a true architect's architect, not a monkey-see-monkey-do sycophant with a dull pencil and worn eraser. If you haven't visited one of his buildings, you're missing out.

After I graduated from high school, my interests shifted again. I knew I didn't have the talent to ever become a great architect, and I didn't want to become a scientist holed up on some university campus in a beige-walled, windowless office, teaching ungrateful kids all I knew about the world and grading their tests and papers just so I could make ends meet. No, I wanted to *do* something. I wanted to become a real mover and a shaker. Doing what, exactly? Who cared? I just wanted to be one of those people in this country who made things happen. And the way I saw it then, and the way I still see it today, making things happen is all about business. It's the heart and soul of America. It always has been and always will be. So the first thing I did when I went to college was to declare a major in business administration.

I am now a vice president of the fourth-largest cardboard box manufacturer in the United States. Laugh if you want. There's a lot more than you probably realize that goes into the production and selling of cardboard boxes. I'm proud of what I do for a living.

But enough about me. Let's go back to that Saturday. I'll set the scene for you by first describing our house. We lived in a large, semiostentatious home on a piece of property in a community called Coto de Caza. This community is located in the dry rolling hills about twenty miles east of the Orange County coastline. It's gated to keep the riffraff out, and it has a very low crime rate. April and I thought this would be the perfect place to start a family, so we moved there and had our two sons.

Our house is quite large—probably larger than we really need it to be. We have a couple extra rooms we use for guests when they visit. We also have a swimming pool, and beside the swimming pool is a pool house with a game room, dressing room, and full bathroom. Our yard is magnificent, thanks to April. She loves working in the yard, and she keeps it manicured and stuffed with flowering plants. I wouldn't know a daisy from a chrysanthemum, but I know what I like, and I like our yard a lot. The only task in the yard that April doesn't do herself is the lawn mowing, which is Jacob's chore. And it's like I said; I had asked Jacob to mow the lawn in the morning, but it was now getting late in the afternoon and Jacob was nowhere to be found. I thought to myself, *Maybe he's working on one of his poems. Sometimes he'll get so involved with a poem that he'll lose track of time and forget to do what he's supposed to be doing.* He did this often. So I went up to his bedroom to find him, but he wasn't there. There was a poem on his desk, sitting in plain sight beside his computer keyboard. I don't usually snoop through Jacob's things, but my curiosity got the best of me. I stepped to Jacob's desk and picked up the poem, reading it. Actually, I read it several times just to be sure. Jesus, did this poem really say what I thought?

"Did you find him?" April asked. She was now standing in the doorway.

"No," I said. "But I found this."

"What is it?"

"We've got a big problem."

"What does it say?"

I handed the poem to April, and she read it slowly. This is what the poem said:

Goodbye

Arcadia calls to me
Like chirping birds from a tree
Harmonizing with the sun
And running one with the sum

Of soda pop brook water
And bubbling fits of laughter:
Ha, ha, and ha it goes through
The lupine blooms, beneath blue

Ceilinged skies with marshmallow
Candy clouds, and don't you know
Even their shadows glow bright
With yellow light, all so bright

That bees and the butterflies
Have to shade their compound eyes.
I lie on the shore and rhyme,
Dreaming of the time I will find

The nerve to up and make a
Run for it. Soon on my way
To Arcadia, sweet place,
Protected safe from God's grace,

Finally trading this life
Of my loneliness and strife
for peaceful and joyous days.
I guess what I want to say

Is goodbye.

April handed the poem back to me. "What does it mean?" she asked.

"This is a huge problem," I said. I was suddenly out of breath. "It means we have to find him now."

"Where is he?" April asked.

"I have no idea. You check the upstairs, and I'll check the downstairs. Check every room. Check every closet. Don't skip anything."

April started looking upstairs, and I ran down the stairs to check the first-floor rooms. I checked the family room and the family room closet. I checked the front room, the dining room, the powder room, and the kitchen. I went into the garage and looked around and under the cars, but he wasn't there either. God, I had no idea what we would find. But I was sure I knew exactly what Jacob's poem meant. He'd been so quiet recently. He had been so blandly morose, which was not unusual for him. I mean, he wasn't always this way, but he did have his moods. And when he got this way, April said it was as though there was a film in front of him. It was a strange and uncomfortable barrier—an invisible barrier, but a barrier nonetheless. And now? Would he really do this? Yes, he would! We had to find him! And we had to find him *now!*

"He's not up here!" April shouted from the top of the stairs.

"You checked everywhere?"

"Everywhere," April said.

"He's not down here either."

"Well, he has to be somewhere."

"Oh, Christ!" I exclaimed.

"What?" April asked.

"The pool house! We need to check the pool house. That's probably where he is."

I ran out the patio door to the backyard. April ran down the stairs and followed me. We ran around the swimming pool and to the pool house. We burst into the game room, but Jacob was not there. We checked the dressing room. Then I ran to the bathroom door.

"I can hear the shower running," I said.

"Knock on the door."

I knocked. I called Jacob's name, but there was no answer. So I knocked again. Still no answer, but we could definitely hear the shower water. "Kick in the door," April said.

"Yes," I said. And I proceeded to kick at the door with my right foot. "Jesus, what the hell is this thing made of?"

"Kick harder!"

With one mighty blow, the doorjamb splintered and the door swung wide open. Then we saw!

"Oh, dear God!" April exclaimed.

Nothing can prepare you for something like this. He is your child. He is your own sweet child, your flesh and blood. He's the boy you raised from his infancy, the boy you taught to catch a football, and the boy you taught to ride a bike. I swear to God, my heart felt like it was going to beat its way right up and out of my mouth.

"Jacob!" I exclaimed.

He was in the shower. He was stark naked, sitting on the shower floor under the downpour of water. His long hair was soaked and sticking to his face in wet strands. His eyes were closed, and he looked unconscious. On the shower floor was a single-edge razor blade. He must have gotten it from my tools and supplies in the garage. His wrists were cut open, and blood was pulsing out of the gashes and streaming like red paint into the water and running down the shower drain. "My baby!" April screamed.

"Go call 911," I said.

"My baby!"

"Call 911. I'm going to try to slow down the bleeding. Go call 911, now!"

April ran to the phone. She made the call. I turned off the water and climbed into the shower stall, hoping to save my boy's life.

CHAPTER 2

THE BOX MAN CAN

———————•●•———————

When I was a kid, we believed. Oh, did we ever! We believed that if you dreamed that you were falling off a cliff and hit bottom before waking up, you would not only perish in your dream but would actually die in real life. The next morning, your parents would find you lifeless in your bed, and no one would know what happened. We also believed that if you dug a hole deep enough in your backyard, you'd reach the mysterious place called China. Imagine that. Being able to access China from behind your house, poking your head up from your hole and hearing everyone speaking Chinese, chomping on chow mein noodles, and lighting firecrackers. I attempted this once, digging a hole to China. I made it down about three feet before I got tired of digging. I set down my shovel and moved on to something else.

When I was a kid, we also believed you would have bad luck if you walked under a ladder, broke a mirror, opened an umbrella inside the house, or allowed a black cat to cross your path. These were not just superstitions. Further, we believed that a silver bullet could kill a werewolf, and we believed werewolves were real. And we knew that if you held on to a frog for too long, you would get warts—ugly little warts all over your palms and fingers.

One thing I always believed, and thought was possible even as an adult, was the idea that while you were dying, you would see your entire life flash before your eyes. Of course, there was no way to confirm this. Once people experienced the phenomenon of dying, they wouldn't be around to tell you if they saw their life flash before their eyes or not. But even as an adult, this idea made sense to me. And on the afternoon when I found Jacob bleeding to death in the pool house shower, the idea was no longer an idea but a frightening reality; for while I was not the one dying, I did see a life flash before my eyes. I saw Jacob's life. I saw all seventeen years of it: every little experience, every word said, every place we ever visited, and every sound, taste, feeling, and smell. And I read every poem he wrote. These memories and images flashed before my eyes on that awful afternoon, and I knew for a fact he was leaving this world.

I recalled Jacob's seventh-grade year. He was taking a creative writing class that year, and his teacher for that class was a wonderful woman named Miss Smyth. I could see Miss Smyth as vividly as if I'd just seen her earlier that same day. I knew exactly what the woman had looked like since April, when I met her during parents' night at the school. I'd guess that Miss Smyth was in her midthirties, although that's only a guess. I have a very hard time guessing the ages of overweight women, and Miss Smyth was quite heavy. She was a big, maternal, and very friendly woman with short blonde hair and mesmerizing blue eyes. April said Miss Smyth would be "a real looker" if she lost about 150 pounds, and I took her word for it. I not only have a hard time guessing the ages of overweight women but also have a hard time picturing them as slender. Even if I squint my eyes and try to enable my imagination, I'm just not very good at it. There's something about the double chins and fatty upper arms that throw me off the task.

Anyway, as I said, Jacob was in Miss Smyth's creative writing class—and how he loved this class. Miss Smyth turned out to be a terrific teacher. Jacob wrote several short stories for her which were quite good, but he especially loved the many poetry assignments she handed out. The assignments were right in his wheelhouse. Jacob did his best for her, wanting to please her, and he would share the poems he wrote with April and me. And I saved all of these poems, keeping them in the box I told you about, in my study closet. For one of his assignments, he was instructed by Miss Smyth to write a poem about a loved one. This could be a mother, father, sister, brother, cousin, aunt, uncle, or close friend at school. The choice was left up to Jacob, and I was flattered that he picked me. Yes, he picked me, and the poem went as follows:

The Box Man Can

Shake hands with my dad, the Box Man.
'Round here we like to call him Stan.
He makes boxes for every need
And turns them out at every speed.

Boxes for hell and for heaven,
One, two, three, four, five, and seven.
Are you missing box number six?
He'll add one more into the mix.

He'll always get your order right,
Summer or winter, day or night.
His machines work around the clock,
And there's no box he doesn't stock.

Moving to a newer abode?
His boxes will carry the load.
Need to store junk in the attic?
He has boxes to do the trick.

Need some boxes to hold your shoes?
With my dad's boxes, you can't lose.
Need to store important papers?
Get a box sooner than later.

Buy all your boxes from my dad,
And he'll make sure you're never sad.
Hopes and dreams, diamonds and rocks—
Nothing you can't store in a box

Made by my dad and all his men
To suit your many needs, and when
You've nothing for a box to do,
He'll sell you a box for that too.

Saints alive, do we even dare
Think of all he did to prepare
Himself for the days he would be
Selling cardboard to you and me?

So let's all give the man a hand,
And thank our stars the Box Man can
Keep all our lives neat and tidy.
Boxes, boxes for you and me!

I liked the poem a lot when I first read it. After reading it aloud several times, I recall saying something like, "Doggone right, Jacob. Doggone good job. Boxes are for everyone!" But isn't it funny how skewed our understanding can be while we're looking right at something? I mean, it can be so out of whack when we're face-to-face with a subject, nose-to-nose. I think I now understand the poem Jacob wrote, all these years after the fact. Jacob wasn't putting me up on a pedestal, admiring me, or bragging about me. He was ridiculing me! I knew he loved me, and I knew he cared a lot about me. And the last thing he would want to do is hurt my feelings, but he also saw my life for exactly what it was. And what was it? What was I? Yes, I was a box man, born, raised, fed, groomed, educated, and now employed to sell boxes. Now I know my ABCs. Watch me color inside the lines! See Dick and Jane run. Ten divided by two equals five. Who was Paul Revere? Who was Eli Whitney? Is water really partly made of oxygen? Yes, there's an equal and opposite reaction to what? Gravity, mass, and the speed of light. Plato's dialogues. The *Iliad* and the *Odyssey*. The law of supply and demand and the Laffer curve. Good job, young man, and here's your diploma. And now, after all this, I was a grown man selling boxes. Yes, let's give me a hand! A big round of applause for Stan Harper, the box man!

Life is interesting, isn't it? I'm thinking of the haphazard way we make connections, and the way things happen. Obviously, I did not plan out my life with the ultimate goal of running a cardboard box company. I suppose there are some people who have firm and indefatigable goals when they are young, and there were times when I had a few, but my goals always morphed into others, or I lost interest in them completely. I think I'm like most people in the world. Many others I've talked to, when I asked them if they had always planned on doing what they currently do for a living, reply with a laugh and a no. Most of us just end up where we end up, like waterlogged pieces of flotsam on this sandy beach or that, jostled about and carried to a final dry resting place by nature's random ocean currents.

I'll tell you how I got my job. It's an interesting story. And the man I now work for is, to say the least, an interesting fellow. It began when I was working as vice president of marketing communications for a website called Viva, which was headquartered in Santa Ana and which hawked all sorts of cheap and unnecessary novelties—T-shirts, embroidered caps, and so forth—to Mexicans living in America. This website was founded and operated by an Irishman named Sean Mills, and I had worked for Sean for six years. He called me his vice president of marketing communications, which was really a pretentious way of saying I was in charge of coming up with a steady stream of dumb ideas to make the site more popular. Not to brag, but I think I was pretty good at my job. Viva was successful thanks in a big way to many of my ideas, and Sean was doing very well for himself. He had a big Mediterranean house in Laguna Beach that looked out over the Pacific Ocean, and he owned a big black Mercedes and a brand-new red Ferrari. He lived the good life. He went to parties every weekend, dated all kinds of beautiful women, and took a lot of vacations—but never to Mexico. And he never dated Mexican girls. "*Nunca comas donde cagas,*" he told me. Translation? It meant, in so many words, "Never eat where you shit."

Anyway, at the time that I was employed by Viva, April was a stay-at-home mom, raising Jacob and Zachary and doing all the things that stay-at-home moms do. Every Friday night, we'd go out to dinner together, just the two of us. This was our chance to get away from the kids and enjoy each other's company while pretending for a couple peaceful hours that we were still free and childless. One evening we decided to go to Maxell's, a fancy restaurant in Newport Beach that looked out over the bay and its yachts, oily water, and seagulls. I was to meet April at seven, but she called my cell phone at six forty-five to tell me the babysitter was going to be a half hour late. Since I was already at the restaurant, and since I now had thirty minutes to kill, I went over to the bar and sat down on a barstool. I then ordered a drink from the bartender. I had planned to nurse the drink by myself and wait for April to arrive. That was my plan. What I hadn't planned on was Harry Bright.

Harry was at the bar, talking to a group of people who were also at the bar. I wasn't sure whether he knew them well or not, or whether he was just being friendly. But they were all listening to him, and they seemed amused. And who wouldn't be amused by Harry? He was an energetic man in his fifties who, in complete discord with the unwritten dress code of this fancy restaurant, was wearing a loud, untucked Hawaiian shirt, black shorts, and brown leather sandals. He was overweight, but I wouldn't call him obese. His hair was thin, but he wasn't exactly bald. I did notice his watch, which was a solid-gold Rolex that was sopping wet with tiny diamonds and rubies. In one hand Harry held his drink, and he waved the other hand around as he talked to the group. If you'd have put a baton in his free hand, he could've been conducting the Los Angeles Philharmonic Orchestra. I imagined Stravinsky's *Firebird*. Wow, could this guy ever talk! Maybe it was just the booze, but he was talking up a storm at this bar. And I couldn't help but hear what he was saying to the others.

He said, "I read it on the internet. Christ, how I love the internet. The whole freaking world is at your fingertips these days. All you have to do is type your freaking question, and up come a hundred answers. It's like having the freaking Library of Congress in a box on your desk. Anyway, I searched for good questions to ask my job applicants, and there it was. It was the perfect question! I could never have come up with something like this on my own. It was freaking amazing! So here's the question—and make sure you listen to it carefully, because there is a perfect answer. And no, it isn't a trick question. It'll make perfect sense to you. You're driving your car down a road, and you come upon a bus stop. The rain is coming down in buckets. I mean, it's really pouring. There are three people at the bus stop, waiting for a late bus to arrive. One of the people is an elderly woman who is obviously very ill and in need of medical help, and the second person is an old buddy who once saved your life. The third person is a lovely girl you are suddenly smitten by and sure is the girl of your dreams. So what do you do? Your car only seats two people. There is no sign of the rain letting up, and there is no sign of the bus. You know you have to help the old woman, and you owe your friend a big favor for having saved your life. And then there's the girl. You are head over heels in love with this girl. So, what do you do?"

Now I was intrigued. No one at the bar had a good answer for Harry. And that's when it hit me! I knew the answer to the question. I mean, it had to be the right answer—at least, it was as good of an answer as any. "I know what I'd do," I said, and Harry turned to look at me. I could tell by the look on his face that he didn't expect me to get it right, but I spoke up anyway. I said, slowly and methodically, "You give your friend the keys to your car so he can drive himself home, and you have him take the old woman to the hospital on his way there. Then you stand in the rain with the girl of your dreams and wait for the late bus."

"Jesus freaking Christ," Harry said, smiling from ear to ear. "Have you heard this one before?"

"No," I said.

Harry stepped over to me and put his hand on my shoulder. "Tell me, what do you do for a living?"

"I do marketing communications," I said. "I'm a vice president."

"For whom?"

"For a website."

"Which website?"

"I'm sure you've never heard of it."

"I'll double your salary."

"To do what?"

Harry laughed. "To run my freaking company. To take charge of the whole kit and kaboodle."

Now, I knew the guy was drunk, and I was pretty sure he was just blowing a lot of hot air. "What does your company do?" I asked for the heck of it.

"We make boxes. Tons of them. We make more freaking boxes than the world knows what to do with." Harry then reached into his pocket and removed a business card. He lost his balance but held on to the edge of the counter with his free hand to keep from falling. Yes, the man was drunk. It was obvious, and his words were beginning to slur. "Come to my office Monday. First thing in the morning. Be there at eight o'clock sharp. Tell my secretary that you're the kid who I met at the bar at Maxwell's. I'll make sure she lets you in. We'll be waiting for you, so don't forget."

"Okay," I said skeptically.

"This is on the level, kid. Eight o'clock."

"Eight o'clock," I repeated.

When April and I sat down for dinner, I told her about my encounter with Harry, and she laughed. Then she said I ought to meet with the man. "You never know," she said. "And maybe he is on the level. And you surely don't plan on selling T-shirts to Mexicans your entire life, do you?"

"I suppose not," I said.

"And everyone needs boxes."

"Yes, boxes are important."

"Can you imagine the world without boxes?"

"I guess not."

It was crazy, wasn't it? Meeting with some guy I met in a bar who was dressed like a stupid tourist—a guy who was three sheets to the wind and who could barely keep his balance without holding on to the edge of the bar. Yet I decided to go through with it. I called in sick to Viva on Monday morning, and I drove to Harry's office. Little did I know, right?

I arrived at seven forty-five, which was fifteen minutes early, and I checked in with the receptionist. I told her I had an eight o'clock appointment with Harry. Then I sat down and waited. I thumbed through an issue of *National Geographic*, looking at the pictures. I remember it occurred to me that I always went for the *National Geographic* magazines in waiting rooms but I had never once read any of the articles. I only looked at the pictures. And I wondered whether everyone was like me—whether the writers for the magazine had any readers at all. They could write about nearly any subject, and make any point, and describe any people, and no one would know the difference. So long as the glossy pictures were interesting, who cared? What a totally ungratifying job it must be, writing articles that no one in the world bothers to read.

"He'll see you now," the receptionist said to me. I set down the magazine and looked up at the wall clock. It was eight o'clock exactly.

Following the receptionist's instructions, I walked down the hall and into Harry's office. The first thing I learned was that it was not his office. In fact, Harry didn't even have an office anywhere in the building. I learned that the office we were in was to be my office if I was hired. I learned that Harry worked out of his home. "This was Jonathan's office for seven years,"

Harry said. "He was a good man. Jonathan was in charge of things until last month. Did a decent job. Could've done better, but also could've done a lot worse. I guess if I was grading him, I'd give him a B. Ah, but now the poor son of a chimp is gone."

"Where'd he go?" I asked.

"It was a major-minor."

"A what?" I asked.

"A major-minor."

"I don't understand," I said.

"He was the victim of a major-minor."

"I guess I don't understand what you mean by 'major-minor,'" I said. And I didn't. I had no idea what Harry was talking about.

"I'm talking about an ostensibly minor event in life that has major consequences."

"I see," I said.

"Here's what happened. Follow along carefully. A woman by the name of Adrianna Nicholson was getting ready to take her six-year-old son to the pediatrician for his annual checkup. She lived in a house not far from here with her husband, Thomas, and their Irish Setter, Max. As I understand it, Adrianna was about to leave the house with her son when the phone rang. It was Thomas who was calling. It was about twelve-thirty, and he was calling from the grocery store. Adrianna had asked Thomas to pick up some dry dog food for Max during his lunch hour, but Thomas called because he was at the grocery store and they were all out of Max's brand of dog food. Thomas wanted to know what he should do. Adrianna told him to try the store again the next day—that the food would probably be stocked by then and that Max had enough food to last a few more days. Are you still with me? It was all innocent enough, right? But that phone call cost Jonathan his life."

"Who's Jonathan?"

"The man who worked for me. Aren't you paying attention?"

"I am," I said. "Sometimes I get confused with names."

"Anyway, fifteen minutes later, Jonathan was dead. Crushed to death."

"What happened?"

"Adrianna broadsided him in an intersection when he was on his way back to the office from the grocery store. She plowed right into him."

"She killed him?"

"Just as sure as you and I are now sitting here now," Harry said.

"That's awful."

"Now do you understand what I mean by 'major-minor'?"

"Not really."

"Think of it," Harry said. "There was a phone call from a husband about dog food. A minor, little thing, right? Innocent enough—a husband asking his wife what to do. But if he hadn't made that phone call when he did, Adrianna would have left the house with her son a couple minutes earlier. And being ahead of schedule by a couple of minutes would've meant she would never have plowed into Jonathan in the intersection when she did. It was a minor event that caused a major incident. It was a phone call about dog food that cost my employee his life."

"I see what you mean," I said.

"Cause of death? A phone call about dog food. A classic major-minor. And they happen all the time, all these major-minors. Once you know what to look for, you'll see that they're freaking everywhere. And once you begin to see them for what they are, you'll realize just how arbitrary and haphazard our life events are."

"Yes," I agreed.

And now I wanted to work for Harry. He was no longer just a boisterous, half-drunk character in a bar that overlooked the Newport Bay. He was a thinker. He was my kind of guy. There was more to Harry than met the eye.

So boxes it was. It would be me taking over Jonathan's old office, tracking and manufacturing and selling truckloads of brown boxes. Me, in a factory of box-making machinery and a sea of rippling cardboard. It would be me calling the shots as if I owned the place. Harry and I talked for over an hour about the CEO job and about my family, my dreams, my experiences, and my education. And we talked about Harry, about his history, and a lot about his boxes. When our meeting was over, he extended his hand and I shook it with gusto. We'd made a deal, and I was now Harry's right-hand man. I couldn't wait to tell April the good news.

That night I sprang the decision on April, and as I was telling her more about Harry, something occurred to me. I had to laugh, and when April asked what I was laughing about, I said, "Major-minor."

"Major what?" she asked.

"It all comes down to our babysitter," I said.

"Down to what?"

"We were supposed to meet for dinner at seven. You were late because the babysitter was late, so I went to the bar to kill time. If our babysitter had been on time, I would never have gone to the bar. I would never have met Harry. I would never have answered his question about the three people at the bus stop correctly, and I would never have been offered a job to run his company. It's exactly like the car accident. It's exactly the same thing."

"What car accident?"

"The one that killed Jonathan."

"Jonathan who?"

"The man whose job I'm taking over."

"You're not making any sense."

I could tell I was getting on April's nerves.

"I can explain," I said. Then I took a deep breath and told her all about the major-minors. And I think April finally did understand how I became a box man, the same silly box man who Jacob wrote about in his seventh-grade poetry assignment. Me, the box man.

Now that I look back, I don't think I ever explained any of this to Jacob. As parents, we often go through our adult lives unintentionally telling our kids less about ourselves than we should. And why is that? Kids naturally look to their parents for answers, and it's important they know where their parents are coming from. It helps them to make sense of the world, and it helps them to make sense of themselves. Life can be very confusing for a young boy or a girl. I think life was confusing for my son. If I'd reached out to him more, maybe he would have understood the decisions I had made during the course of my life. Then again, maybe he wouldn't have related at all. But now, as Jacob sat bleeding to death in the pool house shower, it was possible that I would never know.

CHAPTER 3

THE TOURNAMENT

———————— •❦• ————————

Did I tell you Jacob was a hippie? I probably did say that, but now that I think about it, saying that he was a hippie' isn't a completely accurate or fair characterization. I mean, yes, he did grow his hair long enough to reach his shoulders. And he dressed like a hippie in his threadbare Levi's, colorful tie-dyed T-shirts, and tire-tread-soled sandals. It was funny. The T-shirts came via UPS from a hippie commune up in Northern California that maintained a shopping site on the internet (proving there's no avoiding the need to make money), and the sandals were made in Mexico for people who couldn't afford real shoes. As for the jeans, Jacob bought them at a Salvation Army thrift store. Because the store relied solely on donations for its inventory, they never seemed to have Jacob's size, so his jeans were always a size too large. In any event, you now have a picture of what Jacob looked like. Or at least how the boy dressed and wore his hair—as I have said, like a hippie.

There were ways other than his superficial appearance that Jacob resembled a hippie. He surely had the attitude down pat. He was, for example, vehemently against evils like greed, war, materialism, intolerance, prejudice, and violence, and he had a serious distrust of the establishment. Like a hippie, he felt the world was way too profit-motivated, and he didn't like the way everyone in the country was obsessed with making money off each other. As far as his musical tastes were concerned, he listened only to sixties and seventies rock, and seldom listened to current bands. And while kids at his school had their heads in those simple-minded Harry Potter books, Jacob was discovering works like *Siddhartha*, *Walden*, and *Zen and the Art of Motorcycle Maintenance*. But I'll also say this about my son: he wasn't into drugs. Heck, the kid didn't even drink coffee. The way

Jacob saw it, most drugs were just an "evil manifestation of our greedy and thrill-seeking society."

There's one more thing you ought to know about Jacob. He was clean. Unlike real back-to-nature hippies (at least those I have known over the years), Jacob was as clean as a whistle. The kid had great personal hygiene. He brushed his teeth and took showers every morning like clockwork. So he was a semihippie, really. Something like one third hippie, one third millennial, and one third clean and drug-abstaining Mormon. I guess you could say, in this age of eclectic lifestyles, that Jacob was a hybrid.

Needless to say, Jacob's unique persona didn't exactly help him to fit in with his peers. In order to understand how poorly he meshed, you will need a description of where we lived. As I told you earlier, we lived in Orange County, California. Have you heard of this place? I am talking about Orange County, as in the setting for the popular and awful *The Real Housewives of Orange County*. To make things worse, we lived in a place called Coto de Caza. Coto was a haven for affluent and I-sure-wish-I-was-affluent lily white all-American families who wasted more money on cars, vacations, wristwatches, and plastic surgery operations than most normal people make in a year. I am not exaggerating about this. Most people in Coto did go to church every Sunday, but pretending to be rich and famous was the real religion. And it was a community in which being a liberal was akin to being a rapist or a mass murderer, I kid you not. You had to have a sense of humor. This was a place where breast-augmented, spray-on-tan moms would park their behemoth Chevy Suburbans in designated handicap stalls, and where their husbands would pay the parking fines as if they were paying another utility bill. Didn't that say it all? And the kids—what about their kids? The poor, entitled, misguided, social-climbing kids didn't have a chance in hell.

I felt as though we were living in Beverly Hills. Their parents bought their children brand-new Audis, Porsches, and BMWs as soon as they passed their state driving tests, and they all had cell phones and credit cards. It wouldn't surprise me to learn that some even had their own attorneys and financial advisors. When we moved to Coto, we were told it would be such a great place to raise our kids. There was such a low crime rate, and there would be lots of God-fearing, Republican neighbors we could invite over for dinner. And the kids were supposedly all good students who were involved in all sorts of sports and after-school clubs. They were good kids, right? They were honest and grounded. They were the kinds of kids a parent could be proud of. But now that I look back, I believe our boys would've been better off being raised in a community where the water ran a little deeper. Maybe not so much Zachary, but certainly Jacob would've had a chance at being happier. But we didn't move. Instead we became a part of the scenery.

Let me tell you a few things about myself, for the more you know about me, the better you will understand my son. I believe that father–son relationships are extremely important. Yes, we moved to Coto deliberately, and I would be lying if I told you that I didn't anticipate some of the things I now get a kick out of complaining about. And it's true also that April and I took part in the Coto lifestyle as much as any other self-absorbed, high-tax-bracket couple with two dependents. I'm trying to be honest here. I'm not going to pretend I was miserable where we lived, or disenfranchised, or offended. I made a lot of money as the captain of Harry's box-making ship, and I wanted to spend it. I drove a big, ostentatious Mercedes, and April drove a gas-guzzling Cadillac Escalade. I belonged to Coto's country club, wore a Piaget watch, and took my family out to dinner often at restaurants that charged too much for their food and way too much for their wine. I also bought my boys cell phones, and I never did question the number of calls and texts they made each month. I even gave each of them a Visa credit card, supposedly for emergencies. So what was I? Wasn't I one of those people you meet in life who does precisely what he complains about all those other people doing? And did that make me a hypocrite? Maybe it did. Yes, maybe it did.

But there was one big difference between me and most other people who lived in our community. I knew better. April, maybe not so much. Zach, definitely not. But I knew better. I knew what I was doing there, and I did it anyway. I let myself get swept up in a lifestyle.

Which brings me to Jacob. As I tell you stories about my son, you should be aware that despite all his incongruous quirks and idiosyncrasies, he absolutely meant the world to me. I may not have always shown it in spades, but I deeply admired his courage. Unlike so many people one meets over the course of one's life (especially where we lived), he was not afraid to be himself. He was not afraid to live unapologetically and proudly to the clicks of an eccentric metronome. I mean, think about it. Seriously? A hippie? Well, okay, a semihippie, as I have already defined him. This was the twenty-first century, wasn't it? Hippies were as relevant as cavemen or knights of the round table. And all the poetry? What was the deal with that? What sort of American boy these days spends most of his time in his bedroom, listening to sixties and seventies music and writing poetry? A sissy, or one of "those kinds of boys?" Nevertheless, I honestly loved my odd son to death, and there wasn't a thing I wouldn't have done for him. Even now, when I think of him cutting his wrists, it makes me want to cry my eyes out, and that's a powerful sign of love. There are very few people in my life that have had the power to make me cry, and Jacob was one of them.

Let's rewind this narrative by several years. We'll go back to the times when Jacob was a clean-cut little hockey player in the fourth grade. I'm talking about roller hockey. I got the both of my boys involved hockey when they were around six years old. In Coto we had a tennis college that thrived before we moved into our home, but shortly after we arrived, the college began faltering. There were now a good number of tennis courts that no one was using. It was kind of sad. But roller hockey was becoming very popular around this time, and some of the dads in the community had the bright idea to turn the ghost town tennis courts into roller hockey rinks. One thing led to another, and the next thing we knew, a deal was worked out with the tennis college so that the courts were converted to rinks. Coto now had its own highly popular roller hockey program. Nestled in a grove of oak trees and surrounded by tall chain-link fences, the place went absolutely wild every Sunday with boisterous moms and dads, and sweaty, cursing boys skating back and forth as if their lives depended on it, whacking pucks with hockey sticks and trying to score goals. Of all my memories of Coto, I like these the best. It was a lot of fun, and we had some great times.

William Caldwell was one of the fathers who volunteered to coach some of the boys. I knew William from the country club. I'd never golfed with him but was introduced to him by a mutual friend while we were having postgame drinks in the country club lounge. It's always interesting to learn what people do for a living, and it turned out that William was a salesman. He sold those big steel overhead doors they use in commercial and industrial buildings. I had no idea how much money there was to be made selling such doors, but the man drove a brand-new BMW and lived in one of Coto's nicer neighborhoods. Furthermore, he played a lot of golf. You have to make decent money to play a lot of golf.

Orange County is loaded with guys like William. Basically, they're a dime a dozen. They have good jobs, and they all make decent money. And they have families to support and mortgages to pay. They all drive nice cars, and their stay-at-home wives usually drive brand-new SUVs. Their migratory habits are very predictable. They fly to Hawaii in the summers, and drive up to Mammoth to ski during the winter. Here's another thing I've noticed about these people. They are all believers. So what do they believe in? Well, God, of course, and they all go to church on Sunday. But just as much as they believe in God, or perhaps even more so, they believe in America. They call it the good old US-of-A, and by God, they believe in the way of life we call capitalism. They believe in the American dream. And they firmly believe in competition. They believe that all men and women ought to work hard and compete with each other, and that no one in this country has a right to complain about much of anything. What makes me laugh is that they all have a story to tell about either themselves or someone they know who started with the odds stacked against them, pulled himself or herself up by the bootstraps, and became a financial success. I can't tell you how many of these stories I've heard since we moved to Coto. If you're not driving a Mercedes, if you still live outside the gates, if you're working nine-to-five, you probably just aren't trying hard enough.

William, it turned out, was married to a woman five years younger named Amanda, and Amanda gave him two children—a boy and a girl. The boy's name was Ricky, and he was Jacob's age. Jacob knew Ricky from school. They weren't in the same class, but they sometimes hung out with the same groups during recess. During the summer hockey season, Jacob and Ricky were put on opposing teams, and Ricky's dad coached Ricky's team. Ricky was a goalie, and a pretty darn good one. Jacob played forward on his team, and I know this is going to sound like I'm bragging, but he was one of the best forwards in the league. Along came the tournament I want to tell you about. It was William's idea. During the middle of the regular season, on the same weekend as Father's Day, William wanted the league to sponsor a Saturday tournament for the teams in our sons' age group. They would compete for a special prize—a Gordie Howe–autographed hockey puck to be awarded to each boy on the winning team. William said he would supply the pucks at his expense. Supposedly he knew a guy who knew a guy who could get him a good deal. This was typical of Coto. Everyone had a connection—a guy who knew a guy—even for acquiring oddball things like autographed hockey pucks.

In the final round of the tournament, Jacob's team wound up playing William and Ricky's team. I was there for the game, of course, and so were April and Zach. And so was a large crowd of other parents, friends, and energetic kids. The championship game began at about three in the afternoon. When the referee dropped the puck to start the game, everyone went crazy. All of a sudden, the game became a very big deal. Who was going to win, and who was going to lose? And who was going to go home with the Gordie Howe hockey pucks? Seriously, it was like the Stanley Cup playoffs, except the players were all a bunch of fourth graders trying to win a puck autographed by a player none of them had even heard of. I'll bet 99 percent of the people there that day didn't even know who Gordie Howe was, or what team he played on, or what he was famous for. But they all wanted one of those damn hockey pucks just like they wanted to win the California lottery.

The game was a good one, and the boys on both teams fought hard to win. There were a few minor penalties for tripping and slashing, but for the most part the boys all played a clean and competitive game. There was a goal scored by each team in the first five minutes. Then the score remained tied at one to one for almost the entire game. It was the last ten minutes of the game that were really exciting. The coaches on both teams were busy shouting and barking orders at their players, trying to get that all-important and elusive winning goal. I remember laughing to myself. It got so intense that I thought one of the coaches was going to burst a blood vessel. Then it finally happened in the last two minutes: Jacob weaved through two of the other team's defenders and took a backhand shot at the goal. The puck sailed over Ricky's left shoulder, hit the post, and then bounced off his back and into the net. The crowd went crazy. And then another goal was scored. This time Jacob took a wild slap shot from thirty feet, and the puck blew between Ricky's legs. April was screaming, and so was everyone else. Christ, you should've seen poor Ricky's face after that second goal. He looked as if his world had just come tumbling down. Seriously, I thought he was going to bawl right then and there.

Well, those two goals were all Jacob's team needed to win the game. The final score was three to one, and Jacob was a hockey hero. When the game was over, the kids on Jacob's team all skated up and hugged him. I remember thinking to myself, "These kids know a winner when they see one!" Yes, it was a great Father's Day present. When the pandemonium finally died down, William brought out all the Gordie Howe hockey pucks and assembled both teams in the center of the rink. Jacob's team sat on one side, and Ricky's team sat on the other. One by one, William called out the names of the boys on Jacob's team, and they skated up to grab their pucks. Each player got a big round of applause from the crowd. Even the kids on the other team were clapping.

However, one kid on the other team was not clapping. It was poor Ricky. Instead he was sobbing like a girl. A couple of Ricky's more empathetic teammates patted him on the shoulder to console him, and near the end of the ceremony, he was finally able to get his tears under control. But I ask myself now, as I tell you this story, did it bother me to see Ricky cry that afternoon? The truth is that it didn't. I probably should have felt bad for the kid. It should bother any parent to see a child in tears. But Ricky's sobbing didn't bother me at all. I figured the kid for a crybaby, and no one feels sorry for crybabies. If I felt sorry for anyone, I felt for Ricky's dad, having to carry on with the ceremony while his kid made such a blubbering fool of himself.

After all the pucks were handed out, the kids skated off the rink and returned to their hockey bags where they took off their gear. The parents and friends around the rink were all talking, mostly about the game, and I was getting all kinds of compliments about Jacob's performance and his goals. It was a great feeling being the father of the boy who had won the game for his team. Then, after about twenty minutes of this, we all dispersed to drive home. I drove Jacob, Zach, and April back to our house for dinner.

That night, April made hamburgers and fries, and the four of us all sat at the kitchen table to eat. "You've got to be starving," I said to Jacob.

"Yeah, I'm hungry," Jacob said.

"You played your butt off today."

"You were so good, Jacob," April said. "You were the star player."

"I guess I was."

"You were tied for so long. But you finally came through for your team. That's got to feel good."

"He was just lucky," Zach said with his mouth full. "That game could've gone either way."

"It probably could have," Jacob agreed.

I said, "If you keep the shooting the puck at the goalie, eventually it'll go in. That's what I always say. Just keep shooting the puck."

"Their goalie stunk," Zach said. "I could've scored on that knucklehead with my eyes closed."

"Not likely," I said. "Ricky is one of the league's better goalies."

"You should give your brother some credit," April said.

"For being lucky?"

"For scoring the game-winning goals."

"Whatever," Zach said. He was paying closer attention to his hamburger than he was our conversation.

"You should be more supportive."

"Let's see the puck," I said to Jacob.

"The puck?"

"The Gordie Howe puck. I didn't get to see it. Where is it?"

"It's in my hockey bag," Jacob said.

"Well, go get it."

"He's eating," April said.

"It'll only take him a minute."

"But I'm hungry," Jacob said.

"You earned that puck," I said seriously. "You ought to want to show it off. Just go get it; I'd like to see it."

"Okay, okay," Jacob said. He stood up from the table and walked out to the garage where we kept all the hockey gear. He was gone for about a minute, but when he came back, he didn't have the puck. I looked at him, and he shrugged. "I can't find it," he said.

"What do you mean you can't find it?"

"I put it in my hockey bag, but now it isn't there."

"Maybe you didn't look hard enough."

"No, I looked hard, but it isn't there."

"What an idiot," Zach said. "He lost it already."

"Maybe if I looked," I said. "Maybe you just need a second pair of eyes."

"You can look all you want," Jacob said. "It isn't in there, I'm telling you. It's gone."

"Someone must have snatched it," April said.

"Yeah," Jacob agreed. "That's probably what happened to it."

"Kids," I said. I was a little angry. "What rotten little thieves they are."

"Maybe William has an extra puck he can give to Jacob," April said. "Or maybe he can get one from his friend."

"That's possible."

"Can I eat my dinner now?" Jacob asked.

"Of course," April said.

"I just can't believe it," I said. But it was true. After dinner, I checked Jacob's hockey bag myself, just to be sure he hadn't missed it. But it wasn't there. I also looked in the car, in the trunk, under the seats, and on the floorboards, just in case it had fallen out of the bag. But the Gordie Howe puck was nowhere to be found.

That evening, we all sat in the family room and watched our TV, and at a little after nine, the doorbell rang. I got up to answer the door, having no idea who it was.

It was William and his son, Ricky, standing on our porch. William did not look at all happy, and Ricky looked terrified. He also looked like he'd been crying again, and I thought, "Jesus, does this kid ever stop blubbering?" William was the first to speak up.

"We're here to return something that belongs to your son," he said. "He'll want to have it."

"Oh?" I said.

"Is Jacob available?"

"Sure," I said. "Hang on a minute, and I'll go get him." I figured it was the hockey puck they were returning—that Ricky was the kid who had snatched it from Jacob's bag.

When I returned to the door with Jacob, however, William said to him, "I think my son has something that belongs to you—something you gave him."

"Here," Ricky said, and he extended his hand toward Jacob, and in his hand was the Gordie Howe puck.

"Ricky told me you gave this to him."

"I did," Jacob said.

"You gave it to him?" I asked.

"I wanted him to have it."

"I just want you both to know that's not how things are done in our family," William said.

"No, of course not," I said.

"Here," Ricky said again. Jacob still hadn't taken the puck from his hand.

"But I don't want it," Jacob said.

"Listen, young man," William said to Jacob. "You won that puck fair and square. That's how life works. You win the game, and you get the prize. Life doesn't hand out its rewards to the losers. If Ricky wanted a puck, he should've stopped you from scoring on him. He should've done his job."

"If Jacob wants your son to have the puck, I don't see the harm in it," I said.

"No, no, I don't want my son thinking that every time he cries like a baby and makes a fool of himself he's going to get someone to give him what he wants."

"I guess I get that," I said. Then I looked down at Jacob, who still hadn't taken the puck from Ricky's hand. To Jacob, I said, "Take the puck."

"But—"

"Just take it, Jacob."

Jacob obviously didn't want the puck, but he reached out and took it from Ricky's hand. "That's a good boy," William said to him. Then to Ricky he said, "Isn't there something you should say?"

By the look on his face, I thought Ricky was going to start crying again, but he didn't. Instead he just bit his lip and said he was sorry.

"You don't have to be sorry," Jacob said.

"Yes, he does," William said. "He accepted something he didn't earn."

"Yes sir," Jacob said to William. I could tell he didn't agree with Ricky's dad, but he was also smart enough to know it would be futile to argue with an adult.

"You'll understand when you're older. Life doesn't reward crybabies and losers. Ricky had a chance to win, but he didn't stop you from scoring."

"I get that," Jacob said.

"That's a good boy, then." Then to me William said, "Well, I guess that's it. We came to do what had to be done. I'm very sorry for the trouble my boy caused."

"He didn't cause any trouble," I said.

"It's nice of you to say that," William said, and finally the man smiled. We all stood there for a moment with nothing to add. Then we said good evening, William and his son walked away, and I closed the front door.

"That was a nice thing that you did," I said to Jacob. "I'm not mad at you."

"Yeah, okay," Jacob said.

CHAPTER 4

VIETNAM

———— •◦• ————

Do you have kids? Don't you wonder what they'll remember, and what they'll soon forget? We all have selective memories, don't we? For example, take my older brother, Jerry. He's five years ahead of me, and while we were raised in the exact same house by the exact same parents, we have completely unique memories of our childhoods. If you were to interrogate us about our pasts, you'd swear we came from two different families. I'm not exaggerating; it's as funny as hell.

So I now wonder what Jacob remembers. I do know one thing for sure: he remembers the incident about the summer season hockey tournament and the Gordie Howe hockey puck. He's never brought it up to me specifically or complained that I had him take the puck back from Ricky. But he wrote a poem in eighth grade that was obviously about that evening. He wrote the poem for his English class, and his teacher gave him an A. When he got the poem back from the teacher, he shared it with April and me. The poem went as follows:

Footrace

Congratulations, boy so fair,
You won the footrace fair and square.
Now the trophy is yours to do
With it any darn thing you choose.

Thumbtack it on your bedroom wall,
Clean it up in your shower stall,
Hang it out in the sun to dry,
Fly it like a kite in the sky,

Chew on it like a stick of gum,
Race it like a Formula One,
Paint it like the Mona Lisa
Treat it to some beer and pizza,
Take it to the beach for some sun,
Tell it, "You are the only one,"
Shine it with polish and a rag,
Or stuff it in a paper bag.

Just one thing that you cannot do,
And that's to give your trophy to
The boy fate tripped while on his way
To winning the race on that day.

I've always wondered if Jacob resented me for not backing him up that evening. To tell the truth, I've always had mixed feelings. As a father, I understood William's point. He didn't want his son to be rewarded for a loss, and he certainly didn't want the boy to be rewarded for crying. On the other hand, I was proud of my son, and I think he taught me a lesson. Jacob went out of his way to do what he thought was right. He showed maturity and compassion. He showed empathy for a boy who was hurting, and he was willing to make a personal sacrifice to make the boy feel better. And this was a good thing, right? I really think so. I think there's an awful lot of selfishness and callousness these days, and there's certainly nothing wrong with one person doing something kind for another. In fact, if more people behaved like Jacob, this world would be a much better place.

It was interesting, wasn't it? I mean, I was supposed to be the father. I was supposed to be the purveyor of wisdom and knowledge, yet with Jacob, it could be the other way around. I would learn from him. Jacob would be the teacher, and I would be the student.

I've discovered that learning from your children is half of what parenting is all about. The Vietnam War comes to mind as an example. I know, I know, it's now ancient history. And it certainly isn't a popular or current subject. I mean, people nowadays don't even want to talk about it. It's one of those wars we'd all just like to forget ever happened. But I bring it up now because it was one of those subjects about which I had strong opinions—opinions that Jacob would come to challenge. And I learned a lot from Jacob. In fact, this amazing boy of mine completely changed my mind. You can ask April. This was no easy feat.

I remember the sixties well. I remember all the hawks and doves. I remember the draft dodgers, draft card burners, and the conscientious objectors. I remember the bumper stickers, posters, protest songs, and marches. I remember all those kids who moved north to Canada. Me? I wasn't going anywhere. I was one of the good all-American boys who believed in his country, right or wrong, who believed in the wisdom of its leaders, who believed his older brother was in that stinking, bloody jungle several thousand miles away, fighting for a righteous cause. I knew that communism was just like those dominos, and that it had to be stopped.

My brother was drafted to serve in 1968, and I remember the day he left. Mom, Dad, and I took him to the bus depot, and we said our goodbyes. "You're a man now," Dad said to Jerry, "and we're all so proud of you. We'll be praying for you every day." So my brother was suddenly a man? This was kind of a weird way of looking at him. It seemed like only yesterday he was a dumb student in high school trying to muster up the nerve to ask Mary Anne Wallace to go to the senior prom. "What am I going to wear if she says yes?" he asked my mom. He didn't even own a sport coat. Heck, I don't think he even owned his own adult-sized necktie.

On the way home from the bus depot, no one said anything. It was eerie, and it was a little scary. Did Mom and Dad know something I didn't? Was it possible Jerry was never coming home? Was this the last we were going to see of him? It was a scene that was played out all over America as families shipped their young boys off to the war. I was just thirteen when Jerry boarded that bus, and here's what I knew: our way of life in America was being seriously threatened, and if we didn't stand up and fight, it wouldn't be long before all we loved and held dear was taken away from us for good. And by everything, I mean ice cream, baseball, chocolate milk, *Gilligan's Island*, the news with Walter Cronkite, bicycles, kites, PF Flyers, James Bond movies, Monopoly games, picnics, American flags, Fourth of July fireworks, and Christmas gifts under the tree. Yes, I mean all of it!

Those were tumultuous times. And who were these people who

opposed the war? They were the naive peaceniks and long-haired hippies. They were those idiots who wore anti-war buttons and smoked marijuana and took LSD and parroted idiotic slogans like "Turn on, tune in, and drop out." Seriously, what right did these people have to call brave young men like my brother cold-blooded killers and murderers? They would say things like, "War is not healthy for children and other living things." Well, no kidding. My brother took a bullet in his thigh that shattered his femur and sent him into surgery, so ask him how healthy he felt when they flew him back to the States in a cast and with his crutches.

So now you're probably asking, How does a fifty-six-year-old dad these days come to discuss this war with his sixteen-year-old son? Enter Mr. Winters. He was Jacob's US History teacher. Mr. Winters assigned Jacob and the rest of the class the task of writing a paper entitled "The Vietnam War: What Went Wrong?"

It was the perfect topic for Jacob, since he had already done a lot of reading on the subject. He worked for days on this paper, and I read it several times before he turned it in to be graded. I'll tell you what the paper said in a nutshell. Jacob believed the Vietnam War went wrong, all right, but not because we lost. The war went wrong *because the war was*. Does that make any sense to you? It didn't make any sense to me when I read the first paragraph of the paper, but that's exactly what he wrote. He said, "The Vietnam War went wrong *because it was*." Or, to put it another way, the war would not have gone right even if America had won. It was, according to Jacob, an inherently unwinnable war. A million people lost their lives for nothing. Jacob wrote, "It was one of the great bloody boondoggles of the twentieth century." A million people? I had to double-check Jacob's death count, and he was right. A million people were killed. It was not just a minor skirmish on the other side of our planet in a country of little consequence. It was a major, horrific, and terribly destructive war.

Do you know how many people a million is? You should think long and hard about it, for it's easy to lose your bearings when talking about big numbers and war casualties. Sometimes it just seems like so much ink on paper. I'll put it in perspective for you. Let's assume that the average person is five feet tall, and let's have the dead stand up on each other's shoulders. Do you now see what I mean? Believe it or not, the top dead person would be about a thousand miles high. So, how high is this? Commercial airplanes typically fly about seven miles above sea level. Outer space starts at about sixty-two miles. And now we're talking about a thousand miles. Do you see what I mean? It's hard to fathom.

Anyway, Jacob's paper for Mr. Winters used a single not-so-well-known quotation as its basis. He quoted Eisenhower when he said that if elections were held in Vietnam, 80 percent of the citizens would vote for the Communist Ho Chi Minh. According to Jacob, this quote alone made the war unwinnable by either side, for if we had allowed a democracy to play itself out, a tyranny would have been voted in, and if we were to fight against said tyranny, we would be fighting against democracy. Likewise, the people of Vietnam got a tyranny no matter what they did. Regardless of whether they sided with the tyranny against the United States or sided with the United States and voted in the tyranny, the final result would've been the same—they would've gotten their tyranny. All those involved with this ridiculous war was screwed no matter what they did.

Jacob wrote, "It was like killing a million people because of a dispute over the answer to a Zen koan. A Zen master would immediately have seen the futility. A true Zen master would've laughed his rear end off, were it not so tragic. Who we needed in office was not a politician from Texas, or a Dick Nixon from California, but a wise and gentle Zen master. He would've seen through it all."

I'll tell you the truth; Jacob's school paper rubbed me the wrong way when I first read it. Why did it bother me? I don't really know. I tried to talk to Jacob about it to help him see the right side of the issue. But the more I tried to express my opinions about the war, the less sure of my opinions I became. This was because Jacob was teaching me. Jacob was showing me the way!

"Are you saying that your Uncle Jerry took a bullet in his femur for nothing?" I once asked.

"No, not for nothing," Jacob said.

"Then what are you saying?"

"I'm saying that he thought he was doing the right thing—that his heart was in the right place."

"But?"

"But he had been misled."

"By the government?"

"By all of you. By the US government. By Grandma and Grandpa. By his friends."

"And, of course, you know better."

"I think I do."

"You're a sixteen-year-old, and you know better than all the experts in our military? You know better than all of our politicians? You know better than your grandparents?"

"I'm only telling you what I think."

"You realize, of course, that if you lived in a communist country, you might not be so free to express your opinions."

"I realize that."

"And?"

"I'm not sure what any of that has to do with what we're talking about."

"It has everything to do with it."

"What I've written about in my paper isn't a political opinion, or a statement about war in general, or a comparison of democracy versus communism."

"Then what exactly have you written about?"

"I've identified a conundrum."

"A conundrum?"

"An unsolvable puzzle."

"I think you've lost me," I said. And honestly, I had thought we *were* talking about democracy and communism. "What is this unsolvable puzzle?"

"It's what happens when you're given an option and you chose not to be given options."

"That doesn't make any sense."

"Exactly. That's what I'm saying. That's the point I'm trying to make. What do you do when you give people a freedom to choose how they'll be governed, and they choose to give up that freedom?"

I have to admit that he had me here. I had no good answer for his question, and I remember exactly what I did. I rubbed my chin and stared at him for a moment. The kid was obviously a lot smarter than I'd realized. Sixteen years old, and he had me stumped. I was finally beginning to see his point. "I guess you go to war," I said sarcastically.

"And that's exactly what we did."

"A boondoggle?"

"In the worst way possible."

I'll tell you something that I regret. And I regret this a lot. I never did tell Jacob that I thought he was absolutely right. I never said, "Jesus, son, I never even thought of the war this way, but you are right. I've been wrong all of these years. Yes, the war was a joke. It was all fought for nothing. It was a gigantic waste of time and resources, and a million lives were destroyed for no good reason."

That's what I should've said to Jacob. Maybe he understood that I did see his point, but I never did come right out and say that I agreed with him.

But back to the sixties. When my brother returned from the war, it had to be one of the happiest days ever in our house. It was such a huge relief that he wasn't killed. But Jerry did return home. He was in a cast and on crutches, but he was quite alive. I remember the day he returned. It was a very big deal. Mom wanted to have a celebration that Jerry would never forget, so she invited relatives and neighbors and friends to our house, and she baked a big cake that morning. It wasn't just any old cake, but a double chocolate chunk extravaganza with the words "Welcome Home Jerry" written on the top with white icing. Mom also made fried chicken, potato salad, and a pot of baked beans. She strung red, white, and blue crepe paper streamers all over the inside of the house, and she poked two rows of tiny American flags along the walkway leading to the front door. There must have been at least forty people at our home by the time Jerry arrived from the bus depot with Dad. When Jerry and Dad arrived, Jerry was the first to walk into the house. We saw him enter, and everyone yelled, "Welcome home, soldier!" Mom started bawling, and Jerry was smiling as though he'd just been dealt a royal flush in a high-stakes poker game.

"Wow, look at all you people," Jerry said.

"Everyone is here," Mom said, sobbing.

"I can see that."

"My son the soldier!"

"Alive and well."

"All in one piece."

"More or less," Jerry said, patting the plaster cast on his leg.

"You must have so many stories to tell."

"I could tell some stories," Jerry said, smiling.

"We knew you'd make it home."

"We were praying for you."

"So were we."

"Thank you," Jerry said. "Thank all of you. It means a lot to me."

"Are you hungry?" Mom asked. She had stopped crying and was now focused on feeding her son.

"I'm starving."

"Mom made fried chicken," I said. "And potato salad. And a pot of beans."

"Sounds good to me, squirt." Jerry was looking down at me. Then he said, "Have you been growing while I was gone? I swear you're a foot taller."

"I probably am."

"Don't get too big. Uncle Sam will want you too."

"The war will be over by the time Stanley turns eighteen," Dad said. "By then those Commies will have had about all they can take from us."

"That's right," Jerry said.

"They're probably getting ready to raise the white flag now," Dad said.

"They're tougher than you think," Jerry said, although he didn't seem to be paying attention to what he was saying. It seemed more like something he just let slip out.

"Come to the kitchen," Mom said. "Let me get some lunch for you. Have you lost weight? You look like you've lost twenty pounds."

"I probably have. I've been dreaming about a decent meal for months."

"Fried chicken is his favorite," Mom said to the guests, nodding her head. The guests all smiled at my mom. And Jerry smiled too.

"Did you kill any Commies?" Jimmy asked. Jimmy was our eight-year-old cousin. He was standing just a few feet from Jerry.

"I killed a few."

"How many?"

Jerry laughed. "I didn't keep count. But I killed my fair share of them." Jimmy pretended he was holding a rifle, and he pulled the trigger.

I was glad my brother was back. And Dad was happy. And I think Mom was the happiest of all of us. Honestly, it was great to see her smiling again.

A strange thing happened, however. And I never told anyone about this—not a single soul. I got up in the middle of the night later on to pee, and I walked past Jerry's bedroom on the way to the bathroom. At first I wasn't sure exactly what I was hearing, but then I was. It was coming from Jerry's room. It was my brother, and he was sobbing. It was so weird, and I had no idea what I should do. Should I go get Mom and Dad? Should I knock on the door? Why in the world was my brother crying? He had seemed so happy to be home.

I decided to ignore it. I used the toilet and went back to my bedroom. I was glad my brother was home. That was all that really mattered, right? And in a day or so it would be like old times.

So now what do I think about that night? Why do I think my brother was crying? I think I might know. I also think that I would've been well served to have had Jacob near me during those years. Jacob would've known what was happening. Jacob would've understood. Me? The all-American boy? Heck, back when I was Jacob's age, I had the insight of a squirrel. No kidding. I was clueless.

CHAPTER 5

HAPPY BIRTHDAY, ZACH

Here's the thing about being a parent. You're allowed to have children without having to train for the job, or study for it, or pass any written tests, or get any special degrees, permits, or licenses. It's just one of those things in life that you're allowed to do no matter who you are, or how stupid you are, or how irresponsible you are. It's probably the most important thing you will ever do in your life, and you're allowed to just wing it. It's amazing, isn't it?

The last time I went to have my hair cut, I noticed that my barber had a license from the State of California that included his picture, a state seal, and a couple signatures. The license was posted next to the mirror, and it suddenly struck me how crazy things were. To cut a person's hair, you had to have this official state-issued paper license, but to raise a child, you needed nothing. All you needed to have is a desire to copulate with a partner of the opposite sex without a condom. Heck, you didn't even have to want the kid.

As I tried to slow down the bleeding from Jacob's wrists, I couldn't help but wonder whether I had been such a great father. I mean, seriously, the boy was now trying to kill himself! He was *my* boy. He was *my* flesh and blood. Wasn't the fact that his wrists were slashed and blood was swirling into the shower drain a pretty clear sign that I screwed things up? He was the product of all my parenting efforts, my talents, my supposed wisdom, and the whole thing had turned into a gory debacle—a complete disaster. There were imbeciles and drug addicts who had done better than I had as a parent.

When Zach turned fifteen, we went out to dinner at a restaurant called John's Steakhouse in Newport Beach. Unlike most other steakhouses I've been to,

John's was well-known for its generous portions. How many steakhouses have you been to? As a rule, I don't care for these steakhouse restaurants because you usually wind up paying through the nose for a really stingy allotment of beef—a portion of meat so small that it's actually humorous, like a scene from a New Yorker cartoon. It's like these places are deliberately trying to make you laugh. The last time we went to one of these upscale steakhouses, I ordered a filet, and they brought me a piece of meat I could literally have devoured in three bites. I think when they set the plate down before me, I said something like, "What the fuck is this—the appetizer?" And if I remember right, the waiter ignored me. This was his way of telling me how gauche I was.

Our waiter obviously had no sense of humor. Do you think he was actually offended by my comment? I think he was. And you should have seen this idiot's face when I then asked for a bottle of catsup. I don't know about you, but I can't eat steak without my catsup.

John's was different than the other steakhouses we'd gone to. One, they had no problem bringing me a bottle of catsup. Two, their steaks were big enough to feed a roomful of hungry ranch hands. They were big and juicy and medium rare, the way a good steak should be served. Three, the waiters at John's were not snobs. I detest restaurants where the servers act like they're doing you a favor. Seriously, who do these people think they are? They're servers, right? Their job is to serve you, to take your order and bring out your food and keep your water glass full. In a word, they are the "help," and they work for you. You don't work for them, and you shouldn't have to waste time and energy trying to impress them. They should be worried about impressing you, and goddamn it, if you want a bottle of catsup with your steak, you ought to be able to get one without your server rolling his eyes. And I don't mean a tiny glass bowl with a red dollop of fancy catsup, but a full-sized bottle of name-brand catsup with an all-American label and a metal screw-off cap.

When we arrived at John's we were taken to a table next to one of the windows. The window looked out over the parking lot, and so did the other windows. In other words, the charm and character of the restaurant were not a result of the views. Instead they came from the unique interior. John himself was a prize fighter who had been popular about ten years ago. He used the money he won knocking the shit out of his opponents to build up this restaurant and immortalize his name. His full name was John

Everette Cassidy; perhaps you remember him? The press called him the Irish Tornado. Now do you remember him? Do you follow boxing at all? I think he had only two losses during his long career of forty or so fights, and for several years he was an undisputed champion. I don't remember which weight class he fought in. Anyway, the inside of the restaurant was filled with photos from his fights, some boxing posters, several framed reproductions of oil paintings of old-time pugilists, and autographed pairs of boxing gloves hung by their laces. It was like a basement man cave that happened to serve steaks and cocktails.

Zach loved this place. Of all the restaurants we'd gone to in Orange County, I think this was his favorite. He especially liked that all the waiters were former boxers. It was a pretty colorful group of men. And I liked the restaurant too. April hated boxing, but she did like a good steak. And Jacob? Well, let's just say there wasn't really anything here to turn Jacob on. The boxing? The steaks? No, these weren't Jacob-type things.

But me? I love steaks. Further, I've always been a big boxing fan. I really do love the sport. I could watch boxing matches for hours and never get bored. I've never been to a match in person, but I like to watch them on TV. A cold beer, a bowl of popcorn, and a good boxing match—what could make for a better evening? I also love playoff hockey, which at times resembles a boxing bout. I guess I like watching men throw fists at each other.

You know what I've always thought? I've always believed that instead of waging wars, we ought to just have boxing matches. I'm not kidding about this. When the US was at odds with Saddam Hussein's Iraq, rather than go to war, we should've had a Mexican-beer-sponsored boxing match at the Staples Center in Los Angeles, or at a similar venue in Iraq. They should've put boxing gloves on Bush and Hussein, spread gobs of Vaseline on their faces, and stuck mouthguards into their mouths. Then they should've let them go after each other in the ring with three respectable ringside judges from neutral countries looking on. Heck, it would attract more TV viewers than the OJ Simpson trial and the latest Super Bowl combined. It would make for the best TV entertainment ever broadcast, and you know what would really be great about this? Imagine the wanton destruction of lives and property that would be avoided. Imagine the fiscal savings to our respective governments. Seriously, imagine it.

You say this could never happen? You say this world leader boxing match idea of mine is unlikely and unrealistic? In fact, you think it's preposterous? Maybe it is, but preposterous compared to what? Compared to the reality we're content to live with? During the Iraq War alone, over half a million lives were lost because of the war, and the United States squandered over a trillion dollars—about five thousand dollars per second. And think of the damage done! Billions of dollars. And all these costs are what to you? Unbelievable? Unacceptable? How about we call *them* preposterous? What is more preposterous, suffering the crippling costs and damages of a full-blown war, or staging a Friday-night boxing match between a couple of self-absorbed leaders? I mean, seriously. People should think about this. It's a darn good idea.

But I'm digressing. Let's go back to John's Steakhouse. Zach, Jacob, April, and I were all seated at the table and looking at our menus. I don't even know why Zach bothered to look at his. He already knew what he was going to get. He got the same thing every time we came to this place. For sure he would order a forty-ounce tomahawk ribeye steak, a steak nearly as big as his adolescent head. Funny as hell, right? Believe it or not, Zach would eat the entire thing. There'd be nothing left on his plate but a Flintstones-sized bone. I wanted to order a porterhouse, and April wanted a little filet mignon. And Jacob? Well, Jacob didn't eat meat, so he was going to order a chef's salad.

"Just once I'd like to see you order a steak," Zach said to Jacob.

"Not going to happen," Jacob said.

"You don't know what you're missing."

"I'm just fine."

"Who are you trying to impress?"

"I'm not trying to impress anyone."

"Is it a girl?"

"Is who a girl?"

"The person you're trying to impress?"

"No," Jacob said. "I just told you; I'm not trying to impress anyone. I just don't like eating meat."

"You don't have to worry about her here. We won't tell her about it."

"There's no girl."

"Leave him alone," I said.

"Yeah, leave me alone."

"Maybe you're trying to score points with God?"

"No, of course not."

"Because I'm telling you God doesn't give a flying Watusi warrior's ass if you're vegan or not."

"How do you know what God thinks?"

"I just know," Zach said. "And any idiot knows that God put cattle and pigs and chickens and sheep and turkeys on the earth for humans to eat. That's what they're here for. It's manifest destiny."

"You don't even know what 'manifest destiny' means."

"Sure I do. Listen, I have a question for you. If you were stranded on a deserted island with a big, fat, juicy cow and a barbecue grill, would you become best friends with the cow and starve to death, or would you cook the damn thing?"

"You're an idiot."

"Well? What would you do?"

"First of all, it's a *desert* island, and not a *deserted* island. And second, no I wouldn't murder the cow. I'm sure there'd be some edible plant life on the island I could round up for food. And third, it's a dumb hypothetical. Why would I be stranded on a desert island with a cow and a barbecue grill? The whole thing makes no sense."

"I was just saying, you know, what if."

"Well, listen, here's a what-if for *you*. What if you were a nineteenth-century Frenchman convicted of high crimes by the Cour de Cassation, sentenced to meet the guillotine? What if they told you that if you could prove that you had an IQ over eighty, you'd be pardoned and set free? What the heck would *you* do?"

"That's dumb," Zach said.

"No dumber than the island and the cow. And the barbecue grill."

"Anyway, it isn't like I'm stupid."

"No?" Jacob said.

"I get better grades than you."

"Since when do you have to be smart to get good grades? You're good at following instructions. You're good at doing what you're told."

"I don't always do what I'm told," Zach said defensively.

"You boys need to stop this," I said. I was trying to sound stern. I really wanted the bickering to stop.

"I agree," April said.

"He started it," Jacob said.

"You're the weird one. You're the one who won't eat meat. You're the one who orders a salad at a steakhouse. You're the one who eats like a rabbit. You're the one who spends all his time writing poetry."

"There's nothing wrong with poetry," I said. I didn't like having to take sides when it came to my sons, but I also didn't want Jacob to feel I didn't support him.

"Roses are red," Zach said. "Violets are blue. Elton John is a fag, and so are you."

"Seriously?" Jacob said.

"That's enough," I said.

"We're here to have fun," April said. "Let's talk about something else."

I didn't like it when people looked at Jacob as being weird because he wrote poetry. True, I may not have understood all of it, and I may have disagreed with some of it. And I may have at times wished he showed as much interest in activities such as sports as he did in rhyming words and counting syllables, but the poetry meant a lot to him. And if it meant a lot to him, then it meant a lot to me. As I said before, I was no poetry expert, but it seemed to me he knew what he was doing. And he was an interesting kid. He was a thoughtful kid. And he was a unique kid who deserved to be treated with respect.

I had a friend in Coto named Ralph Anderson. I met Ralph at the roller hockey games. His son was on one of Zach's teams, and I came to like Ralph a lot. He was a building contractor—a real salt-of-the-earth, nuts-and-bolts sort of guy. He cussed a lot, which didn't bother me—I figured it was a consequence of hanging around construction workers all day. There was nothing fancy about this man, and what you saw was what you got. He invited me to come over on a Saturday evening and watch a Laker game with him, and I arrived at his house about seven. I was looking forward to spending a good down-to-earth couple of hours watching the TV. Ralph had beer, tortilla chips, and guacamole waiting for us on the coffee table, and he had one of those gargantuan TVs. I mean, the thing was gigantic. I met Ralph's wife, whose name was Elaine, and she wasn't your typical Coto housewife, in that she was slightly overweight and dressed like she did her clothes shopping at Walmart. But she was very friendly, and I think she was the one who made the guacamole. We sat down on the sofa, and Ralph clicked on the big TV. And just a minute or so later, I heard something that surprised me. It was piano music coming from the front room, and I recognized it right away. I know a thing or two about classical music, and I recognized it as Debussy's "Clair de Lune."

"Someone here play the piano?" I asked.

"That's my older son."

"He's good."

"Yeah, he's very good. It's beautiful, isn't it?"

"Debussy?"

"Not sure what it is," Ralph said. "But it makes the house a home. We're going to miss him when he goes to college. He's going to a music school. He got a full scholarship."

"You don't say?" I said. A budding concert pianist, the spawn of a guy who cusses a lot and erects buildings for a living. It was amusing to me.

And I was impressed. I mean, Ralph probably didn't know Debussy from Mozart, yet he was so proud of his boy. It was obvious to me. And it was the same way I felt about Jacob and his poetry. I didn't know Keats from Longfellow. Hell, I wasn't even positive the two of them were poets, but I was so proud of Jacob.

During the week following our dinner at John's, Jacob wrote a poem about the outing. He didn't give it to April and me to read. Instead I found this one in his wastebasket. Maybe he wasn't happy with the way it turned out. Or maybe he just wrote it to get his feelings off his chest, having no use for it after it was done, crumpling it up and throwing it away. In any event, I saved the poem, and it went as follows:

Dinner at John's

You have to see this place to believe it.
You have to smell it to understand.
All the waiters look like they've been hit
By too many jabs and left hooks and

Right crosses and uppercuts and knockout
Punches. They inquire how you choose
To have your steak prepared, and you shout out,
'Cook that bitch until it's black and blue!'

We're all there for Zach. Yippee and wahoo,
We're singing the happy birthday song.
Look like a monkey, and smell like one too,
And I promise you I am not wrong

When I say I wish I was Zach, at times.
How nice it would be to fit into
This world like a shoe the perfect size,
Or like one and one making two,

Or like a joyous mockingbird, or like
A cat's whiskers, or like a dog's nose,
Or like a paper boy on his bike,
Or a gardener with his rubber hose

Full of water, or like car with its
Tank full of gas, packed up and ready
For a road trip, or like a man who sits
On his porch watching the world fly by.

Or maybe like a big cloud in the sky
That looks like a big brontosaurus,
Or Abe Lincoln's face, or like the old guy
Who sings in the local church chorus.

Zachary, deep as a sheet of paper.
Happy birthday, dear brother of mine.
Maybe we can talk for a while later
And you can teach me to smile and shine.

That's my goal.

One of these fine days I'm going to unlock
All the secrets of your shallow soul.

Yes, that is my goal.

That was the first poem I remember Jacob writing where he spoke of admiring his brother. It also conveyed his discontent. It was not a discontent with his family, or school, or friends, or anything external. It was a discontent with himself. Jacob was experiencing unhappiness. Jacob was understanding himself as odd and wishing he was different. I didn't see this when I first read the poem, but I see it now.

I think there were times when I could've done a better job as a father. I could've been more in tune with Jacob's unhappy feelings. I could've paid closer attention to him. I could've read his poetry more carefully. But you know what they say—that hindsight is twenty-twenty. It's so true, isn't it? If you'd asked me years ago if I thought I was doing a good job as a father, I would surely have told you that yes, I was being the best that I could be. And why not? I was a good man, and I loved both of my sons. If you're a good person, how can you go wrong? If you're a good person, what more could you possibly need to be?

Oh, to be a dog, a furry, panting, four-legged, dog food–eating dog. We had a dog when I was a boy—a golden retriever named Rudy. He was a great dog. He was my best friend. The best way I know to describe Rudy to you is by describing not what he was but what he wasn't. He wasn't anything like the rest of us. He was a dog.

Rudy got up every morning at the crack of dawn. Unlike the rest of us in our family, he didn't care if we were out of milk for our cereal or if we were out of half-and-half for our coffee. Heck, he didn't even care if we were out of coffee. He actually needed a caffeine boost like he needed a hole in his head. Rudy didn't care if the morning paper was wet from the sprinklers, or if the toast was burnt, or if we were running late for school. If it was raining buckets outside, then so much the better. Rudy loved the rain. If the work traffic was unbearable, Rudy couldn't have cared less. Rudy never did learn how to drive, and traffic meant nothing to him. When the boss at the office was impossible, or when fellow workers didn't pull their weight, or when the office phones went down, it didn't bother Rudy. Not even in the slightest. Our troops overseas could lose another battle in Vietnam, or protestors could throw more rocks and bottles at police, or neo-Nazis could be marching up and down Main Street—it didn't matter to Rudy. Rudy didn't care a lick about politics. When the president was callous or ignorant, or when Hollywood was hypocritical, or when athletes took performance-enhancing drugs, or when the bottom fell out of the stock market, or when pharmaceutical companies overcharged sick people for their pills, it just didn't matter to Rudy. And when Dad drank too much, or Mom ate too much, or when my brother got caught shoplifting a baseball mitt at the local five-and-dime, Rudy just shrugged. And when the TV went on the fritz right before the Super Bowl, Rudy was just fine and dandy. The repairman said it could take a month to get the part he needed. No problem for Rudy. In fact, Rudy seemed to be happy no matter what was going on.

I'm not going to lie to you. There have been days when I wished I was Rudy. As we used to say, he had it "made in the shade."

CHAPTER 6

BOBBY FISCHER

———— •◆• ————

I think I already told you that if I wanted to put my finger on the year Jacob began to change, I would aim for around the time he turned thirteen. I mean, he was still Jacob, but he also wasn't. He just wasn't the same happy-go-lucky kid he was before that age. And he was more mature. Sometimes when talking to him, I felt as though I were talking to adult. I guess the best way to explain this transformation is to give you an example of what I'm talking about, and the best example I can think of is the interest Jacob had concerning the great chess player Bobby Fischer. Bobby passed away just a few days following the day we all celebrated Jacob's thirteenth birthday. Are you old enough to remember this man? Do you know very much about him? I don't think Jacob even knew Bobby existed until he died, but following his death, Jacob suddenly became very curious about the eccentric and often unlikeable man. Assuming you don't know a lot about Bobby Fischer, I'll throw some facts at you.

Bobby Fischer was born in Chicago in 1943 and would grow up to become one of the greatest chess players of all time. He started playing at age six, and he later dropped out of high school just to become a better chess player. Dropping out of school did him good. He eventually became the youngest chess grand master in history at the age of fifteen, and he won his first world championship at the age of twenty-nine. His name became a household word in the sixties and seventies. He was like a living legend and attracted unprecedented and worldwide attention to the game. He was winning matches right and left. But you should also know this about Bobby: he was a really queer duck. He was irascible and difficult to get along with. He was opinionated. He was antisemitic and paranoid. And he was always getting himself into all kinds of trouble. If you want a detailed list of all his difficulties, go ahead and read up on him. Plenty has been written about Bobby, and I'm not going reiterate it all here. I'm just going to say that Jacob was fascinated, and he was especially interested in the series of statements Bobby made about the attacks on the World Trade Center and Pentagon on September 11. Bobby will always be known as the genius-turned-idiot and traitor who actually praised the attacks.

So what did he say exactly? He said that he was "happy that the airliner attacks happened." He also said, "This just shows you, what goes around, comes around, even for the United States."

Never in a million years would I have figured this kind of inflammatory talk from a screwball chess champion would have an effect on my son, but it did. And it did in a big way. Bobby's September 11 comments were published in a news article about his life that appeared in our local paper the day after he passed away. Jacob read the article, and he agreed with and related to many of Bobby's statements. Bobby said things that Jacob had believed to be true—namely that the United States was not the benign doer of good around the world that it pretended to be. In fact, in many cases, the US was an outright villain. Case in point? There was always Vietnam, where one million people were brutally killed for no good reason. Of course, there was also the Iraq War subsequent to 9/11, in which another half-million notches could be carved into the handles of our guns. According to Jacob, Bobby was right when he claimed we had the September 11 attacks coming to us. Sure he told me, it was immoral for terrorists to take three thousand lives, but we had asked for it. Or, as Bobby said, "what goes around, comes around."

Had Jacob kept these controversial musings to himself, I'm sure nothing would ever have come of them. But that's not what happened. In his eighth-grade history class, the students were charged with writing papers describing their feelings about a recent historical event. The man teaching this class was Mr. Maloof, an instructor I knew very little about. Inspired by what he had just read about Bobby Fischer, Jacob wrote his paper about September 11. He quoted Bobby Fischer and then argued that the US had simply gotten its just desserts. Mr. Maloof was so impressed with Jacob's arguments and insights that he encouraged Jacob to submit the paper to our local newspaper as a guest opinion piece. Well, wouldn't you know, the paper chose to publish it, and all hell broke loose. Who would've thought a thirteen-year-old boy who spent most of his time listening to outdated music and writing harmless poetry could stir up such a contentious hornet's nest?

After Jacob's paper was published, just about everyone in Orange County wanted to know not just more about Jacob but also more about who in the hell his teacher was. They asked what sort of imbecile would encourage his students to author such a pile of unpatriotic crap. Within weeks, the fur began to fly. Responding to the public's outrage, the paper published an in-depth article about Mr. Maloof that was written by a staff reporter. The reporter painted a shady picture of the teacher as being a thirtysomething Syrian-born immigrant schoolteacher who claimed not to condone terrorists and their methods but who also sympathized with many of their causes. The article said Mr. Maloof flew to Syria to visit with his family regularly, but "who really knew what he did while he was there?" The reporter also said Maloof earned his degree from UCLA, and that prior to coming to Orange County to teach white upper-class kids about history, he was teaching dark-skinned Syrian immigrants how to speak and read English at a Los Angeles mosque that supposedly had ties to ISIS. You could practically hear every conservative patriot in Orange County say at the same time, "I knew it!"

Needless to say, it wasn't long before the administrators at the school took action and showed Mr. Maloof the door. They published a response to the public's outrage, apologizing for having hired Mr. Maloof and for not having done a better job investigating him before putting students under his wing. This apology seemed to calm down the parents. I mean, it calmed them down until the national news media caught wind of the story and stoked up the flames again. But forget about Mr. Maloof. His goose had been cooked, and he was history. The public wanted to hear from Jacob. It was bizarre. Every day we got more and more requests from reporters for interviews and invitations for Jacob to appear on TV talk shows. After talking to Jacob about the pros and cons of meeting with the media, Jacob decided he wanted to appear on *The Chester Hill Show*.

It was true that Chester had carved out a niche in the talk show business as a calm, rational, and kindhearted host who was neither a liberal nor a conservative. He was more like a kind of political eunuch. Jacob had watched his show, and he liked the guy. He liked the way he seemed so open-minded. And after discussing the matter at length, we came to the conclusion that there were a lot of mistruths and misunderstandings floating around in the country, and that a meeting with Chester Hill might clear the air. It was something that just needed to be done, so I called back Chester and agreed to have him meet with Jacob. I wanted Jacob to be on friendly territory; thus the meeting was to take place at our house. Chester had no problem with this, and ten days later he was at our home with his cameras, microphones, and crew.

I remember when they arrived. It was daunting, and I began to wonder if we had made the right decision. After all, Jacob was only thirteen years old. I felt a little like he was being fed to the lions, but after chatting with Chester, I got the feeling that we had made a wise decision. Did you happen to catch this show on TV? A lot of people tuned in that night. Jacob and Chester sat in our front room. Chester was dressed casually in a maroon sweater and a pair of khaki slacks, and Jacob wore a T-shirt and threadbare jeans. I sat off to the side, near the window and away from the cameras, and as the interview proceeded, I crossed my fingers. I figured Jacob could use all the luck he could get.

Lights, cameras, action. They were off and running, and Chester spoke first.

"We're in the home of the Harper family in Orange County, California," he said. "I'm talking to thirteen-year-old Jacob Harper. We're going to be talking this evening about an opinion piece that Jacob wrote. The piece was published in his local paper and was subsequently picked up by every news service in the country. A lot of hairs went up on the backs of a lot of necks. You've created quite a stir, young man."

"I guess I have," Jacob said.

"Did you think there would be such an emotional response to your paper when it was first published?"

"I was a little surprised."

"The paper was written for your history class—is that correct?"

"Yes," Jacob said.

"Your teacher asked you to write about a historic event in the twenty-first century."

"Yes, we were supposed to describe it and tell how we felt about it."

"And you chose 9/11?"

"I did."

"Is there a reason you chose this particular event?"

"Bobby Fischer had just died, and I read about him in our paper. And I read about his comments. I thought what he said was interesting."

"He commented on 9/11?"

"He did," Jacob said. "Right after the attack. I think he was living in the Philippines when the attack took place. I think he was on the run. The US authorities wanted to lock him up in prison."

"And what did he say about 9/11?"

"Basically, he said the United States deserved what it got. He said we should've seen it coming. And he said he was happy that the attacks occurred."

"And you agreed with him?"

"In part, I did. I didn't agree with everything."

"What didn't you agree with?"

"Well, I wasn't happy about it. The attacks did not make me feel happy. It was a terrible tragedy. It was upsetting and frightening, and I felt for the people in those buildings. I felt for the families of the victims. And I felt for the first responders."

"Then what *did* you agree with?"

"I agreed that the United States deserved the attacks. It should have come as no surprise. I believe our country has just been asking for it."

"Asking for it?"

"Because of the way we walk all over other countries. Because of our arrogance. Because of the things we do."

"Can you give me an example?"

"There are many, but I can give you the worst one."

"Which is?"

"The Vietnam War."

"That was a little before your time, no?"

"Maybe so, but I know a lot about it. And whether it was before my time or not, it happened."

"And what does it have to do with 9/11? I don't think I've ever heard anyone blame 9/11 on the Vietnam War."

"It wasn't a direct result of the war. That's not what I mean to say. I mean to say it was a result of the Vietnam War attitude."

"The attitude?"

"The attitude of Americans."

"And what attitude is that?"

"We think we're always in the right. Yet we're not always right. Often we are completely wrong."

"You don't think we were right to help the South Vietnamese get a democracy?"

"They didn't want a democracy. And they especially didn't want capitalism. They wanted a communist government, and they wanted Ho Chi Minh to run it."

"They did?"

"When US involvement in the war started, 80 percent of Vietnamese wanted communism. That's a fact. They wanted Ho Chi Minh to take charge of the country. That was according to our own President Eisenhower. He said it, not me. If Vietnam had been a democracy at the time, they would've voted capitalism and democracy out and communism in. But we didn't want them to choose, because we didn't like their choice. We wanted them to be just like us, whether they wanted to or not, because we believed we were in the right—that our way was the only right way for them to go. So what did we do? We fought against the communism that they wanted and killed over a million Vietnamese in the process."

"But don't you think most Americans these days view the Vietnam War as a mistake?"

"Yes, but not for the right reason. America hasn't learned a lesson at all."

"Oh?" Chester said.

"You know what we've learned? We haven't learned to accept that some people are different from us. We haven't learned that there are other kinds of governments that are appropriate to other kinds of people. What we did learn is simple. We learned not to pick a fight with a country if we're not sure we can win the war."

"I suppose that's one thing we learned."

"It's the only thing we learned. We learned that losing a war really sucks. The important lessons of that conflict went completely over our heads. And this is why there are so many people in the world that hate our guts. If you ask the average American why the Vietnam War was a tragedy, he'll tell you it was because we lost, and because we lost so many soldiers, and not because we slaughtered a million people who simply wanted to govern their country the way they saw fit."

"I'm still not sure what this has to do with 9/11."

"It has everything to do with it."

"So you think that attacking the World Trade Center and the Pentagon was justified? You think it was okay to murder three thousand innocent people because of our involvement in Vietnam?"

"No, that's not what I'm saying."

"Can I ask about your teacher?"

"Mr. Maloof?"

"Yes, him."

"Go ahead."

"How much influence did he have on your school paper? Is he the one who gave you these ideas? Is he the one who brought up Vietnam?"

"No, the ideas were all mine."

"And Mr. Maloof did nothing?"

"He only graded my paper and then suggested I send it to the newspaper. He told me that it was worthy of being read by the public."

"What grade did he give you?"

"He gave me an A."

"And then he said he thought it would be appropriate to have it published?"

"Yes, that's what I just said."

"And you thought the paper would be received well by Orange County readers?"

"I really didn't know what to expect. But I didn't think people would get as mad as they got."

"How about your classmates at school? What did they think of your paper?"

"Most of them didn't even read it. A few who read it said they liked my ideas, but most kids got their opinions from their parents, and those kids didn't like it at all."

"Would you say all this has made you less popular at school?"

"I was never very popular to begin with."

"If you had all this to do over again, would you do the same thing? I mean, would you even write the paper? And would you have it published?"

"I would write the same paper, but I'm not sure I would publish it. I really didn't want to make everyone angry with me. That wasn't my intention."

"Do you understand why some people are angry?"

"I guess."

"Don't you see how you might've upset some people deeply—how you touched a very raw nerve?"

"Actually, I think it's kind of weird."

"Weird?"

"Ever since I was a little kid, I've been told what a great country it is that we live in. It's great because its citizens are free. We are free to think and form our own opinions about this and that. We are free to express ourselves. And we are also free to disagree with others. Yet it seems that as soon as I came up with an opinion of my own that happened to be a little different from everyone else's opinion, people not only wanted to tell me how wrong I was but also wanted to tell me how my opinion was un-American. I get that I'm only thirteen years old and that I have a lot to learn. But I ask you, how can an opinion be un-American when being free to have your own opinion is what America is all about?"

Chester didn't answer Jacob's question, and that's where the interview was stopped. I was pleased that Chester had given Jacob the last word. In my opinion, the interview couldn't have gone any better. In fact, if I didn't know better, I'd have thought Chester did agree with Jacob. He would never say whether he agreed or disagreed. That wasn't Chester's style. But like I said, I don't think the interview could've gone any better.

So now you're probably curious about the public's reaction to Chester's show. How did Jacob fare in the court of popular opinion? The truth is that the interview kind of fizzled and did nothing, like a wet firecracker. Apparently people weren't as interested in an adolescent's musings as the producers of Chester's show had predicted. The big news at the time, the blood in the water, was the current Great Recession and all the problems it was causing. So, sure, years ago a handful of deranged terrorists flew airliners into a few buildings, and three thousand people were killed as a result. But now? Well, now real estate values were plummeting, and the stock market was in serious trouble, and thousands of Americans were losing their jobs, and some of the country's largest and most respected institutions were threatening to file bankruptcy. Maybe the airing of Jacob's interview was just bad timing—or, now that I think about it, maybe it was good timing. I guess it depended on how you looked at it. Me? I was just glad to see the spotlight off my son. I was pleased to see things getting back to normal.

A week after Jacob's interview aired on TV, Zach's roller hockey team was playing in a weekend tournament at a facility in Irvine. April and I went to the tournament, but Jacob didn't want to go. The place was crawling with parents, children, and young hockey players. Zach's team did very well that day. They made it all the way to the finals, and when the final game was being played, there must've been a hundred people watching. The first half of the game was a little slow. I mean, all the boys were trying hard to win, but nothing was happening. No goals were scored, and the audience was quiet. But the action heated up in the second half, and that's when Zach really picked up his game. He scored two goals and then he was thrown out of the game.

What happened? I'll tell you exactly what I saw. Zach was skating with the puck, and there was no one in front of him to slow him down. He was on his way to take a shot on the goal when one of the defensemen from the other team skated up behind Zach and began whacking at Zach's calves repeatedly with the heel of his hockey stick. He was hitting Zach hard, over and over, where there was no protection, and the closer Zach came to the goal, the angrier he got. Finally, instead of taking a shot at the goal, Zach slammed on the brakes and turned around to face the kid. The kid stopped too, and for a moment they just stood face-to-face. Then Zach raised his stick, and with a sudden violent blow, he cross-checked the kid right in his throat. He hit the kid pretty hard, and the boy fell backward. He landed right on his butt, and he began bawling and kicking his legs and skates. He was also holding on to his throat and coughing. The ref immediately skated up to Zach and grabbed his jersey. He then threw Zach out of the game, giving him a major misconduct penalty. Zach didn't bother to protest. He just skated off the rink and went to the locker room to take off his gear and climb back into his street clothes.

Since Zach was one of the team's best players, you would think that losing him would cause a lot of problems. But this was not the case. The misconduct penalty to Zach actually got the team even more fired up to win, and win they did. The final score was five to two. The trophies were handed out after the game was over, and as the official called out the winning names from the players on Zach's team, they came to the center of the rink to get their awards. It was great. I mean to say that I was really proud that afternoon, for when Zach's name was called out loud, everyone cheered like crazy. They had all seen what that other kid had been doing to Zach, and they loved the fact that Zach stood up for himself. And, of course, they loved that they had won.

As we were leaving the hockey facility, I was approached by one of the moms from the other team. She caught my attention and then frowned at me. "Aren't you that boy's dad?" she asked. "You should be ashamed of yourself."

To tell you the truth, I didn't know how to respond. I didn't know if she was referring to Zach and his cross-check or to Jacob and his interview with Chester Hill. A lot of people saw that interview. So what did I say to her? I simply said, "Lady, I'm proud of both of my sons. Enjoy the rest of your afternoon." Seriously, what do people like that think you're going to say?

CHAPTER 7

THE BLUEST SKIES

—•●•—

Here's a question for you. Can a fourteen-year-old boy fall in love with a girl, or is fourteen just too young? When Jacob was that age, I thought it was perfectly reasonable to say he might become infatuated with a girl, but falling in love? I honestly didn't know. It just seemed like falling in love was something that more mature kids did. Maybe they'd fall in love when they were seniors in high school. Maybe even as juniors. But now that I look back to those years, I realize he probably had fallen in love with Mary Parker. The poor kid. I could see the heartbreak coming from a mile away, and so could April. But there was nothing either of us could do.

Ah, sweet little Mary Parker. She was the daughter of Ed and Karen Parker. Dr. Ed was an oncologist at Hoag Hospital in Newport Beach, and Karen was an interior decorator who worked for clients in Coto. I knew the couple from cocktail parties April and I had attended over the years, and they seemed like a nice enough pair. They liked to travel a lot and always had interesting stories to tell about their trips to various parts of the world. I enjoyed talking to them at these parties because they didn't brag about their travels the way a lot of people around here do. Seriously, I think some people travel just to prove they can afford to do it—just to prove they can pay for the first-class plane tickets and pricey hotel rooms, and just to prove they can take time off of work. Have you met people like this? I find them to be very annoying—almost as annoying as people who brag incessantly about their bright and athletic children, assuming that you care. But I didn't find Ed or Karen annoying at all. The stories they told were actually interesting.

Ed and Karen took Mary on nearly all their trips. A lot of couples leave their kids home with babysitters when they travel, but not Ed and Karen. As a consequence, Mary, at the young age of fourteen, had been all

61

around the globe. She had experienced a lot for a kid her age, seen a lot of sights, heard a lot of foreign languages spoken, and eaten at a lot of crazy, exotic restaurants. Perhaps this explained her precocious worldliness and self-confidence. Maybe April and I should have travelled more over the years, taking the boys with us and exposing them to other ways of life. I think they would probably have benefited from it, but there was an obstacle in the way of doing this: I hated hotel rooms. I had a real problem with sticking my face and nose into hotel bed pillows on which God knows how many snoring and disgusting strangers had drooled while they slept. Seriously, it made me want to gag. I don't mean that I just disliked hotel rooms, more or less. I mean I truly hated them, and since travel involved unavoidably staying in hotels, I kept away from travelling like I avoided going to the dentist. Ah, the good old dentist. I am convinced to this day that these doctors of our mouths are just bullies and sadists of yore who've grown up and discovered a socially acceptable means to torment and torture their fellow human beings. No, I don't like dentists at all. Never have, and never will. But back to the subject at hand. Back to Mary.

Mary came over to our home often—especially during the summer, since the Parkers didn't have a swimming pool. It was easy to see why Jacob was so fond of this girl. First, she was a real looker. Everything about Mary's countenance said, "I'm young and beautiful, and I have my whole marvelous life ahead of me." When she was over at our house, I sometimes found it difficult not to stare. It was not a dirty old man kind of stare, but rather the way one stares at an amazing painting or sculpture in a museum. But the things I think made her especially attractive were her personality, her carefree laugh, and her joyous sense of humor. She was one of those teenage girls who absolutely loved the idea of being alive, who cherished every step forward she took while growing up, and who wouldn't trade her young lot in life for all the gold in Fort Knox.

We had Mary over for dinner several times while Jacob was in the ninth grade. Like Jacob, Mary wasn't interested in her own generation's styles, trends, current events, politics, art, music, or literature. She was fascinated by the sixties and early seventies, and so it was no wonder she got along so well with Jacob. And I guess it was also no wonder she got along so well with us, since we were from that era. It turned out that Mary's all-time favorite artist was Bob Dylan. Despite the fact that I was something of a square as a kid, I too was a fan of Dylan when I was younger, and I thought I knew a lot about him. But there wasn't anything about Dylan's life that Mary didn't know, and there wasn't a single song he wrote that she didn't nearly know by heart. I think she had me beat by a mile. And it was funny. Whenever someone pointed out something that was more or less obvious, Mary would quote Bob and say, "Well, you don't need a weather vane to know which way the wind blows." I swear I heard her say this line at least ten times.

Obviously, I wasn't privy to their private conversations, so I don't know if Mary ever told Jacob she loved him, or if she said she just liked him a lot, or if she said anything about her feelings for him at all. But it was obvious that Jacob was head over heels smitten. And like I said, April and I both knew this girl was going to break Jacob's heart. We could just tell. I can't put my finger on anything she said or did to make me feel this way about her, but I felt it for sure. Maybe it was just that she was such a free, lithe, and independent spirit that I knew she would never allow herself to be shackled by a boy's feelings, no matter how much she cared for him. And I thought she cared for my son a lot. But as she would say, you didn't need a weather vane. No, you most certainly didn't. I didn't see the relationship lasting a long time. But what do you do when you're a parent? It's not like you can explain this to a love-mesmerized, inexperienced adolescent kid. If I had brought up my concerns to Jacob, it would only have made him angry, and he would've told me to mind my own business.

In the meantime, they had some great times together. And I liked it when Mary stayed for dinner. She was such a charming and interesting girl, and it was nice to see Jacob so happy. Do you remember the swine flu? I remember the flu was going around the year we had Mary over for dinner on the Fourth of July. I remember talking about it and all the people who were sick and dying. I don't know why I remember that specifically. I just do. Then we talked about the pollution at the beach. They were finding medical syringes on the sand, trying to figure out who the littering culprit was. Then, since it was the Fourth of July, we talked about the Declaration of Independence. It was amusing to hear the kids talk. It was like having little test tube clones of Jane Fonda and Jerry Rubin over for dinner as fourteen-year-olds. Seriously, it was pretty funny.

Anyway, we all got to talking about the United States and the

Declaration of Independence, and Jacob said he'd written a poem for us. "Well, it isn't really a poem," he said. "I wrote some new lyrics for 'America the Beautiful.' Real lyrics, about a real country."

"Go get them," Mary said.

"Yes," I said. "I'd like to hear what you wrote."

"You sure about that?" Jacob said, smiling. "Be careful what you wish for."

Jacob stood up from the dinner table, and he walked to his bedroom to retrieve the lyrics. "Do you have any idea what he's written?" I asked Mary.

"I haven't got a clue," Mary said.

"Okay, okay," Jacob said, returning to the table. "I'm not going to sing this, because I'm a lousy singer. So, you'll have to use your imagination and pretend someone else is singing the lyrics to you."

"I can do that," I said.

"Okay," Jacob said. "Here it goes." And Jacob proceeded to read the following lyrics to us:

America the Beautiful

O beautiful for spacious skies,
For amber waves of grain.
For shopping center parking lots,
For freeways, trucks, and cranes.
America! America! All natives step aside.
Men with plans and calloused hands
Have come to turn the tide.

O beautiful for nail salons.
For gas stations, signs, and roads.
A thoroughfare of steel and glass,
And asphalt rolled in loads.
America! America! Home of brave and free,
Relieved of pain and entertained
By the crap on their TVs.

O beautiful for movie stars,
And guitar-strumming bards.

64

For record labels and magazines,
And radio talk show 'tards.
America! America! God help the man who strays
From the norm, despite the swarm,
Finding his own way.

O beautiful for laying blame.
Nothing is our fault.
Fault lies with the other guys,
We had no chance to halt.
America! America! Lock and toss the key.
If you had a role, you want to extoll,
That's fine, just don't blame me.

O beautiful for praying to
The glorious bottom line.
Success is cash, and cash is king,
And kings are all divine.
America! America! If you think you've won,
Count the bills, and add the change,
And judge the final sum.

O beautiful, the irony
Of fearing storm-tossed masses.
How easily we forget
Our fathers had no passes.
America! America! Let's keep our country free
From the droves of immigrants
Invading our country.

Oh beautiful, our fighting might;
They guard against oppression.
How often do we kill and maim
Without justification?
America! America! We have a deadly lust.
Dropping bombs on dads and moms.
You'd better watch for us.

O beautiful, the Fourth Estate.
They feed us all our news.
News, that is, as they deem worth
Their cameras, men, and crews.
America! America! Beware of what you see.
Trash and lies sell drums of ink
And make for great TV.

O beautiful, our right to speak,
To satire and lampoon.
There's more I could say for sure,
But I'll stop singing soon.
America! America! I tip my hat to thee.
Truth is that there's no other place
Where I would rather be.

That was all of it. Jacob set the piece of paper down on the table, and Mary applauded vigorously. "That was wonderful," she said. "You are so talented!"

"What do you guys think?" Jacob ask April and me.

"I thought it was interesting," April said.

"I thought it was quite good," I said. "Yes, I thought it was very good. Maybe a little too critical, but I liked the ending."

But the truth? I actually wished Jacob had written lyrics that were a little less cynical. I mean, everything he said in his lyrics was true, but there were an awful lot of good things about our country he could've mentioned. As I've gotten older, I've realized that you have to take the good things in life with the bad. You can dwell on the negative, as Jacob just did, or you can dwell only on the positive, or you can be a mature adult and accept the whole ball of wax that we call America as an imperfect but pretty darn good place to live. But I didn't say any of this to Jacob. I figured he'd discover it for himself as he grew up, and there was no reason for me to be overly critical of a poem he was so obviously proud of.

I guess it's a style of raising your children that we're talking about. I know a lot of parents who would not have held back. I know a lot of parents who would not have been able to resist adding their two cents' worth. And is this really wrong? After all, aren't parents supposed to provide their wisdom and guidance to their kids? Aren't they supposed to speak up when their kids do and say things that could be better done and said? Hindsight is twenty-twenty, but now that I look back to this poem of Jacob's, and others, I think maybe I should have spoken up and said that a lot of a person's ability to flourish in the world comes from within and not from things external. I might now be oversimplifying, but maybe, just maybe, if I had said something to Jacob, maybe he wouldn't have plummeted into the depression that led him to slash his wrists.

Arcadia! Jacob was always dreaming of that place he called Arcadia—a utopia that was described in ancient literature but that never truly existed. No, it did not exist. Not anywhere, and never. True, we lived in a land of shopping centers and parking lots and greed and sacred bottom lines. But Arcadia? Was it somewhere over the rainbow, maybe? Sing, Judy, sing, and turn on the Technicolor. Yes, over the rainbow, maybe. But even Oz had witches and flying monkeys and trees that threw their apples at you.

Several weeks following our Fourth of July dinner, Jacob took Mary to the beach. I say he took her, but actually April was the one who drove them, since they were both too young to drive themselves. She dropped them off early in the morning, and would pick them up in the late afternoon. It was a clear day, and there was lots of sun. When April finally did pick them up, they were both as red as cooked beets. But their red sunburns told only half of the story. April told me the kids were quiet all the way home, not because they were tired, but because something had happened between them that day. It wasn't that they were angry, pouting, or deliberately ignoring each other; it was just that they had nothing to say. When April dropped Mary off at her house, the kids didn't even speak up to say goodbye.

Jacob never came right out and told us what happened that day, but we could figure it out for ourselves. Well, at least we could take a good guess. And what we figured was that Mary had told Jacob that they were no longer a pair. This is to say that Mary no longer wanted to be considered as Jacob's steady girlfriend, that she wanted to see other boys, and that she wanted her freedom. And I can't say I could blame her. I mean, she was only fourteen; it's not as if she were in her twenties or thirties, on the prowl for a husband. It just didn't make any sense for a youthful fourteen-year-old girl to commit to one boy.

Despite the fact that the breakup was inevitable (at least that's how

April and I both saw it), Jacob was devastated. For months after that day at the beach, he stayed in his room for hours and hours. He'd come out to eat his meals and use the bathroom, but that was about it. I wished like hell there was something I could do, but I was powerless. I tried to discuss Mary with Jacob several times, and he would just tell me he didn't want to talk about her. He told me to leave him alone. So in his room he stayed, listening to sixties and seventies music and writing poetry.

A year later, I found the following poem folded up in his desk drawer. As I said earlier, I didn't like to snoop, but I guess I did. I'll say this in my defense: when you're a parent and you're worried about your child, sometimes you have to find out what's on his or her mind. And we did worry about Jacob. I didn't like doing it, and I didn't like being a spy, but it was my duty as his father to understand what was on my child's mind and to get a handle on what was happening. Anyway, the poem I found went as follows:

The Bluest Skies

Did I ever tell you how we met?
We were eating lunch at school and she let
Me sit beside her. I was nervous
Because it was just the two of us,
Now sitting and eating and talking
And soon to be done with lunch, walking
To our class. The sun was out that day,
And I was thinking of things to say
To the prettiest thing I had seen
Ever, anywhere, in a sunbeam.
Golden blonde hair and the bluest eyes,
Who knew it was just sorrow's disguise?

Did I tell you about our math class?
I'd rather eat spoonfuls of ground glass
Than go back in time and listen to
Boring lectures from that teacher who
Loved math more than he loved his own wife.
I think it was his entire life.

ARCADIA

What was that dude's name again? Was it
Mr. Schmidt? I remember how he'd sit
At his desk and go on and on for
An hour. I would just stare at her
Golden blonde hair and her bluest eyes,
Who knew they were just sorrow's disguise?

Did I tell you about our first date?
Went to see *Avatar*. It was great
If you like cartoons, but we agreed
It wasn't for us. We should have seen
James Dean in *Giant* on the TV,
Sometimes the best things in life are free.
I remember standing at her door
When our date was over and no more.
She gave me a good night kiss. And I
Walked home and saw her in the night sky.
Golden blonde hair and the bluest eyes,
Who knew they were just sorrow's disguise?

Did I tell you how much my mom and
Dad liked her? They were her biggest fans,
"Such a sweet young girl," they liked to say
Call and ask her if she'll come and stay
For dinner and dessert. We'd like to
Get to know her better and see who
Can win at Parcheesi after we
Put all the dishes away. Then we
Can tell some jokes, like the one Dad knows
About the two apes in women's clothes.
Golden blonde hair and the bluest eyes,
Who knew they were just sorrow's disguise?

Did I tell you about how we told
Each other's secrets both small and bold,
Promising not to laugh or reveal
To a soul how each of us did feel
And worry and scheme and hope for our

Futures to turn out? We had no more
Reason not to trust each other than
We had to believe that those pigs can
Fly, as they say. Or that the sun might
Tumble down to the earth from the sky.
Golden blonde hair and the bluest eyes,
Who knew they were just sorrow's disguise?

She said Robert Zimmerman was true
When he said he was all tangled blue.
I said we can make things as we wish,
But you said there was no point to this,
And that the future that we called ours
Belonged to the planets and the stars
And the coyotes that howl all night
And all those birds that get lost in flight,
High above the roofs and trees, never
Questioning anything, not ever.
Golden blonde hair and the bluest eyes,
Who knew they were just sorrow's disguise?

Did I tell you how she broke my heart
The day she tore all our love apart
And told me she wanted to go out
With other boys? I wanted to shout
At the top of my lungs, but instead
I was quiet and just hung my head,
Knowing there was no use objecting
To the needs of the girl rejecting
Me, and saying but we'll always be
Very good friends. Our love sped off to sea,
Golden blonde sails to the bluest skies,
Who knew they would be sorrow's disguise?

Jesus, I nearly cried when I read this poem. I found it to be very
upsetting. I wasn't angry with Mary for hurting my son, because I knew
the breakup was unavoidable, but I felt for the kid. I really did. He had
obviously lost something that was very dear to him, and he felt robbed and

betrayed. And who could blame him? I'm convinced that if he'd had had his way, he would've been with Mary for the rest of his life. She was his first love, and first loves always evoke a lot of emotion in a boy. And they say that first loves are forever. The candle never really burns out.

Jacob had one other girlfriend in high school who followed Mary. The girl's name was Veronica Schaffer, and the kids were a pair for about three months. Jacob met the girl in his art class at school when he was sixteen.

We wanted to get to know Veronica, so we invited her over for dinner. She was an odd duck of a girl, about four or five inches taller than Jacob with jet-black hair and huge, almost comical eyelashes. Seriously, her eyelashes looked totally fake, but they weren't. In fact, this girl wore no makeup or anything fake at all. She wasn't by any means a beautiful young girl like Mary. If I were to call her anything, I guess I'd call her interesting. To be honest, I wasn't quite sure what Jacob saw in her appearance. They looked like a total mismatch when they were together.

As I said, we had Veronica over for dinner. Unlike our meals with Mary, we did not talk about politics or governments or Europe or Africa or South America or societies in general or science or literature or art or music. Instead we talked about astrology. How do I best put this? It was bizarre, and it took April and me totally by surprise. Astrology? It was like we were being visited by some tall black-haired creature from outer space, from some other planet, who had befriended our earthling son. It made April and me worry even more about Jacob. What in the world was he thinking?

Listen, I think astrology is for kooks. It's that simple. As this girl went on and on at our dinner table talking about cusps and ascendants and critical degrees and signs and houses and quadrants, I was asking myself what damage this *jeune femme folle* was going to do to our son. And hadn't the poor kid suffered enough? Why were we now adding pseudoscience into the mix? But it turned out I was worried about nothing. I suppose, looking back, I can say it was just a safe place for Jacob to go after his heart had been broken. It was just a fleeting phase. No, it was nothing for us to worry about, but, jeez, was it ever alarming.

I guess we should now be grateful that Veronica Schaffer wasn't into witchcraft. Those kinds of girls were out there too, you know. There were thousands of them, maybe millions, all those creepy, spell-casting, cat-loving teenage females influencing and tainting the minds of heartbroken boys. It's a little scary, when you think about it. So, yes, we were better off with the astrology. It was relatively easy for Jacob to make a clean break.

Jacob said goodbye to Veronica after about three months of going steady. I never did find any poems he wrote about her, so I don't think she had a big effect on his life. I think she was just a diversion, and it's natural for kids to have diversions. I remember when I was in high school, I had my own brief and silly diversions. I remember for a few months I was determined to become an astronaut. I was going to walk on the moon. Maybe even on Mars. I think this was when I was in tenth grade, and I checked out every book on the subject of astronauts that I could find in the library. Then it happened. Our family took a trip up to Big Bear to play in the snow, and while driving up the twisting and turning highway, I got carsick. I mean, I was as sick as a dog. My head was spinning like the worst whirling carnival ride, and my stomach was churning like a cement mixer. Dad pulled the car over, and I ran to the bushes, puking like there was no tomorrow. It was awful. I puked up everything but our sofa and the kitchen sink. When I got back into the car, Dad said, laughing, "You couldn't handle being an astronaut if your life depended on it." And he was right, of course. A couple weeks later, I dropped the crazy astronaut dream like a hot potato.

CHAPTER 8

THE ORIGIN OF MAN

———— •●• ————

T he thing I really loved about Jacob, besides the fact that he was my son, was his creativity. Sure, he was bright, and his IQ test scores revealed he was smarter than 99 percent of the population. But it's one thing to be bright as in having a high IQ, and altogether another thing to be creative. On the creative scale, from one to ten, I'd give myself about a four. I was just so-so, but I'd give Jacob a solid eleven. And I'm not just talking about his poetry.

I'll give you an example of what I'm talking about so you can see for yourself. When Jacob was in fifth grade, he was told by his teacher, Mr. Steinway, to write an essay on the origin of mankind. This was a touchy subject, so Mr. Steinway handled it in an interesting way. He gave his students a choice as to which explanation for the origin of man they believed and wanted to write on, with one acceptable explanation being the Bible-driven creation of man by a god, and the other being the more scientific version—the creation of man through millions of years of evolution. Fair enough, right? The plan was to then have the kids read their papers to the class, each side of the issue illuminating the other as to their beliefs. Parents were invited to the readings. The idea was to be 100 percent fair to both sides without one side ridiculing or denouncing the other. I suppose this sounded like a good idea, and there were few complaints from the parents after the assignment was handed out. Everyone seemed to be on board. And everyone, kids and parents alike, looked forward to the opportunity to publicly confirm their beliefs.

Here's something you have to understand about Jacob. I've said this earlier on, and I'll say it again here. The boy was not like every other kid in school. He lived his life according to the clicks of a rather eccentric metronome. Mr. Steinway, in his infinite wisdom, and in so many words, told me that Jacob went completely off the rails. He said this to me when I met with the man to complain about the grade he gave Jacob. The idiot gave Jacob a D.

I'll tell you (in my own words) exactly what Jacob wrote. He said first and foremost, there is all the stuff—the stuff on Earth, being things such as planes, boats, cars, chair legs, pencils, erasers, computer monitors, bats, baseballs, lions and their cubs, tree branches, blossoms, ice cubes, aspirin tablets, and so on and so forth. Then, he said, there are also the things that exist outside of our world, such as moons rocks and craters, the icy rings around Saturn, supernovas, comets, asteroids, stars, solar systems, wormholes, and so on and so forth, on and on to infinity. Then, as if this weren't enough for us to contend with, there are all the invisible things—the thoughts, dreams, ideas, theories, longings, loves, dislikes, fears, anxieties, worries, thrills, chills, hopes, and so on and so forth. These were the sorts of invisible yet very real things scientists couldn't see with microscopes or telescopes. And what, Jacob asked, are all these things made of? What do they all have in common? In one way or another, they are all made of atoms, neutrons, molecules, electrons, cells, elements, gases, solids, liquids, and so on and so forth—trillions upon trillions upon trillions of tiny building blocks. No, in fact, not just trillions or even quadrillions, but an infinite number of them, and an infinite number of combinations, and an infinite number of entities, and an infinite number of infinities. So when you're being asked to explain in an essay where we all came from, you're being asked to explain all of this. In essence, you're being asked to explain infinity.

According to Jacob, neither the theory of evolution nor creationism fit the bill. They were both flawed explanations that man, in his stupendous shortsightedness, came up with to explain away the most amazing, remarkable, and mind-boggling miracle of the universe, which *is* the universe. It was the one, the all, our universe, with all of its idiosyncrasies. It was the universe, both as colorful as a rainbow and in shades of gray, flaming hot and ice cold, bright and dim, as clear as clean air and pea-soup foggy, as graceful as a ballerina and as clumsy as an ox, and simultaneously inspiring and disappointing. It was all of it! It was every shaded nook and cranny, and every wide-open vista! And according to Jacob, creationism and evolution were both woefully inadequate explanations. Calling upon either of them to describe the universe was like trying to contain Mount Saint Helens inside a thimble or trying to stuff a supernova into a cardboard box.

Jacob began his essay by talking about creationism and the concept of God. According to Jacob, humans invented God; God did not make humans. Human beings, in an attempt to make sense of themselves and their surroundings, made up the concept of an omnipotent, all-knowing, all-encompassing master of the universe. These early men were not too bright. They said that in just a matter of days, God made the earth, and God made the sun, and God made the oceans and the mountains and the valleys. God then made man, and from man, God made woman. God made all the animals and plant life. God made the weather, and God made the rain, snow, wind, and heat. It was so easy this way, just saying that God made everything. How, exactly, did he do it? Who cared? It didn't matter. He was God, and he could do anything he wanted to do. He was all-powerful. And there, Jacob said, is where the entire story fell apart. Because no one, not even God, could be all-powerful. It just happened to be inherently impossible.

Why did Jacob say this? Believe it or not, it was from a simple and casual question he heard a kid ask. A kid, mind you. The kid was named Bobby Murphy, and he was standing in line with Jacob, waiting for the teacher to open the classroom door after recess. Bobby was talking about church, and about God, and he asked Jacob, "If God is truly all-powerful, can he make a rock so big that even he can't lift it?" It was just a joke, but to Jacob it was a revelation. It was astonishing! It said it all. The importance of this question hit Jacob like a freight train full of freight. It was undeniable proof that it was, in fact, impossible for anyone or anything to be all-powerful. There was now no doubt in Jacob's mind. Everything he'd learned as a boy about God, and everything he had been asked to believe, was a blatant falsehood. No, this all-powerful God of his childhood did not exist, because he could not exist. In other words, God simply wasn't.

And if God wasn't, then creationism was a lie. It was all a great story, but that's all it was. It was a story. It was a work of fiction. It was mythology.

So now you probably are thinking that, given his rejection of God, Jacob was an evolutionist. But not so fast. Jacob didn't find evolution more satisfactory as an answer. In fact, he believed it was even worse than the God angle. And why was it worse? It was worse because it claimed to have its roots in science as an honest, rational, intelligent, and impartial analysis of facts. But it was no such thing. Rather, it was an emotional and irrational obsession with an alluring little all-star formula they called "the survival of the fittest." That was the battle cry—a trite and oversimplified rule of thumb that was, in reality, a rule of nothing. No, no, how did this rule even begin to explain everything Jacob saw around him in picture books, in glorious nature, and in his own backyard? The answer is that it didn't. It didn't even come close.

How did the rule explain away the fluttering butterfly's psychedelic wings? How did it explain a painted toucan? Or an astonishing peacock? Or how about the giraffe? And how about the zebra? And why didn't the giraffe have stripes, and the zebra spots? And why can't all wild cats run as fast as the cheetah? And why don't all fish in the sea inflate themselves like a porcupinefish fish, and why are so many tropical fish so bright and colorful? This helps them to survive how, exactly? Do predators avoid eating them because they are so vibrant and pretty? And what about the Venus fly trap, or the 350-foot-tall redwood tree, or the once-in-a-lifetime bloom of the century plant, or the Wolffia flower and fruit, smaller than a grain of rice? In Jacob's paper, he listed about a hundred examples of nature's living wonders, asking what any of them had to do with survival of the fittest. According to Jacob, evolution as an ultimate explanation fell totally short when it came to the details. And it made no more sense to believe in it than it made to believe that an all-powerful God is the creator of everything we see around us.

So if not God, and if not evolution, then what? That was the question. Here's what Jacob's paper proposed. He said he believed that life was never ending—not in the way that living things never die, but in the way that they constantly give birth to new offspring. So life in the universe was fleeting for the individual but everlasting for life itself. Life was and always has been, backwards in time infinitely, and forward in time forever. Thus, we were not actually created in the literal sense of the word. Instead we were really just a continuance of something that has always been and always will be. We are a very small segment of an infinite line. And who knows who the Johnny Appleseed was who put life in motion on Earth. You can call him a god, but he is no god. He is no more a god than a farmer who plows his fields and plants his crops.

There is no God who made man from soil, or made woman from man's rib, or tempted them both with the apple of self-awareness and wisdom and guile. All of it—the electrons, atoms, molecules, air, blood, tree sap, leaves, opposable thumbs, dreams, morals, schemes, loves, and hates—is just rejuvenating specks of light in the great forever, all rolling over each other, time and time again.

Well, whether you're buying into this explanation or not, this is what Jacob wrote in his paper. I thought it was pretty darn thoughtful and sophisticated for a fifth grader. But I am his father, and I tend to be biased.

You should've been there when Jacob read his paper to the class. As I said, the parents were all invited. As Jacob talked, the parents and kids just sat there, dumbfounded. It was as if Jacob were speaking Greek. Seriously, I don't think anyone in the room had the slightest idea what he was talking about. Mr. Steinway sat at his desk, squirming in his chair as though he had a bad case of hemorrhoids. Not a good sign, right? I could tell by watching the man the he was going to give Jacob a lousy grade. But leave it to Jacob. He had dared to color outside the lines.

When Jacob brought the graded paper home from school, he dropped it angrily on the kitchen table. There was a big red D marked at the top margin. Not even a D+.

"Check this out," he said.

"That's your grade?" I asked.

"A big fat D."

"What the heck?"

"Mr. Steinway said I didn't follow his instructions."

"His instructions?"

"I was supposed to write about either creationism or evolution."

"But you wrote about both of them."

"I was supposed to pick one or the other and agree with my choice."

"Says who?"

"Says Mr. Steinway. I just told you."

"That's absurd," I said.

"Tell that to Mr. Steinway."

Well, that's exactly what I planned to do. I called the school and asked for Mr. Steinway to call me. The next day he called me back, and I told him I wanted to meet. "About your son's grade?" he asked. What a genius.

I said yes, about the grade, and he said I could come in after school the next day. April asked me if I wanted her to come along, and I said no. I really wanted to deal with this idiot man-to-man.

I didn't tell Jacob I was meeting with Mr. Steinway. I thought he might try to talk me out of it since he didn't like attention being drawn to himself. I figured he would be content with accepting the poor grade and moving on. So, unbeknownst to Jacob, I went into the classroom after school. I waited until all the kids were gone so Jacob wouldn't see me and so none of the other kids would tell Jacob I'd been there. I stepped into the classroom.

I would guess that Mr. Steinway was in his thirties. He wasn't particularly tall; nor was he short. He was very clean-cut. He looked like the kind of guy who shaved a second time in the middle of the day. Either it was that or his facial hair just didn't grow very fast. There are some men who don't get a five o'clock shadow even after a couple days of beard growth, if you know what I mean. Mr. Steinway was dressed in a neat plaid shirt and pair of black slacks. He wore leather loafers—the kind you can put pennies in. Right away I didn't care much for the man. Honestly? I never trusted men who dressed and groomed themselves too perfectly, and Mr. Steinway looked like a mannequin in the Macy's menswear department. He smiled at me and reached out his hand at I approached.

"I'm Stan Harper," I said, shaking his clammy paw. "Thanks for agreeing to meet with me."

"My door is always open," he said.

"I guess you know why I'm here."

"Yes," he said.

"It's about this paper," I said. I set the graded paper on Mr. Steinway's desk. He then motioned for me to sit down, and he took a seat in his chair.

"You don't like the grade," Mr. Steinway said.

"I don't think it was appropriate."

"I see."

"Jacob worked very hard on this assignment. I don't know how else to put it. The grade seems inappropriate."

"Did you read the handout?"

"The handout?"

"The handout I gave to the students for the assignment."

"No, I've never seen it."

Mr. Steinway opened his desk drawer, and he went through some papers until he found the paper he was looking for. He then handed the paper to me. "This is the handout," he said.

"I see."

"You should read it."

"Okay," I said. I put on my reading glasses and looked over the paper. It was titled, "The Origin of Man," and there was a short paragraph describing the class project. It said, "There are two opposing beliefs in our society concerning the origin of mankind. One is God and creationism, and the other is evolution. Your assignment will be to write a 500-word paper describing which explanation you believe and why you believe it. You will then all read your papers to the rest of the class. It will be a chance for us all to listen and learn from each other, and to respect each other's beliefs. If you feel uncomfortable with this assignment, an alternative assignment will be given to you. Parents will be invited to the readings. This is a chance for everyone to be involved."

I set the handout on Mr. Steinway's desk, and I looked at him. "So what was the problem?" I asked.

"Jacob didn't follow the instructions."

"He addressed both creationism and evolution."

"But he was supposed to pick one or the other, not make up a lot of nonsense about—well, what was his paper even about? I don't even remember what your son wrote."

"You don't remember?"

"I have thirty-two students in this class. I have to grade each one of their papers thoughtfully. If they don't follow my instructions, it's like throwing a wrench into the works."

"So that's it?"

"Do you understand?"

"Not really."

"Mr. Harper," he said. I could tell just by the way he said my name that he was going to give me a lecture. It was ridiculous. I was going to get a lecture from a kid who was about twenty years younger than me. But I remained seated, and I listened politely. He said, "Here in my class we don't just teach our students facts and figures. We don't just expose them to theories and established ideas. Here in this high school, we attempt to prepare these young men and women for the world they will face after they graduate. And a big part of that effort involves teaching them how to follow instructions like good and productive citizens. In the real world, they'll be asked over and over to follow a superior's instructions, and they're not going to get anywhere if they haven't learned how to do this. Why did I give Jacob a D? I gave very explicit instructions to your son on how to write his paper and what his paper was to be about. I don't think I could've made myself any clearer, yet he decided to do his own thing. Picture him at a job when he's older, when he's asked to complete a task. What happens when he decides not to follow instructions? What happens when he does things his way?"

"I guess I get that," I said. But why did I say that? I didn't actually get it at all.

"I don't want your son's grade to suffer."

"Neither do I," I said.

"This is the first time I've had a problem like this with Jacob. Usually he's a good student."

"That's good to hear."

"I'll tell you what I'm willing to do. Let's just call this a lesson learned. I'll give Jacob the opportunity to complete an extra-credit assignment that, if he does it properly, will raise his essay grade to a C. Does that sound like something your son would be interested in?"

"I can run it by him."

"Just have him see me after class. I'll let him know what I want him to do."

"Fair enough," I said. But I didn't mean to say that at all. Yet what was the point in arguing with this dope? It would've proved pointless. You know, when I was Jacob's age, I would've done exactly what the teacher had asked for. Which would I have chosen? Creationism or evolution? I don't know for sure, but I would've picked one of them. As I said earlier, I was not a particularly creative boy, but now, as an adult, I found myself longing for that same place Jacob held sacred in his thoughts. I longed for Arcadia—not for myself, but for my dear son. What did he say in that poem he wrote?

The sum of soda pop brook water and bubbling fits of laughter:
ha, ha, and ha, it goes through the lupin blooms, beneath blue-ceilinged skies with marshmallow candy clouds.

It was the right place for Jacob.

When I got home from my meeting with Mr. Steinway, it was nearly time for dinner. I watched a little TV for a while, and then Jacob, Zach, April, and I sat at the kitchen table. April had made a bowl of chicken fettuccini Alfredo with asparagus spears and hot rolls. "I went to see Mr. Steinway today," I said to Jacob.

"What'd you do that for?"

"I talked to him about the grade he gave you on your paper."

"You did what?"

"I thought I should say something to him."

"What grade did you get?" Zach asked.

"I got a D."

"What a retard."

"He didn't deserve a D," I said.

"Then why'd he get it?"

"That's why I talked to his teacher."

"I wish you hadn't done that," Jacob said.

"He told me why he gave you a D."

"He gave me a D because he's an idiot."

"You shouldn't talk that way about your teachers," April said.

"He was trying to teach you to follow instructions."

"His instructions were bullshit."

"Language," April said.

"I worked something out with him," I said.

"I'm not going to rewrite the paper."

"You won't have to rewrite it. But Mr. Steinway said he'd give you an extra credit assignment. He said if you did a good job on the assignment, he'd raise the grade to a C."

"Well, that's just great."

"Take what you can get, retard," Zach said, his mouth full of fettuccini.

"He said to come see him after class if you're interested."

"I think you should do it," April said.

"I'll think about it."

"I know it's not ideal," I said. "But it is something. I mean, at least the guy is making an effort."

"I can't wait until fifth grade is over," Jacob said. "I'm so done with Mr. Steinway. I'm so done with his class. I'm done with it all."

CHAPTER 9

THE POLK HIGH GRIZZLIES

———————— •●• ————————

As far back as grade school, Jacob had his moody weeks, but he always seemed to snap out of them. When he was fifteen, these weeks turned into months, and that's when April and I grew concerned. Sure, we understood that adolescents had their good and bad days, and that they had their moods, but with Jacob it seemed a little more serious than mere adolescent angst and malaise. I think I've said this to you before—that April told me it was like there was an opaque film in front of Jacob's face. He would be there, yet he was strangely hidden behind this film. He would be sitting or standing right there with us, yet he wouldn't be there at all. We could've attributed his moodiness to his breakup with Mary, but it also seemed like it was more than that.

I discussed Jacob with our family doctor, and I described Jacob's morose and detached deportment. He suggested that if things didn't improve, we would be wise to consider taking Jacob to a psychiatrist. He gave me the name and number of a doctor who he said had an excellent reputation, and a month later I gave the doctor a call. Her name was Dr. Erskine-Garcia. She had an office in Newport Beach, and when I called, she said she could fit Jacob in that very week. Apparently she had had a recent cancellation. We set up the meeting for five in the evening, and I told her I would be there with Jacob and that I looked forward to meeting with her. Then came the hard part—telling Jacob I wanted him to see this doctor. I would tell him about the appointment when Jacob and I were alone together. I suppose it would've been okay for April to be there, but for reasons that should be obvious, I didn't want Zach or anyone else to know about this.

The night after I made the appointment, Jacob was locked away in his room and listening to the Grateful Dead. I knocked on his door, and he told me it was okay to enter. I then came in and closed the door behind me. "The Dead recorded some good songs," I said. "I used to listen to them."

"They're good," Jacob said. His voice was monotone and quiet.

"I need to talk to you about something."

"What is it?"

"We need to talk about you."

"About me?" Still his voice was monotone, and he seemed bored with me.

"Your mom and I are worried about you."

"There's nothing for either of you to worry about."

"We think there is."

"Like what? My room is clean. I do most of my homework. I brush my teeth, and I do my chores."

"That isn't what I'm talking about."

"What is it, then?"

"You don't seem happy to us."

Jacob thought about this for a moment. Then he said, "Give me something to be happy about."

"There are a lot of things to be happy about."

"For you guys, maybe. You have your boxes, and Mom has her garden. And Zach has his college plans."

"We'd like you to see someone."

"See someone?"

"See someone who I think can help."

Again, Jacob dismissed my stated concerns. "I'm fine, really. I'm really okay. I don't need to see someone."

"I made an appointment."

"An appointment?" This caught Jacob's attention, and he seemed a little surprised.

"To see a psychiatrist."

"You mean a shrink?"

"Yes, a shrink. She comes highly recommended. I think she might be able to help."

"And what if I refuse to go?"

"I'm not going to make you see her. But I'm asking you. I would like you to do this for me. If you would, please, just do this for me. Just one meeting is all I'm asking for. If you don't get anything out of the meeting, you can stop going. I'm leaving it all up to you."

Jacob stared at me. His Grateful Dead music came to an end, and he pressed the play button on his CD player to start it up again. He wasn't making any eye contact with me, and it was hard to judge how he was feeling about my plan. Then, still with no eye contact, he surprised me and said, "Okay, I guess I'll go."

"You will?"

"I'll give it a try. One meeting, right? Then it will be all up to me?"

"Yes, good," I said.

"And if I don't like going, or what I hear from this shrink, I can quit going any time."

"Yes, at any time."

When I told April later that Jacob would go to this doctor, she was surprised. "I thought he'd turn your down for sure," she said.

"I asked him to do it for me."

Ah, now I felt as if we were getting somewhere. And I think April felt as good about this as I did. He hadn't even seen the doctor yet, and we felt we'd accomplished so much. We felt as though we were going to get our son back. At a little before five on the evening of the appointment, Jacob and I walked in through the doctor's office door. It was the first time I'd been in a psychiatrist's office, and to be honest, it was weird. There was no receptionist or secretary, but there was a receptionist's desk at which the doctor could do paperwork. Oil paintings of European town scenes hung on the walls. I guessed the doctor had a thing for Europe. There was also a coffee table with a pile of magazines, and a couple of sofas that faced each other. We took a seat to wait. The doctor's office door was closed, but we could hear indecipherable, muffled talking from behind the door. The doctor was finishing up with the patient before us. Then there was some laughter, and then the door opened. A mother, father, and daughter came out of the office. They were all smiles, which I figured was a good sign. Then came Dr. Erskine-Garcia. Let's just say she was nothing like what I had expected.

She could've been the opening act in a 1940s Berlin nightclub. I could picture this place full of Nazi officers dressed up in their starched uniforms, their bellies bloated with beer, smoking cigarettes and laughing and singing songs about the *Vaterland*. This image was so powerful that I expected her to open her mouth and speak like Marlene Dietrich. But no, to my surprise she had no accent at all. In fact, her voice was as American as America gets. Around her neck was a long fox stole, the kind that still had the poor fox's head attached. Her dress was a blousy and billowing abundance of orange and white floral-patterned material that disguised the shape of her body so much so that I had no idea if she was heavy or slender. And her hair? It reminded me of Phyllis Diller. Do you remember her? I guess it depends on how old you are. And I half expected to hear a brass band marching behind her in step and playing "Beer Barrell Polka" while she petted her fox stole and glided toward us.

"You must be Jacob," she said.

"Yes ma'am," Jacob said.

"And you're Dad?" she asked me.

"I am," I said.

"Come in, come in," she said, motioning for us to enter. "I've been looking forward to meeting both of you."

"Thanks," I said.

"Take a seat," she said, and we sat down in a couple of overstuffed chairs. There was one larger chair positioned so that it faced the others, and I figured this was where the doctor liked to sit. And I was right, because after she closed the office door, she plopped into the big chair. "So here we are," she said. "Let me tell you both a little about myself before we begin. Then I'll ask each of you to tell me about each of you so I know who you are."

"That sounds fine," I said.

"My name is Dr. Erskine-Garcia. I'm now thirty-eight years old. I graduated from medical school at UC Irvine, and I worked for five years under the wing of one of Orange County's most respected psychiatrists, Dr. Eugene Wall. Maybe you've heard of him? He specializes in adolescent mood disorders and substance abuse issues. Wonderful man. I've been on my own ever since I left Dr. Eugene's clinic, and you can sum up my practice with four simple words: "I like to help." That's me in a nutshell. Whatever I can do to help you with your problems, you can rest assured that I'll find a way. I want both of you to fully enjoy your time on this earth and to live healthy, happy, and very prosperous lives. What is it that Spock used to say instead of goodbye on Star Trek? Live long and prosper? That's me in a nutshell. I want you to live long and prosper. Now tell me a little about yourselves." She inclined her head toward me. "Maybe you should begin."

"My name is Stan," I said. "And this is my son Jacob. I am fifty-four years old. I'm CEO of a large box company located in Anaheim. I don't have any special talents or hobbies except that I play golf now and again. But mostly, I just work. And I like to spend time with my family. I suppose you could say that is my favorite thing to do. We do a lot of things together. I don't know what else you want me to say."

"If you're done, you're done," the doctor said. Then she looked at Jacob. "How about you?"

"My name is Jacob." He said his name, and then he just sat there saying nothing.

"He's very bright," I said. "And he likes to write."

"Ah, a writer?"

"He writes poetry."

"Sometimes I do," Jacob said.

"And he likes music."

"I listen to it in my room when I write."

"What kind of music?"

"Mostly sixties and seventies."

"Are you happy, Jacob?"

"I guess it depends on how you define 'happy.'"

The doctor stared at Jacob. She smiled and said, "Would you feel more comfortable talking to me alone? I can ask your dad to leave."

"No, I want him here."

"Fine, fine. Well, let's see what we can do for you."

"His mom and I have been worried."

"And what makes you think you should be worrying?"

"Jacob doesn't seem himself."

"How can I be anybody but myself?" Jacob said. "That would be impossible."

"You're not happy," I said. "You're no longer laughing, or full of life, or excited about doing anything. You're just not the same—not since you broke up with Mary."

"Who's Mary?" the doctor asked.

"She was my girlfriend."

"Do you miss her?"

"I suppose I do."

"Did she hurt you?"

Jacob thought about this, and then said, "She probably did. I didn't want to break up with her."

"I'd like to try something," the doctor said. "I'd like the two of you to reverse roles for me. Stan, I want you to be Jacob, and Jacob, I want you to be your dad."

"Okay," I said.

"Can you do this?" the doctor asked Jacob.

"Sure, why not," Jacob said.

"Then let's have you go first, Jacob. Pretend you're Dad. You've just come home from work, and you're talking to you. So, go ahead and talk."

"Hello, son," Jacob said.

"Hi Dad," I said.

"We had another big success at work today."

"Oh?" I said.

"A real coup, my boy. We landed the Little Sis-A-Lee Pizza account. We'll be making all their takeout pizza boxes for the next ten years."

"That's good news."

"I hear their pizza tastes like crap, but they're going to have great boxes. Jesus, they sell millions of them. Have you and your friends ever eaten a Little Sis-A-Lee pizza? There's one about a half mile from here."

"I've seen it, Dad."

"Have you eaten their pizza?"

"Can't say that I have."

"Maybe you kids should try them out."

"Kids?"

"You guys, you dudes, you young men. I never know what you want to be called."

"You guys is fine."

"You and your brother have grown up so fast. Right before my very eyes. I keep thinking that you're still my boys. You were such cute kids. Did I ever tell you what I was doing when I was your age?"

"About a thousand times," I said. This was precisely what Jacob would've said to me.

"I was going to be an architect," Jacob said. "I checked out stacks and stacks of architecture books from the good old public library. It wasn't like today. Of course, now you have the internet. The internet changed everything. Have you ever even been in a library?"

"Of course I have, Dad. We have one at school."

"I mean a *real* library."

"I wouldn't even know where to look for one. Didn't they tear them all down?"

"No, of course not. At least I think not. I haven't been to one in years. You know, I met Sally Stanfield in our public library. Did I ever tell you about Sally? I met her before I met your mom."

"She had red hair and green eyes."

"So I've told you about her?"

"About a thousand times."

"Did I ever tell you about the night we went to the school football game? We were playing our crosstown rivals, the Polk High Grizzlies. Sally's parents dropped her off at the game, and my parents dropped me off. Sally was a noisy and wild kid. It was ironic that I met her at the library, if you know what I mean. Being in a public library certainly wasn't her idea of a good time. She was a librarian's nightmare. Especially the way she liked to talk and talk. Man, I swear this girl could talk your ear off. She never stopped talking. Anyway, the night of the football game, we met up with a group of Sally's friends. A couple of the kids were seniors, and one of them had a car. It was an old '55 Chevy Nomad station wagon, and we all piled into it and took off from the game. Do you know where we went? We went straight to Polk High, figuring the place would be empty since everyone was at our school, watching the game. And we were right. There wasn't a soul there. We went around the main building, and in the middle of the interior courtyard there stood the beloved statue of the school mascot, a big grizzly bear standing on its hind feet. One of Sally's friends had a wrench with him, and he got on his knees and unbolted the bear's two feet from the concrete base. Then we all lifted the statue up off the ground. Jesus, the thing weighed a ton. We carried the bear to the station wagon, and loaded it into the back. Did I ever tell you what we did with it?"

"About a thousand times," I said.

"We drove it to the front of the school. At the front lawn, there was

89

an old wooden flagpole, and every morning, they would raise their flag. And every night they would take it down. We tied the flag-hoisting rope around the neck of the bear, like a noose. Then we all pulled on the rope and hoisted the statue up to the top of the pole. Jesus, you should've seen it! It was hilarious, that stupid bear hanging by its neck fifty feet up in the air! I tell you, I laughed so hard that my sides hurt. We were all laughing. Then we piled back into the station wagon and drove back to our school. We made it in time to get in the bleachers and see the last ten minutes of the game. It was in the newspaper the next morning—a photo of the bear hanging at the top of the Polk High flagpole. The article said the police were investigating the crime. Too funny, right? Investigating what crime?" Jacob stopped talking and was laughing. Rather, I should say, he was pretending to laugh. He was pretending to be me, laughing stupidly at his own story. I felt like kind of an idiot. Is that how I looked to Jacob? I mean, how many times had I told him this story so he knew it by heart? Then Jacob said, "High school, son. Some of the best years of my life."

"Let's stop here for a moment," the doctor said. "Tell me, Jacob, what you're feeling?"

Jacob said, "Like my dad is going to tell me that same story over and over until the day he drops dead."

"And how does that make you feel?" the doctor asked me.

"Kind of silly," I said.

"Let's move on," the doctor said. "No more role-playing. Now I want you to be yourselves. Stan, you've just come home from work and found Jacob locked away in his bedroom. You knock on the door, and he says to come in. He is listening to music. He is all by himself. He seems sad to you, and you want to make him feel better. What do you say?" I stared at the doctor for a moment, and she said, "Look at Jacob, and not at me. Tell Jacob what you're feeling. Go on, let's hear what you have to say."

"Jacob," I said. But that was all I said. I couldn't think of anything to say.

"Go on," the doctor said.

"I don't know what to say," I said.

"How about you?" the doctor asked Jacob.

"How about me what?"

"Do you have anything you'd like to say to your dad?"

"Not really."

"Do you feel he loves you?"

"Yes, I know he does," Jacob said.

"He seems to want to talk to you."

"But he isn't saying anything."

"Can you tell your dad how you're feeling?"

"Truthfully?"

"Yes, tell him exactly how you feel."

Jacob stared at the doctor and then at me. Then he surprised me. He said, "Most of the time my dad talks to me, I just feel like killing myself."

"Jacob," I began to say, but the doctor put her finger over her lips. She wanted me to keep quiet.

"Do you know why you feel this way?" she asked Jacob.

"No, I don't." Jacob said.

"Do you love your father?"

"Yes, of course I do."

"But he makes you feel bad?"

"I can't really explain it. But yes, that's what happens to me."

"Have you ever tried to take your own life?"

"No," Jacob said.

"But you think about it?"

"I do," Jacob said. "Sometimes the pain seems like more than I can bear. Sometimes it's just overwhelming."

"The pain?" I asked.

Again the doctor put her finger over her lips to keep me from talking. "Can you describe the pain for me?" she asked Jacob. "Do you know where it's coming from?"

"From life," Jacob said.

"From life?"

"From the act of living. It begins with the dreams I have first thing in the morning. You know, when I was a kid, I truly looked forward to my dreams. I'd dream I could fly. Have you ever had a flying dream? I'd just jump in the air, and presto, off I would go, flying over our neighborhood, over the rooftops and TV antennas, over valleys and mountains, over rivers and streams, high up with the white clouds and high-flying birds. And I'd think to myself, "Wow, I didn't know I could fly," but there I would be, flying. I love flying dreams. I've never had a bad flying dream, and I used to have them all the time when I was a kid."

"And what do you dream about now?"

"Never about flying. I dream about being embarrassed. I dream about people laughing at me. I dream about losing things. I dream about getting bad grades in school."

"Go on," the doctor said.

"Well, the dreams are just the tip of the iceberg. They are just the overture. You asked me about my pain. Maybe my mornings are the worst. Mornings should be full of promise, right? They give us a new day, and new opportunities, and new adventures. But I don't see any of these things anymore. You know what I see in the mornings? I see myself doing the same boring things over and over, like a programmed robot. I get out of bed and pee in the toilet. Then I go to the kitchen and pour some cereal into a bowl. I add in the low-fat milk, and I sit down to eat. I look at the cereal box, and it's exactly the same as it was the day before. And the cereal tastes the same. And Mom says the same old things that she says every morning. "Looks like it's going to be a nice day! Did you get all your homework done last night? I'm going to the store today. Is there anything special you'd like for dinner?" Then Dad bursts into the kitchen, and he looks the same as he does every day. He's wearing a suit and tie. He has a clean-shaven face, nicely combed hair, and a leather belt that holds up his pants. And then there is Zach, my big brother, with his million-dollar smile. He's talking about school. Maybe he's yakking about a teacher, or maybe about some kid. He is a ball of high school spirit and energy. He steals the cereal box and milk from me and makes his breakfast. And all the while that this *Saturday Night Live*–type skit plays itself out in our kitchen for the umpteenth time, all I can think of is standing up and going to our cabinets. I'll remove a serrated steak knife from the drawer and, holding the knife to my wrist, I'll slice it into my skin and sever my vein or artery so that the blood spurts out like it's gushing from Old Faithful, splashing and dripping all over my arm and hands, puddling on the linoleum floor. And I can hear mom at the top of her lungs. "No, no, no!" she screams, and Dad lunges toward me, trying to get the knife out of my hand. And Zach? He's still eating his cereal, but the milk in his cereal has turned into warm blood. He has no clue what's even going on."

CHAPTER 10

SANDCASTLES

———————— •●• ————————

When the boys were small, April and I would take them to the beach. There was one problem with living in Coto: we weren't exactly close to the ocean. And the traffic on the weekends was awful, so we would go during the week. I remember one weekday we took the boys to the Newport Peninsula. Jacob was seven, and Zach was eight, making me forty-six and April forty-four. The reason I remember this day so well is because it was April's birthday. It was April's wish to go to the beach. She packed a picnic lunch for us, and I filled a cooler with ice and soft drinks. We got to the Peninsula around eleven and then spent twenty minutes hunting for a parking spot. Even in the middle of the week, the beach was busy. We carried all our stuff to the sand and picked out a spot to lay down our towels. There wasn't a cloud in the sky. It was a perfect day.

The first thing the boys wanted to do was to run into the ocean. The water was cold, but they didn't seem to care. They splashed, dived, and jumped into the waves. I was out there with them, knee deep in the water and making sure they were safe. They knew how to swim, but with the ocean you just never knew. Eventually they wore themselves out, and they came back to the sand, huffing and puffing, and then running toward April. She gave them towels to dry off, and they each took a cold soft drink out of the cooler.

"I'm going to make a sandcastle," Jacob said.

"So am I," Zach said.

"I'm going to make the best sandcastle on the beach."

"Mine will be better than yours," Zach said, puffing out his little boy's chest.

Jacob just ignored him.

"Here are all your tools," I said. I dumped a plastic bag full of little buckets, shovels, and plastic molds on the sand, and the boys went after the stuff. "Make sure you boys share," I said. "There's plenty there for both of you."

"I think you should give an award," Zach said.

"An award?"

"To whoever makes the best castle."

"This doesn't have to be a competition," April said. "Just enjoy yourselves."

So away they went, working on their sandcastles while April and I sat on our beach towels, watching them. I remember looking at April and thinking to myself how lucky I was to have her as my wife. Honestly, even at forty-four, she was truly beautiful, and she still looked great in a swimsuit. Probably, to anyone else at the beach, she looked her age, but to me she looked like a sixteen-year-old.

I guess this is as good a time as any to tell you how April and I first met. It was, of course, at the beach. In fact, it was only about a hundred or so feet from where we were with the boys, on her birthday. April was crazy about the beach. She loved everything about it: the sand, the ocean, the waves, the coconut-scented sun lotion, the beach balls, the radios, the Frisbees, and the Coleman coolers full of cold drinks. On the day we first met, April was with her girlfriends, lying in the sun. I was with a few of my buddies, and we were walking along the shore, tossing a football among us.

It was Neil who broke the ice. I mean, he was the one in our group who wasn't afraid of girls. He walked right up to April and her friends and asked them what high school they went to. That was his way of getting the conversation going, and it worked. Nine times out of ten, girls didn't mind talking about their high schools. I think it made them feel safe. And it's important to feel safe when you're a girl. God knows there are a lot of weirdos at the beach.

Anyway, it turned out the girls went to Washington High, not too far from our own high school. "I know a couple girls from Washington," Neil said. "Do any of you know Suzie Pierce or Holly Bruce?" They all shook their heads. Of course they didn't know these girls; Neil had just made the names up. But now the girls were even more comfortable with us, since we knew a few other girls from their school. Once Neil had their guard down, he introduced us, one by one. And they told us their names. "Can we sit with you for a while?" Neil asked, and the girls said yes. We each took a seat on the sand, and I sat a few feet from April. It wasn't by accident. I deliberately positioned myself to sit as close to April as possible. That was exactly where I wanted to sit.

I had kept my eye on her since we first approached the girls. Honestly, she was the cutest thing I'd ever seen. And she smiled at me when I looked at her, and at that age, a smile meant a lot. It meant "I'm interested in you." I noticed she had a book in her lap—Carlos Castaneda's *Teachings of Don Juan*. The book wasn't open, but there was a bookmark in it to keep her place. "I see you're reading *Don Juan*," I said.

"Oh, this, yes," she replied.

"Do you like it?"

"It's okay."

"I read it last year," I said. "I thought it was pretty weird. What page are you on?"

"I'm on page twenty-four."

"Don't let her fool you," one of April's friends said.

"Fool me?"

"She's been on page twenty-four for the past three months."

The girls all laughed. Then another girl said, "April carries that stupid book around with her everywhere she goes, but she's always on page twenty-four."

"She wants people to think that she reads," another girl said.

April just smiled at me. I could tell she was a little embarrassed, so I said, "Don't feel bad. I don't like to read much either."

"I planned on reading it," April said.

"What's your name again?" I asked.

"April," she said. "And yours?"

"They call me Stan."

As I tell you this little story, it occurs to me that this was one of Harry's wonderful major-minors. A group of teenage boys comes upon a group of teenage girls, and one boy sits down next to one of the girls. It was a minor event, right? The only thing we had in common was a paperback that April hadn't even read, and that I didn't even really like, and the next thing I knew, we were married and two full-blown human lives were created, one of them being my son Jacob—a complicated, sensitive, creative, intelligent boy who was unlike any living human creature I had ever met. If Neil hadn't asked the girls what high school they went to, Jacob wouldn't exist. Or if the girls had snubbed him. Or if we hadn't been walking along the beach on that day. It could just as easily have been overcast, and all of us could've stayed home.

But we didn't.

You should have seen the look on Dr. Erskine-Garcia's face. I think Jacob's kitchen suicide fantasy really took her by total surprise. It was not what she expected. When Jacob was done talking, she stared at us for a moment. She scribbled a few lines of notes down on a pad of paper, and then she spoke. She said, "Jacob, do you mind if I speak privately with your father? I would like to talk to him alone for a minute. It won't take long."

"That suits me," Jacob said.

"If you could, please wait outside the office."

"Okay," Jacob said, and he stood up to leave.

"I'll get you when I'm ready."

"Fine," Jacob said.

When the two of us were alone in her office, the doctor's demeanor changed. She was no longer so carefree and friendly. Instead she was dead serious, as if she were about to tell me someone had died. She leaned forward in her chair, looking me right in the eyes, and she spoke softly so Jacob couldn't hear her through the door. "I'm afraid this is more serious than I realized," she said.

"I never said it wasn't serious," I said. I was a little defensive.

"When kids start talking about suicide, and when they start to visualize it, and when they fantasize about it, it is cause for alarm. It's a huge red flag. Let me ask you, has Jacob been giving any of his possessions away to others? Have you noticed him doing this?"

"No," I said.

"Does he talk about suicide often?"

"This is the first time I've heard him speak of it."

"Have his eating habits changed?"

"Not that I know of."

"Does he have difficulty sleeping?"

"I don't think so."

"How about friends? Have there been any changes in his friendships?"

"Honestly, he doesn't have many friends," I said. "He's always kept pretty much to himself. He did have one regular friend earlier this year, but I haven't noticed them doing much together lately. I think the kid's name was Paul. Seemed like a nice boy, but I haven't seen him around recently."

"I've seen young people like Jacob before," the doctor said. "Things didn't turn out well for them."

"No?"

"I'm just being honest. I'm not doing you any favors by pretending your boy is just a little morose, a little down in the dumps. It's my opinion that your boy is in jeopardy. Yes, that's it in a nutshell."

I'll tell you the truth; this doctor was kind of freaking me out. This was not what I expected to happen when I brought Jacob in to see her. What did I expect? Maybe I expected some helpful advice. Or maybe some tricks and techniques Jacob could learn. Or maybe some useful changes we could make to Jacob's life. "What do you suggest we do?" I asked.

"Well, there are some excellent medications on the market that would be appropriate."

"Medications?"

"I know some parents are opposed to giving their children medications, but my advice is that you strongly consider it. I can prescribe something that will help your son. It's done all the time. Are you agreeable to this?"

"I don't know."

"You'll probably want to talk it over with your wife."

"Yes, I would want to do that."

"And, of course, we would need to get Jacob on board. He has to agree to it."

"Of course," I said.

"If it's all right with you, I'd like to have Jacob come back in so I can explain this option to him."

"Okay," I said. I felt as though things were moving a little too fast. Honestly, I felt as if I were being railroaded, but I was also very concerned. And I didn't want to do the wrong thing by my son. The doctor opened her office door, and she told Jacob to come back in.

"Did you have a nice little talk about me?" Jacob asked.

"We did talk about you," the doctor said. "I'm not going to beat around the bush. You concern me, Jacob. I'm going to present an option to you. Your dad hasn't agreed to this, and your mother will also need to be involved. But I think you would be best served by taking an antidepressant. Do you know what that is? Does that sound like something you'd be willing to do?"

"You want to drug me?"

"Well, yes, it's a drug."

"It might help you feel better," I said.

"Taking drugs isn't really my thing."

"Lots of young men and women your age take antidepressants, and they have had great results. We've had a lot of success with these medications."

Jacob looked at me. He wasn't angry. Nor was he scared. Nor was he confused. He just looked at me more as if to say, "What the heck are you getting me into?" I really felt for the kid.

"Let me do it this way," the doctor said. "I'll write you a prescription, and you can take it home with you. Then you can all sit down and make a decision as a family. You can talk and think about it, and even research it on the internet. If you decide this is what you want to do, simply take the prescription to the pharmacy and have it filled. If you decide against it, you can throw the prescription away."

"That sounds fair to me," I said.

"It's okay with me," Jacob said.

The doctor walked to her desk and wrote out a prescription. She handed it to me, and I looked at it. I had no idea what she had written. I then folded the scrip it in half, stuffing it into my pocket.

The doctor looked at her watch and said, "I guess that's our session. I'd like to see both of you in a month. Is there a time that works best for you? This five o'clock slot is very popular. Kids are out of school, and it's not yet time for dinner."

"Five works for us," I said.

The doctor got her appointment book and opened it. "Let's see what we have open," she said.

I finally agreed to a certain date, and the doctor gave me a reminder card to go along with the prescription. I knew what Jacob was thinking. Our deal had been that he would come for one visit and then continue on with the sessions if he thought they were helpful. Yet I didn't even bother to ask him if he wanted to come again. I just went ahead and agreed to a date. We would have to talk about this on the way home.

The boys spent about two hours on their sandcastles. It was nice to see them both so focused on something other than teasing and provoking each other. When they were done and ready to move on to the next activity, Zach still wanted April and me to pass judgment on which sandcastle was the best. There was no way we were going to pick one over the other, but I asked the boys to explain what they had done, pretending to be a judge. "We'll start with Zach," I said. "Tell me all about your castle. Who lives in it? Why was it built? What country is it in?"

"It's in America," Zach said. "Duh. Where do you think it is? It's here on the beach."

"There's no story behind it?"

"It's a castle for the sand crabs," Zach said, saying this only because I had asked for a story. But that was all he could come up with.

"How about your castle?" I asked Jacob. "Tell me the story behind yours. Where is it? Who lives in it?"

Jacob got down on his knees so he could point. He said, "This is the greatest castle in all of Europe. It was built in France by Frenchmen. The king of France lived right here in the middle building with his beloved queen. He was a good king. He took good care of all his subjects, and everyone in France loved him like a father. The queen was the most beautiful woman in all of France. Her name was Lucy Marie, and that's what she preferred to be called. No one called her Queen or Your Majesty or Your Highness. They just called her Lucy Marie. Before the castle was built, the king and Lucy Marie lived in a different castle in a different part of France that was destroyed by the Spaniards when they tried to take over France. It was a long and bloody war, but the French people finally won. The hero of the war was a general by the name of Claude de Claude. He led his French troops into battle against the Spaniards and drove them out of the country. His home was destroyed in the war, so the king and Lucy Marie said he could now live here in the new castle, and they built this little square house for him to live in, right here, right next to the palace for the king and Lucy Marie."

"You've put a lot of thought into this," I said. "What's this building here?" I asked, pointing to a damp cylinder of sand next to the palace and Claude de Claude's house.

"That building is to store all the gifts the people give to the king. His people adore him, and they send him gifts all the time. He doesn't know what to do with most of the stuff, so he stores a lot of it in the building."

"And this building?" I asked. I was pointing to a larger building that had four seagull feathers poked into it, one at each corner."

"That's for the king and queen's animals. The king and Lucy Marie love animals. They collect them from far and wide, and they live in this building. The animals are specially trained so they all get along with each other. There are no fights, and they are well fed and taken care of. They have no need to kill each other. There are lions, elephants, zebras, gazelles, ostriches, peacocks, bunny rabbits, kangaroos, goats, laughing hyenas, and many, many others. Once a year, the king puts on an animal parade. The trainers let the animals out of this building, and they all march in a line through the streets of the city for all the citizens to see. The people are allowed to come up close to the animals and feed them, pet them, and talk to them. It's called the King's Parade of the Animals, and everyone in town turns out to see it. In fact, people come from miles around just to see the parade. There is music played by minstrels, and there are jugglers, magicians, and exotic dancers from the Orient. But that's only one day out of the year. For the rest of the year, they live in this building."

"And what is this place?" April asked. She was pointing to a dome-shaped sand pile that was covered with pressed-in seashells.

"That's the schoolhouse. The king and Lucy Marie believe that education is very important, so they put the schoolhouse inside the castle walls, keeping it safe from marauders. There is one teacher in the school, and he is a famous sorcerer named Mergon. Everyone in France knows who Mergon is. In fact, all of Europe knows of him. When the previous king of France tried to overtax his subjects, Mergon turned the king into a fat pig. Then the people butchered the pig, and they had a great feast at which the royal pork was served for dinner. Ever since then, Mergon has held a special place in the hearts of all Frenchmen. And it was Mergon who chose the current king of France to be the king. And he chose Lucy Marie too. Some say that Mergon is the true king of France, but he denies it. He says he is totally satisfied just teaching history, language, and mathematics to students at the castle schoolhouse. He says he's a teacher and not a leader or a politician. Over here, to the side of the schoolhouse, is Mergon's wife's house. Her name is Regina, and she's been married to Mergon ever since she was a young girl. She sleeps in this separate house because Mergon has a snoring problem."

I laughed at this.

"Here comes Godzilla," Zach said, and he held out his arms and stomped through his own castle. He stomped on it and made Godzilla sounds until there was nothing left of the sand castle. He completely destroyed it."

"Why did you do that?" I asked.

"Because my castle sucks."

"Your castle was fine."

Jacob looked at his brother, and I think he felt sorry for him. He had destroyed his own castle, but why? I think Jacob understood. He stood up from the sand, and screeching like Godzilla, just like his brother, he marched and stomped through his own castle, crushing the king and queen's palace, crushing the gift warehouse, crushing Claude de Claude's new home, and totally obliterating the animal building. He stomped through all of it until there was nothing left but footprints and shells and bent seagull feathers.

"Why did you do that?" I asked.

"I didn't do it," Jacob said. "Godzilla did it."

"Let's go back in the water," Zach said.

"Yeah," Jacob said. "Back in the water."

"Are you coming?" Zach asked me.

"Yes," I said. "I'm coming." I stood up and followed the boys to the water. Then April stood, and she joined us. April brought our beach ball, and we took turns slugging at it, keeping it up in the air.

Listen, I loved Zach to death, but Jacob was a special boy. He was truly one of a kind. And now? Never in a million years did I think we'd find ourselves in some nutty psychiatrist's office talking about medications, talking about suicide, and putting Jacob's life into the hands of a woman who saw patients while wearing a fox stole around her neck. She was so serious with me, and yet she was also something of a joke, wasn't she?

Who knew? Who knew if the woman knew what she was talking about? I certainly had no idea.

When Jacob and I returned home from the appointment, it was time for dinner. April had made chicken curry, one of Jacob's favorite dishes. He piled the stuff on his plate as though he hadn't eaten for weeks. There was certainly nothing wrong with the boy's appetite. Or maybe the meeting with Dr. Erskine-Garcia just made him hungry.

April and I had decided to tell Zach about the doctor. He was probably going to find out eventually, one way or the other, so why try to hide it from him? And we thought it would be better if we talked to him, explained it to him, and told him how important it was that he didn't belittle or tease Jacob about his issues. I told Zach, "We're a family, and Jacob is your kid brother. It's all our jobs to look out for each other, and it's your job to look out for your brother."

So what's the first thing Zach said at the dinner table? He smiled and asked Jacob, "So what was it like?"

"What was what like?" Jacob said.

"Seeing a shrink? Did she have you lie down on a couch? Did she hypnotize you? Did she ask about your dreams?"

"None of the above," Jacob said.

"Did you cry?"

"No, I didn't cry."

"Did you blame everything on me?"

"No, of course not."

"What the heck is wrong with you, anyway?"

"That's enough," April said.

"It's a fair question," Zach said.

"We talked about this," I said.

"Talked about what?"

"About our family. About each of us supporting the other, and cheering each other on."

"Who's supporting me?" Zach asked. "Who's cheering for Zach? I'm the one who does his homework and gets good grades. I'm the one who works his butt off after school to excel in sports. I'm the one who's trying to get into a good college. I'm the one who's normal around here. So, tell me, why isn't anyone paying attention to me?"

CHAPTER 11

HARVEY ASKS FOR A RAISE

———— •◦• ————

Jacob decided to try the doctor's prescription. This surprised me. It didn't seem like something he would opt for, but maybe he felt even worse than we suspected, and maybe deep inside he was ready to try about anything to help him snap out of the way he was feeling. So I went to the pharmacy and came home with a bottle of pills. He was supposed to take one pill a day, but we were told the medication wouldn't take effect for a couple of weeks. A couple weeks later, how did Jacob feel? We were all hoping, right? By "we" I mean April and me and Jacob. We were hoping that this miracle of modern science and chemistry in a pill bottle would make a noticeable, optimistic, and uplifting difference. But the truth was that Jacob felt nothing. There was not even a placebo effect. He told us, "I may as well be taking a couple of Tums each day."

Meanwhile, Jacob had been working on another poem, and when he was done, he gave the long poem to April and me to read. It went as follows:

Take a Pill

All the weeds keep growing in your bed,
And that fly's buzzing around your head,
And you keep forgetting what you said.
You can now take a pill.

Your mom keeps telling you what to do,
And your dad gives his two cents' worth too,
And your children don't listen to you.
You can now take a pill.

Those new lightbulbs barely last a week,
And that spot in the floor always creaks,
And the faucet continues to leak.
You can now take a pill.

Seems your car always needs a new part,
And the doors all attract shopping carts,
And the old engine will never start.
You can now take a pill.

Your cat claws your brand-new leather chair,
And your dog clogs your vacuum with hair,
And all of your pets pee on the stairs.
You can now take a pill.

Your boss says you always come in late
And says your results are not so great
And tells you you're not pulling your weight.
You can now take a pill.

On the way home, you are low on gas,
And the car ahead won't let you pass,
And the cop says you're driving too fast.
You can now take a pill.

A man holds up a store with a gun,
And kids spray-paint building walls and run,
And teenagers kick winos for fun.
You can now take a pill.

Addicts leave their needles all around,
And the homeless excrete on the ground,
And thieves steal from the lost and found.
You can now take a pill.

Hypocrites tell us all not to sin,
And athletes take drugs so they can win,

And bigots march against colored skin.
You can now take a pill.

The president is a steaming heap,
And the Congress can't a promise keep,
And the public votes them in like sheep.
You can now take a pill.

Husbands are all cheating on their wives,
And all children tell their parents lies,
And grandparents waste away their lives.
You can now take a pill.

The old war machine is in full swing,
And those fine young men sign up to bring
Mayhem and horror; let freedom ring.
You can now take a pill.

A small child of six is killed one day,
And a mother is killed the same way,
And a father swears they will make us pay.
You can now take a pill.

Hatred as deep as the day is long.
And the weak bite ankles of the strong,
And the strong say we all have them wrong.
You can now take a pill.

Meanwhile the rich stomp on the poor,
And the poor hold up markets and stores,
And our streets are lined with working whores.
You can now take a pill.

The middle class whines about prices,
And businessmen try to entice us,
And the news calls it all a crisis,
You can now take a pill.

It's like there is no end to it all,
And there is no bottom to the fall,
And above our heads, the endless pall.
You can now take a pill.

And when pills are coming out your ears,
For longings, anxieties, and fears,
And none of them do anything near
What you need them to do,

There will be pills for all those things too,
So don't ever feel sad or blue.
The good doctor will take care of you.
Just take another pill.

Did you like that poem? Me? I happened to like it a lot. April thought it was too cynical, but I thought the poem said some things that truly needed to be said. And there's nothing cynical about calling a spade a spade.

Did the poem depress me? Did it depress Jacob? I can't speak for Jacob, but I can speak for myself. I learned long ago that life is neither a bowl of cherries nor a stinking cesspool of waste. It is all things. And a good life is a life is that in which one masters the art of weaving every thread and string together into a tapestry of the good and the bad, the sad and the happy, the sweet and the sour, the bright and the dark, the warm and the cold, and so on. A good life is not all rainbows and unicorns; nor is it the brimstone and hell some people make it out to be. It is best when it is all things, and everything under the sun.

I have described for you some of Jacob's disappointments, but he certainly had some happy times. For example, I haven't mentioned Ralph. Good old Ralph. The year was 2008 when Ralph came into our lives, and Jacob was thirteen years old. Ralph was a young German shepherd; we never were sure of his exact age. Back then the country was flailing from the advent of the Great Recession; people were moving out of their houses right and left. Many of them were moving into apartments where pets were forbidden, and a lot of these people, believe it or not, would simply abandon their dogs and cats when they moved out of their houses, leaving them to fend for themselves. Ralph was one of these victims. Jacob found him wandering around in our neighborhood.

When Jacob first found Ralph, it was pathetic. The poor dog was lost, sad, emaciated, and dehydrated. Jacob brought Ralph to our house, where he fed him some raw hamburger and gave him a clean bowl of water. Do you think dogs are grateful? Do they have the capacity for gratitude? Ralph certainly seemed to appreciate Jacob. April took Jacob to the grocery store, where they bought a big bag of dog food, some pig ears, and a large rawhide bone. It seemed this poor beast had found a new home—our home.

At first we kept Ralph in the backyard. We didn't really want this stray dog in the house. Then April and Jacob took Ralph to the vet for shots, and then to a dog groomer for a nail clipping and a bath. Seriously, it was unbelievable, and it was incredibly heartwarming. This dog took to our family as if he'd belonged to us for years. He loved all of us. It wasn't long before he was in the house, curled up by the fireplace at night while we watched TV. It wasn't long before he was sleeping on Jacob's bed every night.

I think Ralph truly brought joy into Jacob's life. They would go everywhere together. And Ralph was totally Jacob's responsibility. Jacob fed him twice a day and always kept his water bowl full of water. He also cleaned up after him. They would play fetch together; Ralph was obsessed with this sport, and he would chase after about anything. And when Jacob locked himself in his room, listening to music and writing his poetry, Ralph was almost always with him. And it was something I never did quite understand. How could Jacob slash his wrists and say goodbye to the world, and leave Ralph behind? How would we be able to explain to a dog why his beloved master was suddenly gone?

Those were good times with Jacob and Ralph. They were good times filled with love, loyalty, joy, and affection, all rolled up into one young-boy-and-his-dog package. Yes, they were so happy together, and no, I never did, and still don't, understand.

I'm going back now to 2011, when Jacob was sixteen. It was a cool fall day, and I had a Saturday afternoon to kill. And I thought it would be nice to do something with Jacob. We hadn't done anything as father and son for quite some time. At least it seemed that way. Jacob had completed his chores, and he was in his room, writing poetry. I knocked on his door, and he told me to enter.

"What's up?" he asked.

"I was going to ask you the same question," I said.

"Just writing."

"And I was thinking," I said.

"About what?"

"How would you like to take Ralph to the beach?"

"Like now?"

"Yeah, like now. You, me, and Ralph. It's a cool day. There will be hardly anyone there."

Jacob looked down at his poem and then over at Ralph, who was on Jacob's bed. Ralph had no idea what we were talking about, but he seemed game. "Why not," Jacob said. "I wouldn't mind getting out of the house."

We drove to the Newport Peninsula. The traffic was light, and it was easy to park. Ralph was very excited. The smell of the ocean was in his nose, and his tail was wagging like crazy. We walked to the water and then strolled along the shore. Ralph was having a ball chasing after seagulls and splashing in the shallow water. I tried to think of something interesting that Jacob and I could talk about, because I loved talking to the boy. He always saw things in his own way, analyzed matters using the brains God gave him, and formed his own opinions. So what did I bring up to talk about? It was kind of dumb, but I couldn't think of anything else. I mean, it was in the news, and lots of people were discussing it. And there were lots of feelings and opinions floating around, so why not bounce the issue off my twenty-first century, long-haired, tie-dye-and-sandal-wearing sixteen-year-old son?

"So, what do you think of this Occupy Wall Street movement?" I asked.

"We are the 99%?"

"Yes, that."

He did not say what you'd expect from him. Everyone thinks that because you have long hair and dress like a 1960s hippie that you're a liberal. After all, aren't all hippies liberals? But if Jacob was a liberal, he was certainly a different kind of liberal. His opinions on the Occupy Wall Street movement were not what I expected.

"They're idiots," Jacob said.

"Who do you think are the idiots?"

"The protestors. I think they're all fools."

"Have you been following the movement?" I wanted to be sure we were talking about the same people.

"Of course I have."

"I would've guessed you'd be on their side. Didn't you once tell me that it was the protestors who ended the Vietnam War? And didn't you say protestors made the country aware of blacks and their civil rights?"

"Totally different causes."

"So now you're for the establishment?"

"It has nothing to do with being for or against the establishment. Or for or against Wall Street. Or for or against the government."

"What do you think it's about?"

"I think it's about irresponsible citizens. Wall Street was asked to do what liberals have been asking them to do for years. They were loaning money to lower-income people with below-average credit histories so they too could have a piece of the American Dream, so they could own their own homes, and so they could have lawns to mow and garages for their cars and backyards for their kids to play in. So, what did these people do when they finally had the chance to get all the amenities they'd been asking for? They went out and bought houses that they couldn't afford. Seriously, what the heck was wrong with them? What were they thinking? They then defaulted on the house payments, and the mortgages went into foreclosure. And what a mess! This whole thing—the collapse of the mortgage industry, and collapse of home values, and the domino effect all this had—was entirely their fault. It is all on them. Don't kid yourself. They're not innocent and stupid little children. It wasn't like those curious kids who want to play with knives, so you keep them away from the knife drawer to keep them from injuring themselves. It wasn't like that at all. These are adults we're talking about. They were grown-ups. And they were being treated like adults. They were finally given a great opportunity to behave like adults, and they screwed the whole thing up. As I said, it's all on them."

"You don't think lenders are to blame at all?"

"Not even a little. They just did what they've been asked to do for years, to loan money to the little guys so they could afford to live better lives. The little guys got the chance they'd been asking for, and they crapped all over it."

"What about the wealth distribution in this country? Don't you think it's lopsided?"

"Wealth distribution has been lopsided in every country around the world since the beginning of time. And 99% of the people in this country are far from poor. People in the United States live very well, especially when compared to most other places. Those who are complaining should move out to another country and see just how well they can live elsewhere. I think people in this country are spoiled rotten, and entitled, and basically full of crap."

It was funny. Under my breath, I laughed. I felt like I was talking to some sixteen-year-old flag-waver from the Orange County Chapter of the Young Republicans. Yet I wasn't. I was talking to Jacob.

Ralph found a piece of driftwood along our walk, and he wanted to play fetch with it. He brought it to Jacob, and Jacob tossed it out into the water. Ralph was fearless. He ran out into the waves to get it. Nothing was going to stop this dog from bringing the stick back to us.

As we continued to walk, we stopped talking. I couldn't think of anything else to say, and Jacob seemed to be deep in thought. He was probably composing a poem in his head about the beach, or maybe a poem about Ralph, or maybe one about Ralph playing fetch with the piece of driftwood.

I thought back to when I was a kid about eight years old. Don't ask me why my thoughts travelled there. Sometimes the shifting of one's thoughts is inexplicable. I recalled when my friends and I would go to the five-and-dime and buy the latest comic books off the magazine racks. Spider-Man was my favorite, and Sandman was my favorite villain. We'd bring our comic books home and sit on the floor in my room to read them with my transistor radio tuned to our favorite AM station. We read them from cover to cover, including all the crazy printed ads—the ads for Sea Monkeys, ant farms, X-Ray Specs, miniature secret agent cameras, throw-your-voice ventriloquist lessons, and those little giftwrapped packages with the big black question marks dotted all over them. Do you remember those? You had to send in a buck or so to get a little box in the mail with a surprise gift in it. I always wanted to send away for one, but I never did. My dad told me the surprise would probably be a rip-off, and the prospect of wasting my precious allowance on a total unknown was daunting.

Speaking of surprise packages, the week before I took this walk with Jacob, a manager at our box facility asked if he could meet with me. Of course, I said yes. My door is always open to my employees. This manager's name was Harvey Culpepper, and he was a good man. He was competent and honest, and he had turned thirty-three just a couple months prior. Anyway, he came into my office, sitting in the chair across from my desk, and I noticed he seemed nervous, as if he didn't want to be there. And yet he did. I mean, there was something he had to ask, and he wished he didn't have to.

"What can I do for you?" I asked. I said it very nicely, because I could see that Harvey was uncomfortable.

"There's something I need to ask," Harvey said.

"Go ahead and ask it."

"I've never done this before."

"You have nothing to worry about. Everyone here is happy with your work, and nothing you say is going to jeopardize your place in the company."

"There's something I need."

"Yes?" I said.

"My wife and I are going to have a baby. We just found out she's pregnant. We just found out last week."

"Congratulations."

"Thanks," Harvey said.

"You need some days off to help out your wife?"

"No, it isn't that. I mean, that would be nice, but that's not why I'm here."

"Okay," I said. "Then tell my why you're here."

"I wanted to ask for ... well, I wanted to see if I could get a small raise."

"A raise?"

"Having a child these days is expensive."

"Yes, I know about that. Do I ever. I have two boys of my own."

"We've just been barely squeezing by on what I'm making now. We don't waste money on anything. We don't eat out a lot, or go to movies, or go skiing in the winter. We buy our clothes at Target and use coupons at the grocery store. We drive cheap cars that get good gas mileage. We haven't been on a vacation since we first got married, and we don't spend a lot of money on birthday and Christmas presents. Yet despite all this, we still live paycheck to paycheck. I haven't been able to save a dime. And now we're going to have a child."

"How much are you making?" I asked, and Harvey told me what his annual salary was. It sounded about right. "Don't forget the benefits here," I said. "You have to consider all the benefits."

"Yes, I considered those, and we appreciate them. But I did some research on the internet. Do you know how much they say it costs to raise a child these days? They figured it all out. They say it costs almost a quarter of a million dollars from the day the kid is born until he or she is seventeen. And maybe it's even more in California. The number they gave was just the national average, and California is more expensive. And the cost they gave doesn't even include a college education. Jeez, how much does college cost? Tens of thousands? Maybe hundreds of thousands? I guess it depends on where the kid goes and what scholarships are available. But there's no way around it. It's an awful lot of money."

"It is a lot," I agreed.

"Will you consider giving me a raise?"

"I'll see what I can do."

"Thank you, thank you. I really didn't want to ask you for more money. I'm not greedy. And I love my job. I don't want to work anywhere else."

"I know you don't."

Harvey stared at me for a moment. Then he said, "I'll let you get back to whatever you were doing. Sorry if I interrupted you."

"It's fine," I said. "Don't worry about it."

Harvey smiled nervously, and he then walked out of my office, closing the door behind him. I leaned back in my chair and thought about what he said and how much courage it took to hit me up for money. It took a lot of guts, and I wanted to help the guy out. I really did.

I am older and wiser today. Now I realize the poor guy had no idea. Money wasn't even the half of it. In fact, money had little to do with anything. Everyone always thinks it comes down to money, don't they? No, Harvey and his wife had ordered a surprise package from the stars, and not even God knew what they were going to get.

CHAPTER 12

GLIESE 581C

———— •●• ————

I have always liked the stage. I have never cared much for big Broadway-type productions, and I don't drag my family to those. What I have always liked are the small, off-the-beaten-path sorts of playhouses you find where the rent is cheap, the crime is a chronic problem, and the parking is inadequate. My favorite in Orange County was the Bitter Thespian, located in a chain-link-fenced-and-razor-wired industrial neighborhood of Santa Ana. The place was great, right up my ally. This theater was run by a man named Clarence Oliver. Clarence wasn't in the business to make sacks full of money; in fact, his little on-a-shoestring theater was always in the red and looking for donations from loyal patrons. Clarence owned and operated the run-down place solely out of his love for the theater. I read an article about him in the paper, and it said he was from New York City and that he had years of intense experience with a good number of very successful productions on and off Broadway. The Bitter Thespian was his answer to that high-pressure daily grind. As I said, the place was right up my ally.

Here's the thing about the Bitter Thespian: they never put on a play that you'd ever heard of, or read about, or read, or seen anywhere else. Every play they put on was one written by an unknown playwright and had never, ever been produced by any other playhouse. Year round, they sought plays from amateur writers, and the less well known you were, the better chance you had of seeing your play produced. So going to see a play at the Bitter Thespian was like looking for the prize in the bottom of a Cracker Jack box, in that you never knew exactly what you were going to get. Sometimes the plays were pretty awful, but often they were much better than expected.

When Jacob was twelve, we took Zach and him to see a play at the

Bitter Thespian entitled *Tram*, a story about a group of complete strangers who are stranded up in a Palm Springs Tramway car for nine hours during a bad windstorm. It was a pretty good story as far as amateur plays go, but not great. But the great thing about this play was that it inspired my son to write his own play and submit it to the theater. Jacob holed himself up in his bedroom and worked for months on his play. The title of his amateur play was *Gliese 581c*. Jacob's story was inspired by a news story he saw on the TV about a planet that astronomers claimed to have found in our galaxy that was orbiting a sun in the distant Gliese system, twenty light years from earth. They said in the TV segment that the planet might be friendly to the sort of life forms that populate Earth. And that would include future colonies of human beings. What if, right? Jacob's young imagination soared.

As I said, Jacob worked for months on this play, and when he was done, he gave it to April and me to read. He didn't just want our opinions. He also wanted us to help him submit it to The Bitter Thespian. April proofread the script, and Jacob made the appropriate corrections. Then April hand-delivered it to the playhouse, and the man there said they would look it over. I saved a copy of the script, and while I'm not going to rattle off the entire thing for you, I'll give you an excerpt. The excerpt is from a scene where Billy Crusher (Gliese 581c's top-of-the-charts popular singing and songwriting star) is talking to Natalie Williams (Billy's manager). They are in Billy's office, waiting for Abe Winchester (Billy's public relations man):

BILLY
After all the things I've done for the people of this planet, it's hard to believe.

NATALIE
The numbers don't lie.

BILLY
When's my next album due to be released?

NATALIE
Next month. Maybe sooner.

BILLY
And what's Abe doing to promote it?

NATALIE

He's doing everything humanly possible. But remember, he's a PR man, not a miracle worker.

BILLY

(shaking his head)
Damn it all.

NATALIE

It's "The Shit Song."

BILLY

Who would've thought?

NATALIE

It was a stroke of genius. That's what the critics are calling it—a stroke of genius.

BILLY

Fortunately, so far for me, critics don't buy records.

NATALIE

I'm just telling you what they're saying. And people are listening to them.

BILLY

Who would've thought that a song about shit would be so freaking popular? I would certainly have never guessed. I've listened to it over and over, and I just don't see what the public sees in it.

NATALIE

Like it or hate it, it's catapulting Julian Jasper to the top of the charts. Everyone on Gliese 581c now knows who he is. And they love him, Billy. They love him to death, and they love his "Shit Song."

BILLY

(whining)
I don't want to step down. I like being in charge. I truly love it. Why is this happening to me? Haven't I been doing a good job?

NATALIE

(in a consoling voice)

We have until the end of the year, Billy. The fight isn't over yet. We're still just in the middle rounds. I've talked to Abe. There are things we can do.

BILLY

Things?

NATALIE

Abe has some good ideas.

BILLY

When's he due here?

NATALIE

He should be here any minute. He knows we're waiting for him. He said he'd be here.

BILLY

Don't the young people on Gliese 581c get what's at stake here? Don't they understand how precious our system of government is? Brave and selfless kids struggled, fought, and even sacrificed their lives during the Great Revolution to rid ourselves once and for all of Earth's old ways. And now? We got exactly what we wanted for the planet. No more voting. No idiotic political parties. No career politicians. No more prune-faced, doddering old fools making a grand and perpetual mess of things. We were to be young! We were to be a fresh new world directed and led by the young, the agile-minded, and the creative. Top of the pop charts for us, baby, and nothing less. Yet Julian mocks it all. Shit indeed. What kind of an idiot writes a song about shit?

NATALIE

There's nothing in the constitution that specifies the subject matter of any performer's song. That was whole point—that the citizens would be given the right to choose as they saw fit, never to be pressured by the status quo.

BILLY

But a song about shit?

NATALIE

(sighing)
I know, I know.

BILLY

(pensively)

Maybe it's just my age.

NATALIE

Your age?

BILLY

Face it, I'm approaching thirty. Of course, everyone knows what that means. It means that it won't be long before I'm obsolete. Retired. Put out to pasture.

NATALIE

Don't even think that way, Billy. Once you start thinking like that, you're bound to go down in flames. No, you're still a young man. You're in the prime of your life.

BILLY

Yes, you're right.

NATALIE

We've just hit a bump in the road. Honestly, I think Julian is a one-hit wonder. I don't think he can sustain his popularity, no matter how young he is, no matter how many "Shit Song" records he sells.

BILLY

But maybe it's the one big hit that will put him over the top. Maybe he only needs one hit.

NATALIE

We need to talk to Abe.

BILLY

Where the heck is he, anyway?

NATALIE

He should be here any minute.

ABE
(walking into the room)
Good morning all!

BILLY
It's about time.

NATALIE
We've been waiting for you. Where have you been?

ABE
Sorry about that. I was at the record company, putting a hold on the release of Billy's upcoming album. Good thing I stopped by this morning. I got there just in time.

BILLY
And why on earth would you hold up the album?

ABE
We're going to add a song.

BILLY
We are?

NATALIE
What kind of song?

ABE
The kind of song that no record-buying citizen will be able to resist. Sales of your new album with this song will be off the charts. I guarantee it. If this song doesn't outsell Julian's "Shit Song", I'll catch the next ship back to earth and live in Philadelphia.

NATALIE
Tell us more. Tell us about this song.

ABE
It going to be the kind of inspiring song that will bring us all together. It'll be a song that tugs at the heartstrings. It'll make every record-buying nut on this planet open his wallet and hand over his credit card to buy Bill Crusher's latest album. The sales are going to go through the roof. We're going to record a patriotic song. A song about the

glory of Gliese 581c. When we get done with this song, young people, the only people that matter, are going to be so darn proud of themselves that they'll be playing and singing along with the song everywhere they go. They won't be able to get enough of it. And they're going to idolize and adore the young man who sang and reminded them of what it means to be a patriot. Trust me; you're going to leave that "Shit Song" in your dust.

NATALIE

Yes, I can see this working.

BILLY

So can I.

ABE

Of course you can.

NATALIE

Tell Billy about your other plans.

BILLY

(perking up)

There's more?

ABE

Yes, there's more. This is going to be a three-pronged attack. We're going to put Julian Jasper in his place once and for all. We're going to swat him like the pesky little fly that he's become.

BILLY

So what else are we going to do?

ABE

First, there is the matter of his birthdate.

BILLY

His birthdate?

ABE

He's been boasting to the press and his fans for the past eight months that he's only nineteen. He's been trying to paint you as obsolete. He's been trying to make you out as too old to be an effective leader. Well, he's going to wish he had kept his mouth shut.

BILLY

How so?

ABE

As we are speaking right now, I have an operative removing all evidence of his birth from his local government offices. There will be no record of his birth at all.

BILLY

Is that legal?

ABE

(smiling)

Hell no, it isn't legal.

BILLY

I don't want to break any laws.

NATALIE

Do you want to stay in power or not? That's what it boils down to. Sometimes you have to take off the gloves, Billy. You have to get down and dirty.

BILLY

What about his school records? Anyone can look them up. Won't those tell how old he is?

ABE

That's the beauty of it all. The idiot was homeschooled by his mother. Can you believe it? There are no school records for Julian Jasper. His age will be whatever we say it is.

NATALIE

We'll be cutting him off at the knees.

BILLY

(thinking about what the others have said, and then speaking)

What's the third prong?

ABE

The third prong?

BILLY

You said this was a three-pronged attack on Julian. We have my patriotic song, and a challenge to Julian's age. What is prong number three?

ABE

Yes, of course. Prong number three. The knockout punch. The stake in the heart. The silver bullet. The straw that broke the camel's back. Did you know Julian didn't even write the lyrics to "The Shit Song"? Sure, he's been taking credit for it. But the fact is that the lyrics are, word for word, taken from a poem that was written by a writer named Theodore Richards over a hundred years ago. We did a little research and found the poem in a self-published collection of poems that Richards tried to market while he was in his forties. Richards is now dead, of course, but we found a copy of the book in the main branch of the Gliese People's Library.

BILLY

How did Julian get ahold of this book?

ABE

Who knows? The point is that the kid is a plagiarist. And we've caught him red-handed.

BILLY

So how are we going to break this news to the public? I don't want it to seem like I've been desperately digging into Julian's past.

ABE

Simple. We'll just find some English major and poetry addict at one of the universities, and we'll pay him or her under the table to come forward to the media and tell them about the old Richards poem. You'll have nothing to do with it. You'll just be able to sit back in your big leather chair, smelling like a rose. And Julian will smell like his song. Like shit.

Anyway, there is your excerpt. The full play is two and a half hours long. Did you enjoy the excerpt? It is kind of a weird play, isn't it? Maybe it was just a little too weird for Clarence Oliver since he turned it down. Or maybe I'm being unfair to my own son's play. Is "weird" really the word I should be using to describe *Gliese 581c?* I certainly wouldn't use the word to describe Jacob, so why would I use the word to describe something he wrote? A better word might be "creative," or "unique," or "special."

The first objection you might raise is to say the premise of *Gliese 581c* is ridiculous. A little too far-fetched, maybe? Too off the wall? After all, what country or planet would ever agree to its leaders being put in place according to the status of their popular music record sales? It's crazy, right? Or maybe not. I've thought about Jacob's play now and again over the years, and I've wondered about it. And I've looked around at the state of the planet that we live on. There are so many different ways people come into power to lead and control their countries, and as accepted as these ways might be, none of them seem to be very effective in producing great and humanitarian men or women. Horrible leaders and terrible politicians are plentiful in today's world. So, I wonder, why not? Why not try out something completely different? Why not shake up the status quo. Why not do away with democratic elections, military coups, revolutions, and purple-royal bloodlines. Why not go for youth, talent, popularity, and, yes, one's place on the music charts? Seriously, why not—especially when nothing else seems to work?

The more I thought about *Gliese 581c*, the more I liked it. It was clever, and it was honest. There's something one could always say with certainty about Jacob: he was not naive and did not pretend people were perfect. I liked how the political characters in his play were just as conniving and self-serving as they are in real life. Would you call in "cynical"? I know for a fact that April was often concerned that Jacob was too jaded with the world, especially for a boy his age. But there was also always hope. There was always that place, even if it was only in his mind. There was always Arcadia, its blue skies and marshmallow clouds and soda pop creeks—that place where people loved, cared, and behaved themselves.

I guess I should give you one more excerpt from the play. I wasn't going to do this, but I now think it's important that you read it. Billy and his wife, Zelda, are at their governor's mansion, eating dinner. The dialogue is as follows:

BILLY

Julian Jasper is history. I heard that sales of his "Shit Song" have plummeted, and it's no longer being played on the radio. I kind of feel for the guy.

ZELDA

He got exactly what he deserved.

BILLY

That's what Natalie says. And that's what Abe says. They say goodbye and good riddance.

ZELDA

The planet is better off. You've done a lot of good things for us. There's no question about it. Having a self-absorbed gnat like Julian running the show would've been a sure disaster for everyone.

BILLY

Don't you find it odd, the choices God gives us?

ZELDA

What do you mean by that?

BILLY

I mean they say the road to hell is paved with good intentions. But isn't it really the other way around? It's the road to God's kingdom I'm talking about. This grand road is paved with schemes, guile, and the sins of men. God knows this. God is the one who set the whole thing up. What on earth do you think he had in mind?

ZELDA

I don't know.

BILLY

Do you believe in Arcadia?

ZELDA

You've described it to me before, and I do believe that you believe.

BILLY

Someday we'll be there, Zelda. Someday I'm going to clear us a piece of land and build a fine house there, and live there, and sleep there. Yes, we'll sleep in peaceful silence on a bed that is always soft, and our dreams will always be pleasant. We'll live the way people ought to live. We'll be kind to our many neighbors, and we won't tell lies or plot behind our neighbors' backs. We won't have to protect ourselves from others, because no one will be out to wreck us, and we'll always have plenty to eat and drink. Then, every morning, the sun will rise in the east, and it will fill the sky with its shining yellow light, and the birds will sing, and a new day will be upon us, and we'll look forward to every second, minute, and hour during which Arcadia is our home.

So there it was again—Arcadia. This had been Jacob's vision for as far back as I can remember. When he was younger, he called it by different names. But it was always the same, a place unattainable, a verdant land sprawling in his dreams with its soda pop creeks and marshmallow clouds and gentle rains and Kodachrome rainbows. When he described it in his poems and stories, I often felt I could reach out and touch the place, and feel it, and live in it.

CHAPTER 13

TARDY TIM

———— ••• ————

The story I'm now going to tell you, I did not witness firsthand. Well, I did witness some of it, but not much. For the most part, I heard bits and pieces of the story from several reliable sources, so I have no reason to believe that the accounts are inaccurate. The story takes place when Jacob was a sophomore in high school.

There was a kid at Jacob and Zach's high school named Tim Cousins. Before I go on, you need to have a picture in your mind of who Tim Cousins was. I saw the boy several times, so I do know what he looked like. He was a short wisp of a kid with thin red hair, cloudy green eyes, and a galaxy of freckles. He was not what you would call effeminate, but he looked barely strong enough to swing open a simple door. I seldom saw him in the street, playing with the other neighborhood boys and girls. When I did see him, he was usually on his way to school or on his way home from school, wearing a backpack full of books and binders that you'd swear could break his back. But apparently his back was stronger than it looked—sturdy enough to carry all those books and binders. He reminded me of an ambitious little ant carrying a morsel of food that was ten times its own weight. Yes, Tim was an industrious little ant, walking to and from school with his big backpack.

I would learn that the kids at school called him Tardy Tim. The nickname was bestowed upon him by his seventh-grade history teacher, Mr. Jeffries, as a result of Tim's chronic lateness to class. This class was right after lunch break, and Tim would often stroll into the class five or ten minutes after the bell had rung. He would try to stroll in unnoticed, but Mr. Jeffries would always spot Tim coming in late and say, "Well, well, so glad you could make it, Tardy Tim. We're all so happy that you decided to come and join us." It was obvious Tim didn't like this attention, but there was nothing he could do about it. His face would turn red, and he would plop his big backpack on his desktop and take a seat. The kids in the room would laugh at him. Then Mr. Jeffries would pick up where he left off before Tim had arrived.

I would learn why Tim was so often late to class. I don't remember how I found this out, but Tim was extraordinarily shy about using the boys' room. By "shy" I mean he couldn't get his plumbing to work with other boys in the room. So what did he do? He waited until the bell rang—until everyone had left the room to go to class. Then he would use the urinal or toilet, whichever he needed, and no one would be there to watch. He'd have the entire bathroom to himself. Then he'd do his business, wash his hands, and arrive at class late. Tardy Tim is what the teacher called him. "Ha, ha, here comes Tardy Tim. One more tardy, and it's detention time, young man."

Tim served plenty of detentions. That was, after all, the rule at the school. Three times tardy to class equaled a half hour of detention, and there was no getting around it. It was the price Tim paid for his shyness, but it was time he would serve willingly, because anything was better than peeing with an audience.

What a strange ritual detention was. Tim definitely did not belong there. The other kids serving detention were, for the most part, the school's ruffians and troublemakers. They were disciplinary problems. They were usually boys, and not girls. They were the kind of kids who disrupted class, picked on the weak, made lewd comments to teachers, and so on. And there, amid these high school problem children, sat well-behaved Tim with his oversize backpack, whose only crime had been his shyness in the boys' bathroom. No, it probably wasn't fair, but rules were rules. And like it or not, high school was all about rules.

Tim was a bright kid. He figured that going to high school was a lot like doing prison time, and he used his head, keeping to himself like a smart inmate. There was no sense provoking anyone or giving anyone a reason to go after him. He would avoid eye contact at all times, stay out of conversations, and try not to laugh or smile about anything unless he was actually with his few friends. Otherwise it would always be "Who the hell are you looking at?" or "Who asked you?" or "What the hell are you laughing at?" Unfortunately for Tim, even the brightest kids get tripped up trying to play this game. Even the most careful inmates can make mistakes, and Tim was no exception.

So this story begins. It happened on a Tuesday after school while Tim was on his way home, walking behind Arnold Wentworth and two of his friends. Tim was about ten feet behind the three boys, minding his own business but listening. About twenty feet behind Tim was Jacob, who was also walking alone. Arnold and his buddies were talking about a girl they knew at school named Candice Kowalski.

"I heard the same thing," Arnold said.

"Who knocked her up?" one of his friends asked.

"Who knows. The way she plays the field, it could be about anyone."

"I heard it was John Applegate."

"Seriously?"

"You'd think he'd have better taste."

"Hell, I'd fuck Candice," one of the boys said.

"You'd fuck your mother's Yorkie if you could get it to hold still," Arnold replied.

"Do you really think it was John?"

"I don't know for sure, but that's what Hank says."

"And how would Hank know?"

"Hank keeps his ear to the ground," Arnold said. "He knows a lot."

"Is Candice going to have the baby?"

"How should I know?" Arnold said.

"I heard a good one about babies."

"Another one of your stupid jokes?" Arnold asked.

"No, this one isn't stupid. It's a good one. Seriously, you'll laugh. Don't you want to hear it?"

"Go ahead," Arnold groaned.

"There's this lady," the kid says. "She's going to have a baby, and her husband rushes her to the hospital. They wheel her into the delivery room, and the husband stays in the waiting area. He waits and waits, and finally the nurse comes through the doors. She tells the man, "I have some really bad news for you, mister." The man is scared. "What's wrong?" he asks. A second nurse comes through the doors, and she is holding the man's child. It is wrapped in a blanket, and the man comes to see his baby. The second nurse peels the blanket away so he can see, and in her arms is a giant eyeball. There is no body, or arms, or legs, or even a head. There is just one giant fucking eyeball. The man says, "Oh my God, what could be worse?" And the first nurse says, "*It's blind.*"

The boys laugh. "That is pretty funny," Arnold said. "Where'd you hear that one?"

"My uncle told it to me."

Tim, still ten feet behind the boys, heard the joke and was laughing too. Suddenly Arnold turned around and asked Tim, "What are you laughing at?"

"I'm laughing at the joke," Tim said.

"Who said we were talking to you?"

"No one. I just heard."

"You just heard?"

"I'm sorry," Tim said.

"Maybe you should be minding your own business," Arnold said. "Maybe we weren't talking to you."

"No one likes an eavesdropper," one of the boys said.

"Especially a little faggot eavesdropper," Arnold said, and now Arnold and the other boys stopped walking. So did Tim and Jacob. "Why are you so close behind us, anyway?"

"Sorry," Tim said.

"Maybe sorry doesn't cut it," Arnold said sharply, and now he stepped up to Tim so that they were nose-to-nose. "Tardy Tim, Tardy Tim, look at him," Arnold said, rhyming his words. Arnold then gave Tim a shove so that Tim fell backward and landed on his butt on the concrete sidewalk. "Come on, come on. Get up off the ground, Tardy Tim. Let's see what you've got. Don't you want to hit me?"

"Yeah, get up," said another boy.

"I don't want to hit you," Tim said. "I don't want any trouble." Tim's reluctance to fight back only made Arnold angrier.

"Oh, you'll get trouble," Arnold said. "If it's trouble that you're looking for, you've come to the right place."

"Kick him," one of the boys said. Tim was still seated on the sidewalk, and Arnold kicked him.

"Kick him harder," the boy said, and again Arnold kicked Tim, harder this time.

"Little faggot," Arnold said.

Jacob had seen enough, and he said to Arnold and his friends, "Leave him alone."

"Who's going to stop me?" Arnold asked, now staring at Jacob. "Are you going to stop me?"

"Maybe I will."

"This is great," Arnold said. "The hippie comes to rescue the faggot. That'll be the day, hippie."

"Just leave him alone."

Arnold walked around Tim and approached Jacob. He shoved Jacob so that he was pushed backward, but Jacob did not fall down. "Why don't you mind your own business, hippie? Why don't you go pick some flowers?"

"Screw you," Jacob said.

"Screw me? No, screw you."

Arnold tried to push Jacob again, but Jacob shoved Arnold's hand aside. "Hit him," one of the boys said.

"Maybe I will," Arnold said.

Arnold stood there for a moment, staring at my son. Then, from out of nowhere, he threw a sucker punch at Jacob's face. Jacob dodged the punch and said, "Why don't you idiots just keep on walking."

"Not until I'm done with you," Arnold said. He threw a second punch at Jacob, and this one connected with Jacob's ear. All this time, Tim was still on the ground, watching. He was surprised that Jacob was standing up for him.

"I warned you," Jacob said, angrily. He quickly removed his backpack and then ran into Arnold, swinging his fists and kicking his legs like a karate black belt with a beehive in his *karategi*. The sudden response took Arnold completely by surprise, and the fight lasted less than a minute. I wouldn't say Jacob won, or maybe he did. He managed to break Arnold's nose.

I would get a call from the school principal the next day. Arnold's parents had complained to him about Jacob, saying he beat up their son on the way home from school. They painted Jacob as some sort of bully, and they said they wanted April and me to reimburse them for Arnold's doctor bill. Can you imagine how surprised I was? Jacob had said nothing about this when he arrived home, and he said nothing while we all ate dinner together.

Have you ever been to a principal's office as an adult? It's a weird experience, to say the least. I mean, I hadn't been in a school principal's office since I was a kid. The last time I was in a principal's office, I had been sent by Mr. Rich, an English teacher who had caught Terry Witherspoon and me smoking a cigarette behind the gym. In fact, I wasn't smoking. I didn't smoke at all. It was Terry who was smoking, and I was just there, well, because I was stupid. I was stupid because kids in high school are generally stupid—a fact I think adults often overlook, because the principal kept asking me, "If you don't smoke, then what were you doing there? Anyway, we were sent by Mr. Rich directly to the principal's office, and Terry and I were given ten hours of detention and a warning that if either of us got caught smoking again, we would be suspended for three days. I remember that visit at the principal's office. I wasn't the kind of kid who got in trouble often, and it was terrifying.

And now here I was, a grown man and a father, being called into the principal's office again. I wasn't exactly terrified, but I'll tell you how I did feel. I felt like a kid who had done something wrong—or, more accurately, like a parent who had done a lousy job raising his child. "We take bullying very seriously at this school," the principal said. "And we have a strict no-tolerance policy when it comes to fighting. We expect our parents to teach their children how to get along with others."

I held my tongue.

Jesus, what a knucklehead this clown was. Did he know anything about my son at all? Did he even have a clue as to what took place?

So what eventually came of this? The principal had Jacob and Arnold meet in his office to shake hands, promising to leave each other alone. I agreed to pay half of the doctor bills for the broken nose, and that seemed to satisfy Arnold's parents. Meanwhile, Tardy Tim was Tardy Tim. He still came in late to class after lunch break. I think he was grateful for what Jacob had done, but to my knowledge he never said thanks. It would've been nice if he had thanked Jacob.

I remember eating dinner on the evening after I met with the principal. I was telling the family about the meeting, and Zach (with his mouth full of tuna casserole) said, "You know, little brother, this is the first time I've actually been proud of you. I didn't think you had it in you."

"Fighting is wrong," April said.

"But a boy needs to defend himself," I said.

"There are ways to resolve differences besides fighting," April said.

"Broke his nose," Zach said. "That freak got exactly what was coming to him."

"Don't talk that way," April said.

"That's the last time that idiot will mess with Jacob. Or Tardy Tim, for that matter."

"You're probably right about that," I said.

"The boxing hippie. Watch out for his left hook!"

"That's enough," April said.

There was a pause in the conversation as everyone ate their food. Then I asked Jacob, "How do you feel about all this?"

"I don't feel anything," Jacob said. "Can I be excused?"

"You've hardly eaten," April said.

"I'm not hungry."

"Well, if you're not hungry."

Jacob took his plate up to the kitchen sink and rinsed it off. He put the plate in the dishwasher and then went to his room. Ralph followed him, wagging his tail. That was the last I saw of Jacob that night. I figured we should just give him time alone. After cleaning our own dishes, the rest of us went to the family room and watched *American Idol*.

Some people are indestructible. Have you noticed this? Let me tell you about Tardy Tim. I know quite a bit about the boy, or should I say the young man. There was an article in the paper about him that I read several months ago. The headline for the article said, "Local Boy Grabs Brass Ring." Tardy Tim, Tardy Tim, look at him. At the age of twenty-four, he was the founder, CEO, and majority stockholder of Aries Technologies. You say you've never heard of them? It doesn't matter. They weren't out to make Aries a household name; instead they were out to make preposterous amounts of money. The article I read said that Tim, now known respectfully as Tim Cousins, went to UCLA after graduating from high school, where he studied computer science for two years before dropping out to start up his own company.

They were calling him a genius. Some called him a young King Midas. Here's the fantasy I enjoy pondering when I think of good old Tardy Tim these days (and remember, it's just a fantasy):

He's a marvelous red-headed cross between James Bond and Bill Gates. He can afford to travel anywhere he pleases. Right now he's in Monte Carlo, enjoying summer and playing roulette in one of the casinos. He is dressed in a tuxedo with his red hair slicked back from his forehead, and there is a cool glass of bubbly champagne in his hand. The croupier says, "Faites vos jeux," and Tim turns to the woman sitting beside him. "Choisir un numéro," he says. She smiles and says, "Onze." He places the bet on the felt and says, *"Onze* it is, lady." The croupier calls off the betting and spins the polished wheel. The little ball bounces around, and no one knows where it's going to stop. Finally the ball comes to a rest. "Onze!" the croupier says. The woman shrieks, and the croupier adds the winnings to Tim's bet. "I couldn't lose if I tried," Tim says. He tosses a tip toward the croupier and walks away with his winnings. The lady is hanging on his arm as he makes his way to the cashier. After cashing in, he turns to the woman and says, "Repas du soir avec moi?" She says, "Oui, oui," and they walk to the nearest restaurant, where he orders for both of them. His order includes a bottle of champagne. They dine and talk French to each other for an hour and a half, and then he looks at his watch, saying, "Je dois y aller" (I have to go), and she pouts a little. He tells her that he'll look her up the next time he's in Monte Carlo (which is a lie).

Tim boards his private jet in Nice, and they fly back to Orange County. On the plane he reads the issues of the *Wall Street Journal* he missed while he was on vacation. When he arrives back at John Wayne Airport, his driver is waiting for him, and they head to his large home in Newport Beach. His girlfriend is in the house, and she's so happy that Tim has returned home. She gives him a bear hug and a wet kiss on the lips and then tells him to sit down in his favorite chair so she can massage his feet and fill him in on everything that he missed while he was gone. She tells him about her younger brother and how he walloped a two-run homer during his college baseball game, about how her mom's skin biopsy came back benign, about how she and her girlfriends all took the Rolls Royce to go shopping at South Coast Plaza for a full day, and about how the gardener replaced those awful orange chrysanthemums at the front of the house with Nikko blue hydrangeas.

And now comes the best part of this fantasy, which is Tim's stable of cars. He has a carpeted ten-car garage filled wall-to-wall with exotic American and foreign cars. Every month, the cars are all detailed. When Tim wakes up the next morning, the detailer is at the front door, ready to begin work. Tim answers the door in his bathrobe with a cup of coffee in hand. "I'll open the doors for you," he says to the man. He goes inside the house, to the garage, and presses the buttons that will open the doors. One by one, the doors lift up.

"Thank you, Tim," the car detailer says.

"Don't mention it," Tim says.

"Does it matter which one I do first?"

"Start with the Ferrari," Tim says. I'm going to be using it in a couple hours."

"Yes sir," the man says.

So, you now ask, why is this the best part of the fantasy? Can't you see the face of the car washer? Don't you recognize him? He's Arnold Wentworth. He's the same Arnold Wentworth who pushed Tim to the sidewalk the afternoon that Tim laughed at that stupid eyeball joke. He's the same Arnold that kicked Tim while he was sitting on the sidewalk. And he's the same Arnold Wentworth whom Jacob punched in the nose. Imagine, when Arnold is done with the cars, Tim will walk around to check out his work. "You missed a spot over here," he will say.

"Oh, of course," Arnold will say. "I'm sorry; let me get that for you."

"And this wheel. You need to clean it."

"The wheel?"

"I think you must have overlooked it. You need to pay closer attention to what you're doing."

"Yes, of course sir."

Ha, this little fantasy slays me every time I play it out in my head. It really makes me laugh. It's all about that big shot, Arnold. How much do you suppose my make-believe Arnold brings in each year cleaning and polishing other people's cars? Enough that he can afford to live in Coto like his parents, or in Newport Beach like Tim? Probably not. My Tim Cousins probably spends the equivalent of Arnold's total annual income on the special dark-roast coffee beans he imports from Costa Rica to brew in his Elketra Belle Epoque coffee machine. Tardy Tim indeed.

CHAPTER 14

ZONKEYS AND SWITCHBLADES

———— •◦• ————

When Jacob was sixteen, I thought that if I could relate some story from my past to his life, I would be able to help him deal better with his moods. It seemed like a very good idea at the time. And wasn't it just the sort of thing a good father would attempt to do? I mean, shouldn't a parent pass forward wisdom and experience to his child? The question was, which story from my personal history would be of the most help?

I decided to tell Jacob about the day my dad took me to Tijuana. "The best way to appreciate the life you have here in America is to pay a visit to another country," Dad said. I remember exactly when he said this; it was when I was hanging out with a kid named Dylan Parks during the seventh grade. My dad didn't care much for Dylan. Dylan didn't have long hair or smell like patchouli oil or dress like a hippie. But he held a cynical view of America. Further, his parents were Democrats, which in and of itself was anomalous in Orange County. When I was a kid, Democrats were rare. Coming across one where I lived was like coming across an albino. Most of us were John Wayne–loving, flag-waving ultraconservatives, kids and parents alike. Just to be clear, to this day, I am convinced that given some form of animalia suffrage, even our canaries, dogs, and cats would have voted Republican.

I remember the afternoon we arrived in Tijuana. We drove across the border and parked on one of the cruddy side streets, then walking to the Avenida Revolucion. I'll be honest (and I don't mean to offend Mexicans), the first thing I noticed was the odor. It was like a disgusting mix of dust, rotten fruit, and disinfectants. The smell of Tijuana is real, and there's no escaping it; it's as if the place has its own atmosphere. We walked up and down the main drag of the Avenida like a pair of gringo tourists. Dad explained we weren't really experiencing Tijuana, not yet, but rather we

135

were experiencing the *turista* section of the town, kept presentable and unsullied (by Mexican standards) for us foreign visitors.

We saw the zonkeys, which were donkeys painted with black stripes to look like zebras. You could have your picture taken with a zonkey, I guess to prove you had been there. Honestly, it seemed like a really stupid idea to me, painting a donkey and palming it off as a zebra, and it seemed sort of cruel to paint an animal and make the poor beast stand on the hot border town street, posing for tourists hours on end. Of course, these people also adored bullfights, so I suppose painting donkeys was humane by comparison.

Up and down the street we walked. We went into many of the shops, run by an assortment of big-smile proprietors with a lot of gold teeth and slick black hair. Here they sold all kinds of shabby, cheap, and worthless souvenirs—and switchblades. Yes, I admit these knives really captured my attention. My dad laughed when he saw me gawking at them, and he decided to buy me one. I think I still have it in a box stored up in our attic. I'm not exactly sure why I've kept it. I suppose it will come in handy if I ever decide to become a foot soldier for *la Mafia Mexicana*.

But it wasn't the tourist nonsense that Dad wanted me to see. Sure, we had some fun there, but once we had our fill of it, we got back in the car and drove to one of the town's ugly residential areas. Wow, it was a real eye-opener; I'd never seen anything like it. If ever there was a place that deserved to be called a shithole, this was it. At least, this rang true for this twelve-year-old boy from Orange County with his very limited travel experience. I had never seen or smelled anything similar, not in person or in pictures. It was like the county dump, except people had made homes out of all the trash. "The next time someone tells you America stinks, remember this awful place," Dad said to me. Of course, not all of Mexico was like this neighborhood; nor was all the rest of the world. I know now as an adult that my dad was giving me a false dichotomy to chew on. Yet there was no denying what I saw that day. There these people were, living worse off than any animals, anywhere, and I came away from the experience with a new respect for my country. I knew exactly what I had seen, and I trusted my own twenty-twenty eyesight, and I trusted my trusty nose. I knew what I saw and smelled.

Are you wondering how I figured that telling any of this story to Jacob was going to be helpful to him? It seemed to me Jacob needed it. I thought he needed to understand how good he had it as an American citizen, living in our spacious house in Coto with its modern appliances, manicured yard, clean bedding, and sparkling, pH-balanced swimming pool. Then I also realized that trying to tell him about what I saw when I was twelve years old would fall short of actually being there. No, he would have to visit Tijuana in person to really have his eyes opened. He would have to drive through the slums and see all the squalor just like I did. You have to see it, smell it, and feel every square inch of it to appreciate how awful it is. So I decided that rather than recite my story to Jacob as if reading it from a book, I would take him across the border the same way my father had been wise enough to take me.

Jacob was sixteen when we went. He wasn't a lot of fun to be around during those months. His attitude was sour, and he had few good things to say about anything. I remember he had just written a poem about America that expressed how he felt about our country, and he asked April and me to read it. You know, I almost said no, knowing it would probably be a downer. And it was; I didn't like it at all. After I read it, I was more convinced than ever that I was about to do the right thing for Jacob; I knew that a trip to Tijuana was exactly what a good doctor would've ordered. By the way, the poem he wrote went as follows:

Don't Look at Me

Once upon a time it was a land
Framed by pristine waters and white sands,
A place where the buffalo were free.
Who's to blame?
Don't look at me.

Redwoods and oaks and maples and pines
And lupine and poppies, winding vines,
And grasses sweeping into the sea.
Who's to blame?
Don't look at me.

River water cold, all pure and clear,
Lakes reflecting the blue skies like mirrors,
Mountains standing all purple and green.
Who's to blame?
Don't look at me.

With swords and disease and gunpowder
They beat the stewards until they were
Burying their hearts at Wounded Knee.
Who's to blame?
Don't look at me.

They stripped and mined and drilled like madmen,
Raising churches so they could amen,
Building cities for the brave and free.
Who's to blame?
Don't look at me.

Manifest destiny they called it,
And if it was open, they walled it.
Yes, it was all surely meant to be.
Who's to blame?
Don't look at me.

Now it is us and no longer them.
Here we live, oblivious to when
Men and women and the land agreed.
Who's to blame?
Don't look at me.

All of us, pseudo kings and queens,
Steak on our plates, and cans of string beans,
And cartons of eggs, and bags of tea.
Who is to blame?
Don't look at me.

Toasters and blenders and electric
Knives and washers and dryers and Bic

ARCADIA

Lighters and stoves and fake Christmas trees.
Who is to blame?
Don't look at me.

When the day is done, just thank God you're
Loving this lovely, wonderful girl,
With her cars, stars, B-movie monsters,
People magazines, shows with sponsors,

Jokers in the deck, stand-up comics,
Rock 'n' roll stars choking on vomit,
Nonprofits, Nazis, Klan robes and hoods,
Cigarettes, airplanes, cops with the goods,

Low-cal beers, dumb slogans on shirts,
Designer drinks, fattening desserts,
Soft porn, hard porn, leather-bound Bibles,
Lawyers who will sue you for libel,

Polluters, politicians, grifters,
Whorehouses, casinos, weight lifters,
Diets, group therapists, horse races,
Uppers, downers, cream for your faces,

Boob jobs, nose jobs, hair restoration,
Ads, jingles, and public relations.
Don't tread on us, and don't ask us why.
We're just as right as the sun up high,

We have brought this great land to its knees,
And we will damn well do as we please.
And who is to blame?
Don't look at me.

Look, my good friend, I was just born here.
I don't really know any better.
So just pour me one more glass of beer,
And let's get good and drunk together.

And we'll sing, "Who, who, who is to blame?
Just give us a goddamn name,
Or two or three,
So long as it isn't me."

I suppose the poem was funny in a way, but I still felt it was too cynical. I felt it lacked worldliness. It was short on maturity, and a little long on inexperience. That's just my opinion. You may feel that Jacob hit the proverbial nail right on the head.

Anyway, we arrived in Tijuana on a hot day in the middle of July. I drove my car across the border and probably should've stopped to get Mexican car insurance. But I didn't. I figured, *What could go wrong?* We were only going to be there for a few hours—just long enough to visit some tourist shops, eat lunch, and drive through some neighborhoods. I parked the car downtown on a side street, and we walked along the crumbling Mexican sidewalks to the Avenida Revolucion.

The place was much like I remembered, except now there were fewer zonkeys and every other store was a pharmacy. No kidding, the pharmacies were now a *big* thing. I didn't know much about it, but I assumed drugs were much cheaper in Mexico. I knew for a fact that they cost a fortune in the US. Were the drugs being sold in Mexico of the same quality? I had no idea.

One thing that hadn't changed in Tijuana was the odor. The place still smelled bizarre. Another thing that hadn't changed was the number of junk-souvenir shops. We went into a few of them, and none had any switchblade knives. I guessed they were now illegal in Mexico, but I wasn't sure about this. I was just guessing.

Jacob wasn't even slightly interested in spending time in the shops. "They all have the exact same crap," he said. "Who buys all this shit?"

"I don't know," I said.

We then went into a Hard Rock Cafe for lunch, and we both ordered hamburgers. I was impressed with the service, and the food wasn't bad. I told Jacob I wanted to take him through the residential neighborhoods when we were done eating, and he said he was okay with that. He didn't seem to care one way or the other what we did. Listen; I know the boy loved me, and I know he didn't want to hurt my feelings. That was the reason he was going along with all of this in the first place. And I wasn't fooling myself by thinking he was actually enthralled with what we were doing. However, he did seem to like the hamburger a lot. He said it was juicy, and he was right. Mine was juicy too.

Have you ever been to Tijuana? Have you ever attempted to drive a car there? The streets are laid out like platefuls of spaghetti, and it's very difficult to make any sense of all the twists and turns to find your way around. Somehow, after about thirty minutes of negotiating the noodles, I was finally able to find one of the residential areas that I wanted Jacob to see, and we drove into it. The roads were not paved, and the slums were built on a hill. There were barefoot and shirtless kids running all around the place, playing soccer, tag, or whatever, and the dirt road was filled with deep ruts and chuckholes. So I drove very slowly.

"This is what I wanted you to see," I said.

"Why?" Jacob asked.

"I wanted you to see how fortunate you are."

"That I'm not a Mexican?"

"That you don't live in a place like this, that you live in our house, and that you live in Orange County."

"What's wrong with these people?"

"They're poor."

"Why don't they do something about it?"

"I'm sure they try."

"Well, they're not doing a very good job."

"Poverty is a complicated issue."

"I don't feel sorry for them," Jacob said. "Not even a little." Jacob's statement surprised me. It was not what I expected him to say. It was more the sort of thing you'd expect to hear from a right-wing blowhard like Rush Limbaugh, right? Or from one of his ditto-heads. I knew that Jacob couldn't stand Limbaugh, so I pressed the issue.

"Have you thought much about it?" I asked.

"Not really."

"So you're just talking without really thinking?"

"Not a lot of thinking is necessary."

"No?" I asked.

"People are people. Give them a whole lot to work with, or give them very little, and they're still just people. And I hate to say it, but people are full of shit. For the most part, anyway. 99 percent of them are full of shit right up to their eyebrows."

"I guess that's one way of looking at it."

"No matter how much money they have or don't have in the bank; no matter where they live or what their house is like; no matter whether their roof leaks or doesn't leak; no matter what kind of food they gobble down for breakfast, lunch, and dinner; no matter if their kids are good looking or ugly; and no matter if they drive a brand-new Mercedes Benz or an old hunk-of-junk pickup truck, they're still, for the most part, just plain old corrupt, greedy, ignorant, sinful, pompous, self-absorbed, and stupid human beings. Add food and they'll grow bigger, but they won't get any better. Add money and you just have a bunch of idiots who have money. Add jobs and you have a bunch of pricks who now have to be somewhere on time each morning. Add college educations and they use bigger words. But they still don't say anything worth listening to."

"That's terribly cynical," I said.

"Is it? I think I'm just being realistic. As you like to say, I'm calling a spade a spade. I thought you liked honesty. I thought you liked people telling it like it is."

"I've met a lot of good people in my life." True, I was now feeling defensive. The fact was that I *had* met a lot of people over the years, and I did not dislike or have any bad feelings about most of them.

"Name one good person," Jacob said.

"Well, there's your mother, for one."

"It's a low blow, but I'll answer it anyway," Jacob said. "I love Mom just as much as you do. But is she really such an admirable person? I mean, what does she actually do day after day? What kind of person is she? If you can forget the fact that you love her for a moment, and that I love her, and look at her critically, you might be surprised at what you see. She is a woman who claims to believe in climate change, for example, yet she leaves a carbon footprint like a Sasquatch. She burns enough gasoline in her SUV waiting for the light to change to power up a whole fleet of illegal Mexican gardeners and their gas-powered leaf blowers. She goes through cases of bottled spring water like she gets the stuff for free. Did you know it takes two thousand times the energy to produce bottled water as it does the same amount of tap water? And that's not all. She claims to worry about the US trade deficit and then does her shopping at Target and Walmart, where 90 percent of their inventory comes from where? From China, of course. Then she worries about illegal immigration, but she tips undocumented aliens at the car wash whenever they do a good job cleaning her car, and she hires them to help her with the yardwork at our house. I think you guys even hired an illegal to babysit me back in the day. Am I right about that? And here's one that really makes me laugh. Last year, near the grocery store, right before Christmas, there was a woman and two scruffy-looking children standing in the parking lot, begging for money. The woman's cardboard sign said, "Lost my job. Anything will help. Happy holidays. God bless you." Mom handed the woman a twenty-dollar-bill and told me, "No one in this country should have to stoop to begging for money during the holiday season." Then a month later, after the holidays had passed, the woman was there again, standing in the same spot with her cardboard sign. Mom said, "If that broad thinks I'm good for another twenty, she's got another thing coming."

I laughed at this. It sounded just like April. And I also thought to myself, *I probably ought to talk to her about all the bottled water she drinks.*

Then a Mexican fellow stepped in front of my car so that I had to stop. He was smiling, but it was not a friendly smile. Then another man came to my side of the car and tapped on the glass, motioning for me to roll down the window. I rolled it down, and now there were three men in front of my car and three men behind it.

"Can I help you?" I asked.

"Tu dinero," he said.

"Sorry," I said. "I don't speak Spanish."

"Your money," he said.

"What about it?"

"Hand it over. Your wallet. Give me your wallet."

He was robbing me, and I was stuck. I couldn't go forward or backward. I couldn't very well run over the six men who were blocking my way. "There's not much in it," I said, referring to my wallet.

"I'll take what you have."

"Jesus," I said. "Are you serious about this?"

"Just hurry it up."

"Okay, okay," I said, and I reached to my back pocket. I pulled out my wallet and handed it to the man. "You can take the money and credit cards, but I need my driver's license to get back across the border."

"Maybe I could use a driver's license."

"Please," I said.

The man looked through the wallet. I went to an ATM before coming over the border. I had over three hundred dollars, and the man seemed pleased to find so much cash. He removed it, and he also took out the credit cards. He looked at the driver's license, but he didn't remove it. "This is a good picture of you," he said.

"Thanks," I replied.

He then handed the wallet back to me. "I'll take the watch too," he said.

"Please," I said.

"It's worth some money, no?"

"It has sentimental value. My wife gave it to me for my birthday several years ago."

The man looked at his friends and said, "His wife gave him the watch." They all laughed. I wasn't sure what was so funny. Then he glared at me and said, "Give me the watch."

"You better give it to him," Jacob said.

"Listen to your son. Or to your daughter. Or whatever he or she is." The man was grinning when he said this, and I figured he was referring to Jacob's long hair.

"He's my son."

"The watch, *por favor*."

"Fine," I said, and I removed the watch from my wrist and handed it to him. I noticed he had small and gentle hands, and this surprised me.

"What else you got?"

"Nothing."

"Get out of the car."

"What are you going to do?"

"Just get out of the car. The boy too. Both of you, out of the car. And leave the keys in the ignition."

"I've done everything you asked," I said. "We don't have anything else of value."

"It's a nice car," the man said. Then he looked at his friends. "Buen coche, si?" The men smiled and nodded their heads. Then to me he said, "We've decided that we like your car."

"No," I protested.

"*Si*, the car. We want the car."

"How will we get home?"

"Use your feet."

"You've got to be kidding."

To his friends, the man said, "Estamos bromeando?"

"No, no," they all said, and they laughed.

"No, we're not kidding. None of us are kidding. Start walking," the man said to us. "Get moving before we take your shoes and pants."

"You can't do this."

"Arre, arre!" the man said, clapping his hands and stomping one foot, laughing.

"I think we should go," Jacob said. "Come on, Dad. Do what he says."

What was I supposed to do? What would you have done? We didn't stand a chance against these guys, so we started walking down the dirt road. "This is fucking horrible," I said to Jacob.

"We'll be okay."

"How are we going to get home?"

"You'll figure out something."

I was glad Jacob had faith in me. To be honest, I had absolutely no idea what we were going to do. I had no plan and no ideas. We walked for about a half hour until we finally saw a police car. "Officer, officer!" I shouted, and I waved like crazy until he saw me. He pulled his car up to us and rolled down his window. All I can say is, thank God he spoke English. "What's the problem?" he asked.

"We've been robbed," I said. "They took my wallet, watch, and my car."

"They?"

"A group of men."

"Do you know who they were?"

"No, I don't know who they were."

"Who is this?" he asked, looking at Jacob.

"This is my son."

"You're tourists?"

"Yes, we're tourists. We're Americans."

"And what are you doing way out here in this neighborhood?"

"We were just driving around."

"Ah, driving around."

"Yes," I said.

"Buying drugs, maybe?"

"No, of course not."

"You were with a prostitute? Maybe two of them? One for each of you?"

"No, no, we were just driving around."

"I see," the officer said. "Then he sighed and said, "Get in the back. I'll give you a ride." He got out of his car and opened the rear door for us. Once we were in, he said, "We'll have to file a report."

"Don't you want a description of my car?"

"It'll be in the report."

"I mean, don't you want it now? You know, so you can get people looking for it?"

"We have to write a report."

Long story short, Jacob and I were taken to the police station, where the officer asked us all sorts of questions and handwrote a long report on a yellow form. He took down my name, phone number, and address in case they happened to find my car. He asked if I had purchased insurance before coming into Mexico, and I said no. "Eso podria ser un problema," he said to another cop. I assumed he meant to say I was out of luck. He gave me a copy of the report, the pink copy, and then drove Jacob and me to the border at San Ysidro. On the way to the border, I looked the report over. The entire stupid thing was handwritten in Spanish.

"What would your generation call this?" I asked Jacob. "An epic fail?"

"Something like that," Jacob said.

That was a perfect name for it.

You should know that three weeks later I got a call from the Tijuana Police. They had my car and wanted me to come and get it. When I got there, I was amazed. Except for the fact that it was covered with Tijuana dust, it was in perfect shape. Say what you want about Mexican police officers; you'll hear no complaints from me.

CHAPTER 15

MY NAME IS FRED

Nothing can prepare you for it. Maybe if you were an uncaring parent, or maybe if you didn't spend any time with your kid, or maybe if you were abusive, or maybe if you were a drug addict or an alcoholic—maybe you would have a reason to expect something like this. But April and I were not bad parents. Sure, we made mistakes like every parent on Earth makes mistakes, but we certainly never imagined in our wildest nightmares that it would all boil down to this—to seeing our son slumped over and naked in a shower stall, blood oozing freely from his freshly slashed wrists. I can't begin to describe in words how painful, tragic, haunting, shocking, disappointing, and bewildering it all felt. I was too distraught to even think about crying.

I honestly had no idea what to do. As I said earlier, I told April to call 911. They answered right away, and they got our address. The lady told April an ambulance was on its way as they were speaking. Then she asked questions about how long Jacob had been bleeding, whether he was breathing, and whether he was conscious. It was all such a horrifying blur. I'm going to tell you what happened, but don't be surprised if I'm not completely accurate or thorough. Seriously, it was very confusing. I remember the 911 operator asking April about the blood flow. She asked whether it was oozing, pulsing, or spraying, and how much blood there was on the floor. April started crying, and she handed me the phone. I told the woman it was sort of oozing and pulsing, but we had no idea how much blood Jacob had lost since he was in the shower and the blood had been going down the drain. Jacob was slightly with us, not totally unconscious. He was moaning and trying to say something. I think he was telling us to leave. Yes, I think he kept saying, "Go away."

"What color is the blood?" the operator asked. "Is it a bright red color, or is it dark?" I told her it looked dark, and she said that was a good sign—that probably a vein or veins had been severed rather than an artery. Then she started giving me instructions. "Get a clean towel, and apply as much pressure as you can to the wounds. You need to get the bleeding under control. Also, raise his hands above his head. That will help a lot. You need to raise the wounds up above the level of his heart." Christ, it was ridiculous. April and I were both on our knees. April was trying to keep Jacobs arms raised, and I was applying the pressure. It was a small shower stall, not designed for three people. It didn't take long for the towels to become saturated with blood, but the operator said to keep using them. "Just be sure to apply pressure," she said. "The EMTs should be there soon."

Sure enough, the EMTs arrived, and they burst into the pool house and bathroom like a whirlwind. They told April and me to get out of their way, and the next thing we knew, they had Jacob loaded up on a gurney and were wheeling him through the house to the driveway. "You can meet us at the hospital," one of the men said. "Don't try to follow us, and don't drive fast. We'll be doing everything we can, and if you get into a car accident, it will only make the situation worse." I told the guy I understood, and April and I climbed into my car.

We didn't follow the ambulance, but I wasn't exactly driving the speed limit. April told me to slow down several times. Then April said something that surprised me. She asked me, "Do you think he's going to die?"

I said, "No, of course not," but now that I thought about it, I really had no idea. No, no, no, he wasn't going to die. Dying seemed too final. So final that it had to be impossible.

Isn't it strange how the mind works? While I was driving to the hospital, I thought back to when Jacob was in the third grade. That year, encouraged by his teacher, Jacob entered the school science fair competition. This teacher's name was Mrs. Hardin, and she adored Jacob. Seriously, she loved the boy to death. She told us he was the brightest and most creative student she'd ever taught. Of course, she was young and had been teaching only three years, but her enthusiasm meant a lot to us. We already knew that Jacob was very bright, and it was a relief to have him in a class in which his teacher recognized his potential. There was only one small problem. Mrs. Hardin was kind of a nut.

You're probably curious to know what I mean by saying she was a nut.

I'll describe her for you, and you can see if you agree. First, there was her appearance. I don't like judging people by their looks, so don't construe what I'm about to tell you to be a judgment. In fact, I happen to like that all people have their own look. I think it would be terrible if we all looked exactly the same, like robots or clones. Vive la différence! And not just as between men and women, but between *toutes les personnes*. But Mrs. Hardin? Honestly, you had to laugh when you saw her. I'll start with her face, which bore an uncanny resemblance to Alfred E. Neuman from *MAD* magazine, except Mrs. Hardin was a female. Unlike Alfred, she always wore bright red lipstick and lots of rouge. She also wore glasses—the kind of wing-tipped, '50s-style plastic-and-rhinestone contraptions you'd imagine on a woman in curlers in some Las Vegas trailer park. She also had very large breasts, almost too large, but she was not overweight. And how did she dress? A couple years earlier, she took a trip with her husband to Hawaii, and ever since she had been addicted to muumuus. Heck, she must have had a hundred of them in her closet.

But we liked Mrs. Hardin a lot. It wasn't just because she was so crazy about our son. We believed several things about her. We believed the woman had a huge heart. We believed there wasn't a mean bone in her body. And we believed she always had the best intentions when it came to anything having to do with each and every one of her students. She never gave us a reason to believe otherwise.

Anyway, it was Mrs. Hardin who encouraged Jacob to sign up for the school science fair. She also encouraged Jacob to be as creative as possible. Forget turning potatoes into batteries, or growing crystals with Epsom salts, or making sparks of static electricity with balloons. Forget any projects that used food coloring, classical music, soft drinks, toothpicks, or colored pipe cleaners. Mrs. Hardin convinced Jacob he had much more to offer, and she convinced April and me as well. For one or two weeks, Jacob stewed over what his project would be about, until one morning at the breakfast table he stood up and shouted, "Yes, I've got it!"

"What have you got?" I asked.

"Whatever it is, don't give it to me," Zach said.

"I know what my project is going to be about," Jacob said, ignoring Zach.

"That's great," April said.

"So tell us what it is," I said.

Jacob walked over to the kitchen counter and put his hand on top of our toaster. "I'm going to do something no kid has ever done. I'm going to prove to the world that toasters are living things."

"You're cracked," Zach said.

"I'm serious."

"Toasters can't think, you idiot."

"Neither can you," Jacob said. "Yet here you are, alive as ever."

"Are you sure this is what you want to do?" I asked. The idea seemed a little strange to me. But as I think I've told you before, I'm not that creative.

"I'm positive," Jacob said.

"You're going to win first place," Zach said. "First place for the stupidest idea ever."

"I think it's a great idea," April said.

"I'm going to call my project 'My Name Is Fred,'" Jacob said. "Fred is the toaster, and Fred is going to tell his story."

And so it started. Jacob began work on his project, first by doing all the research required. He was on the computer for days, visiting internet sites, reading, and taking notes. Then he began to write. Christ, he must have handwritten twenty or thirty pages in his composition book. He wrote first drafts, second drafts, and third drafts. When he was done writing, he had April take him to Target to buy some poster boards, glue, colored tape, felt pens, and all the other things he would need to prepare his project display. I hadn't seen him this excited about anything since we bought him the latest Alanis Morissette album for his seventh birthday. He was crazy about her. This was before he grew interested in '60s and '70s music.

When he was done, Jacob's completed project consisted of two parts. The first part was the poster board triptych he had put together using photos, drawings, titles, and some limited text. The second part was his written and bound report that went along with the display. In my opinion, what he had done was very clever. Rather than writing a dry and fact-upon-fact third-grade-level scientific report, he wrote his paper all in first person, the narrator being a toaster named Fred. It was funny as hell. It really was. I got quite a kick out of it, and April liked it too. Later I decided to save the report in the same box I used to contain all his poems. After all, it was kind of like a poem. I mean, it wasn't really a poem, but it was so darn clever and creative that it deserved to be stored in the company of poems. Word for word, his report went as follows:

> My name is Fred. I am a living thing. I am not a human being, or a disobedient dog, or a muddy hippopotamus, or a sperm whale, or a redwood tree, or a poison oak plant, or a freshwater trout, or a powerful swordfish, or a tree-swinging monkey, or a clucking chicken, or a diamondback rattler, or a dung beetle, or a praying mantis, or a speck of bacteria, or an elephant, or an amoeba, or a gentle brontosaurus, or a saber-toothed tiger, or a violin spider. But I am as much a living thing as any of these lifeforms I have listed. I am a toaster.
>
> Yes, I am an everyday, run-of-the-mill, variable setting toaster. I belong to the Harper family, and I reside on their kitchen counter at 384 Willowbrook Lane in Coto de Caza. I get up early every morning and go to work, and I spend the rest of the day relaxing. Sometimes I have to work late at night when one of the Harpers is having trouble falling asleep and wants a midnight snack. But that isn't very often. All in all, the Harpers are pretty sound sleepers, so for the most part, I am a morning person.
>
> I was born in China six years ago, but I don't consider myself to be Chinese. I am as American as Mom and apple pie. What could be more American than a toaster? Now I know some of you reading this are skeptical. You're saying, "Fred, you weren't really born. You were manufactured. Without human beings to make you, you wouldn't even exist." Oh, we toasters have heard this argument a thousand times. But since when does reliance on the activities of another life-form nullify a life? I give you the fruit tree as my example. Is a fruit tree a living thing? Of course it is! Yet none of you human beings argue about whether the fruit trees in your backyards are alive like you would argue about me being alive. Would fruit trees be able to produce fruit and reproduce without bees? Just because the trees are dependent upon bees, do we say they aren't living things?

Einstein said, "If the bee disappeared off the face of the Earth, man would only have four years left to live." Of course, this is probably an exaggeration, but he still makes a vital point. It's called symbiosis, folks. I'm not making this up. Symbiosis occurs when a lifeform benefits from the existence of another life form. You should know that there are three types of symbiotic relationships: mutualism, commensalism, and parasitism. Mutualism is where both partners benefit from the relationship, and commensalism is where one species benefits while the other is neither helped nor harmed. The third type, parasitism, is where one species benefits, causing harm to the other. As regards human beings and us toasters, the symbiotic relationship is one of mutualism. The toaster benefits from human beings in that the humans are necessary for reproduction. The humans benefit from the toaster in that they enjoy eating the toaster's excrement.

You're laughing at this—the idea that human beings eat our excrement? What happens when you feed a person food? They chew it up, and it goes down their gastrointestinal tract. It passes through all those slippery, hollow organs that are joined in a long, twisting tube from the mouth, to the esophagus, to the stomach, to the small intestine, to the large intestine, and out the anus. The food is processed. It goes in as food and comes out as excrement. Well, the toaster is really not that much different. You feed it a slice of bread, it is processed, and it comes out as crap. It comes out as toast. The process is just a lot simpler for a toaster than it is for a human being, but being simple does not mean the toaster is not a life-form. We call an amoeba a lifeform, right? An amoeba is about as simple as a lifeform gets. It doesn't have a mouth, esophagus, stomach, small intestine, large intestine, or anus, yet we say it is alive. I would say that we toasters have both mouths and anuses. They just happen to be in the same place. Yes, it's kind of weird, but nature produces all sorts of weird things. I happen to think that dung beetles are weirder than toasters. Or the black widow spider too—what could be weirder than killing and eating your mate after you've had sex?

Another argument I've heard against toasters being seen as living things is that they spend most of their time turned off and do not come to life unless they are turned on. Thus, most of the time they are dead. But, no, no, we're not dead at all. People who make this claim completely misunderstand death. Is a hibernating grizzly bear dead? Is a dormant tree during the cold winter dead? Look at a dormant tree—no leaves, no color, and no life. Sure, it looks dead, but it isn't, and we all know that it isn't. Well, a toaster not being used is no more dead than a dormant tree or a hibernating bear. Plug me into the wall, stick a piece of bread in me, push down the plastic thingamajig on my side, and I immediately wake up, bright-eyed, to do my job. Have you heard of the burrowing frogs in Australia? When food resources are scant, they bury themselves in the mud and turn themselves off not just for months but for years. Yet they are still alive. Compare that to me, the toaster. I'm usually dormant only from one breakfast to the next. Or maybe I'm quiet for a week or two if the Harpers go on vacation. But I'm certainly not dead—not by any stretch of the imagination.

Here's another bone for you to chew on. Do you believe in evolution? If you believe in science, then I assume you're an evolutionist—at least to a degree. So, tell me, what could fit Darwin's model for the development of life-forms better than me, the everyday toaster. You don't have to dig holes in Africa to find my ancestors. All you have to do is visit junkyards and antique stores. The evolution is obvious. We toasters have our stove-top ancestors, our rococo side-loading ancestors, our top-loading '50s chrome Airstream trailer–looking ancestors, and our modern stainless steel and plastic models. We're no different from humans. We have our aforementioned ancestors, just like you have your Neanderthal, *Homo habilis*, and *Australopithecus*. No, I can't think of anything more obvious.

Which brings me to the ultimate conclusion of life, which is death. We toasters die just as humans die, just as animals die, just as trees die, just as plants die, and just as the tiniest one-celled life-forms die. We simply do not live forever; no lifeform does. Some of us live for a very long time, but none of us lives for eternity. It is further proof that we are, in fact, living things. To die, you must have once been alive.

I do not have arms or legs, or hands or even feet. I do not have eyes or ears or a nose or a taste-bud-laden tongue. Nor do I have a high-functioning brain. But what I do have I hold dear. I have my life, and I have my purpose in life. I serve a well-defined function on this earth. Just as trees turn carbon dioxide and water into oxygen, and just as honeybees turn pollen and nectar into honey, and just as certain worms make silk, and just as palms grow dates, and just as chickens lay eggs, and just as maple trees make syrup, I transform your sliced bread into toast. I can handle all kinds: sourdough, white, rye, pumpernickel, or whatever else you've brought home from the grocery store. I don't ask for much in return for my service, except to be respected for what I am. I am a friend and a slave. And I am a living thing.

Not bad for a third-grader, don't you think? I told you that Jacob was exceptionally bright. Now I suppose you're wondering how Jacob's project did in the science fair. I'll tell you exactly who won what.

The third-place ribbon went to some girl named Sally who grew plants from seeds, nourishing them with assorted liquids. It turned out that the plant watered with Diet Coke grew the tallest. The second-place ribbon went to a boy named Tom who made four fly traps by cutting plastic water bottles in half. The idea was to see which bait attracted and drowned the most flies. He used molasses, corn syrup, honey, and maple syrup. The maple syrup won. I guess the question I had was why they had so many flies in their house. In our home, we've never had much of a problem with flies.

The first-place ribbon did not go to Jacob. It went to a girl named Madison, who made a model of an eardrum by stretching some Saran Wrap over a ceramic bowl and pouring some candy cake sprinkles on top of the Saran Wrap. When you got close to the bowl and hummed or sang, the cake sprinkles would dance about, and supposedly this was what your eardrum did. Of course, she also had a written report to go along with the project. She probably wrote a lot about sound waves, frequencies, and hearing ranges. I mean, there had to be more to her project than the stupid bowl with the cake sprinkles in order for her to beat all the other projects and win first place.

It was a tough lesson for Jacob. It was something I had learned a long time ago by watching others. People in general do not like creativity. You can argue with me about that all you want, but I think I'm right. I've seen evidence of this time and time again. Creativity and deviation from the status quo make most people feel uncomfortable. In fact, they just don't like it.

At the end of Jacob's third-grade school year, Mrs. Hardin had the parents of each student come in for a private meeting. She wanted to discuss each child's progress, and she wanted to make suggestions for what the parents could do over the summer months to prepare their children for the next year. When April and I showed up for our conference with Mrs. Hardin, the woman was all smiles. As I said earlier, she really liked Jacob a lot. And she liked talking to us, the parents who created him. "I only hope that his future teachers can see what I see. This world has a way of being a little harsh with boys like your son. I hope he learns to stand his ground. He has a lot to offer the world."

"Yes," I said. "We agree."

"Don't let the system change him. He's a very special young man."

"We'd like to think so," April said.

CHAPTER 16

WHEN I WAS SEVENTEEN

———•◦•———

When April and I arrived at the hospital, we parked my car in a lot adjacent to the emergency entrance. We then walked into the building and got the attention of the woman at the desk, who entered Jacob's name and birthdate into her computer. She said, "He just arrived. I'll need your insurance information, and you'll need to fill out some forms."

"How is our son doing?" April asked.

"I don't know."

"Doesn't it say anything on your computer?"

"It just says he was admitted fifteen minutes ago. I need your insurance information. And the forms."

"Fine," I said.

The forms were attached to a clipboard, and I took the clipboard. April and I stepped to a pair of open seats in the waiting room. We sat down, and I proceeded to fill out the papers.

"Do you think he's okay?" April asked.

"I'm sure he fine," I said.

"How do you know?"

"I'm sure they're taking good care of him."

"What if they can't help him?"

"I'm sure they've seen a lot worse."

"People die in hospitals, you know."

"I don't think Jacob is going to die. They would've said something to us."

"Maybe he lost too much blood. Maybe his heart stopped. Maybe they have a sheet over his face right now."

"Here," I said. "You fill this top page out. You know more about

Jacob's medical history than I do. In fact, go ahead and fill out the rest of the pages." Honestly, I knew as much about Jacob as April did, but she needed something to keep her mind busy. Her worrying was driving me crazy. I handed April the clipboard and pen, and she put on her reading glasses to go to work.

"You know all this stuff," she said. "I don't see why you couldn't be doing this."

"Just fill out the forms."

"Do you have your insurance card with you?"

"I do. It's in my wallet."

"Are you sure he's okay?"

"He's where he needs to be. I'm sure they know what they're doing."

"How much blood do you think he lost?"

"I don't know. I know as much as you."

Finally, April was quiet for a couple minutes while working on the forms. Meanwhile a man and his wife came in through the main doors. The man had a bloody towel wrapped around his hand, and he was holding it in place with his free hand. The woman had a jar filled with ice, and in the ice was the man's severed finger. I figured he must've cut off the finger with a power saw while doing some weekend home improvement project. Judging by the way he was gripping the towel, and judging by the look on his face, he was in a lot of pain. The couple stepped quickly up to the lady at the counter, and I heard the receptionist say, "So what have we here?"

"My husband accidentally sawed off his finger."

"Oh my. I need you to fill out these forms. Someone will be out to get your husband soon." She handed the woman a clipboard similar to mine.

"I have the finger here, in this ice."

"I can see that."

"Shouldn't they take him back there now? You know, before the finger dies."

"They'll be out soon," the receptionist said. "Do you have insurance?"

"Yes, we do."

"I'll need to see your insurance card. And please sit down to complete the forms. The sooner we get the paperwork done, the sooner we'll be able to get your husband to a room with a doctor."

The woman and her husband took a seat in the waiting area, and no sooner did they sit down than a filthy homeless man stood up from his chair and walked to the counter. "I've been waiting here for over an hour," he said. "Is a doctor going to see me or not?"

"We'll get to you, Mr. Spanner. You need to be patient. We're very busy this morning."

"My throat is killing me."

"I understand that."

"If I keel over and die here in your waiting room, it's not going to look very good for you."

"You're not going to die, Mr. Spanner."

"How do you know?"

"Please just take your seat, and we'll get to you."

The man glared at the receptionist for a moment and then returned to his chair. Everyone else in the room pretended not to see or hear him when he suddenly shouted, "I really hate this fucking place. I fucking hate it. I could die right here, and what would they care?"

I leaned over to April and said softly into her ear, "Well, I wouldn't care."

"You shouldn't say things like that," she said.

When I was seventeen, good old President Nixon started up the space shuttle program and surprised the world by visiting the People's Republic of China, and the RMS *Queen Elizabeth* was destroyed by fire in a Hong Kong harbor, and Shirley Chisholm announced her candidacy for US President, and pictures of Mars were transmitted back to earth from *Mariner 9*, and *The Godfather* and *Fritz the Cat* were released, and George Wallace was shot and paralyzed, and Jane Fonda travelled to North Vietnam, and George Carlin was arrested for public obscenity in Milwaukee, and Israeli Olympic athletes were murdered by Arab terrorists, and you know what? I couldn't have cared less about any of this stuff. None of these events were on my radar. The main thing I cared about at age seventeen was Cindy Kerry—lovely, blonde, beautiful Cindy Kerry.

Cindy was in my English class. She sat across the room near the windows, and it was a morning class, so the warm sunlight would pour in through the windows and ignite her like an angel in a colorful Renaissance oil painting. It was a sight to behold. Every morning I looked forward to staring at her and dreaming about what it would be like to be noticed by her, to talk to her, to be loved by her. She had long, golden blonde hair that was always straight and perfectly brushed so it fell across her shoulders. There was never a single hair out of place, and she couldn't have looked more perfect. Her eyes were sky blue, her nose was rather small, and her lips were like a pair of rose petals. How I longed to feel those lips touching mine. My guess was that her kisses tasted like candy, or like maple syrup, or like wine. Jesus, I mean I really had it bad for this girl. And her body? It was supple, soft, and warm, dressed so perfectly—I don't think there were any clothes she couldn't make look just right. Every sweater, pair of jeans, skirt, or dress she wore to school looked as if it had been tailor made for her alone to wear.

When I was seventeen, nothing else mattered. So I schemed and planned. I had to figure out a way to meet this girl, and I had to do it without looking like an idiot. Could I make her like me? Was it even possible?

I thought and thought. We had no common friends. We were in no common clubs or groups of any kind. We didn't even sit close to each other in that English class. She sat over by the windows, and I sat clear across the room. So I decided what I would have to do, and it would take a lot of guts. I would be swinging for the fences, but I would do it. I really had no choice. I decided to approach her from out of the blue and ask her to go out on a date with me. I would ask if she'd like to go see a movie. And what would she do? Would she politely say no, or would she lie and say she had other plans, or say that her parents didn't allow her to date? Or would she laugh in my face? Did she even know I existed? Would she say, "What is your name, and who the heck are you?" Would I embarrass her, annoy her, or make her angry? There was only one way to find out.

I checked the movie listings in the newspaper. I searched for a movie I thought she might enjoy. I weighed the options and decided on *The Poseidon Adventure*. Lots of kids at school were talking about this movie, and everyone seemed to like it. I would make my move on a Wednesday. I remember this because it was every Wednesday that our English homework was due, and I had turned in my homework that morning and then followed Cindy out of the classroom. I followed her out the door, down the hall, and then down another hall until we reached her locker. She stopped to drop off her English book and to get what she needed for her next class. As she stood at her open locker, I approached her. Jesus, I was scared out of my mind, but I didn't wuss out. It was now or never.

"Hello, Cindy?" I said.

She turned to look at me. "Hi," she said.

"My name is Stan."

"I know what your name is."

"You do?"

"You're in my English class."

"Yes, I am."

"Did you want something?"

I cleared my throat, and then said, "I wanted to ask you sort of a question."

"A question?"

"I was wondering to know, I mean, I wanted to know if you would like to go to a movie with me."

"A movie?"

"*The Poseidon Adventure*." Cindy didn't say anything at first. She just stared at me. I said, "They say it's a good movie."

"Yes, I've heard about it," she finally said. Cindy then smiled. "Are you asking me out on a date?"

"Something like that."

"I don't even know you."

"That's true."

"We've never even talked."

"No," I said. "We haven't." This wasn't going well. I was sure now that she was going to shoot me down and say no. I was prepared to walk away.

"When?" she asked.

"When what?"

"When did you want to go?"

"I was thinking Saturday," I said. "But it doesn't have to be Saturday. I mean, if you're busy."

"I'm not doing anything Saturday."

There was now a lump in my throat the size of a melon. "Does that mean you'll go?"

"Do you have a car?"

"I was going to use my dad's car."

"Maybe it would be fun."

"It's supposed to be a good movie."

"You are kind of cute."

"I am?" I said, and now I was blushing. I could feel it in my cheeks.

"Do you know where I live?"

"No," I said. Cindy then wrote her address down on a piece of paper along with her phone number, and she handed the piece of paper to me.

"What time are you going to pick me up?"

"Around seven."

"Okay then, I guess it's a date."

"Thanks," I said. It was kind of dumb to say thanks, but that's what I said. Then I smiled like an idiot and walked away, toward my next class. I felt like a Roman general who had just conquered a city. I hadn't grown an inch, yet I felt ten feet tall.

Son of a gun. Cindy Kelly! We were going to a movie, just the two of us. She had called it a date. We were going out on a date!

I arrived at her house at seven fifteen on Saturday, and her mom answered the door. She said Cindy was upstairs getting ready, so she had me step into the family room to meet Cindy's father. It turned out the guy was a doctor. He was a tall man, which I discovered this when he stood up from his easy chair to shake my hand.

"So you're Stan," he said. "I understand you two are going to a movie?"

"*The Poseidon Adventure*," I said.

"Sounds like fun," Mrs. Kelly said.

"Who's in the movie?"

"I'm not sure."

"I think Gene Hackman is in it," Mrs. Kelly said. "You like Gene Hackman."

"He's a good actor," the doctor said.

"It's about a sinking ship, isn't it?"

"Yes," I said.

The doctor stared at me. He had a nice face and kind eyes. He asked, "Are you a senior in school?"

"Yes, I'm seventeen."

"You're in Cindy's English class?"

"I am," I said.

"How do you like your class?"

"It's okay."

"Cindy says the class is reading *The Sun Also Rises*."

"Yes, by Hemingway."

"What do you think of it?"

"I've only read the first couple chapters."

"It's a terrible book," the doctor said. "I'm surprised they're having you read it. Hemingway wrote some much better novels. I liked *The Old Man and the Sea*."

"Don't discourage him," Mrs. Kelly said. "Maybe he'll like what they're reading."

"Maybe he will."

"Our teacher says it's an important book."

"Do you have a curfew?"

"You mean from my parents?"

"Yes, what time will you have Cindy back?"

"I have to be home by eleven," I said, "so, we should be back here before then."

"If you're a little late, it's okay. We want you two to have a good time."

"Thanks," I said.

"Do you have your own car?"

"I'm driving my dad's car."

Just then Cindy appeared in the room. "There she is," the doctor said.

"Are they driving you crazy yet?" she asked me.

"No," I said. "We were just talking."

Cindy seemed to be in a rush to get out of the house. We all said goodbye, and Cindy and I walked outside and to my dad's car in the driveway. We climbed in, and no sooner had I backed into the street than Cindy had opened her purse and removed a joint. "Does the cigarette lighter in this jalopy work?" she asked.

"I think so."

"Then let's fire this up," Cindy pressed in the lighter, and when it popped out, she lit the end of the joint and started puffing. After she put the lighter back into its hole, she took a long drag and held the smoke in her lungs, handing me the lit joint.

So that was how this strange evening started. I had smoked marijuana before, so it wasn't like I was being asked to partake in something I'd never done, but it did take me completely by surprise. I just never expected Cindy to light up that joint. Nor did I expect her to ask us to forget about the movie and go to a party instead. The party was at an old house near Chapman College and was being thrown by a college student Cindy knew who went by the nickname of Gado. This was a house that was being shared by Gado and three other Chapman College students. The place was packed with college kids, and the bathtub in the bathroom was filled with ice and cans of Coors, and the music was loud, and the air was thick with cigarette and marijuana smoke. The first thing Cindy did was find Gado and introduce me to him.

"This is Stan," she said to Gado. "He's in my English class."

"Cool," Gado said. He was weird looking. He had a big bird beak of a nose, and dark brown eyes that were way too close together. He parted his long, wavy hair in the middle, and it looked wet, as if he'd just taken a shower. "I guess I should be thanking you."

"Thanking me?"

"For bringing my old lady to the party."

"We told my mom and dad we were going to a movie," Cindy said. "They think we're watching *The Poseidon Adventure*."

"Far out."

"Yeah," I said. "Far out."

"Beer is in the bathroom," Gado said to me. "Help yourself. There's plenty for everyone."

"Thanks," I said.

"It was really cool of you to bring Cindy over here. Her parents don't like her seeing me. And they won't let me pick her up. They think I'm too old for her."

"It was no problem," I said stupidly.

"I'm so glad you made it," Gado said to Cindy. He put his arm around her and pulled her close to him. Then he held his arm out, as though getting ready to make a speech, He said, "I do much wonder that one man, seeing how much another man is a fool when he dedicates his behaviors to

163

love, will, after he hath laughed at such shallow follies in others, become the argument of his own scorn by falling in love." When Gado was done speaking, he looked at Cindy.

"I love it," Cindy said.

"Know who wrote that?" Gado asked me.

"Shakespeare?"

"Yes, yes, you're right. Are you a Shakespeare fan?"

"It was just a guess," I said.

"Well, it was a good one."

It turned out that Gado was a drama major. Of course he had memorized some Shakespeare. Honestly, I didn't know if I liked the guy or hated him. Sure he was friendly enough, but he was also Cindy's boyfriend.

"Here's someone I think you should meet," Gado said to me. At his side was a young girl. She didn't look old enough to be a college student, yet there was something about her eyes that told me she was no little girl. She looked smart. And she looked like she knew a few things. She had black hair and the most amazing pair of brown eyes. Her complexion was clear and somewhat dark—not as if she was tan, but as if she just happened to have dark skin. "This is Monica," Gado said. "She's in high school too. She's a sophomore. She's a friend of my little sister."

"My name is Stan," I said to her.

"Well, Stan, it's nice to meet you."

Gado and Cindy then left us, walking into the crowd to talk to others. I stood there with Monica, not sure what I should say. "What high school do you go to?" I asked.

"If I told you, would it matter?"

"I suppose not."

"Isn't it funny how we ask each other questions like that when we first meet?"

"I guess it is."

"Ask me something else."

"Such as?"

"I don't know. You're doing the talking. You're the guy, so come up with something deeper. Ask me something I can sink my teeth into."

I don't know why I asked. It was the only thing I could think of, having been put on the spot. I asked, "Do you believe in God?"

Monica laughed. "Well, that's jumping right into the frying pan," she said.

"Well, do you?"

"Let's find a place to sit down."

"That sounds good to me," I said. We stepped out of the house through the rear doors, and in the backyard we found a patio table and chairs that were not being used. We sat down next to each other.

"You want to know if I believe in God?"

"Yes," I said.

She scooted close to me and put one hand on my cheek. Then she leaned in and kissed me on the lips. She looked me in the eyes, and she did it again. She grasped my right hand, and she guided it up under her sweater so that it was now on her warm breast. She wasn't wearing a bra. Her breast felt soft and firm at the same time—it was kind of amazing. Then she kissed me again, but longer this time. I mean, it was a long and full kiss, wet and warm and indescribably pleasant. Her hand was on my thigh now, up close to my crotch. This went on and on for several minutes. I'm not sure exactly how long it was, because I was kind of lost in the moment, lost in our sudden closeness. Finally she stopped kissing me, and I pulled my hand out from behind her sweater. She put her own hand on my cheek again, and she asked, "So now you want to know if I believe in God. Well, I do believe in God. I believe God is love."

I was speechless. I was just staring at this lovely girl, trying to think of something intelligent to say. Finally I said, "That was nice."

"That was God."

"It was?"

"How else can you explain it?"

"I don't know," I said. Was that God? Show me the dotted line. I was ready to sign.

Monica and I talked for a couple hours, until Cindy finally came and got me. It was time for me to take her home, and again Gado thanked me for bringing her. Monica gave me her number on a piece of paper, and I put the paper in my wallet. Then I took Cindy home. She fell asleep on the way, so we didn't get to talk much.

The following Monday in English class was the next time I would see her. She was sitting in the sunlight, as beautiful as ever. But this time it was different. She looked at me, and when our eyes met, she smiled. And from that day on, we were friends—not as boyfriend and girlfriend, as I had originally hoped, but we were good friends, and we sat together during lunch break and talked, and I enjoyed our friendship.

And what about Monica? We also became good friends. I'd call her on the phone often, and we would talk until our parents told us to hang up. She lived too far away for me to call her my girlfriend, but we remained close all through high school. And whenever I went to church with my parents, and when I would listen to the sermons about God, I knew what the rest of the congregation didn't know. I knew who God was; I had experienced him at Gado's party, in his backyard, at that patio table with my good friend Monica. Our hands on each other, and our mouths pressed together—amen to that, right? Every time I think of Monica, it puts a smile on my face.

CHAPTER 17

THE PARAGRAPH

S everal months before Jacob's suicide attempt, while Jacob was still at school, I was snooping in his room and found a lengthy piece of writing lying on his desk. It wasn't another one of his poems. It wasn't a short story or an essay. I'm not sure exactly what the heck it was. It was a sole paragraph that was handwritten on several pieces of paper. There were no scratch-outs, erasures, or corrections of any kind, so it was most likely a final draft.

I didn't want Jacob to know I'd been in his room, so I took the papers to my office and ran them through my copier. I put the original back on Jacob's desk exactly where I had found it. Then, in my office, seated at my desk, I proceeded to read what Jacob wrote. There was no title, but word for word, it went as follows:

> What an evil, violent, hungry, flesh-ripping, bone-chewing, sadistic, cruel, shit-producing world we all live in. God must have been in a really bad mood that week. You know the week I'm talking about. Abracadabra! Let there be light! Watch me pull a rabbit out of my hat! Behold the miracle of life! Focus your microscope and get an eyeful of the lonely, living amoeba, this curious little one-celled blob, this invisible team mascot, this teeny-tiny violent killer. It's always hungry. Yes, it has to eat. It isn't so much different from you and me, this shapeless speck on a microscope slide. Can you see it? Look closer, and turn the knob to get it focused. Killing, eating, killing, and eating. Cytoplasm flows around the prey and engulfs it. The cytoplasm produces enzymes. Poor hapless algae and bacteria, doomed, consumed, and

destroyed. Nothing left but undissolved residue. A pile of bones. Consumption for consumption's sake, all to stay alive. It is the ultimate model. It is God's will, right on up the line. Life consuming life to stay alive: pursuit, violence, death, and ultimately food. Spiders spin their webs. Venus fly traps open their mouths. Snakes strike with venomous fangs. Birds peck at insects. Coyotes chase down rabbits. Cheetahs go after the young and lame. Crocodiles go after everything—chomp, chomp, chomp! Everybody is after everybody. Make no mistake about it; our primary purpose on Earth is to eat and be eaten. That is God's will. It is what life is all about—death! Living is all about dying and being digested. And what about us human beings? Are we really any different? Do you know how many animals human beings kill for food? The answer? About 150 million each day. It's hard to fathom, isn't it? It doesn't even seem like we're eating the flesh of dead animals. We're eating dishes. We're eating beef stroganoff, chateaubriand, barbecued short ribs, and coquilles Saint Jacques. We're eating hamburgers, cheeseburgers, and foot-long hot dogs. We've turned the bloody murder and consumption of other life forms into an art form, and into a business, and into a recreational activity. But make no mistake about it; the model remains the same—we hunt, kill, and consume just like the amoeba. Dumb as dirt. Stupid and violent. Stick a knife in it, or shoot it with a gun. Slit its throat so it bleeds to death. Lop off its head—just be sure the damn thing is dead. Humans are the worst. It isn't just the food we eat. It's the money we make, and the power we seek, and the leisure time we acquire, and the discoveries we make, and the tall buildings we erect, and the rivers we cross, and the ships we build, and the liquid and solid resources we bleed and mine from the earth. We are earth's greatest predators. We are mankind. There is no end to our quest. There are no satisfactions or final, realized goals. We have God to thank for all of this. We can thank God that there are doctors and hospitals who will gladly pocket our life savings to prolong our lives, to improve our days, to look a little younger or better. We can thank God we have attorneys to attack our enemies and prevent our enemies from successfully attacking us—for a fee, of course. We can thank God we have Hollywood to take advantage of our stupidity. We can thank God we have the IRS to steal our hard-earned money and spend it on things we couldn't care less about. We can thank God we have businessmen to convince us to buy things we have no real need for. We can thank God for everything. He is, after all, the one who got the ball rolling. This whole dog-eat-dog world was his vision. But wait, you say, what about all the wonderful things in the world? What about love, and music, and art, and altruism? What about nature's beauty? What about ethics? Oh, hell, can't you see what's going on here? It's all shit window dressing and ornament. It's all peacock feathers and cumulus clouds and purple mountain majesties. It's a ruse. It's just lipstick on a pig. If and when you put all your faith in love, music, art, altruism, beauty, and ethics—and I mean really put your faith in it—you soon learn you have fallen in love with the girl's clothes and not the girl. And what about the girl? She is nothing at all like you imagined. She devours you, and she breaks your heart. All the time when you thought you were flying, you were actually caught in the threads of a web. And the spider approaches. Now it's either you or him, and he's holding all the cards. Once upon I time, I thought God was all things good. I honestly believed this. I would've staked my life on it. But now I know better. Now I can see. And so I dream about Arcadia, not as a place God created but as a land that God had nothing to do with. Someday my feet will stand upon its Godless soil, and my lungs will fill with its fresh and Godless air, and my ears will hear the Godless laughter, and my eyes will take in all there is to see—Godless vistas warmed by the sun, caressed by a gentle breeze, made musical by the birds in the Godless trees.

Having read this, I really started to worry. What was all this crazy talk about God? I didn't think Jacob even believed in God. And I asked myself what the heck I should do. Should I do anything at all, or was this just an adolescent phase Jacob was going through? Or was it more serious? And all this talk about Arcadia was making me very uncomfortable. It didn't seem to be a healthy obsession.

We had tried the psychiatrist route with Jacob, but that was a bust. All Dr. Erskine-Garcia wanted to do was prescribe Jacob drugs. I was no expert, but that just didn't seem like a good solution—not for Jacob. I'm not sure any kind of therapy would've helped him either. In fact, I'm not sure what would've helped. Then it occurred to me that I now needed help; in fact, maybe I needed it even more than Jacob. I was anxious, worried, and fearful, so I sought out my own shrink. I thought that if I could get a better grip on my own feelings, I would be better equipped to help out Jacob. I called our family doctor, and I asked him if he had the name of a competent psychiatrist for adults. He said he did, and he referred me to Dr. Henry Ness. I called Dr. Ness, and he agreed to see me.

When the afternoon of our appointment arrived, I was hard at work, trying to get a contract finalized for providing boxes to one of the country's largest moving companies. It would've been a tremendous coup. I was dictating a long letter about some details of the contract to my secretary when my cell phone chimed to remind me of the appointment. "I've got to go," I told my secretary. "We'll finish this later. I should be back in a couple hours."

I arrived at Dr. Ness's office; there was a waiting room, but there was no receptionist. There was just a pair of sofas, a coffee table, and a stack of magazines. There was a painting of a ship at sea on one of the walls, but except for the ship painting, the walls were bare. Next to the door going into the doctor's office, there was a brass plate with a button and a small red light. A sign on the plate said to press the button for the doctor and take a seat. I pressed the button, and the red light lit up. I then took a seat and stared at the ship painting, since I didn't feel like thumbing through magazines. Five minutes later, the doctor's door opened. Dr. Ness was in the doorway, and he said, "You must be Stan Harper."

"I am," I said.

"I'm Dr. Ness. Please come in."

My first impression? The man was into ships. There were paintings of ships. There were parts from ships, clocks from ships, bells from ships, big thick ropes tied into lumpy knots, binnacles, lanterns, diving helmets, and some other maritime paraphernalia I didn't recognize.

"Please take a seat," the doctor said.

"Which chair?" I asked. There were several of them.

"Take your pick."

"I guess I'll sit here," I said, sitting down. Dr. Ness took a seat behind his desk. It was weird. I felt like I was visiting Captain Nemo.

"So what brings you to see me?"

"My son, I guess."

"You're not getting along with your son?"

"No, it isn't that. We get along fine."

"I see," Dr. Ness said. He rubbed his chin and waited for me to continue talking.

"I'm worried about him. I found this on his desk. It's a paragraph he recently wrote." I had brought the copy I made of Jacob's paragraph. It was folded and stuffed in my pocket. I unfolded it and handed it to Dr. Ness.

"You want me to read this?"

"Yes, please."

"Does your son know you have it?"

"No, he doesn't. I made a copy of the original. He still has the original."

"Do you ordinarily go through your son's private things?"

"On occasion," I said.

"Because you're worried about him?"

"Yes," I said.

Dr. Ness put on his reading glasses, and he took the papers from me. He then leaned back in his chair and read. He was a fast reader, and I was surprised at how quickly he was turning the pages. When he was done, he set the pages on his desk and leaned forward toward me. "I'm not sure what you want out of me," he said.

"You just read it, right? You're a psychiatrist. Doesn't it cause you to be concerned?"

"You'll need to tell me a little about your son."

"I can do that," I said. "His name is Jacob, and he's now seventeen years old. He's a senior in high school. He's a very bright boy. He scored very high on his IQ tests. They said he was in the top 1 percent, and he is very creative. And he writes a lot of poetry. He thinks he's a hippie." And on and on I went, talking about Jacob for about fifteen minutes. Dr. Ness sat at his desk, listening quietly, and when I was done, he picked up Jacob's paragraph and leaned forward to hand me the pages.

"Without meeting Jacob in person—and I'm not making any kind of diagnosis—it sounds to me like what you have on your hands is a perfectly normal, confused, overly dramatic, self-absorbed, and immature teenager writhing in the throes of his growth. Remove the extraordinary intelligence, and subtract the obvious creativity, and you have a normal boy, just like every other Norman Rockwell boy, who is becoming an adult and trying to make sense of the adult world he is facing. Do I think you have anything to be worried about? Well, one always worries when it comes to teenagers. It's a very dangerous time, and teenagers do dangerous things. You've been honest and shared your reality with me, so I'm going to do the same for you. I'm going to tell you the story of Henry Ness. Are you paying attention?"

"Yes, of course," I said. I guess he caught me looking around the room at his ship junk.

"When I was a teenager, my goal was to run off as soon as I was done with high school and spend the rest of my life sailing on the high seas. I was utterly and hopelessly enthralled with anything to do with ships and boats and oceans. I was in love with the heaving green waters, the seaweed, the seagulls, the pelicans, the storms at sea, the doldrums, the majestic morning skies with their religious sunbeams, and the sunsets. Christ, I would've been in heaven as a sailor. I wanted to race porpoises and dolphins and whales, and I wanted to eat food prepared in a galley, and I wanted to smoke a pipe, and I wanted to sleep in a creaky bunk alongside all the other tossing and turning snoring sailors. I wanted to tell stories and jokes, and I wanted to get good and drunk on rum, and I wanted to sing out of key with the toothless guy who squeezed music from his concertina. Aye, matey—that was my dream as a boy. That was my dream until I woke up."

"Until you woke up from what?"

"From the dream."

I thought about this for a moment. "I was going to be an architect," I said. "That was my dream."

"See what I mean?"

"And Jacob's dream is what?"

"To live in this place that he calls Arcadia," the doctor said. "Isn't that obvious?"

"Where did he ever get this idea?"

"Who knows? Maybe he read about it in a book. Does he like to read? When I was in high school, I read *Treasure Island* over and over. I'll bet I read it ten times. I knew every chapter by heart."

"How old were you when you abandoned your dream?"

"As you can see from my office, I never really abandoned it. But I did learn to go with the flow. My parents urged me to go to college, and so I went. It was when I was in college that I discovered psychiatry. At first it was like diverting a child from an old cruddy toy with a shiny new one. But I can tell you eventually what happened. It wasn't just a matter of switching toys. I was growing up. I was becoming a man. The dream took a backseat to my adulthood."

"And you think this will happen to Jacob."

"I'm pretty sure of it."

"So, in the meantime, what can I do?"

"You can try not to worry so much. And you can cross your fingers like every parent does and hope that Jacob crosses the raging river without falling off the bridge."

Here's something you may or may not know. Doctors and nurses don't like suicide attempts. You would think that they would have had some empathy for Jacob, but instead of feeling sorry for him, they were angry with him. I suppose saying that all doctors and nurses behave this way is an unfair generalization. This anger may not be the norm for doctors and nurses at every hospital in the country. But it was certainly the truth at the hospital we were in. Granted, Jacob was being very difficult and uncooperative, and they had to restrain him in order to sew up his wrists. But the negative vibe was obvious. They really didn't like my son. It was as if they resented being asked to save his life.

I talked to the doctor. He said, "Your son was out of control, so we had to restrain him. He was making our job very difficult. I don't think he appreciated what we were trying to do. He kept telling us to leave him alone."

"He's upset," I said.

"Yes, we noticed," the doctor said curtly. He didn't roll his eyes, but he may as well have. "I'm having him transported to a county mental hospital for observation. They'll keep him for seventy-two hours, or until they're sure he's not going to try this again."

"A mental hospital?"

"It's standard procedure with all suicide attempts. The nurse will have some papers for you to sign. The ambulance should be here soon to pick up your son."

"I think he'd be better off coming home with us."

This time the doctor did roll his eyes. "Apparently being home with Mom and Dad hasn't been helping him a whole lot." I thought this was kind of a rude comment for a doctor to make to a troubled father, but before I could think of a response, he had turned and walked down the hall. Then the nurse approached me with the papers. What would you have done? Of course, I signed the papers.

So a mental hospital it was. April and I were not allowed to visit until the following day, which was a Sunday. We were told to come at two in the afternoon to meet with the doctor who was put in charge of Jacob's case. Her name was Dr. Rosenblatt, and we had no idea what to expect from her. Neither April nor I had ever been in a mental hospital or talked with anyone who worked at one. It was very weird. It felt a lot like going to our first teacher-parent conference. It was that same pregnant combination of curiosity and dread, and I had the same sorts of questions. Was the doctor going to give us any good news? Did she like our son? Did she think we were good parents? Had we been letting Jacob stay up too late at night, or disciplining him too little, or allowing him to watch the wrong kinds of TV shows? I can't speak for April, but I felt guilty as all hell before we even talked to anyone.

It turned out that Dr. Rosenblatt was very friendly, and she had a nice smile. This helped to put us at ease. I guessed she was in her early sixties, approaching retirement age. An orderly had brought us to her office, where we found her seated and expecting us. "My name is Dr. Rosenblatt," she said. "You must be Jacob's parents."

"We are," I said. "I'm Stan, and this is my wife, April."

"Have a seat."

"Thank you," I said, and April and I both sat in the chairs across from the doctor's desk. She then opened a file folder on her desk.

"I had a nice long talk with your son."

"How is he doing?" April asked.

"He's doing fine. It was a little rough going last night, but he's doing much better today. As I said, we had a nice talk."

"What did he tell you?" I asked.

"I promised him that our conversation would be private. I can't tell you specifically what we talked about."

"I see," I said.

"But he's doing better?" April asked.

"Much better, I think."

"When can he come home?"

"Well, that's what I wanted to talk to you about. We had a nice, long talk."

"Yes, you said that."

"It's my opinion, after talking with him, that Jacob should stay in a hospital for a while."

"For a while?" April asked.

"By 'for a while' I mean for a week or two. Or maybe three. I think there's a lot that can be done for him."

"That's not what I was hoping to hear," April said.

"This isn't a punishment."

"No, of course not," I said.

"Nor does it mean your boy is seriously ill. It just means I think a hospital stay can help him."

There was a pause in our conversation, and while the doctor looked at us, April and I looked at each other. Then we looked back at the doctor. "What do you think is wrong with him?" I asked.

"I need more time to make an accurate diagnosis, but just from our talk this morning, it's my opinion that Jacob may be bipolar."

Well, hell.

I'm going to stop right here. I'm going to tell you what went through my mind as I sat there with April and the doctor. I was looking around at the office walls. There were diplomas and certificates and some framed clippings of published articles written by Dr. Rosenblatt. Clearly this doctor knew what she was doing. I mean, they don't hand out diplomas to any idiot who asks for them, and they don't publish articles written by morons. Also, given that this woman was in her early sixties, as I had guessed, she had certainly seen a few things. In other words, she wasn't some wet-behind-the-ears puppy fresh out of college. She was an experienced doctor, and that meant a lot to me. I valued experience.

But let me tell you what I was thinking about. I had been learning a few things about psychiatrists. I'll preface what I have to say by telling you I believe most of them are well-intentioned and reasonably intelligent. But that being said—and maybe this is just the nature of the beast—I was a little surprised at how different they all were. You'd think that after going to school and learning all there is to know, they would all be on the same page—that they would be handing out similar advice. But I had now talked to three shrinks about Jacob. First there was Dr. Erskine-Garcia. Then there was my own shrink, Dr. Ness. And now there was Dr. Rosenblatt, who seemed very capable. So what was I being told? I was being told stories ranging anywhere from "These are just your typical growing pains" to "We'd like to keep your bipolar son locked up in a mental hospital."

And where did that leave April and me? We had a decision to make. What if we decided that Jacob was just experiencing some adolescent growing pains and we brought him home with us—what if it turned out he actually was bipolar? Or what if we had him stay at a hospital and let them treat him as if he was mentally ill, when in fact he wasn't—what damage would that cause to our boy, and what would a false diagnosis do to his self-image? Seriously, it seemed like we were screwed one way or the other. God bless them for trying, but it seemed as though seeking help had only made things worse, and more confusing, and further from a solution than they were before we sought the help from these so-called professionals.

What to do? April and I told Dr. Rosenblatt we wanted to go home and discuss the matter before taking (or not taking) her advice. I told her we would have a decision for her the next day.

CHAPTER 18

PACIFIC ACRES

———— •◦• ————

I was probably the worst person imaginable to be making any kind of decisions concerning someone who had just attempted suicide. I had no experience at all with the subject. Suicide had just never played a role in my life, nor in the lives of any of my family members, nor in the lives of my friends, nor in the lives of my neighbors, nor in the lives of any of my work associates. The only person I ever knew who killed himself was a boy in high school named Edward Hardy. We weren't what you'd call friends, but we knew some of the same kids. The closest I ever got to Edward was during the winter of 1973 when a group of us boys went to Big Bear on a skiing trip. I was asked to come along because I was a friend of one of Edward's friends, a kid named Alex Hillsdale.

As I said, Edward and I were not actually friends, but I certainly knew a lot about him, mostly just because he was one of the more popular kids at school. I mean, everyone knew about Edward. The first thing you noticed was his acne. The kid had it bad. It was all over his face, and most likely all over his back and shoulders. But the acne didn't hold him back—not like it would've held back other kids. The boy had a personality as large as Jupiter, and it outweighed his skin condition a hundred to one. Everyone adored Edward, and even the teachers and the principal were very fond of him. Was he good-looking? I'd say that without the acne, he would certainly have been one of the best-looking kids in our school. Even with the skin condition, he had no problem getting girls. It was amazing. While the rest of us numbskulls were stumbling ineptly over our words trying to talk to even the most average-looking girls, Edward was dating and going steady with the best of the best. Just because of that fact alone, I admired the boy. What I wouldn't have given to be more like him—to be self-confident, outgoing, funny, and sure of myself.

Another thing about Edward you would notice right off the bat after talking to him is that he was as smart as a whip. He got top grades in his classes, and he even spent time after school tutoring. No kidding, he was like an expert at every school subject. If it wasn't for Bobby McQueen, the school's Einstein-clone, briefcase-toting resident genius, Edward would surely have been our valedictorian. And as if it wasn't enough to be so smart, Edward was also a first-rate athlete. He played basketball and football, and he was captain of the baseball team. What wasn't the kid good at? I had no idea. It seemed like he had all the bases covered.

Edward's dad was a successful attorney who made a ton of money suing people, defending clients, and negotiating deals between people who couldn't get along. I guess it was Edward's parents who were paying for most of our trip to Big Bear. We drove there in their brand-new station wagon, and we stayed in their mountain cabin. We dined out on Edward's credit card. It was unheard of for a kid back then to have his own credit card, but Edward had one. The only thing the rest of us had to pay for was the ski equipment rental and lift tickets. Of course, Edward had his own skis, and his dad had purchased season lift tickets for their entire family. The other thing Edward said we had to pay for was our own beer. This was no problem. We all pooled our money together each evening and then stood in front of the local market, asking adults if they would buy us our beer. Amazingly, even if it took an hour or two, there was always some adult eventually willing to make the purchase for us.

The skiing was great that weekend. It had snowed like mad the entire week before, and the slopes were thick with powder. But it was the evenings that we all looked forward to. We'd invite as many kids as possible to the cabin, and we would all drink beer and party until late at night. I can't even describe how much fun it was. There was no adult supervision. There was all the beer a person could drink. There were potato chips and corn chips and little plastic tubs of guacamole dip. And there were girls. This was a few months before I met April, so I was still free to meet, and flirt with, and kiss other girls to my heart's content. Jesus, I don't remember ever having so much fun in my life.

It was on a Sunday night that I got to know Edward better. Our party was over, and the rest of our group had gone to sleep. Edward and I were the only kids still awake. It was early in the morning, about two or three, and the two of us were still drinking. Who knows how many beers we had consumed that night, yet neither of us felt like turning in. We sat on the sofa and talked. And we drank more beer. And we nibbled at what was left of the potato chips, corn chips, and guacamole. Edward was pretty drunk, and I guess I was too. We hardly knew each other, yet thanks to all the beer, and thanks to the late hour, it was as if we were best pals.

"Did you ever have Mr. Krantz for math?" Edward asked me.

"I did," I said. "I had him for algebra."

"Did you ever notice how often he said 'the-uh?'"

"No," I said. "But now that you mention it, I guess I do remember that." I laughed and took a sip from my beer.

"Do you know who Teddy Michaels is?"

"I know who he is."

"He sat next to me in Mr. Krantz's class. You know what he used to do?"

"What?" I asked.

"He kept a sheet of paper on his desk, and he would make a mark every time Mr. Krantz said 'the-uh.' He would keep track of every one of them. Before class each morning, Teddy and I would make a bet. We'd bet on how many times old Krantz would say 'the-uh,' and the one of us closest to our number would win a dollar from the other. Don't ask me how, but I won the bet every time. Then one morning, I said fifteen and Teddy said sixteen. So anything sixteen or higher, and Teddy would win the bet. Then Teddy kept track, making the marks on his paper. Toward the end of the class, Mr. Krantz hit number sixteen, and Teddy looked over at me, smiling. Then he slapped his hand down on his desk, and he shouted, 'I win! I win!' Well, hell, you should've seen the look on Mr. Krantz's face. He had no idea what the heck was going on. Then I started laughing, and then Teddy laughed. 'Would you boys like to fill the rest of us in?' Mr. Krantz said. Teddy just replied, 'I can't believe I finally won!' It was funny as hell. Mr. Krantz just shook his head and continued with his lecture."

"That's funny," I said.

"He said 'the-uh' four more times before the bell rang."

I laughed.

"You want another beer?"

"Sure," I said. Edward got up from the sofa and went to the refrigerator. He came back with two beers and handed one of them to me.

"What do you think of Mr. Giles?" Edward asked.

"The principal?"

"Of course, the principal. Do you know anyone else named Mr. Giles?"

"He's okay, I guess."

"Did you know he's a homo?"

"He is?"

"Just as sure as I'm drinking this beer. Why do you think he never married? Did you know he's never been married?"

"I didn't know that."

"He's fifty-three, and he's never tied the knot with anyone. He has a boyfriend, you know."

"No kidding?"

"A lover. That's what they call each other. They call each other lovers. Kind of gross, isn't it?"

"Yeah," I said.

"You know how I know all this? My dad is his attorney. My dad has been his attorney for over fifteen years. My dad knows everything about the guy. So you might ask yourself—and it would be a fair question—what would a high school principal need a lawyer for? I mean, seriously, why would he need one? Can you think of a reason?"

"Not really."

"Do you know what a pedophile is?"

"I think so. Isn't it someone who has sex with dead bodies?"

"No, no, no, that's a necrophiliac. A pedophile is an adult who has sex with kids."

"Is Mr. Giles a pedophile?"

"Well, that's the question, isn't it? Mr. Giles hired my dad fifteen years ago when he was working as the dean of boys at a high school in San Diego County. The parents of one of the boys went to the principal and accused Mr. Giles of making some sexual advances to their son while the boy was in his office. I don't think they accused him of actually doing anything to the boy. They said he just made advances, and they wanted him to be fired. They also wanted to keep the incident quiet. They didn't want their son to be humiliated, and who can blame them? If the other kids at school got hold of the information, the poor kid would never have lived it down. So the parents wanted Mr. Giles to be fired, and they didn't care what the principal used as an excuse. They just wanted Mr. Giles gone, and they wanted him gone right away. Tough, right? What would you have done if you were the principal?"

"I don't know."

"They had no proof. It was the kid's word versus the word of Mr. Giles."

"Did they fire him?"

"Well, not exactly. Mr. Giles hired my dad, and he had my dad negotiate a deal with the principal. It turned out that Mr. Giles had had his eye on an opening at our school for a new principal, and Mr. Giles wanted the job. He had all the right qualifications, except for the fact that he was a fag and possibly a pedophile. My dad told the principal that Mr. Giles would voluntarily leave the school without an embarrassing battle if the principal called up our school and recommended Mr. Giles for the job opening. It would be about all that was needed, since the principal was very highly respected and since Mr. Giles had an impeccable record—well, except for the recent complaint against him. As to the complaint, my dad told the principal that he had to talk the boy's parents into signing an agreement promising to tell no one about their son's claim. I mean not *ever*. The parents agreed to this because they didn't want to fight over the matter. They just wanted the whole thing to be over and done with, nice and quiet, swept under the rug. So they agreed to my dad's deal, and a month later, thanks to the recommendation of the principal, Mr. Giles was hired as *our* school principal."

"Wow," I said.

"You can't tell anyone any of this."

"I won't."

"Seriously, my dad would kill me if he knew I told you. He'd cut off my head."

"I can keep a secret."

"Now it's your turn."

"My turn for what?"

Edward took a long swig from his can of beer, and then said, "You tell me a secret. Tell me about something you'd get killed for if your parents found out that you opened your big mouth to someone you hardly knew."

"Okay," I said. I thought, but nothing came immediately to mind. My dad wasn't an attorney. He wasn't privy to everyone's dirty little secrets.

"Go on," Edward said.

"I can't think of anything."

"There's always something. Think harder."

"Well, I suppose there's one thing."

"Out with it," Edward said, smiling. He then drank some more beer, and so did I.

"It's about my uncle."

"Your dad's brother, or your mother's brother?"

"My mother's brother."

"And?"

"My aunt and uncle lived up north in San Jose. They were visiting with us. This was about three years ago. My mom, dad, and uncle were up late talking at the kitchen table. My aunt had gone to bed. So had my cousins. Mom and Dad thought I had gone to sleep too. But actually I was wide awake, and I had come down the stairs to get something to eat in the kitchen. I could hear the adults talking, and something my dad said caused me to stop at the foot of the stairs."

"What did he say?"

"He said, 'I can't believe you actually had sex with a hooker.'"

"Ha!" Edward laughed. "He was talking to your uncle?"

"Yes," I said.

"How did your dad know his brother had sex with a hooker?"

"I guess my uncle told him."

"That's funny."

"But that's not the half of it."

"Oh?" Edward said.

"My uncle said the hooker gave him gonorrhea."

"No kidding," Edward said, laughing. He took a long sip from his beer.

"And that isn't even the worst part," I said. "My aunt didn't know anything about it. And my aunt and uncle were still having sex."

"Jeez, seriously?"

"My mom and dad were reading my uncle the riot act. They were doing it quietly, of course. They didn't want anyone to hear. But I could hear from the foot of the stairs. I could hear all of it. Heck, I now knew more about my uncle's dick than his wife did."

Edward laughed. Then he said, "Adults are so strange, aren't they? When you get right down to it, they're really a bunch of freaks and weirdos. They're supposed to be the ones setting an example. And they wonder why so many of us are so messed up."

"No kidding," I said.

I liked having this conversation with Edward. We stayed up past five in the morning drinking more beer and sharing jokes and stories. Edward knew a few good jokes. One that I remember is about a boy who comes home from school. The mother asks her son what he did at school that day, and the boy tells her he had sex with his teacher. He is grinning from ear to ear, proud of himself. The mother is furious, and she tells the boy to go to his room until his father gets home. When the father gets home, the mother tells him what the boy said, and the father goes to the boy's room. "I hear you had sex with your teacher," the father says, and the boy nods his head. The father can't help it. He's just as proud as hell. "I'm so proud of you son," the father says, "I'm going to take you to buy that bicycle you've always wanted." So they go out and buy the bicycle, and the father tells the boy, "I'll drive, and you can ride home on your brand-new bike." The boy says he can't ride the bike, and the father asks why. The boy grimaces and says, "Because my butt still hurts."

Maybe it was because of all the beer, but I laughed like hell when Edward told me this joke. Maybe you find this joke in poor taste, and in retrospect, it probably is. But you have to realize that I'm talking about the seventies, the years that I was in high school, and not about our enlightened times. Back then gay jokes were funny, and back then we called gay men fags. I'm not trying to offend anyone, so please don't be angry with me. I'm just telling you how it was.

Anyway, it was a month later that Edward took his own life. The entire school was shocked out of their socks when they heard the news. So what exactly happened? I know that Edward was on his way home from school, and he was walking alone. He came to a freeway overpass, and he set down his books. He climbed up over the chain link fence of the overpass and watched the cars speeding on the freeway below. Then he did it. He jumped from the overpass, landing right smack in the path of an eighteen-wheeler. They said he died instantly. I heard they also shut down the entire north bound lanes of the freeway for an hour or two. He left no note, and gave no one any kind of warning or explanation. It was one of the school year's great, tragic mysteries.

I went to the memorial service for Edward at his family's church. I wasn't exactly invited, but Alex (our mutual friend) said I could come along with him. Alex and I sat in the pews and listened to people speak about Edward. They had so many good things to say about him, and he probably did deserve all the praise. In my book, he was a decent guy. I remember some of the girls at the service were crying. But here's what's odd. I don't remember anything about Edward's parents. I'm sure they were there, but I don't remember seeing them. And I think it's strange how kids live in their own kid world and how parents are really just wallpaper. Seriously, if there were any people sitting in the church that afternoon who deserved my sympathy, they weren't the crying girls or the long-faced boys; they were Edward's parents. Now that I'm a parent myself, I can see this. It's so clear to me. It's the parents who take the brunt of the blow. It's the parents who hurt the most. It's the parents who really suffer more than anyone else when a child commits suicide or attempts it.

So April and I were faced with a decision to make. Should we have Jacob stay a few weeks in a mental hospital under the care of someone like Dr. Rosenblatt, or should we bring him home with us and do—what? Who knew?

That evening, I went into Jacob's room. In his desk drawer there was a stack of poems he'd recently written. I knew they were recent because I didn't remember seeing them previously when I'd been snooping. I hate to use that word, 'snooping,' but that's exactly what I'd been doing, wasn't it? Fuck it. Let's call a spade a spade. Yes, I had been snooping. He was my son, and I had every right in the world to do everything possible to understand why he had tried to take his life. Among the poems, I found several pages of haiku that caught my attention. Some of them are as follows:

Innocent children—
they like to hurt your feelings
and make your eyes cry.

Girls made of sugar
and spice are not all that nice.
Lots of broken hearts.

Boys and girls who try
to be different are just
the subjects of jokes.

I live in a land
where wise men are foolish and
dumbbells are leaders.

If people were bees,
they would buzz around and sting
everything in sight.

I had a dream in
which all the teachers wanted
their students to learn.

One day all babies
will be born with a tag that
says, "Made in China."

My dad studied hard
and earned a degree so that
he could sell boxes.

If you want to be
successful in life, learn to
torture bugs and cats.

Your dog doesn't care
about the trade deficit
or about sales tax.

I had a plastic
soldier that could never be
killed by anything.

Money can't buy you
happiness, but it will buy
you a brand-new bike.

Governments kill men
women and children like they're
shopping for new clothes.

The miracle of
life is all about buying
fast cars and houses.

    I called Dr. Rosenblatt as promised, and I told her what April and I wanted to do. We decided that, yes, we would agree to Jacob being in a hospital, so long as Jacob was willing. I was surprised to learn that Jacob was on board. It didn't seem like the kind of thing he would've liked, but obviously I had misjudged his desire to get well. Clearly he didn't like being so unhappy or feeling as though he had to take his life. He wanted to give his shot at life another chance, and this was a good thing, right?

    We had Jacob transferred from the hospital he was at to a new, very reputable hospital near the beach that Dr. Rosenblatt recommended. The name of this hospital was Pacific Acres, and it was run by a psychiatrist named Dr. Arnold Bloom. I checked out their website on the internet, and it looked like a decent place. It was a complex of new Mediterranean buildings built on twenty acres of nicely landscaped land. They had a big swimming pool, two volleyball courts, and a rock-lined and koi-stocked fish pond. Seriously, the place was like a hotel—the sort of place people would go to on purpose. The only thing I didn't like about it was the price they demanded for Jacob to stay there. I thought the cost per day was too high, but this was, after all, our son we were talking about. And all said and done, we could afford it, so we were willing to part with the money.

The doctor put in charge of Jacob's case was a young man named Dr. Terrance Trill. He had been working at the hospital for three years. Dr. Rosenblatt said Dr. Trill had a good rapport with his younger clients, so we didn't object to his lack of experience.

When April and I drove to the hospital to meet Dr. Trill for the first time, April asked me, "Are you sure we're doing the right thing?"

"I thought we already decided."

"We can always change our minds."

"I guess we can."

"I suppose it will depend on what this new doctor is like—whether we like him and whether Jacob likes him."

"Yes," I said.

April looked out the side window for a moment, thinking, and then asked, "What do you think Jacob will be like a year from now?"

"A year from now?"

"Yes, what do you think?"

"I have no idea," I said. "I can't even guess. But it's a very good question."

CHAPTER 19

THE GAME

————————•❦•————————

Dr. Trill came out and met us in the nicely furnished reception area. He then took us back to his office, and we all sat down. I have to say that the doctor's boyish face and thick brown hair made him look younger than I had anticipated, but he was also reassuringly mature. He spoke well, both intelligently and eloquently, and after several minutes of listening to him talk, I felt good about him handling our son. He seemed to know what he was talking about, and much of what he was saying made good sense. There was one thing, however, that I didn't like, and that was the doctor's insistence that we not visit with Jacob in person for the upcoming two weeks. But I went along with the plan, and so did April. We both wanted to follow the doctor's instructions, since it was obvious that what we'd been doing on our own wasn't working.

So we waited two weeks. April brought clothes for Jacob to wear, and she also went to Jacob's school, where she worked out a deal that allowed Jacob to do his schoolwork while away. They had an in-house educator at the hospital who was qualified to substitute for teachers. Homework and tests would be exactly the same.

Are you wondering if Jacob planned on going to college? In fact, he had no desire to attend college at all. We had argued about it, but Jacob was adamant. He just refused to go. All he wanted was his high school diploma, and to be honest, I'm not sure if he even cared about that. When April and I asked him what he planned to do after high school, he never had much of a plan. He just said he would find a job "doing something." We were hoping that Dr. Trill was more adept than us at talking Jacob into college. Ideally, I hoped the doctor would convince Jacob to go. We were paying this hospital a small fortune, and it would be nice to get our money's worth.

So where was Zach during all of this? He was finishing his first year at UCLA. He had declared a business major, just like I had. He was getting good grades (as usual), and he was making a whole new group of friends. He called us every Sunday to let us know how things were going, and we let him know all that was happening with Jacob. He just sighed and said, "Jesus." It was not a 'Jesus' as in 'Jesus, poor Jacob,' but rather a 'Jesus' as in 'Jesus, what a mess my little brother has caused.'

After two weeks passed, it was time for us to come in and meet with Jacob in person at the hospital. It had only been two weeks, but it felt like months. The meeting was on a Saturday morning. April and I arrived on time, and Dr. Trill met us in the reception area and then took us back to his office. He wanted to talk to us alone at first, and then he would bring in Jacob. Dr. Trill was nicely dressed that morning in a tasteful polo shirt, slacks, and brown leather shoes. He looked the way one would want one's psychiatrist to look: in control, as neat as a pin, and tastefully put together. He looked like he cared. He looked like his job mattered to him.

"Well," I said, "I guess today's the big day."

"The big day?" the doctor asked.

"To see our son."

"Yes, of course."

"We do get to see him, right?"

"Yes, but there are some things we need to discuss before I bring him in."

"Fire away," I said. This whole thing was not exactly uplifting, but I tried to sound upbeat.

"First I need to manage your expectations. Turning around a patient's life is often a long and arduous task. Things don't happen overnight."

"I understand," I said.

"Often when parents leave their children with us, they expect instant results. They think we just wave a magic wand, and presto—a new person."

"I think we both understand," I said. I looked at April, and she nodded.

"That being said, we have made a lot of progress. We have been doing what we always do with new patients. We've been making Jacob aware—making him aware of his feelings, aware that he has a problem, aware that there are better ways to deal with his feelings than suicide, and aware that his actions affect others. He is not yet *fully* aware, but like I said, we have made a lot of progress. I think you'll notice a difference."

"That's what we're hoping for."

"Your son is very bright."

"We know that."

"And inquisitive."

"Yes," I said.

"This makes him especially hard to treat. He questions everything we ask him to do."

"I can imagine."

"This is going to sound sort of inappropriate coming from a psychiatrist, but I'm going to be frank with you. The dumber a patient is, the easier it is to help him. It is easier to make dumb people happier. They don't teach you this in school. It's just something you learn from experience."

"Okay," I said.

"You should think of this as a long cross-country road trip to the East Coast. We're going to get there just fine if we have faith in our GPS. But right now, we're barely out of the state. Does this make sense to you?"

"Yes," I said.

"And does it make sense to you?" the doctor asked April.

"Yes," April said. "I think I get it."

"Okay, then sit tight for a moment, and I'll go get your son. I'll be right back."

When Jacob was a sophomore in high school, he was taking a world history class taught by a teacher named Mr. Abrams. For one of the assignments, Mr. Abrams asked the class to write a paper about a custom or ritual in some other country that was different from what we were accustomed to in the United States. I thought it was a great idea for a paper. I thought it was good to expose kids to the ways of life in other countries, and I was curious to see what Jacob would write about. But leave it to Jacob to turn over the applecart. I mean, he really flipped the entire thing over. His remarkable paper was titled *The Game*, and here it is. See what you think of it:

The Game

Come one, come all, to Arcadia. You won't find the land of Arcadia anywhere on a world map, or in a history book, or in a dusty old encyclopedia, or in a James Michener novel. But it is a real place—as real as any other place in the universe. They say, "I think, therefore I am." I say, "I can think of it, therefore it is."

This paper is about sports—one sport in particular. There are many varied sports in Arcadia, most of them being the same as the sports played in the United States. There is basketball, soccer, baseball, golf, football, badminton, tennis, gymnastics, wrestling, boxing, and so on and so forth. There is also their most beloved, which is ice hockey. This exciting sport attracts athletes and fans from every corner of Arcadia. Some people say it is more than a mere sport. Some people say it's an actual way of life. Some people in Arcadia go so far as to say it's a religion.

In Arcadia, ice hockey is played much the same way as we play it here. The players wear ice skates and protective gear, and they whack a puck around the ice with hockey sticks. There is a goal for each team, and there is a goalie protecting the goal. There are five skating players on each team who try to score goals for their team while trying at the same time to keep the other team from scoring on them. The rules are much the same as ours. There are penalties assessed for slashing, high-sticking, tripping, cross-checking, boarding, charging, and so on and so forth. But despite all the similarities, there is one fundamental difference between the way we play the sport and the way it is played in Arcadia. They don't play so that one team beats the other. The objective in an Arcadian hockey game is to achieve a tie score. If the game is not tied at the end of regulation time, overtimes will be played until both teams have the same number of goals.

Don't let this objective fool you. They play just as hard in Arcadia as they play here in our country. They try to score goals, and they try to prevent goals from being scored on their goalies. It is very intense. Fights break out, and noses are broken. Blood is spilled, and teeth are lost.

If a player on one team is significantly better than a player on the other, he is expected to help the other player improve his game. This does not mean that he lets the other player get the best of him. No, this means exactly what I just said—that he helps the other player improve his game. Time-outs are taken to give players time to do this. The whole point is for all players and teams to perform to the best of their ability, to play at the same high level. If the teams are both performing well, running on all cylinders, the result should be a tie game—exactly what the fans came to root for. And at the end of each season, awards are given not to those who defeated their opponents but to those who were the most helpful to them. The trophies go to the best teachers. Yes, the awards go out to those who best represent everything Arcadia stands for.

This is so much the opposite of sports in the US that it's difficult for us to comprehend how it even works. But it does work. It works in Arcadia, a place where people aim to help one another rather than to defeat enemies and create losers. There are no losers in Arcadia. It isn't us versus them. It's us for all of us.

It's a way of life in Arcadia. This spirit of cooperation isn't just found in its sports. It is everywhere. It is the goal of all that goes on in this society. Take social issues, for example. There are people who will advocate for one side of an issue, and others who will advocate for the other side, just as in our country. But what do they do? In Arcadia there can be no winners or losers. Both sides get together and help each other argue opposite sides until they discover they are actually arguing for one thing, which is the right thing. And by putting themselves in each other's shoes, they see each situation for what it actually is and they reach an agreement. This is the opposite of what we do in our country, and it's difficult (maybe even impossible) for us to understand. We are taught to seek lopsided victories at the expense of others. Arcadians, on the other hand, are taught to seek ties.

In Arcadia it's called "The Game." A game as we have come to know it is a competition in which one side schemes and makes moves to defeat others. Not so in Arcadia. The Game in Arcadia is a competition between two sides that scheme and make moves to bring out the best in each other and reach for a common goal. It's hard to fathom if you're an American. But believe it, because like I said, Arcadia is real.

Mr. Abrams gave Jacob an F on his paper. With red ink, he wrote in the upper margin, "You were specifically asked to write a paper about a custom or ritual in a real country, not in a pretend one. You did not follow the instructions. Please see me after class." Jacob did see Mr. Abrams after class, and Mr. Abrams gave Jacob the opportunity to redo his paper. But Jacob refused to do it. The truth was that Jacob didn't really care what grade he got, and I knew this. I found the poorly graded paper in Jacob's wastebasket at home, crumpled into a ball. I didn't ask him about it, because that would've revealed that I was snooping through his things. And I didn't call the teacher, although I was greatly tempted. I would've loved to have given the idiot a piece of my mind. So I did what I did with most of Jacob's other writings, putting it in the box with his poems and other writings.

When Dr. Trill brought Jacob into his office, Jacob sat between April and me, and Dr. Trill sat behind his desk. It was kind of weird. April and I should've stood and hugged the boy, but we didn't. We were both apprehensive.

Jacob looked no different than he had a few weeks earlier. His long hair was tied into a ponytail with a rubber band. He was wearing one of his tie-dyed T-shirts, worn Levi's jeans, and Mexican sandals. There were white gauze bandages taped around both of his injured wrists.

"Well, now we're all here," the doctor said.

"Hello, son," I said.

"Hi, Dad."

"Are you doing okay?" April asked.

"I'm doing okay."

"We've been so worried about you."

"Are they treating you okay here?"

"They're treating me fine."

"Are they feeding you well?"

"The food is fine."

"When you come home, I'll fix whatever you want for dinner. Whatever you feel like. Just name it."

"Thanks, Mom."

"Zach said to say hi," I said.

"Did he?"

"We've all been thinking about you."

Everyone sat and stared at each other for a moment without saying anything. Then Dr. Trill said, "Jacob and I have talked a lot over the past two weeks. Haven't we, Jacob?"

"Yes," Jacob said.

"He has some things he'd like to say to you."

"We'd like to hear," I said.

"Jacob?" the doctor said. "You have the floor. What would you like to say to your parents?"

Jacob looked at the doctor and then at April and me. He said, "I guess I want to say I'm sorry. I really am sorry for what I did. I know that you both love me, and what I did was hurtful to you. I wasn't thinking about either of you. I guess I want you both to know that I wasn't trying to make either of you feel bad, or make you worry, or frighten you, although I know that's probably what I did. I guess I wasn't thinking clearly. What I did was wrong. I know that now."

"Don't worry about it," I said.

"We're just happy you're alive," April said.

"Don't let him off the hook too easy," the doctor said.

"Off the hook?"

"Jacob has to understand what he did to both of you. We don't want this to be forgotten as a minor blunder. It was a very big deal, and Jacob needs to understand this. He needs to understand that his actions can have serious consequences."

"Okay," I said.

"So tell Jacob exactly how *you* felt."

I thought about this. April was looking at me, waiting for me to answer. I said, "It scared the living shit out of me. It was fucking horrible."

"And?"

"It hurt, Jacob. It was like someone stuck a knife into my heart and twisted it. It really hurt like hell. Both of us love you to the ends of the earth, son. You need to understand that."

"I know you love me."

"Then why? We both want to know why."

"Why what?"

"Why would you try to kill yourself?"

"I guess I wasn't thinking of either of you." At this point, Jacob looked at Dr. Trill. It was if he was hoping the doctor would do the rest of the talking.

"Go on," the doctor said to Jacob.

"I was in so much pain," Jacob said. "I just wanted to make it go away."

I didn't know what to say. This hurt a lot. Why was he in so much pain? April and I had done everything in our power to give Jacob a good life. Isn't that how one feels as a parent? I mean when one is a good parent. And we were both good parents. Jacob's life could certainly have been a lot worse, and that was a fact. I guess I didn't understand why Jacob was so miserable. April spoke for me when she finally said, "We've done everything possible to give you a good life. Honestly, I don't know what else we could've done."

"It had nothing to do with either of you," Jacob said. "It was all me. It had nothing to do with you."

"I believe him when he says this," the doctor said.

"You're good parents," Jacob said. "You always have been good parents."

"Yet here we are," I said.

"Yes," Jacob said.

"Tell your mom and dad what you told me."

"About what?"

"About the spaceship dream."

"The spaceship dream?" I asked.

"We've never heard of this," April said.

"Go on," the doctor said to Jacob. "Tell them exactly what you told me."

"I have this dream," Jacob said. "I have a dream that I'm a NASA astronaut. Dad, do you remember how you told me you wanted to be an astronaut when you were a kid? Well, in this dream I actually am one. I've flown a solo mission to the moon, and I'm returning to Earth. I'm looking out the small window of the space capsule, and I can see Earth below, but then something goes wrong. The gauges and lights start going crazy, and I veer way off course. I'm no longer headed to Earth. Instead I am orbiting it, not able to do anything to correct it. And I now realize I am trapped in an orbit—that I'm just going to go around and around, and never return home. I'll run out of food, and I'll run out of oxygen. Earth is right below me, like I can reach out and touch it. Yet I am drifting, orbiting, all by myself, trapped and soon to be dying."

"Then what happens?" I ask.

"I wake up."

"Well, at least you wake up."

"I wake up, but I don't feel any different. I still feel like I'm orbiting the earth, out of control. And the feeling doesn't go away. It just gets worse and worse until it becomes so painful that I can't stand it."

"That sounds awful," April said.

"It's how I feel every day."

"Which is how, exactly?"

"Disconnected from my flight plan and orbiting the earth, home except not home at all, and consumed with loneliness and pain."

Jesus, do you have any idea what it's like to hear your own child speak like this? It is horrible. That morning, his pain became my pain, and his loneliness hit me like a ton of bricks. And I was just as helpless as him, orbiting the planet Earth, running out of food and oxygen, starving, suffocating.

"I think Jacob's dream is very descriptive," the doctor said.

"Yes," I agreed.

Out of the corner of my eye I could see April nodding, although she didn't say anything.

"So the question is, how do we bring the capsule safely to Earth? This is the question I've been exploring over the past two weeks with your son."

"Okay," I said.

"What have you come up with?" April asked.

"Do you two have any ideas?" the doctor asked.

"You're asking us?"

"You know Jacob better than anyone else."

"Jeez," I said, and I thought for a moment. I was sure April was thinking too.

"We were hoping you would know," April said.

"Yes," I agreed.

"Just thought I would ask," the doctor said. "I wouldn't want to start treating your son without getting input from you first."

"Well, I can tell you that I'm not crazy about giving Jacob medications," I said.

"Neither am I," Jacob said.

"When we first talked with Dr. Rosenblatt, she said she thought Jacob might be bipolar. Is that what you think?"

"I'm glad you brought that up."

"Well?" I asked.

"I'll be honest with you. I don't like mental disorder classifications. I think every patient is unique. The brain is an astonishingly complex organ, and these classifications have been written to pin down things that can't be pinned down. Now, you'll find a lot of people who disagree with me. You'll find a lot of smart and well-educated people. But here's exactly what I promise to do. I will look at Jacob's issues as being all his own, and I will do my best to come up with appropriate actions I feel will best help him to land his spaceship—to lead a healthy and happy life. If you're looking for someone to give a name to your son's problems, you're probably having him see the wrong psychiatrist. Are we on the same page? If we're not, now is the time to say so. There are lots of psychiatrists in Southern California who would be willing to take your money and lead you in a different direction."

I liked this. I liked what this doctor was saying. I turned and looked at April, and she smiled at me. I think the smile meant she agreed with me.

"We'll support you," I said, looking back at the doctor. "We like what you're saying, and we believe you're the right person to help Jacob." I then looked over at Jacob. "How do you feel about this?" I asked.

"I'm good with the doc," Jacob said. "We're getting along fine."

Then I looked at the doctor. He was leaning back in his chair, staring at me. I said to him, "This brings us back to my earlier question. What are we going to do?"

"I'll tell you exactly what we're going to do," the doctor said. "I've written a poem."

"A poem?" I asked.

"That sounds right up my alley," Jacob said. April and I laughed at this. At first, the doctor didn't seem to understand why we were laughing.

"Jacob writes a lot of poetry," I explained.

The doctor smiled and said, "This will be Jacob's mantra." He handed each of us a sheet of paper with the poem printed on it. "Follow along with me," he said, and he read the poem out loud to us.

CHAPTER 20

THE MANTRAS

————————— •●• —————————

The human brain is a phenomenal organ. When you stop to think about it, it's actually not just phenomenal; it's completely beyond comprehension. They say it's made of a hundred billion neurons, and we do know a few things about how it works. But the truth is that we know next to nothing. We're like idiots when it comes to our brains. We are science cowboys riding our horses in our absurd science rodeos, trying to throw lassos around what? Around a hundred billion neurons? Good luck with that endeavor. Do you have any idea how many neurons a hundred billion is? If each little neuron was the size of a golf ball and we lined the balls up end to end, they would go to the moon and back *thirty-three times*. And that just in one brain—one lowly human brain encased in one human skull, between a pair of fleshy ears, behind one pair of eyes. Think of this: there are seven and a half billion people on this planet, so there are seven and a half billion individual brains! Think of the scope of this! Think of the number of golf balls! And we go to psychiatrists who have a few years of higher education so they'll what? So they'll unlock the mysteries of these ultraphenomenal, blood-drenched gray matter miracles? It's like us asking a colony of amoebas to design and build a spacecraft that will fly them to Mars and back. It really is about that ridiculous.

And now comes the question at hand, the question Dr. Trill was trying his best to address. How did a hundred billion tiny Jacob-neurons get together and decide it was time to take their own lives? And what could be done about it? What cure did our trusty doctor come up with? What did he want Jacob to do? He wanted him to memorize a poem. I didn't laugh or smirk as the doctor read his poem to us, his proposed mantra for our son to repeat over and over, a rhyming lifeline for climbing out of the deep hole he was in. How did the poem go? The doctor read the poem out loud to us, and we silently read it along with him. It went as follows:

> It didn't cost you one thin dime,
> So why are you inclined to whine?
> Ride it to the end of the line.
> Thank the conductor for his time.

That was it. Those were the four lines that were going to save my son's life. I could hear the hundred billion neurons in Jacob's head listening, snapping, popping, firing, and changing their minds. Was I skeptical? Maybe I was a little. But was I hopeful? Yes, I was as hopeful as hell.

Ronald Reagan said, "They say the world has become too complex for simple answers. They are wrong." Never mind his politics for the moment. (You probably either hate him or love him.) This is a beautiful quotation, and I believe it's entirely accurate. I've seen it for myself.

I'll give you an example. I'm going to tell you a little more about my brother, Jerry. I already told you how he fought in the Vietnam War back in the sixties. Now I'm going to tell you about a war he fought after he returned. I know for a fact that he wouldn't mind me telling you this story. These days he tells the story to anyone who'll listen, so I'm not revealing any personal or sensitive secrets.

Jerry didn't talk much about the war after he came home; in fact, he didn't want to talk about it at all. So I could only imagine how horrible it was. It was probably even worse for me not knowing the true details, because without real information, the mind can travel to some very dark places. And I saw those dark places in Jerry's eyes whenever anyone brought up the war. In order to forget his experiences, Jerry turned to alcohol. I don't mean that he was an instant alcoholic, because that's not the way it happened. But he did party a lot. He would go out on Friday and Saturday nights, and he wouldn't come back home until the early morning hours. And he'd be drunk and loud when he did come home, and I remember him arguing with my dad in the kitchen. My dad didn't like Jerry's drinking.

It was at one of these parties that Jerry met the love of his life, Rachael

Waters. I say she was the love of his life because that's what Jerry called her. What did I think of the girl? I thought she was nice, but I also thought she was the wrong kind of girl for my brother. Jerry needed a girl who was bright and understanding, and who had both of her feet on the ground. Rachael was anything but that. Rachael was a walking, talking, blue-eyed, mai tai–guzzling bundle of short-fused dynamite sticks. She drove my brother crazy, but he loved her. And the two of them became great drinking buddies not just on weekends but also during the week. When they announced their engagement, Mom and Dad congratulated them, but I could tell they weren't happy. One night at dinner while Jerry was out of the house, Dad said, "It'll never last." Mom said, "You never know," but I could tell she felt the same.

Jerry and Rachael were married, and everyone was invited to the wedding. The reception was wild. All Jerry and Rachael's party friends were there, and they drank, ate, and danced, but mostly they drank. Jerry and Rachael got so drunk that neither of them was okay to drive, so my dad drove them in their car to their hotel in Laguna Beach. Mom followed them and then drove Dad home.

My brother's marriage lasted five years. It was the booze that drove them apart; it was my brother's strong desire to stop drinking and Rachael's refusal to get sober. It was during the fourth year of their marriage that my brother decided he had had enough and started going to AA. He hated going to the meetings alone, so he asked me if I would join him. I have never had a drinking problem, but I was curious about what went on in these meetings. I also wanted to help my brother out, so I went with him. The meetings he went to were held by a group of Vietnam veterans every Wednesday night in a Methodist church in Norwalk. I didn't really belong there, but I went for my brother. I remember one night after a meeting, we were all standing outside and drinking coffee. My brother introduced me to a guy named Curt. Curt had long dirty blonde hair that he kept tied back in a ponytail, and he had a bushy beard that looked as if it hadn't been washed or brushed for weeks. He was dressed in denim, and he wore a pair of wire-rimmed glasses. He was very friendly to me even though I was neither a veteran nor an alcoholic.

"So you just missed the war?" he asked.

"It ended right when I got out of high school," I said.

"Lucky you."

"I appreciate everything you guys did over there."

"What'd we do?"

"You know," I said. "Fighting for our country."

"Didn't you tell him?" Curt asked my brother.

"No," my brother said.

"Tell me what?"

"The war was a joke," Curt said.

I didn't know what to say. So I stood there and said nothing.

"It was a fucking joke. Why do you think so many of us veterans are drug addicts or alcoholics?"

"I don't know," I said.

"We don't talk much about the war," Jerry said to Curt.

"Well, you should."

"I'd rather forget it and move on."

"Yet you can't."

"No, not yet," Jerry agreed.

"Uncle Sam fucked us over royally, and now here we are, standing outside of a fucking church and drinking shitty coffee, telling everyone our problems." Curt now looked at me. "Do you know why we go to AA meetings? It's because the fucking things are free, and all of us alcoholics and addicts are broke."

My brother laughed at this.

"Do you believe in God?" Curt asked me.

"I think I do," I said.

"If you want to work AA, you'd sure as hell better believe in God."

"Or a higher power," Jerry said.

"God or a higher power—six of one, half a dozen of the other. Not fooling me."

"Do you believe in God?" I asked.

"Sure, and I believe in Santa Claus and the tooth fairy and Peter Pan. Shit, anyone who's fought in a war knows that either God doesn't exist or that God is a fucking asshole. What kind of sadistic bloodthirsty freak would have allowed it? God is all powerful and loving. That's what they like to say, isn't it? All powerful and loving, yet perfectly content to watch men kill and maim each other. Believe me, if you've ever seen a man step on a land mine, you'll think twice about all the warm feelings you once had about the mighty fuckhead we worship on Sundays."

"Amen, brother," a veteran said. He was standing several feet away and had been listening to Curt talk.

"If you don't believe in God, then what are you guys doing here?" I asked.

"It's the only game in town," Jerry said.

"And it's free," Curt said. Jerry and Curt both laughed at this again. "And they say it works."

"Does it work for you?" I asked.

"Let me put it this way. I keep coming because, who knows? Maybe I'll change my mind about God. Maybe a miracle will happen. He's all about miracles, right?"

On the way home from the meeting, I rolled down my car window for some fresh air, and I asked my brother, "Do you believe in God?"

"It's a problem," Jerry said. "These AA people want me to turn my life over to him, but do I even think he exists? I just don't know. I really don't know. If he does exist, then he must be very cruel. And if he's so cruel, why would he care if I stopped drinking."

Jerry was sober for a few years. When he sobered up, he divorced Rachael. He also got a new and better job working as an assistant manager at a warehouse. The owner of the warehouse hired Vietnam veterans deliberately because he thought it was a patriotic thing to do. My brother did well during these years, and he seemed to finally put the war behind him. He met a woman who was a secretary at the warehouse, and eventually they got married. Her name was Natasha, and six months after they were married, Natasha was pregnant. She soon gave birth to a boy, whom they named Peter. Then, when Peter was one year old, Jerry started drinking again. At first it didn't seem like a big deal. Jerry was behaving himself. But within a year, the drinking got much worse—even worse than it was when he went to the veterans' AA meetings. I was in college at the time, still living at home. I remember when Natasha, Jerry, and their baby came over for dinner and my father confronted Jerry about the drinking.

"Enough is enough," my dad said.

"Since when is it everyone's business whether I drink or not? Do I tell you what to do?"

"You're our son. And you're Natasha's husband and Peter's father. It's everyone's business."

"I have a good job. I bring home enough money to pay the bills. No one's wanting for anything."

"Your family is wanting for a husband and father."

"Says who?"

"Says me," Natasha said, speaking up.

"We know what's been going on," my dad said.

To Natasha, Jerry said, "You've been talking to my parents? Behind my back?"

"We're worried about you."

"That's right," my dad said.

"Why weren't you so worried when you drove me to the bus depot and shipped me off to Vietnam? I didn't see anyone doing anything to stop me back then. Now you're worried? You can check my math, but I'd say you're about eight years too late."

"The war is over, son."

"The war will never be over."

"Maybe you should see a psychiatrist," my dad said rather suddenly. He wasn't being a wise guy. He was dead serious, and my brother knew it.

There was a pause in the conversation, and looking up at the ceiling, Jerry said, "Maybe I should."

A month later, my brother went to his first meeting with a psychiatrist. This doctor supposedly specialized in treating people who were addicted to alcohol and drugs. I never met the guy, so I can't provide a description of him. I can, however, tell you what Jerry told me. He said, "This doctor has a diagram that he keeps in his briefcase. It's been drawn on hundreds of times, because he uses a ballpoint pen to explain the thing to you. He circles the circles, and draws lines over the lines, and he underlines the words. He's like some kind of mad scientist." Jerry then explained the diagram to me, and I forget exactly what he told me. So I can't tell you just what the doctor said, but it was rather complicated. Supposedly this psychiatrist had invented this diagram, and he was the only shrink anywhere who used it with his patients. After explaining it to me, Jerry said, "So what the hell? If this guy's diagram was so helpful, why wasn't everyone using it?" Then the doctor told Jerry, with a straight face, to start going to AA meetings again. He said, "AA is your best bet when it comes to getting sober."

I felt for Jerry. I think deep down he really wanted to quit drinking, but he wasn't getting good advice. Instead of improving, the drinking got worse. And now Jerry was beginning to experience some of the telltale problems that were commonly associated with alcoholism, which is to say he was arrested for drunk driving while coming home from a night out with Natasha and, worse yet, he lost his job at the warehouse. After putting up with his drinking for four years, Natasha said she couldn't take any more. She filed for divorce, and she sued for full custody of Peter. She still had her job at the warehouse, so she was able to pay her bills. Jerry moved back home. Dad had read up on the subject, and he decided the best thing to do was to send Jerry to a rehab facility. Jerry agreed to go. As I said before, deep down he really wanted to be sober, and he'd tried AA and a psychiatrist. Rehab now seemed to be the only option.

Obviously I was not at the rehab facility with Jerry, so I don't have any firsthand information. But I can tell you what Jerry told me when he returned home after putting in his twenty-eight days as an inmate. The two of us went out to dinner so he could tell me about his experience without Mom and Dad hanging on his every word.

"The first thing I noticed about the place was that my six-foot-four, two-hundred-eighty-pound roommate snored at night. I don't mean that he snored a little. I mean it sounded like I was sleeping in the same room with a sick hippopotamus. Jesus, I didn't think I was going to make it through the first night, let alone through twenty-eight days."

"That sounds awful," I said.

"The second thing I noticed was the tattoos."

"The tattoos?"

"Everyone in the place, including the counselors, had tattoos on their arms, legs, necks, backs, shoulders, and God knows where else. There were more tattoos there than you'd find at a Hell's Angels convention. Seriously, it was so weird. What is it about being addicted to alcohol or drugs that makes a person want to have someone ink pictures on their skin? One of the guys there had 'Fuck you' tattooed on his neck. Jesus, can you imagine?"

"That's crazy," I said.

"The third thing I noticed was that everyone cussed. Every other word out of their mouths was either 'fuck' or 'shit.' I mean, I'm no Goody Two-shoes, but they cussed so much that it was even a little much for me."

"So what did they do there?"

"We had lots of group therapy sessions. And we had some lectures. They had one doctor come in and explain how nerve cells worked. He talked all about synapses and receptors and dopamine, but I have to be honest with you—I didn't have a clue what the idiot was talking about. I may as well have been listening to a lecture about paleontology, another subject I know and care absolutely nothing about. And it all seemed so strange to me."

"What seemed strange?"

"It seemed like they were saying that addictions are the result of our physiology."

"Why is that strange?"

"Because the solutions they gave us to tackle the problem never had anything to do with anything physical. The solutions were all spiritual. They said a lot of prayers. They read from a lot of spirituality books. Hell, they even taught us how to meditate. What the hell was that all about? So your nerve cells are messed up? Now the solution is to sit on your butt, close your eyes, and imagine you're on a tropical island with a naked girl massaging your shoulders? This made no sense to me at all. Does it make sense to you?"

"Not really," I said.

"Then they talked a lot about family dynamics, as if the way we were raised made us addicts. Then the next day they told us that scientists believed that alcoholism and addictions are hereditary. Well, listen, either it's in your DNA or it isn't, right? I'm no scientist, but even I know that. Seriously, the whole thing was one big clusterfuck of theories, ideas, facts, and wild guesses, none relating to the other. By the time my twenty-eight days were done, I was ready to leave. It was like I had been going to a school run by the Three Stooges, and I haven't even told you the worst of it. Do you know what their suggestion was for me to remain sober after being discharged? They told me to go to AA meetings, and they said AA was the only real way I was going to make it. Can you believe that crap? After all their reading, lectures, meetings, and group therapy sessions, their final solution to the whole thing was for me to just go to AA. Jesus, it was unbelievable."

"Are you going to AA meetings?"

"No," my brother said.

"Are you sober?"

"So far, so good. But I have no idea how I'm doing it. It probably won't last. That's just between you and me."

And it didn't last.

Three months after leaving rehab, my brother was drinking again. His drinking was even worse than before. I think it was worse because he now thought of himself as a failure and lost his self-respect. Dad finally put his foot down, and in a fit of tough love, he kicked Jerry out of the house and told him to get his life together. Mom was against sending him away, but it had to be done. They were enabling him. They were prolonging Jerry's misery by providing for him. At this point, Jerry and I were no longer talking. I didn't like him. It was as if he was a completely different person—a man I no longer knew. After Dad had kicked him out, Jerry took on odd jobs as a construction laborer, and he lived in a one-room dump up in East Los Angeles. This went on for over a year, until Dad met a man at work named Harold Milton. It would turn out that Harold would save Jerry's life.

Harold was a very interesting man. He was my dad's new supervisor, and he'd just moved to California from New Jersey. The owner of the company knew about all the problems my parents were having with Jerry, and he gave Harold all the details. It turned out Harold was a reformed alcoholic, and the man had not touched a drop of booze for eighteen years. He was not in AA. He did not go to a psychiatrist, and he had never been to rehab. But he had stopped drinking, and he was now leading a productive and happy life. Harold talked to my dad about Jerry, and my dad asked him to help. He asked if Harold would meet with Jerry and share his secret to staying sober. Harold told my dad it was no secret, but that he would be happy to talk to Jerry. It took some time to finally get Jerry to agree to the meeting, but the two men finally got together for lunch. I was not there, so I can't tell you exactly what was said. But I can tell you what Jerry told me six months afterward. Believe it or not, he was now sober. He was still working as a construction laborer, and he was still living in that one-room dump. But he was also planning to move soon to a much nicer apartment, and he had a steady job lined up. He looked so different. His eyes were clear, his clothes were clean, and his hair was cut. Seriously, I hardly recognized him.

"I think I'm going to make it this time," he said.

"That's great," I replied.

"This guy Harold—I really like the guy. And I think he may have saved my life."

"What did he do?"

"It's not what he did. It's what he said."

"Well, what did he say?"

"Something no one else ever said to me. This guy has been sober for eighteen years, and do you want to know how he did it? He follows a simple rule. When he first told me his rule, I thought he was crazy. I did, and I thought the rule was lame. Then I thought more and more about it, and I don't know how to explain what happened, but something just clicked. Suddenly, it all made sense. I'm not sure you'll understand, since you're not an alcoholic. It was so simple."

"What did he say?" I asked.

"Five little words: 'Don't take the first drink.' It's my new mantra."

"That's it?"

"I told you that you wouldn't get it."

"I guess I don't."

"Those five words changed my life."

"Well if it works for you, I'm all for it."

"It works for me."

And that's all that mattered. If it worked for Jerry, then it worked, period. I'm not an alcoholic, so I'm probably the wrong person to ask why these five words are so significant. But they are to my brother. Jerry is now happily married and working as a building contractor up in LA County. He got a license and started his own business. The last time we talked, Jerry said he was taking his family to Hawaii for a three-week vacation.

So you see, I am not at all averse to simple solutions to complex problems. And maybe Dr. Trill's simple little poem for Jacob would be just what he needed. His poem. His mantra. A gate to be opened.

CHAPTER 21

A CLOSE CALL

—— •●• ——

I took the piece of paper with Dr. Trill's poem for Jacob home with me, and later that evening I looked at it again. I was sitting at my desk in my study, and I read the poem out loud to myself. I read it again and again:

> It didn't cost you one thin dime,
> So why are you inclined to whine.
> Ride it to the end of the line.
> Thank the conductor for his time.

It was a good poem. I thought about it, and then I closed my eyes and opened them. The next thing I knew, Jacob had been released from Pacific Acres, and he was now wearing a crimson mortarboard and gown, graduating from high school. He still had absolutely no plans to go to college, but he did have plans. He wanted to move out of our house, and he wanted to earn his own living. His outlook on life had improved significantly thanks to the time he'd been spending with Dr. Trill. Just one month after graduating, he got a job at the Berkshire Real Estate Company installing signs on their properties. I had heard of Berkshire. Who hadn't? Their real estate signs were all over Southern California. They said they'd provide Jacob with a pickup truck and the tools he would need, and they gave him a credit card to buy gas. The job paid just a few dollars above minimum wage, but Jacob was fine with that. He found a one-bedroom apartment to live in that was located in a lousy part of Santa Ana. April and I told him he could live at home to save some money, but it was important to Jacob that he be independent.

Meanwhile, life at the box company changed, and in a rather big way. Do you remember me telling you about the owner of the company, Harry

Bright? Well, there's something you should know about Harry. He was a thrill-seeker. He would go on these crazy adventurous vacations all over the world, and then he'd come back and tell everyone how he'd risked his life. I'm sure there are other people like this, but I'm not one of them. And whenever Harry told me about one of these vacations, I'd sit and listen politely, thinking to myself, "What kind of idiot would do something like that?" To me, vacations were all about swimming and splashing in pool water, lying in the sun, reading paperback books, drinking tropical drinks, and looking at young women in their swimsuits out of the corner of my eye. Risking my life was never part of the plan. But Harry? He did some of the craziest things, one of them being riding a bicycle downhill on the Yungas Road in Bolivia. I knew about this road; it was called "the most dangerous road in the world." Look it up on the internet. I kid you not.

Harry signed up for a bicycle tour. He and the others were rolling merrily downhill when they came up to a rock. The rock had rolled down from the face of the mountain above. The rock, which was about the size of a grapefruit, was right in Harry's path, so he tried to steer clear by jerking his handlebars. Unfortunately, he jerked them too hard, and the bike and Harry went tumbling out of control, sailing right off the cliff. He bounced off the mountain face over and over, like a grotesque rag doll, until his broken and bloody body lay dead. When he signed up for the tour, they told him twenty-two cyclists had died on the road since 1998. I guess they could now make that twenty-three.

It was one of Harry's major-minors, right? It was a single rock the innocuous size of a fruit, coming loose at precisely the wrong time and at the wrong place. Who would've guessed? What were the odds such a minor event would not only take Harry's life but would also turn my own world upside down? One little rock, and the next thing I knew, Harry's vile shrew of a wife was in charge of the company I worked for. She was now the sole owner, and I answered directly to her. Two weeks after Harry died, she called on me to come over to her home to discuss my future with the company.

"I've been going over some things," she said. "One of them being your contract."

"My contract?"

"Yes, are you aware your contract comes up to be reviewed in six months?"

"Yes, I'm aware of that."

"You do realize this is a family-owned business, right?"

"Yes," I said.

"And now that Harry's gone, you understand that I'm calling the shots?"

"I understand that." At this point I knew the news she was about to give me was not going to be good.

"Do you remember meeting my little brother?"

"I'm not sure I do."

"He comes to the Christmas parties. Surely you must've met him. His name is Kaleb."

"Maybe I did meet him."

"Here's the thing about Kaleb. He's bright, and he's hardworking. He's responsible, clever, and he gets along well with people. But his life has been disappointing. It's been one disappointment after the other. The poor kid has never caught a break the way some people do. You caught a break, Stan. You caught a break when you met Harry at that bar in Newport. Why do you suppose some people get all the breaks?"

"I don't know."

"Well, now it's Kaleb's turn."

"I don't follow you."

"It's my brother's turn to catch a break, and I'm the one who's going to give it to him. Do you get my drift?"

"Not really," I said.

"How long have you worked for us?"

"About sixteen years."

"And you've been paid well?"

"I'm very happy with my salary."

"So you can say you got your money's worth out of Harry, right? My husband always treated you well, didn't he? You don't have any complaints?"

"No, I have no complaints."

"Well, now it's Kaleb's turn."

"I'm not sure what that means." I did understand. I just didn't want to believe it.

"It means it's Kaleb's turn to run the company, and it's your time to step aside. You said you got your money's worth. You said you have no complaints."

"Are you firing me?"

"No, I'm not firing you. You still have six months left on your contract. I'd like you to spend this time teaching Kaleb everything you know about the company, showing him the ropes, so to speak."

"You want me to help him take over my job?"

"Yes, something like that."

"I see," I said. Christ, I can't even imagine the look that was probably on my face. I was flabbergasted. But what could I do or say? The woman was right about one thing—she was calling the shots.

I went home after my meeting with Audrey, and I told April the horrible news. She couldn't believe it, and the upcoming months were like a bad dream. I simultaneously had to train Audrey's couldn't-catch-a-break brother to take my place, and I had to look for a new job.

I will not forget the first day I met Kaleb for as long as I live. No, I didn't remember ever meeting him at a Christmas party. If I'd met him, I would've remembered. Jesus, what a dork this guy was, and it was infuriating to think Audrey felt this was the sort of character who was qualified to replace me. What she must've thought of me.

The first thing I noticed about Kaleb was his ridiculous moustache. As a rule, I detest moustaches, but this one really took the cake. Listen; there are men who can wear moustaches successfully. Burt Reynolds and Tom Selleck come to mind. Even William Powell pulled it off (although his wasn't much of a moustache). But Kaleb? He looked like a cross between a third-rate male porn star and a two-bit grifter. Although I suppose if he were a porn star, they would also have had him wear a nice toupee to disguise his balding head. He wasn't bald, but he was getting there.

The second thing I noticed about Kaleb was the way he dressed. Jesus, did this guy have any idea we were living in the twenty-first century? How long had he kept his same clothes? He looked like a *Newlywed Game* contestant from the 1970s who had just gotten done bickering with his fat wife about the answer to some idiotic Bob Eubanks question. Damn it all, they weren't going to win the refrigerator or the washer and dryer. They were going home with nothing.

The third thing I noticed about Kaleb was his New Jersey accent. It was the icing on the cake. I figured Audrey was also from New Jersey, and although I wasn't impressed with her, at least she had the good sense to lose the New Jersey accent somewhere along the way. There's something about New Jersey accents, isn't there? I mean, they're fine if you live in New Jersey, since all the people there talk like aspiring mafiosi. But talking like that in California? Kaleb may as well have worn a sign around his neck that said, "Where should I bury the fuckin' body?"

The first day Kaleb came to the plant, I took him on a long tour and showed him everything. I kept an eye on his face as I took him around, watching to see if he was actually absorbing the tremendous amount of information I was feeding to him, and it was weird. I felt as if I were giving the tour to a kid with Down syndrome. That's probably not a very politically correct thing to say, but that's exactly what it felt like. I didn't feel as though my effort was going anywhere. When we were done, I asked Kaleb what he thought, and he said, "I still can't believe you don't have a lock on the supply closet. Anyone can just go in there and take anything they want. That's the first thing I'm going to do. I'm going to put a lock on that door. I want everyone here to know I run a tight ship."

I laughed. He was Captain Queeg's twin brother with a New Jersey accent and a bad moustache. Wait until the employees got a load of this guy and all his plans to run a tight ship. This idiot didn't know what he was in for.

Then there was the job hunting. As if it wasn't bad enough that I had to spend time training Kaleb to take over my job, I also had to find a new job for myself. The first interview I had was with a man named Chad Montgomery. Chad was starting up a brand-new windshield wiper company with funds he had borrowed from his father. He showed me a sample of the wipers, and he told me the ingenious new design was patented. "There won't be anyone in the country who can compete with us," he said. "We'll have the entire market to ourselves."

Well, yes, I thought. *You'll have the market to yourself, except for the fact that the market is already being served just fine.* Seriously, what is so wrong with the wipers that have been selling for years? I don't remember having any pressing concerns about the wipers on my own car. It rains on my windshield, then it gets wiped away, and then it rains on the windshield again. When I asked Chad how much his newfangled blades would cost consumers, he said he was working out a deal with a manufacturer in China so that the blades could sell for only about twice what blades were selling for now. I told Chad I didn't really get it, and he said I obviously wasn't the kind of forward thinker he was searching for to take the reins of his company.

Another company I found was a cosmetics corporation in the market for someone to take over the management of their skin care products division. The man I met with was Wilbur Farmer. Wilbur seemed like a nice enough guy, and the sales figures he showed me for the past five years were impressive. I knew next to nothing about skin care products, so I took him on his word that everything was on the level. "We're looking for someone to come aboard right away," Wilbur said. "The sooner we hire, the better." This opportunity was interesting, and I told Wilbur I would think about it that night and call him the next day. That night I went on the internet and did some research. I found out that the company had just been hit with a billion-dollar class action suit for selling skin care products that were causing an alarming rate of severe skin rashes among its steady users. The rashes started out as small red patches that eventually grew into colonies of painful blisters and scabs that left unsightly scars on the faces of women. I guess Wilbur wasn't such a nice guy after all. Seemed he was looking for a sucker to go down with his sinking ship, not someone to run a thriving skin car division. I didn't bother to call Wilbur the next day, and he didn't bother to call me.

Another opening I looked into was a position as the vice president of operations for a large Mexican restaurant chain called Vida Frijoles. I'd seen them around. They had restaurants all over California, Nevada, and Arizona. I'm not sure how many stores there were altogether, but there were a lot. Their corporate offices were in Irvine, on the sixth floor of a small high-rise office building. I'll describe the place to you. As soon as you get off the elevator, you're met by a security guard at a big built-in desk who wears a gun, uniform, badge, and cap. At his desk are several TV monitors and a bank of buttons, lights, and switches. There is also a computer monitor and keyboard, and when you give the security guard your name, he checks his computer to see if you're on the official list. Then he asks for your driver's license or passport to confirm you are who you claim to be. Once your identity is confirmed, you have to give the guard a thumbprint on a small device, like the device they use at the DMV. You're then asked to stand perfectly still while the guard frisks you and passes his metal detector wand up and down your body. If you're deemed okay, the guard clips a color-coded ID tag on your shirt and unlocks a big door. On the other side of the door is a woman dressed in a white lab coat. She is carrying a clipboard, and she asks you for your name, scribbling it down on a sheet of paper. "Right this way," she says, and you follow her down a hall to another door. She knocks on this door, and it opens. And guess what? There's another stupid uniformed security guard with a gun, and he leads you to your destination, holding your elbow to keep you from veering off course. In my case, the destination was Colonel Rank's office. Colonel Rank just so happened to be the owner of Vida Frijoles. Yes, I was being interviewed by the top dog, a man who obviously took his company very seriously. "It's a jungle out there," he said as I entered, and he motioned for me to take a seat. He hadn't asked me even one question, and I knew this wasn't the right place for me.

Of course, I'm telling you about some of the worst job openings I found, but still, it was becoming clear to me how much I liked my job at Harry's box company and how little I wanted to work anywhere else. Why did Harry have to die? Why did that little rock have to roll? That goddamn rock!

Then it was like a miracle. Three months after the fateful evening I met with Audrey the Shrew, and three months into my frustrating search for a new job, an old friend of Harry's made Audrey an offer she couldn't refuse. He wanted to buy the box company, and he wanted to pay all cash. Audrey jumped at the offer, greedy as she was, and the next thing I knew, Kaleb was gone and I was back in charge. The new owner was a man named Art Fagen. If I wasn't such a flaming heterosexual, I would've grabbed Art by both ears and kissed him on his seventy-two-year-old lips. Jesus, what a relief!

During this period of uncertainty, I became keenly aware of something. For several months I had lost track of Jacob. He was no longer living at our house, so I didn't see him in the mornings for breakfast or in the evenings for dinner. And I hadn't talked to him on the phone. On one hand, it was a nice little interlude, focusing only on myself and my own problems, but I also missed my son.

April had been in touch with Jacob during these months, so she knew what he was up to. But rather than have her give me a rundown of his life, I decided to call Jacob and ask him to have lunch with me. It would be a great opportunity for the two of us to catch up, and we decided to meet at a café in Newport Beach. April thought this was a good idea. She also said I was going to be surprised. "How so?" I asked. She said that if she told me, it wouldn't be much of a surprise. "Just brace yourself," she said.

We were to meet at a small place on the peninsula that served salads, soups, and sandwiches. I arrived early, and I took a seat at one of the outside tables. I ordered a cup of coffee, and I waited for Jacob to show up. He was right on time.

Well, I just about spit my coffee across the table when I saw him. In fact, I blinked my eyes several times and pinched my arm just to be sure I wasn't dreaming. But it was Jacob, all right. The long hair was gone. He had gotten himself a haircut. It was shorter than my hair, cut close to his skull—not like a marine, but pretty darn short. He looked so different, and it wasn't just the haircut. He was dressed in slacks with a brown leather belt, leather shoes, and a plaid button-down shirt that looked as if it'd been ironed flat just an hour ago. And he was wearing a watch. In the eighteen years I'd known him, I don't think he'd ever worn a watch. Not once.

"Holy moly," I said. "Look at you!"

"You like?" Jacob asked.

"You look great. But aren't you a little overdressed to be putting up signs?"

"I'm no longer putting up signs."

"Are you working somewhere else?"

"No, I'm still at Berkshire."

"Then what are you doing there?"

"I'm an assistant coordinator."

"Meaning what?"

"I help out the salesmen and brokers."

"Well, I'll be damned," I said. "How did you come to get that job?"

"One of the brokers I was installing signs for took a liking to me. I don't know why, but he did. His name is Hank Mathews. Hank asked me if I had a desire to do something other than put up signs. I said, "Sure, why the heck not?" So he talked to his boss, and it turned out they had an immediate opening for an assistant coordinator. Hank told his boss he thought I had a lot of potential and that he would like to see me fill the position. So I cut off my long hair and bought some new clothes. Mom helped me pick out the clothes. Then I went in and got interviewed by Hank's boss, and I guess he liked me too. They offered me the job, and now I'm making twice what I made before. And I like my job. In fact, I think I like real estate. I signed up for a real estate course on the internet, and they guarantee that after I take their classes I'll be able to pass the state exam and get a license. That's what I'm shooting for—to get my license. I think I could be good at this."

"Jesus," I said. "This is great news."

"What are you going to get?"

"Pardon me?"

"For lunch."

"I thought I'd get a tuna salad sandwich," I said.

"I'm going to get soup. They have great soup here."

"Sounds good to me."

"You want to hear a joke?"

"A joke?" I asked. Seriously, I couldn't recall Jacob ever telling me a joke. "Yes, let's hear your joke."

"There's a man and a woman in a restaurant, and they're eating lunch. The waitress is near their table, and she notices the strangest thing. For no apparent reason, the man has slid under table. The waitress steps up to the woman, and she says, "Honey, your husband seems to have slipped off his seat." The woman says, "Oh, no, you're wrong about that. My husband just walked into the restaurant.""

I laughed.

"Where'd you hear that one?"

"From Hank. He knows a million of them. He has a joke for every occasion. He told me that one the last time we went to lunch together."

Would you have been worried? I probably shouldn't have been fretting, but I was. The transformation seemed too fast and perfect. How long ago was it that April and I found Jacob bleeding in our shower stall? I did the math in my head. It had been about nine months. Jacob had gone from a kid trying to take his own life to a young man having lunch with his dad, ordering soup, and telling a waitress joke.

"I know another one," Jacob said. "You want to hear it?"

"Sure," I said.

"A woman goes into a restaurant with her seven sons. The boys all start horsing around, and the woman says, 'Tommy, stop it right now and sit still.' The boys all stop goofing around, and they behave themselves. The waitress asks, 'Did you really name all of your boys Tommy?' The woman says yes, she sure did. Then the waitress asks, 'What do you do if you just want to talk to one of them for some reason?' The woman smiles and says, 'I just call him by his last name.'"

"Funny," I said.

"Not as good as the first one?"

"I liked them both."

"I know some others that are kind of gross."

"No need to go there," I said.

"Have you talked to Zach lately?" Jacob asked.

"I talked to him yesterday."

"How's he doing?"

"He seems to like college. It's not as easy as high school for him, but he says he's getting Bs and Cs."

"I used to wish I was more like him."

"You did?"

"Sometimes I did."

"How about now?"

"I think I'm happy, Dad."

"That's good to hear."

But I was still worried about him. He could've told me a hundred more jokes. He could've been wearing a three-piece suit and a Rolex watch. He could've been driving a brand-new red Ferrari, but it wouldn't have mattered. I was so used to worrying about Jacob that it had now become a reflex. Let me tell you something: When you find your son in your shower with his wrists slashed, and with his blood spurting from his body, the image of that doesn't go away. It haunts you. It stays with you a long, long time.

CHAPTER 22

THE PARTY

—•—

Several days after Jacob and I had lunch in Newport, I stopped at the grocery store on the way home from work to buy a bag of dog food for Ralph. Yes, Ralph was really Jacob's dog, but Jacob wasn't allowed to have pets in his apartment, so April and I were taking care of the animal.

At the grocery store, I pushed my cart down the aisle, and you won't believe who I ran into. It was good old Mrs. Hardin. If you don't recall, Mrs. Hardin was Jacob's wonderfully buxom third-grade teacher—the one who adored Jacob, and the one who talked him into entering the school science fair. She looked exactly the same as she did when Jacob was younger. She wore a blue-and-white Hawaiian muumuu, and her hair was a disheveled disaster. She wore bright red lipstick and too much rouge, and she still wore those weird, pointy glasses. Her face lit up like a Christmas tree when she recognized me.

"Mr. Harper!" she said.

"Mrs. Hardin," I replied. "It's good to see you."

"It's so great to see you."

"Still teaching at the school?"

"Teaching the fourth grade now. But I'm still at it. How is Jacob doing?"

"He's doing well," I said.

"How old is he? Wow, how the time does goes by. Has he graduated from high school yet?"

"He graduated this year."

"Is he going to college?"

"Not to college. He didn't want to go."

"Oh?" Mrs. Hardin said. She seemed a little surprised to learn this.

"We tried to talk him into it. I just don't think school is his thing."

"Such a shame."

"He'll be okay."

"What is he doing now?"

"He's working for a real estate company. He's some kind of a coordinator. He's going to get his license soon. He signed up for a course."

"Real estate?"

"He seems excited about it."

Mrs. Hardin gave me a curious look, and then she said, "I have a hard time picturing him selling houses."

"His company sells and leases commercial and industrial properties. They don't get involved in houses. It's a whole different ball of wax."

"I see."

"He seems happy. I think that's what matters."

"Of course," Mrs. Hardin said. She stared at me for a moment, and then said, "Do you remember that science fair project?"

"The toaster named Fred?"

"Yes, yes, the toaster. God, how I loved your boy. He was so darn bright, and so creative. He should've won first place that day."

"I think he would agree with you."

"Do you remember his civics lecture?"

"Civics lecture?"

"When he gave our class an hour-long lecture on how he would reorganize our government."

"I don't recall that one."

Mrs. Hardin thought for a moment and then said, "Well, of course you don't. How silly of me. You weren't even there that day. But I wish you had been. I asked each student to stand up in front of the class and tell the other kids something they would like to see done that would make our world a better place to live. If I remember right, one child said summer vacations should be made a couple months longer, and another kid said children should be allowed to drive when they turned fourteen. Another kid said wars should be made illegal. It was the usual third-grade stuff, until your son Jacob stood in front of the class and spoke."

"What'd he say?"

"He had everything worked out in his head. He said we had to revamp our entire representative government. He said that everything wrong with the country was the fault of adults, and the older the adults were, the worse their influence was. His idea was to establish a government operated exclusively by children. I raised my hand and asked him if he didn't think experience was important, and he said experience was a hindrance and a detriment, and not an advantage. He said experience was basically just the accumulation of prejudices, hatreds, greed, corruption, and vices. He said your average child had none of these debilitating flaws in his or her personality—that the flaws were handed down to them by their parents. He said the perfect and uncorrupted mind was not the mind of an older man or woman, but the mind of a child who had not yet been tainted—the mind of a child whose intellect was tapped before adults had a chance to corrupt it. In his ideal government, children, rather than adults, would be selected according to their raw intellect and put in all positions of power. This way the country would be run by the closest thing we could get to unsullied intelligence and thoughtfulness. I'm not doing as good of a job as your son did explaining this idea, but I have to tell you—your son was very persuasive. His plan actually made a lot of sense to me. Unfortunately I don't think the rest of the class had any idea what he was talking about."

I laughed. "Jacob had a special way with words and ideas," I said. "He also had a way of confusing people."

"Had?" Mrs. Hardin asked.

Her question caught me by surprise. "Well, I guess he still does. I mean, yes he does."

"I certainly hope so."

"How's Mr. Hardin?" I asked, changing the subject.

"He's doing fine."

"Do you two still visit Hawaii?"

"Every year. Got to stock up on muumuus, you know. And macadamia nuts."

"It was nice to see you again."

"Tell Jacob to drop by the school. I'm always there for an hour or two after class gets out. I'd love to see him if he would come by."

"I'm sure he'd like to see you too."

"I have all these kids in my classes. I seldom get to see them when they grow up."

"That's a shame."

"It is, isn't it? Well, I guess I'd better get going. It was so nice talking to you."

We said goodbye to each other and went our different ways. As I pushed my cart toward the store cashier, I thought about the science fair and Fred the toaster. It made me smile for a moment. Jacob was one of a kind. Now Jacob was telling jokes and studying to get a real estate license, and honestly I now wasn't sure exactly how I felt.

Shortly after Jacob turned nineteen, he passed his state real estate test. It was a very big deal. They threw a party for him at the Berkshire offices, and Jacob invited April and me to come. He wanted us to meet all the people he worked with, and we wanted to meet them. The party started at five on a Friday evening, and there was a catered buffet so everyone could get food in their stomachs to absorb all the alcohol they were drinking. There was a full bar that had been set up near the conference room, and the drinks were on the house. There was loud music, and the furniture had been moved against the walls in the reception area to create an area for people to dance. I was impressed at how much trouble they went to on Jacob's behalf. Or maybe these people just liked having an excuse to throw a party.

I was surprised at how many people were there. They were still all dressed in their work clothes, but many of the men had loosened or taken off their ties. When we arrived at the party, nearly everyone had a paper plate full of food in his or her hand. April and I approached the buffet and loaded up our own plates with an assortment of hors d'oeuvres. Jacob said he wanted to introduce us to a few people, and the first person he led us to was Hank, the broker who was responsible for getting our son into the real estate racket; he was the one who had taken a liking to our son. I was surprised at how short Hank was. He was a fireplug of a man, very nicely dressed and groomed, and as soon as we met, he shook my hand as if he were pumping water from an old water pump.

"It's nice to finally meet you," he said.

"It's nice to meet you," I said.

Hank handed me a business card, and I stuffed it in my pants pocket. Then Hank said, "I've heard a lot about both of you."

"You have?"

"Jacob talks about you all the time."

"Not all the time," Jacob said.

"I think family is very important," Hank said.

"Yes, so do we."

"I wish my parents were behind me."

"Your parents don't support you?"

"They wanted me to become a doctor. Anything in medicine would've made them happy. Dad is an oncologist, and Mom is a pediatrician. I think they really wanted me to keep the royal bloodline going. The last thing they had in mind for me was to become a real estate broker."

"That's too bad."

"But I love what I do here."

"Well, then that's good."

"Yes, a person needs to follow his own dreams, right? I would've been miserable as a doctor, poking and prodding sick human bodies all day, examining bodily fluids, looking into ears and down throats and up rear ends. No, no, that wasn't meant for me."

"No," I said. "I don't think I'd would've liked that either."

"You run a box company?"

"Yes," I said.

"Jacob told me."

"I enjoy it," I said. "It's challenging and rewarding. And the pay is good."

"I should put you in touch with Ned Andrews. He's a broker here. One of his clients is one of the largest moving companies in the country. I'll bet they buy a ton of boxes. Who knows? Maybe they'll buy them from you."

"Who knows?"

"I'll introduce you to Ned before you leave."

"Thanks."

Hank picked up a tiny bite-sized sandwich from his paper plate, stuffing it past his lips. With his mouth full, he said, "People don't realize how important real estate is. Yes, we basically just help clients to buy, sell, and lease property, but we're also like the central nervous system of the county. Everything goes through us. We're on a first-name basis with anyone who has any skin in the game. When a company needs a building or property to conduct their operations, who do they come to?

They don't come running to their doctors, or lawyers, or gardeners, or dry cleaners. They come to us. They need us, and they depend on us. Business is the flowing lifeblood of the community, and you can count on this; the business world couldn't function without us."

"I never thought of real estate that way," I said.

"You'll find some very bright people working here. Your son will feel right at home."

"That's good," I said.

"Jacob is very bright."

I could see this embarrassed Jacob. He was, of course, very bright, but he didn't like people talking about it in front of him. "Yes, he is," I agreed.

"I've still got a lot to learn," Jacob said.

"He's just being humble," Hank said, smiling. "The kid has what it takes. He's going to be a big success here."

"We're glad you think that," April said.

"You did a good job raising him."

"Thanks," April said.

"Who have we here?" a man said. He had joined our group, and like everyone else, he had a paper plate full of food in his hand. He was tall and sturdy, like a tree, and he had a low baritone voice.

"These are the kid's parents," Hank said. Then to April and me he said, "This is Clyde Clauson. He's our in-house attorney."

"Nice to meet you," I said.

"Here's my card," Clyde said, and he handed me his business card. I stuffed it in my pants pocket.

"I heard two new ones," Hank said to Clyde.

"I've probably heard them."

"I don't think so."

"What are you talking about?" April asked.

"Attorney jokes," Hank said.

"I've heard them all," Clyde said.

"I'd like to hear them," Jacob said.

"Go on," Clyde said to Hank. "The kid wants to hear them. This is, after all, his night."

"Very well," Hank said. "The first one is about a man who is sent to hell for his sins. As he's being led by Satan to the hot depths of his eternal torment, he sees a lawyer passionately kissing a very beautiful woman. "What the heck is this?" the man asks Satan. "I have to roast my butt off in hot flames for all eternity, and that lawyer gets to spend all his time kissing that beautiful woman." Satan just snarls and says, "Who are you to question how I punish that woman?"

Everyone laughed. "That was pretty good," I said. "I've never heard that one."

"Okay, I'll admit I've never heard it either," Clyde said.

"What's the second one?" Jacob asked.

"It's about a fifty-year-old lawyer," Hank said. "The guy is sent to the pearly gates for judgment. The lawyer tells St. Peter, "There must be some mistake. I'm only fifty years old. That's far too young to die." St. Peter looks at his big book and says, "Well, that's odd. When we added up the hours you billed to your clients, we figured you were at least eighty-three."

I laughed and said, "That was even better than the first one."

"Everyone likes to pick on attorneys," Clyde said. He was smiling when he said this.

"If you all weren't such sleazy snakes in the grass, maybe people wouldn't pick on you." Clyde was still smiling. It was all in good fun.

"Excuse me," Clyde said. "I see someone I need to talk to. I've been trying to reach him all day."

"It was nice to meet you," I said.

"Likewise," Clyde said, and he left our group.

"That man is a lifesaver," Hank said. "He's gotten me out of more little legal jams than I care to admit."

"Aren't you going to introduce me?" a girl's voice said. I say she was a girl, but she was probably in her early twenties. She was standing beside Jacob as if she knew him well.

"This is Amy," Jacob said to us.

"Amy Jackson," she said. She reached out, and we took turns shaking her hand.

"Amy is one of the secretaries here," Jacob said.

"I've worked here for three years. I adore your son. I've been looking forward to meeting you."

"Oh?"

"Jacob has told me so much about you."

"Not that much," Jacob said.

"How much has Jacob told you about me?" Amy asked. She was batting her eyelashes.

"They don't know about you," Jacob said.

"Shame on you, Jacob," Amy said.

"I was going to tell them all about you. I just haven't gotten around to it."

"Is there something we should know?" April asked.

"I'm going to leave you four alone," Hank said.

"You don't have to go," Jacob said.

"Seems you have some explaining to do to your parents," Hank said to Jacob. "I'll see you all around." Hank then left us to join another group. Amy was smiling as if she was proud of something. I'll describe Amy before I continue. She was about Jacob's height, but she was a little heavy. She was not what you'd call fat or obese, but she certainly wasn't thin. She had short red hair, a lovely smile, and porcelain skin. She was dressed tastefully, the way you'd expect a professional secretary to dress at a reputable real estate company. This evening she was wearing a green sweater and green skirt that made her own green eyes appear greener than they probably were. If someone had been taking bets, I would've bet she was an Irish American, or at least a good part Irish. But she had no Irish accent. She sounded Californian.

"Jacob and I are an item," she said.

"An item?" April asked. She was looking at Jacob.

"I was going to introduce you to her tonight," Jacob explained.

"Any friend of Jacob's is a friend of ours," I said. I didn't want Amy to feel uncomfortable.

April said nothing.

"I suppose Jacob hasn't told you about the trip?"

"The trip?" I asked.

"We're going to Rio next month."

"Rio de Janeiro?"

"My mom and dad are paying for it."

"They've met Jacob?"

"Oh, yes. They both love him."

"You're going to stay in a hotel together?" April asked.

"Yes, Mom," Jacob said. "That's usually how it works when you go on a vacation."

"I see."

"I think that's great," I said.

"Have either of you been there?" Amy asked.

"No," April said. "We've never been to Rio."

"My parents go there all the time. They love it there. They've taken me with them several times. It's a long plane flight, but it's worth it."

"Whenever I think of Rio, I think of *The Girl from Ipanema*," I said. "The Stan Getz version."

"What do your parents do?" April asked Amy.

"My dad is an executive at a pharmaceutical company, and Mom is an attorney."

"Where do they live?"

"In Newport Beach. That's where I grew up. They moved out here from North Carolina twenty-five years ago. Jacob tells me you live in Coto de Caza."

"Yes," I said.

"We met at the beach years ago," April said.

"I don't think I could live in a place like Coto," Amy said. "I need to be close to the ocean. I love being close to the ocean. I love everything about it."

"I used to feel the same way," April said.

"We were told Coto was a better place to raise children," I said. "Too many weird things happening near the beach. And the kids there are spoiled."

"I think I turned out fine," Amy said.

"I'm sure you did," April said. "Where do you live now?"

"I'm living with my parents. There's no way I can afford a decent place on what they're paying me here at Berkshire."

"Did you attend any college?"

"I graduated last year. I was a straight-A student and a philosophy major. That's why I'm a secretary at a real estate company."

I wondered why Amy's successful parents hadn't guided her toward a more useful degree. But who knows why people do what they do? Maybe people were looking at me and wondering why Jacob wasn't going to college at all.

"Do you want to see where I work?" Jacob asked us. "I can show you my cubicle."

"We'd like that," April said.

Jacob then took us to his workstation. It wasn't much to speak of, a little space surrounded by portable partition walls, but I was suddenly so proud of him. Seeing where he worked made the whole thing seem very real. There were some pictures of the family thumbtacked on the wall, as well as a couple pictures of Amy. Also on the wall was the poem Dr. Trill had given to us a couple years ago. I stepped up to the poem, and I read it out loud:

> It didn't cost you one thin dime,
> So why are you inclined to whine?
> Ride it to the end of the line.
> Thank the conductor for his time.

"I read it every day," Jacob said. "Usually first thing in the morning."

"It makes more sense every time I hear it," April said.

"Jacob made a copy of it for me," Amy said. "I have it in my office."

"You like it?" I asked.

"I love it."

I didn't mention anything to Amy about Dr. Trill or Pacific Acres. I had no idea how close Jacob and Amy had become. I had no idea how much about his life he had revealed to the girl. For all I knew, she thought he was just another really smart kid who was raised in Orange County and who opted out of college to work in the real estate business. Talking to Jacob now, one would never have guessed how badly the boy was hurt and tortured as a child and an adolescent, or how unhappy he had become, or how he had, on one otherwise normal Saturday afternoon, decided to remove all his clothes and climb into our pool house shower to slash open his wrists with a razor blade. One would never have guessed that the hospital staff had to tie him down to a gurney in order to sew him up, or that they had transferred him to a mental hospital, or that he spent over a month in yet another mental hospital, fighting for his mental health.

Jesus, I now hated to even think about those days. They were not pleasant memories.

"Do they have any champagne here?" I asked.

"I'm sure they do," Amy said.

"Let's all go to the bar and get some champagne. I feel like making a toast. I feel like toasting my son, the real estate tycoon-to-be."

"Sounds good," Amy said. She led the way, and the rest of us followed behind her to the bar. We got in line. I wasn't even thinking about Jacob being underage.

While in line, April said to me, "Do you think we should be encouraging Jacob to drink?"

"One glass of champagne isn't going to kill him."

"I guess it's okay, April said.

When we reached the bartender, everyone got their glasses of champagne, and we walked back to where we were earlier. I raised my glass up high and said, "This is to Jacob passing his state exam."

"Hear, hear," Amy said.

"And here's to Rio," Jacob said.

"Sure," I said. "Why not. Here's a toast to Rio. Let's hear it for Rio."

CHAPTER 23

THE CRAB PALACE

———— •●• ————

When Jacob was about to turn twenty-one, I found myself alone in my study, reminiscing with his box of writings. I had taken off the lid and was going through the papers. Reading all these poems was very nostalgic, and it brought back an avalanche of memories. It was funny, but I hadn't added anything new to the box for several years. There were mostly poems about all sorts of topics, and there were other bits of writing as well, some of which I've already shared with you. One I haven't yet shared was a fable Jacob wrote in high school for his English class. They were reading *Aesop's Fables*, and the teacher had the kids make up and write their own fables. The teacher gave Jacob an A for his effort, and I remember when he gave me the story to read. It was titled *The Marksman*, and it went as follows:

The Marksman

Once upon a time in the dry hills of California, a family of field mice lived among the weeds and bushes. They fed off wild berries and seeds that were plentiful. Not far from where they lived, there was an old farmhouse occupied by a marksman. He lived alone, but on his property he had two horses, a donkey, three hogs, a German shepherd, and three cats. One cat was solid gray with white feet, another was a calico, and the third was a brown tabby. One day one of the young field mice strayed from its mother while foraging for wild berries, and it found itself near the marksman's property. It came close to the backyard, where the calico cat was sleeping in the sun, and upon seeing the cat it thought,

My, what a large and colorful mouse it is who lives here at this house.

Undaunted and inexperienced, the small mouse crept up to investigate the large mouse, and its little footsteps woke the cat up. The cat looked around, finally seeing the little mouse approaching. "A mouse!" the cat said under its breath, and it got down low and crawled toward the little creature. Meanwhile, the mother mouse had noticed that her child was missing, and she was calling for it. But the little mouse was too far away to hear her. Slowly the cat approached the little mouse, and then, without any warning at all, the cat pounced upon the young mouse and grabbed it with its sharp claws. Realizing this was no mouse and that its life was in imminent danger, the little mouse shrieked at the top of its lungs. But there was no one nearby who could hear it. After pawing and cruelly playing with the little mouse, the cat finally bit into its head, and then into its back, and then into its head again. Before the mouse knew it, it was bleeding and as good as dead, and finally the cat proceeded to eat it.

The next day, the calico cat was sleeping in the same spot in the backyard, in the warm sun. While the cat slept, a mangy old coyote came up to the property. The coyote was hungry, and it hadn't eaten for days. The coyote sniffed and sniffed until, much to its surprise, it caught the aroma of the sleeping calico. "A lovely, lovely cat!" the coyote said softly under its breath. "It's just what the doctor ordered!" The coyote followed the scent until it was within several feet of the calico, and it paused, its mouth salivating and its stomach rumbling. Then, in a frenzy, the coyote attacked the sleeping cat, biting down on its back with all its might. The cat woke up and swung its claws at the coyote, but it was no use. The coyote kept the cat in its strong jaws, and with a violent series of shakes, it snapped the poor cat's neck. The cat was as good as dead, and now, with the fatally wounded cat in its mouth, the coyote ran off into the field to eat.

The next day, the coyote returned to the property, thinking that where there was one cat, there might be more. But the coyote didn't realize that the marksman had already missed the calico. He had called the three cats in for dinner, and only the gray cat and the tabby showed up to eat. "Goddamn coyotes," the marksman said, and he unlocked his gun cabinet and removed his favorite rifle. He loaded the rifle the next day and took a seat on a backyard chair. He waited patiently. He waited for the mangy coyote to show up looking for a second cat, and sure enough, in the afternoon, the coyote appeared in the near distance. The marksman raised his rifle and took careful aim. Then he squeezed the trigger, and the rifle fired. The next thing he knew, the coyote toppled over sideways, bleeding from the bullet in its brain. "Right on the money!" the marksman said. "See how many cats you can kill now!"

The next day, the marksman planned to drive into town to do his weekly grocery shopping. "Some nice, thick steaks would be great," he said to himself, and he climbed into his pickup truck and drove down the highway. Little did he know that coming up the highway from the opposite direction was his neighbor, Ned Elder. Ned had been out all the previous night partying, and he was drunk and exhausted. He could barely keep his car on the highway. He turned up the radio and rolled down the window, trying to keep himself awake. He even slapped his own face when he felt himself nodding off. Then it happened. As he drove with the marksman coming the opposite direction, he fell asleep at the wheel. His head fell forward, and his arms fell to his sides. The unmanned steering wheel pulled the car directly toward the marksman's pickup truck. By the time the marksman knew what was happening, it was too late. He plowed head on into Ned's car, and both men died instantly.

All good fables have a moral. This fable is no exception. The moral to this fable is, "If you truly believe that God is love, I've got some beachfront property in Arizona you might be interested in buying."

It was a brutal little fable. Actually, I was surprised his teacher gave him an A. But at least at the time he wrote it, Jacob still had a slight sense of humor. Once we lose our sense of humor, all is lost.

For Jacob's twenty-first birthday, I took everyone to the Crab Palace for dinner and drinks. By 'everyone' I mean Jacob, Amy, April, Zach, and Zach's girlfriend, Janet Brown. I was the designated driver that night. Everyone else planned on drinking and having a good time, and I was fine with being the sober one. The truth was, I was a little old to be out pounding down drinks, but I wouldn't have missed the night for the world. After all, your kids only turn twenty-one once.

If you haven't been to the Crab Palace, it's a restaurant in Newport Beach in an old refurbished brick building on the bay that overlooks the oily bay water, the boats, the buoys, and the noisy seagulls. The place has been in business forever—meaning, in California years, for longer than a decade. It hasn't been a hotspot all these years because of the superior quality of its food. People go there because it's a great place to eat like a slob and get good and drunk. April and I had been there with friends a couple times, but honestly, it just wasn't our type of establishment. But it happened to be perfect for celebrating Jacob's twenty-first birthday.

Zach and Janet drove down from Los Angeles, and the plan was to have them stay that night at our house. We would pick up Amy on the way to the restaurant. When Zach and Janet arrived at our home, Zach had a brown paper bag, and he told Jacob he had brought a present for him. Then he pulled a bottle out of the bag. "This is for you, little brother. Straight from Mexico." It was a yellowish bottle of mescal, with a colorful label and a dead worm at the bottom. "Are you up to it?" Zach asked. "They say if you eat the worm at the bottom, you'll hallucinate like a mother."

"Crack it open," Jacob said.

"Seriously?"

"Let's see if it's any good."

Zach pulled a sliced lemon and a salt shaker out of the bag. He had come fully prepared. "You drink this stuff just like you drink tequila."

"Whoa," I said. "Are you guys going to get drunk before we even get to the restaurant?"

"Maybe we are," Zach said, and the boys both laughed as Zach unscrewed the top from the bottle.

For a while they took turns drinking the mescal straight out of the bottle, licking salt from the backs of their hands, and biting into the lemons. Janet didn't want any, so she just watched. "You guys are going to get sick drinking that awful stuff," she said.

"So what if we do?" Jacob said. "You only turn twenty-one once." The boys laughed, and Janet rolled her eyes. "You want some?" Jacob then asked me. He held the bottle toward me.

"No thanks," I said. "I'm driving."

"One little swig?"

"Seriously, no thanks."

"The only difference between the saint and the sinner is that every saint has a past, and every sinner has a future."

"What are you talking about?" Zach said.

"Oscar Wilde," Jacob said.

"We should probably get going," April said. It was early to be leaving, but April wanted to interrupt the boys' drinking. She was smart to do this. They were already getting drunk, and the evening hadn't even started.

"To the Crab Palace," Jacob said, setting the bottle down on the kitchen table. He pointed up as though we were all going to fly there as superheroes.

Zach screwed the top back on the bottle, and we all walked out of the house and stepped to April's SUV in the driveway. We piled in, and I backed out and into the street. "I don't know where I'm going," I said. "You'll need to give me directions to Amy's house."

"No problem," Jacob said. "And while we're driving, put on this CD." Jacob was reaching over the seat, handing me a CD he had brought along.

"What is it?" I asked.

"Bruno Mars."

"Bruno who? Seriously? Who in the hell names their child Bruno?"

"Bruno's parents. Just stick it in and turn it up. I think you'll like it."

"I thought you only listened to gay hippie music," Zach said to Jacob.

"Times change. In the immortal words of the illustrious Robert Zimmerman, 'You better start swimming, or you'll sink like a stone.'"

"Who the fuck is Robert Zimmerman?" Zach asked.

"Just play the CD, Dad."

"Okay, okay," I said.

"Here, I'll do it," April said, and she took the CD out of my hand. Then to Jacob she said, "Don't bother your dad while he's driving."

April put the CD into the player.

"Take the toll road to the 73," Jacob said. "Then take the 73 into Newport and get off on Newport Coast."

"Got it," I said.

The CD was playing, and Jacob sang along, "Easy come, easy go. That's just how you live."

"Is your little girlfriend rich?" Zach asked.

"Her name is Amy."

"Okay, is Amy rich?"

"Her parents have money. They're both doctors. I think her dad owns a clinic."

"Not everyone who lives in Newport is rich," April pointed out.

"And not all doctors are rich," I added.

"They're just like us," Jacob said. "They make enough money to live well, but not enough to get out of paying income taxes."

"That's actually very funny," I said.

"It's the mescal," Jacob said. "You can thank your older son for that one."

"Yeah," Zach said. "Thank me."

Janet laughed. Then she said, "Both of you are getting really annoying."

"You haven't seen anything," Jacob said.

"Yeah," Zach said. "Just wait until Jacob starts quoting more Oscar Wilde."

Jacob laughed and said, "Consistency is the last refuge of the unimaginative."

"What does that even mean?" Zach asked.

"It means you're consistent."

Zach thought for a moment, and then said, "I think I liked you better when you were a hippie."

"No you didn't," Jacob said.

"You were a hippie?" Janet said. No one said anything for several seconds, and then everyone laughed.

When we arrived at Amy's place, I pulled April's SUV into their driveway, and Jacob hopped out to get her. He spent a while at the front door talking to Amy's parents, and finally Amy and Jacob came to the car.

They climbed into the far backseat, and Jacob said, "This is my brother, Zach, and his girlfriend, Janet."

"Nice to meet both of you," Amy said. Then she turned and looked at Jacob. "Have you been drinking already? I can smell it on your breath."

"It's my fault," Zach said.

"My brother is evil," Jacob said.

Jacob and Zach laughed at this, and Janet turned around to Amy and said, "They've been acting like idiots the whole way here. I'm glad you're here. We needed someone to balance the scales."

"Ah," Jacob said. "One can live down anything except a good reputation."

"What's that even supposed to mean?" Amy asked.

"He's quoting Oscar Wilde again," Zach said. "Don't try to make sense of it. It's the mescal talking."

"We should've brought the bottle with us," Jacob said.

"No, no, no," I said, laughing.

When we finally arrived at the restaurant, I found a place to park, and we all climbed out of the car. Our table for six was ready for us as soon as we walked in, and we sat down in our places. The waiter showed up promptly, and he brought us menus. He asked if we wanted anything to drink, and Jacob spoke up and asked him, "What's the strongest, biggest, most butt-kicking drink your bartender makes?"

"That would be our Tahitian Typhoon," the waiter said.

"No kidding?"

"Yes, that would be it."

"Then bring me one."

"Can I see your ID?" the waiter asked.

"Yes," Jacob said. "As a matter of fact, you can." Jacob was grinning, and he reached to his back pocket for his wallet. He then handed the waiter his driver's license. The waiter looked at the license and smiled.

"Happy birthday, sir."

"Thank you," Jacob said.

"I'll have one of those Tahitian things too," Zach said. "And make mine a double."

Zach and Jacob laughed.

Janet, Amy, and April ordered wine, and I asked for a cup of coffee. When the waiter brought out the Tahitian Typhoons, we all laughed. The glasses were big enough to use as goldfish bowls.

"Just one of those ought to be plenty," April said.

"Heck, we're just getting started," Jacob said.

"I'll race you," Zach said to Jacob.

"You're on."

"I think I could drink four or five of these."

"What are you going to get for dinner?" Amy asked. She was trying to change the subject and slow down the drinking. She was looking over her menu.

"You have to get the Captain's Special," Jacob said. "It has everything. It comes in a metal pail. You get crab legs, corn on the cob, a sausage, some shrimp, french fries, melted butter, cocktail sauce, and a roll."

"And you eat it with your hands," Zach said.

"You get to wear a bib," Jacob said. "They put a bib on you so you don't get the food all over your clothes."

Amy looked around and saw how many people in the restaurant were wearing bibs. "Looks like it's a popular dish."

"It's the only thing to get," Jacob said.

"I thought you only ate vegetables and weeds," Zach said to Jacob.

"Ancient history."

"You've changed?"

"He even tells jokes now," I said.

"No kidding?"

"I'd like to hear one," Janet said.

"Are they clean?" April asked. "I don't like raunchy jokes, and Amy and Janet probably don't either."

"I know some clean ones," Jacob said.

"Tell them the one about the couple in the restaurant," I said to Jacob.

Jacob had finished off his Tahitian Typhoon. The waiter walked past us, and Jacob got his attention. "Another Typhoon," he said, and then he looked at the rest of us to tell his joke. "There's a couple eating in a restaurant," he said. "They're sitting and eating, enjoying their meal. Suddenly the man gets a funny look on his face, and he slides off his chair so that he's under the table. The waitress notices this, and she comes up to the woman and says, 'Excuse me, ma'am, but your husband just fell off his chair.' The woman at the table says, 'No he didn't. He's in the restaurant.'"

Everyone stared at Jacob without laughing. "I think you messed up the punch line," I said.

"This Tahitian Typhoon is a lot stronger than I thought."

"How does the punch line actually go?" Zach asked.

"The woman is supposed to say that her husband just walked into the restaurant," I said.

"I don't get it," Amy said. "Who is the man under the table?"

"He's the woman's lover," I said.

"I get it," Zach said. "He's hiding from the husband."

"Why would the husband be coming to the restaurant in the first place?" Amy asked.

"What does that matter?" Jacob asked.

"It makes no sense to me," Amy said.

"If Jacob hadn't screwed up the punch line, it probably would've been funny," Zach said.

"Everyone's a critic," Jacob said. "I'd like to see you do better."

"I can tell a good one," Zach said. "An elderly man and his wife are sitting in their church. The old gal suddenly leans over and whispers to her husband, 'I just let out a long and silent fart. What should I do?' The man says to his wife, 'First things first—you ought to replace the battery in your hearing aid.'"

We all laughed.

Finally the waiter returned, and everyone at the table ordered the Captain's Special, and ten minutes later the waiter brought out the pails of food. By now the boys were each on their second Tahitian Typhoon, and believe me, neither of them was feeling any pain. It was funny to watch the kids eat. Jacob and Zach were feasting on their meals like a pair of drunken Roman soldiers, while their girlfriends were trying to be as neat as possible. Jacob started talking about his work at Berkshire, and he was telling us about a land lease for a fast-food restaurant he'd been working on. Then he suddenly set his crab leg down and looked up at us. Little bits of crab were clinging to his buttery chin.

"Look at me," Jacob said. He was laughing. "Just look at me. I'm just like the rest of them."

"Like the rest of who?" I asked.

"Like *them*."

"It's about time, little brother," Zach said. "Welcome to the land of the living. Glad you could make it."

I just told you about Jacob's twenty-first birthday because it was a fun night. But I don't want to give you the impression that Jacob was a big drinker, because he wasn't. In fact, he never was. He was a very responsible young man, and he took his behavior seriously. And he took his job seriously. As Hank predicted, he fit in fine at Berkshire. By the time he was twenty-one, he was making enough money to rent a nice house in Laguna that had a view of the ocean, and that was a short walk from the beach. He drove a mid-sized BMW, and he had a closet full of moderately expensive clothes. He was also saving up to purchase his own house, and April and I were counting down the days before he'd ask Amy to marry him. In our opinion, it was inevitable.

As for Zach, he was also doing well. When he graduated from college, he got a job as a loan officer at a bank in LA. Jacob was probably making more money than Zach, but I don't think Zach minded. Not yet. I think Zach figured that in the long run he would make more than his brother because of his college degree. The job at the bank was just the first step toward what was sure to be a high-paying career. Was this true? I honestly didn't know, but for the time being the boys were getting along well. They weren't bickering like they did when they were younger, and April and I liked this.

Speaking of April, you might be wondering what she spent her time doing now that the boys were adults. I got her a job as an administrative assistant for a friend of mine who had a software company in Irvine. It worked out well. April liked being a part of the working world, and she liked the extra cash she was earning. However, I think she threw herself a little too vigorously into her job at times; it was probably to help her forget about the fact that she was no longer raising our boys. Being a mother had been important to her. It had been her top purpose in life, but life goes on, right?

I felt the weird dread of being older too. I was now sixty, closing in on my golden years. Jesus, I really didn't want to retire.

CHAPTER 24

THAT AWFUL SMELL

───── •◦• ─────

I never met Sid Sanchez. Not face-to-face. But I knew a lot about the guy. He was kind of a real estate legend in Orange County, the sort of a legend who was a legend because he said he was a legend. In other words, he had some good public relations people working for him who were able to get his name in the news every time he bent over to pick up a penny. The guy loved being written about, photographed, and, above everything else, envied. He was known as "the man who owned half of Orange County," which was, of course, an impossible feat for one man, yet somehow the overblown description stuck to him like "the king of rock 'n' roll" stuck to Elvis.

Sid's real estate development company had recently built a large shopping center not far from our home in Coto. The place was impressive; it had been designed by the well-known Orange County architect Chet Burrows. We had several shopping centers already in the area, and they were very nice, but Sid's new center was a step above them all. The name of the new center was Rancho Rodeo—Rancho because it was located in the city of Rancho Santa Margarita (next door to Coto), and Rodeo because Sid wanted people in the area to think of it as their own South Orange County version of Rodeo Drive. It would, of course, be nothing like the real Rodeo Drive. It was just a name gimmick, like naming a Buick after the Riviera or a Chevy after Monte Carlo.

Sid didn't seek any tenants prior to construction, because he didn't think they'd see what a great idea it was until it was actually built. Sid believed people had lousy imaginations, and he was probably right about this. Since the project was being funded with Sid's own money, there were no lender requirements for him to have tenants before breaking ground. Several real estate companies were competing to be the leasing agent for the project. Always with a flair for the sensational, Sid said he would announce the chosen broker to the public on the Fourth of July. There would be a barbecue and live music, and at night there would be fireworks. And everyone in the community would be invited, including the mayor, who had used his influence to get the project approved by the planning department. If you're wondering why I'm telling you all this, hang on. I'll explain in a minute.

First I need to tell you about Jacob. Sid had another shopping center in the city of Orange, also not far from Coto. This center was about six years old. It was nothing fancy, just a mundane assortment of retailers that had a space on one end of the main building that had been designed for restaurant use. When the center first opened, the restaurant that went into the space was a nice little hamburger joint called Wally's Burgers, a mom-and-pop venture owned by a nice little man named Wally Andrews. Wally's Burgers executed a five-year lease but stayed in business for only about six months. The space then sat empty until it was leased by an Indian restaurant. This restaurant also signed a five-year lease, but they kept their doors open for just a little less than a year. After the space sat vacant for another twelve months, a new restaurant came into the picture. This place served waffles, and it had a proven track record up in LA. It was very busy when it first opened, and everyone thought the restaurant would last. But after only ten months, they shut down the restaurant and vacated the space. People began to talk, saying that the location was cursed. And for two years the space remained vacant, until Jacob came into the picture. Jacob had a client from Phoenix who owned a pizza chain called Arizona Pizza, and they were looking to expand into the California market. Jacob convinced the owners to lease the spot in Sid's shopping center.

Construction started as soon as the lease was signed, and the owners spent a fortune revamping the space, turning it into their pizza restaurant. Several months later, they opened their doors to the public, and it was a great success at first. The new tenant couldn't have been happier, and Arizona Pizza was selling its pizzas hand over fist until the day they found out why all the other restaurants had left. There was a smell. It was an awful smell, like raw sewage. Maybe it was raw sewage, and maybe there was something wrong with the underground waste lines. They called out some contractors, but none of them could figure out where the smell was coming from. Nor could they figure out why it came and went. One week the place would smell fine, and then the next week it would be intolerable. But the writing was on the wall. Arizona Pizza closed its doors after being in business only four months.

Now the fur would fly. The owner of Arizona Pizza was no pushover. The owners of the other restaurants had been happy just to have their leases terminated so they could move on and open their restaurants elsewhere. But not the owner of the Arizona Pizza. His name was Ernie Blackstone, and he was a sixty-eight-year-old Vietnam veteran, but not the kind of veteran who suffered from post-traumatic stress or feelings of guilt or any other of the things he referred to as weaknesses. You'd swear this guy ate broken glass and nails every morning for breakfast. He didn't care if Sid did own half of Orange County, or half the judges, or half the politicians. By God, the bastard was going to pay Ernie back for every dime he lost by opening his restaurant in Sid's shopping center. He hired the best California attorney his money could buy, and they prepared a case against Sid that demanded payment for all the money spent on opening the store and all the funds spent on employees, insurance premiums, food, supplies, taxes, and city fees. He was also demanding a huge sum of money for damage to his reputation and for cutting into his expected and deserved profits. It was clear that the amount being sought by Ernie was going to be above and beyond anything Sid would ever agree to pay. The little molehill had officially turned into a mountain, and guess who got caught in the middle of this? You guessed it. It was Jacob.

Jacob had known nothing about the smell problem when he negotiated the lease between Arizona Pizza and Sid's company. He knew other restaurants had closed their doors after short stints in business, but he thought their closings were the result of either poor management by the proprietors or maybe just the fickle whims of the eating public. When Jacob learned about the smell, he was truly surprised. It didn't take long for Sid to secure an attorney to plan a counterattack. Sid called for a meeting, and Jacob was told to come. Jacob was there in the attorney's office, along with Sid and Hank. Joe was the name of the attorney.

"You're the key to us surviving this whole goddamn fiasco," Sid said to Jacob. "You're holding all the cards, kid."

"I am?" Jacob said.

"That's the way we see it."

"Hear them out," Hank said.

"Hear them out for what?"

"They're going to offer you a deal, Jacob. It's a good deal. Think about it carefully."

"You're new to this racket, aren't you kid?"

"Yes, more or less."

"How old are you?"

"I'm twenty-one."

"Do you know how many twenty-one-year-olds in this business mean diddly squat to me?"

"I don't know."

"Just one."

"Me?" Jacob said.

"Yes, you."

"Before we go on, you need to understand something," Joe said. "What is being said in this room today isn't really being said. Do you understand? If you tell anyone about what is said here, we'll deny all of it. All of us will. This is a conversation that is not taking place."

"I think I understand."

"This pizza asshole you signed up to move into my shopping center is now threatening me with a lawsuit," Sid said. He was obviously very angry.

"It's a very large suit," Joe added.

"He's an opportunist," Hank said.

"He wants to be paid a ton of money for something that's no one's fault."

"How much is he suing for?" Jacob asked.

"We don't know yet."

"We heard through the grapevine it will be for millions," Joe said. "I have that from a reliable source."

"Millions?"

"And he has a case against us," Joe said. "He's going to win something. Maybe not millions, but certainly more than he deserves."

"Unless …" Sid said.

"Unless what?"

"Unless you're smart enough to see a good thing when it's falling right into your twenty-one-year-old lap. Are you smart enough to see it?" Sid asked.

"I guess not," Jacob said. He was a little confused. "I mean, I don't know what opportunity you're talking about. How exactly do I fit in?"

"You'll have to spell it out for him," Hank said.

"We're only going to tell you once," Sid said.

"And we'll deny we ever said it," Joe added. "It stays within these walls."

"Understand?" Sid asked.

"I get it," Jacob said.

"We want you to lie for us. We want you to tell a flat-out, 101 percent lie."

"Lie?" Jacob said.

"Under oath."

"You mean commit perjury?"

"Now you're catching on," Sid said. "Can you guess what we want you to say?"

"Not really."

"It's simple, really," Joe said. "We want you to say that you told Ernie Blackstone that the space he was leasing had an occasional yet substantial odor problem."

"You did meet with Ernie several times, didn't you?" Sid asked.

"Yes, I met with him."

"We want you to say you're not sure when exactly, but that you positively recall telling Ernie about the problem. And we want you to say Ernie told you that he would deal with it when his plumber came out to install his tenant improvements. He said he'd take care of it."

"That's it?" Jacob asked.

"That's all of it," Sid said.

"It will blow their entire case right out of the water," Sid said.

"Do you understand?" Hank asked.

"I think I do," Jacob said.

"Of course, you will be handsomely compensated," Joe said.

"You mean like a bribe?"

"No, we can't do that."

"Listen to them," Hank said. "This is a good deal. It's not a bribe."

"We're going to put you in charge of a highly visible and lucrative project."

"With Hank to help you, of course."

"I'll be with you all the way," Hank said.

"What project?" Jacob asked.

"You're going to be the primary agent leasing my Rancho Rodeo center," Sid said. "Do you know what this means? You'll be negotiating high-dollar leases. There will be lots of fat commissions. Every store you lease will be written up in the paper. It'll put you on the map, kid."

"With Hank by your side, of course," Joe said.

"I'll be right there with you," Hank said. "You can depend on me."

"And what do I do when Ernie Blackstone throws a fit and calls me a liar?"

"It'll be your word against his," Hank said. "That's the beauty of it."

"The guy is an asshole," Sid said. "No one will believe a word he says. Everyone knows he a litigious, self-serving bastard."

"And what if he comes after me?"

"Witness tampering," Sid said. "He may be an asshole, but he isn't stupid. He'll know better. We'll have him by the goddamn short hairs. He's going to see what we've done, and he'll cut his losses and move on."

"You'll have nothing to worry about," Joe said.

"It's a good deal," Hank said. "Sid can't force you to do it, but think about it. This is a good deal."

"You have two days to think it over," Sid said. "Don't call Joe or me about any of this. Just give Hank your answer, and he'll tell you what to do."

Obviously I made the above conversation up. I mean, it's by no means a transcript of the meeting, but from what Jacob told me, and from what I know about Sid, Hank, and attorneys, I think it's a pretty close reenactment of the conversation that took place. And this brings me to Sid's grand Fourth of July celebration at Rancho Rodeo. Are you wondering what Jacob finally decided to do? Several hundred people were there at the celebration to get the free hot dogs and listen to live music. At four in the afternoon, Sid's silver Rolls Royce pulled up and parked on the grass. Sid got out of the car, and he made his way through the crowd to the stage. The singer for the band introduced Sid to the audience and handed Sid the microphone. Sid then made the following little speech, which I can tell you is accurate nearly word for word, because I was in the audience and heard all of it.

Sid said, "For those of you who don't know me, my name is Sid Sanchez. I'm the guy who is throwing this party for you. I'm the guy responsible for this great shopping center being built in your wonderful community. I'm not going to break up the party, but I did promise I would make an announcement today. So here I am, and this will only take a minute or so. It's been very important to me that we get the best possible mix of stores and restaurants in this center. Finding the best tenants means using the best and most talented real estate agent. I searched all over Orange County for just the right agent, and I've made my decision. I want to announce that the Berkshire Company will be filling this center with tenants in the months ahead—tenants who will be here to serve you. And in charge of this effort at Berkshire will be one of their most creative and fastest-rising stars, a fine young man who grew up right here in this community with the rest of you. His name is Jacob Harper. Let's hear it for Jacob!"

It was then that Jacob climbed up on the stage and stood alongside Sid. The crowd cheered, and Jacob said thank you several times. I knew this was coming, but April didn't. Jacob had told me his decision earlier on, and he had asked me to bring April to the barbecue. He wanted her to be surprised, and was she ever. April knew nothing about the actual deal to lie, because Jacob made me promise to keep the whole thing quiet; and for better or worse, if there's one thing I know how to do, it's keep a secret.

Some say the people never change, but I say that Jacob had definitely changed. For the better? For the worse? Or maybe for neither? I'm sure you have now formed your own opinion of my son's behavior, and you have a right to it, just as I have a right to mine. Can you figure out what I was thinking? I'm not going to tell you. You've been listening to me go on and on about Jacob for some time now, so I'll let you use what you've learned and guess.

Jacob didn't exactly get rich off his deal with Sid, but he did make a name for himself. And business was subsequently good for him—good enough, he decided, that it was time to do something he had been planning to do for some time. It was time to ask Amy to marry him. April and I both knew this was coming, maybe even before Jacob figured it out. It was obvious to us that the two were in love and destined to tie the knot. And we liked Amy. She was more than welcome in our family. She was, without a doubt, one of the best people to come into Jacob's life since the day he met Dr. Trill.

Speaking of Dr. Trill, Jacob still went to see the doctor, but now they met every four months. I still didn't know how much Jacob had told Amy about his past and his suicide attempt, or whether he had told her that he was still seeing a psychiatrist. It wasn't something we talked about much anymore. What we did talk about, and what really got Jacob excited, was gardening, believe it or not. I guess he picked this up from April. It was one of the primary reasons that Jacob wanted to own his own home—so he could plant a spectacular garden he could call all his own. The kid had a green, green thumb, as green as Amy's Irish eyes. And yes, Jacob did finally ask her to marry him. She said yes, and the next thing we knew, they set a date and were planning their wedding.

Prior to the wedding, Jacob found a house for them to move into. It was in Corona del Mar, a little community right next door to Newport Beach. Amy's parents and I all contributed to the down payment, and escrow closed just a month before the wedding. The place didn't have much of a yard, but it was big enough to satisfy Jacob. It had three bedrooms, so the house itself was plenty large. It was a fixer-upper, meaning that there was a lot of work to do. Jacob told me he looked forward to working on the house. It's great to be young, isn't it? I can't imagine anything I would look less forward to than working on fixing up a house.

I'm going to tell you a few things about the wedding, but first I need to tell you about Amy's parents. I think I already said her dad was an executive at a pharmaceutical company and her mom was an attorney, and that both of them lived in Newport Beach. April and I met them in person when they invited us over for dinner when the kids were dating. The dad was Joseph, and the mom was Sonja. Like us, they believed the kids were headed toward marriage, and they wanted to vet us. I mean, they didn't say this, but I think that was the point of the dinner. April and I were being checked out to see if we were an acceptable branch to be grafted to their family tree. On that evening, while we were getting ready to leave, I told April we should show up dressed like Hells Angels.

They were actually very nice people, and I didn't blame them for wanting to learn more about us. I was also curious about them, so I guess it's fair to say that the vetting process was actually working both ways. Joseph was a tall man, and I imagined he was often asked if he'd played basketball when he was young. Seriously, the guy was at least six foot six, and he had hands that were the size of dinner plates. I didn't ask him if he used to play ball. I thought if he had, and he wanted me to know about it, he would've mentioned it on his own. Besides, who really cared what sport a person played when he was young? I played a lot of baseball, and so what? It had nothing to do with me as an adult. We did trade information about where we went to college and what we studied. There was one odd thing that I noticed about Joseph, and I'm sure April noticed it too. The man's voice was too high for his large body. You expect tall people to have low voices, but this guy sounded like a shrimp. It took a little getting used to, but it bothered me less and less as the night went on.

Sonja was a slender, blonde Scandinavian. She had a very pleasant accent, and she seemed like an attorney. She was well put together, and she spoke deliberately and eloquently, as if she were getting paid to convince us of something. It turned out that she practiced family law, and she told us sadly of all the married couples she'd seen who couldn't get along. "Marriage is such serious business," she said. "But no one takes it very seriously while they're saying their vows. They recite their vows like they're ordering a hamburger and fries at Burger King. The next thing you know, they're coming to me, writing checks for my services, having their fates decided by judges who barely know them."

"If they all got along, you'd be out of business," Joseph said. He was smiling when he said this.

"I'd *like* to be put out of business," Sonja said.

I found this hard to believe. It was one of those things people say to impress others with their goodwill toward others, but I wasn't really all that impressed.

"You know," April said. "There's a good chance that Jacob and Amy will be getting engaged soon." Ha, now I was actually impressed. Leave it to April. She went right after the elephant in the room.

"We've thought of that," Sonja said.

"That's why we've invited you over," Joseph said.

"And we like your son."

"He's a good kid," I said. That's exactly what I said to our hosts, but do you know what I felt like saying? I felt like telling them a few truths. I felt like taking a deep breath and saying, "Jacob isn't your average kid. Not by any means. Did you know that in third grade he actually put together a science fair project on how toasters are living things? Did you know he was interviewed on TV, telling the country how we had an event like 9/11 coming to us? Did you know he doesn't believe in God any more than he believes in evolution? Did you know he longs for a place called Arcadia? Did you know he thinks this place is real? Did you know he tried to go to there by closing his eyes and slashing his wrists? You heard me right. Did you know they locked him up in a county mental hospital? Did you know he still sees a shrink? How much do you really know about our son? You may think you know him, but you don't know the first thing about him."

Of course, I would never say any of these things to Sonja or Joseph. As far as they knew, Jacob was just another clean-cut kid from a pair of loving Orange County parents who lived in a big house with a swimming pool and well-tended garden. We were the sort of parents who worked hard, told the truth, saluted the flag, went to occasional cocktail parties, and played golf when our busy schedules allowed. And Jacob was a boy becoming a man, now working for the same reputable real estate company as their daughter. He was a boy who knew the difference between right and wrong, up and down, left and right.

I can say this: our dinner with Sonja and Joseph went superbly, and I think our family met with their approval thanks in large part to my skill at lying and withholding the truth. I mean, they were getting a great son-in-law; there was no doubt about it. But let's keep it real.

CHAPTER 25

YOUNG MAN DANCING

————— •◦• —————

I believe in the institution of marriage, and I'm glad that I married April. My marriage means the world to me, and so does April. But I detest weddings. I do everything within my power to avoid them no matter how close I am to the participants or their parents or relatives. So while I'm going to tell you a few things about Jacob and Amy's wedding, don't expect me to get carried away in all the boring details.

Here are a few words about the wedding itself. It was a traditional tuxedo, cake, and limo affair, complete with a modest family church, flowers, a maid of honor, bridesmaids, a best man, a bevy of handsome ushers, a flower girl, and a five-year-old ring bearer. Jesus, a lot of invitations were sent out, and a lot of people showed up. There weren't so many relatives as there were friends. The ceremony was a bit long for my taste, but ten minutes would've been too long for me. I thought the vows were interesting. Amy wrote the vows herself, and there were a lot of references to quotations from famous philosophers. If you'll remember, Amy was a philosophy major in college; I think people tended to forget this fact since she was now just a real estate secretary. One quote I liked was from Albert Camus, who said, "Don't walk behind me; I may not lead. Don't walk in front of me; I may not follow. Just walk beside me and be my friend." I thought this quote was especially appropriate for a newly married couple.

The reception was held at the Marriott in Newport. Amy and her mom had one of the ballrooms decorated from the floor to the ceiling. The people sitting at our table were me, April, my brother and his new wife, Hank and his wife, and an amazingly gregarious woman named Adriana who was a friend of Amy's family. Everyone was getting along well and chatting about the bride and groom. Adriana, whom I'd never met before, was doing most of the talking. Seriously, if you had put this woman at a table all by herself, she could've carried on a nonstop conversation. She probably wouldn't even have noticed she was alone. Finally she stood up and said she was going to mingle with the other guests. Others, including my April, then also left the table to mingle. This was when Hank and I began to talk about Jacob. I had asked how Jacob was doing at his job and was looking forward to what Hank had to say. Of course Hank couldn't give me a straight answer without telling a joke first.

"Did Jacob tell you about the two doctors he negotiated a lease for?"

"No," I said.

"A psychiatrist and a proctologist. He didn't tell you anything about them?"

"No," I said again.

"They're starting up a clinic together. They're going to call their practice Odds and Ends." Hank laughed at his own joke.

"Good one," I said, also laughing.

"Sorry about that. Force of habit. One of my dumb doctor clients told it to me."

"He must be a barrel of laughs."

"We meet all kinds of crazy characters in the real estate business. But seriously, you want to know how Jacob is doing? I keep forgetting how young he is and how much you still care, being his father and all. Well, he's doing terrific. I don't think I've ever seen anyone at his age grasp things the way he does."

"That's good to hear."

"And he's a good kid. He has good morals."

"Yes," I said.

"You must've done something right when you and your wife raised him. You must be very proud."

"Thanks," I said. "We are very proud. But we did nothing special. We just did our best, like any loving and responsible parents would."

"We've had other kids his age in our office. They come and go. It feels like one flash-in-the-pan after the other. And to tell you the truth, they crack me up. They think they're going to get rich, and quick. They think they're going to close a big fat deal or two and then retire to some tile-roofed villa in Costa Rica with servants and big Cadillacs and chauffeurs.

They dream of living like kings, you know. But not Jacob. The boy has a level head. Steady as she goes. Yes, I think he's going to go far."

Hank wasn't the first person to compliment me on how I had raised Jacob. I received the same compliments about Zach, and it always caused me to wonder, especially in Jacob's case, just what the heck it was that I did that was so great? And what was there about Jacob's childhood that anyone would want to emulate? The truth was that Jacob's younger years were frustrating and scary, and despite all my love for him, those years culminated in the worst of all scenarios—a bloody and nearly successful suicide attempt. Surely there were things I could've done to prevent this. Surely I was not the ideal parent that people were making me out to be. But what could I have done different? Honestly, I had no idea, but isn't this lame ignorance the thing that made me such an inept parent, and not someone special to be admired? I didn't know. The truth was that I never really did know what the hell I was doing, and the good place Jacob was now in was really due to dumb luck more than anything else. It was dumb luck that his suicide attempt wasn't a success and that he was now still alive and breathing. It was dumb luck that he was sent to see Dr. Rosenblatt in that county mental hospital and dumb luck that she knew Dr. Trill. It was dumb luck that Dr. Trill actually knew what he was doing and that he wasn't another fox stole–wearing nut like Dr. Erskine-Garcia. And it was dumb luck that Jacob came upon an employment ad in the newspaper for someone needed to install real estate signs for the Berkshire Company, and it was dumb luck that Hank came to know him and that he noticed Jacob's potential and took him under his wing. Dumb, dumb luck.

"Do you have any kids?" I asked Hank.

"I have a boy," Hank said.

"How old?"

"He'll be eight in a month. He's here this afternoon. He's at a table with some of the other kids."

"Do you think you're a good father?"

"Of course I do. Do you think I'd tell you I was a bad father?"

"What exactly makes you a good father?"

"I don't know. Because I love him, I suppose. Because I care. Because I try to set a good example. Because I set rules and boundaries. Because I'm moral."

"What are you going to do if none of those things work?"

"Why wouldn't they work?"

"Just suppose," I said.

"I guess I'd try something else."

"Like what?"

"I don't know. I guess I'd have to think of something. Where is all this coming from? You obviously did a great job raising Jacob."

"If you were told that you could teach only one thing to your child, what would it be? I mean *only* one thing."

"One thing?"

"Just one thing."

"I guess I'd teach my boy to have a sense of humor."

"That's it?"

"You asked, and I answered."

"Fair enough."

"What would you teach *your* boys?" Hank asked me.

"I've thought about this," I said. "And you know what? I like your answer. But I've always thought more along the lines of teaching them to accept imperfection. I think when we're young, we tend to look at the world very critically, and we're obsessed with just how messed up things are compared to how we think they ought to be. I think children are born as little idealists, and I truly believe that unless they learn to accept all the imperfections, they will be terribly unhappy with their lives."

"Makes sense," Hank said.

"Although maybe you and I are saying the same thing."

"How so?"

"Maybe what I'm teaching my children is not just to accept imperfections but also to laugh at them. Maybe that's part of what having a sense of humor is all about."

"Maybe," Hank said.

"Anyway, it was just a hypothetical. Obviously we get to teach our children more than one thing. That's what parenting is—teaching many things."

"I have a joke for you about parenting."

"Okay," I said.

"Two little boys are talking, and the first boys says, 'I'm really worried.

My dad gets up at five in the morning and goes to work for twelve hours a day just to bring home enough money to put food on our table and pay all our bills, and my mom works her fingers to the bone cooking meals for us, keeping the house clean, and looking after me. I'm worried sick!' The second boy says, 'What are you worried about? It sounds like you've got it made.' Then the first boy says, 'Yeah, but what if they try to escape?'"

"How do you remember all these jokes?" I asked, laughing.

"Did you like it?"

"Yeah, it was very good."

Hank thought for a moment, and then he said, "It's funny that you would've asked me what one thing I would choose above others to teach my children. I remember something my own dad said to me when I was a teenager. It was when he was dying in the hospital. Dad died of cancer when I was seventeen. 'If there's one thing I want you to take away from your childhood, it's that it's okay to be average.' That's all he had to say to me that day, and the next day he was dead. Those were the words I was supposed to carry with me for the rest of my life. It was weird, because all during my childhood, my father pushed me to be the best at everything I did. When I played football, it wasn't enough that I made the team. I had to be the best at my position come hell or high water. When I did an assignment for school, anything less than an A was not acceptable. If I got a B, he would never say, 'Good job son, I'm proud of you.' It was always, 'You could've done much better. Next time put your shoulder into it and get an A.' Then, in his hospital room the day before he died, he just threw it all out the window as if everything he'd told me for the past seventeen years was bullshit. I had been on the highway toward happiness, and it was as if someone had stopped me in my tracks and said, 'You're on the road, pal. This is the road for suckers. The road you want is over there.'"

"Wow," I said. "Why do you think he did that?"

"Maybe he felt guilty."

"Maybe," I said.

"I think dying makes you stop and think about your life, and about the lives of the ones you love and the things you have told them."

"Apparently," I said.

"Do you know any good jokes about death?" Hank asked me.

"I'm not big on jokes," I said.

"I know a few."

"Of course you do," I said, laughing.

"Have you heard the one about the middle-aged woman who has a heart attack?"

"No, go ahead," I said. I could tell Hank was dying to tell me this joke. And I kind of wanted to hear it.

"There's a middle-aged woman," Hank said. "And she has a serious heart attack. They take her to the hospital, and while she's there she almost dies. She has a near-death experience in which she meets up with God. She asks him, "Am I going to die? Is this it for me?" God says, "No, my dear. Your time is not up. You have another thirty-seven years, three months, and seven days to live. When she recovers from the heart attack, the woman decides to stay in the hospital. She figures she may as well make the best of it. She has them do a face lift, liposuction, a nose job, and a tummy tuck, and she even has someone come in and dye her hair a different color. When she leaves the hospital, she crosses the street to get her ride. As she crosses the street, a truck plows into her and kills her on the spot. She goes to heaven, and when she meets with God she says, "I thought you said I had over thirty-seven more years to live. Why didn't you stop that truck? God looks at the woman and says, "I didn't recognize you.""

I laughed at this.

"You ought to be a comedian," I said.

"I'm in real estate. Close enough."

"Look at that," I said, now changing the subject. I was pointing toward the dance area where Jacob and Amy were having their first dance. I didn't recognize the song they were dancing to.

"I don't see how you can watch them without crying," Hank said.

"It isn't easy."

"Do you see them?" April said. She came over to make sure I saw Jacob and Amy.

"Of course I see them."

"What song is that?"

"I haven't got the slightest idea."

"Where's the photographer? He should be getting pictures of this."

"He's right over there," I said.

"Oh," April said, now looking at him.

"Don't worry so much. Everything is under control."

"You're right, of course. But it's a mother's job to worry." April then left to rejoin her friends.

Then Hank stood up. "Excuse me," he said. "Need to visit the men's room."

"Okay," I said.

And I sat alone, watching as other people began to join my son and his wife on the dance floor. How does that old song go? "Happy, shiny faces?" It's something like that. All those happy, shiny faces having a good time, and there I was at the table, suddenly so alone. I'm not a person who ordinarily gravitates toward morose feelings, but I felt a strange and chilling wave of discomfort envelop me. What exactly was it? I should've been happy, but I suddenly felt like weeping—like a dumb little girl. I was sad, and why was I sad? I was feeling loneliness. I was feeling as though something was being ripped away from me—and something was, in fact, being taken away. I was losing Jacob. I was losing my son. He was moving forward into his new fixer-upper house with his sparkling new wife and his real estate work life while I was left with April and my cardboard box company. Fuck! It was awful! As I said, I wasn't used to this kind of emotion, and now I wished I'd never come to the wedding.

Hank was right, you know. The most important thing in life to keep is your sense of humor. Just a minute ago I had been laughing, and it felt good to laugh. Anything was better than the way I was feeling now. Where the hell was Hank? What was taking him so long? Had he just left, or had he left fifteen minutes ago? Jesus, I was losing it. The room started to spin, well, not really spinning, but spinning. All those happy, shiny faces! All those suits and ties and dresses and necklaces, all whirling around my head in a horrible blur. All that talking with nothing being said.

"Still here?" Hank said.

I looked over at him. He was sitting back down in his chair. "Barely," I said.

"You don't look so good."

"I'm feeling a little light-headed."

"Can I get you something?"

"Get me something?"

"A glass of water? A cup of coffee? A good stiff drink? The drinks are on the house, you know."

"Yes, I know," I said. "No, I'm fine."

"How about a joke?"

"A joke, of course."

"A joke about weddings?"

"No, nothing about weddings," I said. "Anything but weddings. How about a joke about a horse?"

"A horse?"

"I'm trying to keep my mind off this wedding."

"A horse, a horse, a horse," Hank said to himself, trying to think of a joke.

"Or a cow."

"A cow?"

"I don't know. Don't you know any jokes about cows?"

"I know one about a pig."

"A pig will do."

"Okay, good," Hank said. "It goes like this. There's a man who's stranded on a tropical island with a pig and a dog. There's plenty to eat on the island, and the weather is good. The man and the animals live for months on the island, but the man finds himself getting increasingly lonely. Strangely, the man begins to find the pig more and more attractive. He soon finds himself approaching the pig for physical comfort, but every time he gets within a few feet of the pig, the dog snarls and barks protectively, keeping the man away. Then one day the man spots something on the ocean horizon. He dives into the water and swims out to see what it is, and he discovers a life raft containing a beautiful unconscious woman. He climbs in the raft and rows it to the shore, where he takes the woman out. Over several days, he nurses her back to health. When she is feeling better, the woman thanks the man profusely, and she asks if there's anything she can do to pay him back. The man nods his head, and he is obviously excited. He puts his hand on the woman's shoulder and says, 'Would you mind taking my dog for a walk?'"

I laughed at this, and Hank smiled. "I didn't expect that," I said.

"No one does."

"What's so funny?" Jacob said. He was now standing at our table with Amy. They were done dancing.

"Just a joke," I said.

"Are you telling my dad jokes?" Jacob asks Hank.

"Just a few."

"It's good to see you laughing, Dad. I'm glad you're having a good time. I know how you hate weddings."

"I could never hate your wedding," I said.

"Where's Mom?"

"She's over there talking to friends," I said, and I pointed to their table.

"Are you going to dance with her?"

"Dance?"

"Yeah, you know, *dance*."

"I suppose we should," I said, and I stood up. Then I looked at Hank. "Take the dog for a walk," I said, repeating the punch line and laughing.

"I thought you might like that one."

"Didn't expect it."

I woke up early the next morning. One son down, and one to go. Zach would probably be asking Janet to marry him soon, and then it would be just April and me.

I climbed out of bed and stepped to the bathroom. I was wearing only my pajama bottoms, and I looked at my naked torso and then at my face. Then I brushed my teeth and rinsed out my mouth. *Jesus, where did the time go?* I went to the closet to put on some clothes, and then downstairs to make coffee. Ralph was in the kitchen, waiting for me, his tail wagging and his stupid dog tongue hanging out. He wanted breakfast, so I filled his food bowl. Then he wanted water, so I filled up his water bowl. This made him happy—what a life. As for Jacob? He had his own house now, the fixer-upper near the beach. After they returned from their honeymoon, they would probably come to get Ralph. That would be okay. Ralph was always Jacob's dog, not mine, and I was letting my sons go, so why not the dog? Jesus, everything and everyone was flying right out the windows.

"What are you doing up so early?" April asked. She had come into the kitchen.

"I don't know."

"It's four in the morning."

"I just woke up," I said. "I wasn't sleepy."

"Are you thinking about Jacob?"

"I am," I said.

"It's weird, isn't it?"

"It is weird. And a little upsetting."

"I remember the night before *we* got married," April said, reminiscing. "I found my dad up in the middle of the night in the kitchen. He was having a sandwich and a glass of beer. And he'd been crying. He wouldn't admit it, but his eyes were red and swollen. I knew he'd been crying, and I asked him what was wrong. I thought he'd be happy that I was getting married, but it was the other way around. He was sad and heartbroken. You know what he said to me?"

"No," I said.

"He said, 'You've lived in our house for all these years, and now I feel like I hardly know you. And now you're leaving us.'"

"What'd you say?"

"I told him just because I was getting married, it didn't mean I'd never see him again."

"Did that make him feel any better?"

"I don't know. I couldn't tell."

"I think I know how he felt."

"But you *do* know Jacob."

"Do I?" I asked.

"Of course you do."

"When I saw him dancing with Amy last night, he looked like a complete stranger. He looked like a young man dancing with his bride—not my son, but a young stranger with his whole life ahead of him."

CHAPTER 26

THE YEARS

Z ach married his girlfriend, Janet, six months after Jacob's wedding. Now both of my boys were married, starting lives of their own. April was still working for my friend's software company. And me? I had my hands full at work. There was no end to the complexities and challenges of selling cardboard boxes.

Last summer April and I decided to take a vacation in the Caribbean, and we asked the boys and their wives if they wanted to join us. We offered to pay for the whole thing, and we were really looking forward to a week of family time. But neither boy wanted to come. They each said they were too busy with work, which I figured was really just an excuse not to be with us. I was disappointed, but April said to put myself in their shoes. "When we had just married, would you have wanted to go on a vacation with your parents? Or my parents?" I thought back and realized April was right about this. I wouldn't have wanted to go on a vacation with either of our parents. It had nothing to do with loving them any less, and everything to do with wanting to be independent and wanting to start our new lives. There was nothing wrong with this; in fact, I decided it was a good thing that the kids turned us down. We didn't need two sons and their brides clinging to us when they should be loving each other and growing up.

I guess I should take a moment to tell you about Zach's wife and her family. The Browns lived up in LA, and Janet's father, Rob Brown, was a firefighter. Her mom, Robin, was a bookkeeper for a large construction company. They lived in a modest tract house in Pasadena, and April and I went there for a Memorial Day barbecue and beer party that they hosted for friends. We were invited because it was becoming clear that our kids were getting serious about each other and the Browns wanted to get to know us. If we hadn't been invited to their house for that party, we probably would've invited them to our house. Janet's parents were very pleasant salt-of-the-earth, beer-drinking, burger-grilling, country-music-loving, Toyota-driving, middle class, American, blue-collar type folks. I know this is going to sound snobbish, but they weren't the kind of people April and I normally socialized with. Janet saw that we were a little lost at the party, so she introduced us to several of the people there.

"These are my boyfriend's parents, Stan and April Harper," she said to one couple. Then to us she said, "I want you to meet Minnie and Albert Bender."

"Nice to meet you," I said.

"Nice to meet you," Albert said. "Where are you two from?"

"We're from Orange County," I said.

"Ah, Orange County."

"Our kids met in college. Our son went to college up here with Janet at UCLA."

"I see," Albert said.

"How do you know the Browns?"

"Rob and I both work for the same fire department. We're both firefighters." There was a pause in the conversation as we tried to think of something to say. Then Albert said, "So what do you do for fun?"

"I mostly work," I said.

"Doing what?"

"Making boxes."

"Do you put in a lot of overtime?"

"Actually, I run the place."

"Ah, you're a boss?"

"I guess so."

"I tried my hand at factory work for a few years when I was younger," Albert said. "I didn't care for it much, doing the same thing over and over. Working for the fire department keeps me hopping."

"I can imagine."

"And there's lots of time off."

"That's good."

"We like to go camping. Do you like to camp?"

"I haven't been camping since I was a kid."

"You ought to take out your family. I can show you some perfect spots. We have a great time."

"Sounds wonderful," I said. I was just trying to be polite. It actually sounded awful.

You can imagine how the rest of this conversation went. I discovered after talking to Albert for about ten minutes that we didn't have much in common; in fact, I discovered after about an hour of socializing with the other guests that I had little in common with any of them. Camping? Really? Who in the hell goes camping?"

But back to last summer's Caribbean vacation. April and I decided to go to Jamaica, and we made reservations at one of those all-inclusive resorts. On the first day, we went to the beach, swimming in the water and lying in the sun. It was awesome. There were a lot of people, and maybe it was even overcrowded, but for some reason all the hotel guests didn't bother us. There was a thatched-roof bar on the beach that served frozen drinks and hamburgers. There was also a steel drum band that played for most of the afternoon and into the evening. We felt as though we were a million miles from home—exactly what we were shooting for when we booked the trip. April and I both brought paperback books to read. I brought *War and Peace*, which I'd always wanted to read, and April brought a popular new book about getting more exercise, drinking water, and eating healthy.

"You should read this," April said, holding her place in the book with her finger.

"No thanks," I replied.

"It would make you feel a lot better."

"I feel fine just like I am."

"Don't you want to feel even better?"

"Not really."

"You don't get enough exercise, and you have some unhealthy eating habits."

"I enjoy what I eat, or I wouldn't be eating it."

"Don't you want to live longer?"

"My dad lived until he was ninety-three, and I think he pretty much ate anything he wanted, and he sure as hell didn't drink a lot of water."

This made April a little angry. She frowned and said, "I guess if you choose to be ignorant, there isn't anything I can do about it."

"You'd be guessing right."

April looked back at her book for a moment, and then she said, "I bet I'll outlive you."

"Have at it," I said. Her statement didn't bother me at all. Outlive me? Heck, I never did want for me to be the last one to go.

We'd have a conversation like this every time April was done with a chapter, and I knew from experience what was going to happen when we got home. She'd start buying only the book-recommended foods for us to eat, and she'd tell me that if I wanted to poison my body with other less-healthy foods, I could go and do my own damn grocery shopping. Of course, I would have no desire to go to a grocery store, so I would eat what she served. This annoying behavior would go on for a month or two, or maybe three, until April grew tired of eating her hamster food and drinking water—until we went back to our old routine. I knew she'd grow weary of the whole thing and give in because this is what happened every time April read one of these inane books. The last time she read one, she had us eating a steady diet of grilled fish and steamed vegetables that got old faster than asparagus. Her enthusiasm soon waned, and then she never served fish at all. We haven't had fish for years. In fact, if I remember right, she went to the store and bought a whole new set of pans because she said her old pans now reeked of smelly fish, and the scent was tainting everything good that she tried to cook.

While we were on our vacation, we met a couple named Frank and Elaine. They were from Georgia, and Frank owned a chain of restaurants located in Florida, South Carolina, North Carolina, and Georgia. The restaurants were called Elaine's Kitchen because all the recipes came from Elaine's side of the family. Other than the recipes, I didn't get the impression that Elaine had much to do with the business. Instead she owned a little antique store in Augusta. This interested April, since she had always been a big fan of antiques. We probably had more antique furniture crammed into our house than Elaine had in her little Augusta store. April asked what sort of antiques Elaine sold, and Elaine said, "I stock American pieces, early American all the way to the 1960s."

"The 1960s are considered antique?" I asked.

"They're some of our most popular items, especially with younger buyers."

"Jeez, that really makes me feel old."

"You *are* old," April said.

"He doesn't look that old to me," Elaine said, trying to be nice. She smiled at me.

"You should see him without his toupee," April said.

"I don't wear a toupee," I pointed out.

"His hair doesn't look fake to me," Frank said, staring at it with one eye open wider than the other.

"I don't wear a toupee," I said. I gave my hair a tug to prove it was mine. "April just says I wear a toupee to cause trouble. She thinks she's being funny."

"Even if it is a toupee, it doesn't look like it."

"Well, it isn't one."

"I don't think I'm ever going to go bald," Frank said. "It doesn't run in my family."

"His dad is eighty-six," Elaine said. "And the old guy still has all his hair."

"Actually, my dad is eighty-seven."

"No, he isn't. Don't you remember? We just celebrated his eighty-sixth birthday at our house."

"That was his eighty-seventh birthday."

Looking at April and me and talking about Frank as if he weren't there, Elaine said, "He may have all his hair, but his memory is going to pot."

"Bah," Frank said.

"Don't feel bad," I said. "My memory is nothing like it used to be. I used to remember everything. Now I'm lucky if I can remember what I did the day before."

"There's nothing wrong with my memory," Frank said. "And never mind what Elaine says. My dad is eighty-seven."

"I bought Stan a bottle of B12 for his memory," April said. "They're in the medicine cabinet, but he keeps forgetting to take them."

Everyone laughed at this.

"I hear omega-3s also help," Elaine said.

"Stan thinks vitamins and supplements are all a big scam put on by vitamin and supplement companies," April said. "He thinks they're some kind of a conspiracy."

"I don't think they're a conspiracy," I said. "I never said there was a conspiracy. I just think it's a scam."

"He also thinks any non-Western remedies, like acupuncture, are another scam."

"Oh, no," Elaine said. "Acupuncture actually works."

"You believe in it?" I asked.

"I definitely do. I pulled a muscle in my back moving a piece of furniture at the store, and I went to our doctor. He gave me pain pills, which didn't help at all. He also gave me some exercises, and they didn't help either. Then I was talking to one of my customers, and she referred me to an acupuncturist in Atlanta, and finally I went to see him. He had me lay facedown on a table, and he poked little needles all over my rear end and upper thighs, and he had me stay there for about thirty minutes. I had six sessions, and after the sixth session, guess what? My back pain was completely gone. So yes, I know that it works. I'm a believer."

"Why'd he poke the needles in your butt if the pain was in your back?" I asked.

"The human body is complicated," Elaine said.

"I think the guy just wanted her to take her panties off," Frank said.

I was the only one who laughed at this.

"You have such a filthy imagination," Elaine said to her husband, and she punched him half-heartedly.

April and I both liked Frank and Elaine a lot. They were good people. We had dinner with them a couple times, and they were a lot of fun to talk to and eat with. They finally left the resort to return home three days before we were scheduled to leave, and we were sorry to see them go. We exchanged phone numbers, and they told us to call if we were ever in the south. Likewise, I told them to call us if they ever visited Southern California.

After a week of relaxing, and 484 pages into *War and Peace*, April and I left the island for home. We met a man on the plane to LAX named Sam. I was at the window, and April occupied the middle seat. Sam was seated on the aisle, and he was flying by himself. He had been in Jamaica too, but at a hotel in downtown Kingston.

Sam wasn't dressed anything at all like a tourist. I mean, most men who were tourists were dressed in T-shirts, shorts, and sandals. And most returning tourists were tan from time they'd spent in the sun. But Sam wasn't tan at all. Unless you knew he had just been in Jamaica, you would never have guessed he'd been there. His skin was pale and pasty, as if it hadn't seen the sun for years, and he was dressed in a full suit and tie. And he was fat. I don't just mean to say he was a little chunky. The guy barely fit between the armrests of his seat, and it was impossible for him to use the tray table in front of him because it fell on his protruding stomach. His suit was white, and his shirt was even whiter. Even Sam's leather shoes were white, and all of this white contrasted noticeably with his uncombed hair, which was thinning and dyed jet black. He looked like a movie actor, as though he belonged in an old black-and-white Orson Welles film with a big cigar in his mouth. I have no clue whether he actually smoked; I'm just describing what he looked like, and when I see a man like this, I picture a cigar.

"Excuse me," Sam said.

"Yes?" April said.

"Can you do me a favor?"

"I suppose so. What is it?"

"Can you reach down by my feet and grab my bag. I can't get it from here. I'm kind of stuck in here."

"Of course," April said.

"Just pull it by the strap."

April was leaning over, and she had the strap in her hand. "I got it," she said.

"Just pull it up here."

April pulled on the strap, and the bag surfaced. It was a black leather satchel covered with zippers. "Here you go," April said.

"Thanks a million," Sam said. He grabbed the bag and set it on his knees. He then opened one of the zippers and felt around inside of the bag with his pudgy hand, finally pulling out a bottle of Pepto-Bismol. He unscrewed the top while we watched. He then noticed us staring at him. "Jamaican food does a number on my stomach," he explained. "I think it's the bacteria."

"Right," I said.

"I don't know how those people eat that shit day after day. They must build up some sort of immunity."

"Were you on a vacation?" I asked.

"On a vacation?" Sam said, laughing. "Hell no. I wouldn't vacation in that shithole if you paid me a million dollars. No, Hawaii is more my cup of tea. I like to keep things American if possible. You can't go wrong if you keep it American."

"Why were you in Jamaica?" April asked.

"Business," Sam said.

"Doing what?"

"I'm in the arts and crafts business. I import arts and crafts."

"That sounds interesting," April said. I don't know if she thought it was interesting or not. Maybe she was just trying to be friendly.

"I suppose if you're not in the business, it might sound interesting."

"Don't you like what you do?"

"It's what I know how to do, so I do it."

"I'm in the box business," I said.

"Then you must know what I mean."

"How do you market your stuff?" April asked. "Do you have a catalog?"

"Not anymore," Sam said. "Catalogs are out. We now have a website. Everything is done on the internet."

"Is there much money in it?" I asked.

"I make enough."

"Do you sell those wood carvings?" April asked. "We went to some crafts markets. I noticed Jamaicans do a lot of wood carvings."

"Sure," Sam said. "Wood carvings, handbags, dolls, all kinds of jewelry and clothing, and those calabash doodads."

"Calabash?"

"It's a gourd. Jamaicans make all sorts of crap out of them. They're very popular."

"Can I ask you a question?" I asked.

"Sure," Sam said. He took another swig of Pepto-Bismol and then stuffed the plastic bottle back into his bag.

"What got you started in the business?"

"My wife," Sam said.

"She likes the stuff?"

"She used to. We used to travel a lot, and for some reason she fell in love with Jamaica. Me? I haven't much use for the place. But my wife was crazy about it. I was working at the time for a mail order women's undergarment company, and my wife thought it was beneath me. She talked me into quitting my job and pursuing Jamaican arts and crafts. I put together a full-color catalog, and I placed some strategic magazine ads. Slowly but surely, the catalog caught on—barely. We weren't exactly rolling in cash. Then we switched over to the internet, and our costs dropped and our profits soared. By 'soared' I mean that I now had a viable business. I'm now selling the crap worldwide. I'll never get rich, but it's paying the bills."

"Your wife must be happy about this."

"I assume she is. She's getting her alimony on time."

"You divorced?"

"She met another man. Never married him, but I think they still see each other. I think he spends a lot of money on her. I really shouldn't have to pay alimony, but so long as the old broad remains single, I'm going to be on the hook."

"Did you have any children?"

"Three daughters. They all live with me."

Sam closed his eyes and leaned his chair back. I assumed he was done talking and that he wanted to nap, so I also reclined my chair. I looked out the window for a moment, and then I closed my eyes. Soon I fell asleep.

I'm going to tell you about the dream I had. It wasn't a long dream. Or maybe it was, and maybe I only remember a part of it. In the dream, I was back in college, and I was in Professor Gable's class. Professor Gable is real, but the class in my dream was not. I'm not sure what the subject of the class was, or what it was called. All I know is that a had a term paper due, and I had to present the paper to my classmates and a panel of judges. None of the judges' faces were familiar to me. They were all old men, and they were dour and bored. They were sitting at a long wooden desk, and I was standing at the head of the class. Each of the judges had a pad of paper on the desk, and their pens were poised to take notes.

I began to talk, and it wasn't long before the judges began to shake their heads disapprovingly. I realized my efforts were not impressing them. I heard one of them say to the judge sitting next to him, "Haven't we heard this all before?" I realized in my dream that I would have to do something drastic to head off what was sure to be an academic disaster. So, while I was talking, I was planning an alternate move, and I remember thinking to myself, "You are multitasking, Stan. You've never been able to do this." And then it hit me like a ton of bricks while I was talking, and I knew exactly what I had to talk about instead. It would be a revelation. It would be an inspiration. It would be like a bright orange-and-white star in space peeking over the horizon of an otherwise dark planet. There would be beams of light, and waves of warmth, and above all else, my genius would shine.

I said, "What I really want to talk about are the years. You are thinking to yourselves, 'what years?' And I'm going to tell you. I'm talking about *the* years—all the boring printed pages between the bookends, all the soft bread inside the crust, and all the track between the start and finish lines. I'm talking about the vast seas and oceans, the blue skies between the horizons. What are these years made of? They are the years you walked your dog over and over, did your house chores, changed the oil in your car, vacuumed your floors, cleaned your windows, mowed your lawn, and pulled weeds from your flower beds—long, eventless, mindless years, dragging on one after the other, day after ridiculous day. They are the death of your birth and the birth of your death.

"Who would've guessed, right? Your lives all started out so fresh and exciting. The beginning was so hopeful. There was lots of joy, yearning, and anticipation. You learned to build with blocks, to glue things together with sticky white paste, to color pictures using your crayons, and you memorized your ABCs. Then you learned to write within the lines, to read between them, and to string verbs, nouns, adjectives, adverbs, and prepositions into coherent sentences. Then a fire was lit inside of you, and you descended on the opposite sex. Soon you lost your virginity. Then you learned to be something. You learned a vocation, or a craft, or a science, or a musical instrument, and you were taught how to earn a living. You had the right to vote, to drink, and to kill (or be killed) in war. You married the girl of your dreams and got your first job, and you bought your first house. It all happened so fast, and it felt as if the excitement was never going to end. But it did end. Or at least everything suddenly slowed down to a crawl. And then they arrived as if from nowhere—all the years, the years: the great wasteland between saying hello to life and saying goodbye to the world. It is that great, vast, empty, dry, lifeless, steady, deceptive expanse that we call being alive. But it's what is left when the dust settles."

In my dream I looked at the judges, and I wondered if they understood what I was trying to say. Did they have any idea how profound these thoughts were? Did I do a good job explaining them? One of the kids in the class stood up and said, "I will not be a victim."

I looked at this student, and I said with certainty, "Don't fool yourself. We all become victims. It is what life is all about. It is the definition of life. It's the one and only thing you can depend on. It's what the oddsmakers call a sure thing. It's a done deal, and you can bet everything in the world you own on it."

Then I woke up from this dream, and I looked immediately to my right. April and Sam were both sound asleep. The man across the aisle was playing a game on his cell phone, and the woman next to him was reading the latest issue of *People* magazine. The bald guy next to her was deep in thought and looking out the window at all the clouds. The second hands on our wristwatches were ticking gradually forward. The sun outside was getting lower, creeping down toward the horizon, and people in the plane cabin were breathing in and out, and their hearts were beating so that I swore I could hear them. *Thump, thump, tick, tock*, wheezing, killing time.

CHAPTER 27

PAYING SALVADOR

———————— •◦• ————————

Last fall I decided it was finally time for us to renovate the employee restrooms in our Anaheim facility. This building was over twenty years old, and while we'd done work now and again to keep the manufacturing areas up to date, we had done nothing to maintain the restrooms. No one was complaining about it, but I thought it would be a nice gesture to reward our employees for all of their hard work. I made some calls and asked around for the names of some contractors, and I got three. I then called them and set up separate meetings.

The first contractor I met with was a guy named Joey Black. He was a thin, hyper mosquito of a man who I would guess was in his late thirties. Joey and I walked through the restrooms, and he was a geyser of expensive ideas. He wanted to tear out just about everything in sight and replace it with new. I originally imagined a mild face lift, not a freaking heart, liver, and kidney transplant. But I let him base his proposal on all that he had in mind. Maybe it would be affordable. Joey scribbled down four pages of ultra-detailed notes, took precise measurements of everything, and snapped a ton of pictures with his cell phone camera. Finally, he gave me a business card and said, "I'll get back to you within a week to give you a price. It'll be a good price. Things are slow right now, and I could really use the work."

The second contractor who came out was a man named Walt Jacobsen. The guy was huge. He was well over six feet tall, and I'll bet he weighed close to three hundred pounds. It was funny. You'd think a guy who was this enormous and imposing would have a handshake like a grizzly bear, yet when we shook hands, it was like squeezing a warm marshmallow. Another thing that put me at ease about Walt was his accent. He was obviously from the South, and he spoke with a marvelous drawl, calling me "sir" and "Mr. Harper," never using my first name. He told me he'd renovated lots of restrooms in his day. "I can do these puppies with my eyes closed," he said, and I told him I'd prefer that he kept his eyes open. He laughed and said, "Yes, sir, of course I will." Walt wasn't like Joey. He saw no reason to get carried away, and he said he'd put together a proposal that I'd be happy with. I liked where Walt was coming from.

The third and final contractor was a Mexican American man named Salvador Rios. He spoke with a heavy Mexican accent, but I had no trouble understanding him. I asked him what he thought we ought to do, and he said, "You just tell me what to do, and I'll get it done." In other words, it was up to me to spell out the scope of work. This bugged me at first, but then I thought, *What the hell, it's only a pair of restrooms.* I ought to know what I want, and it wasn't like we were designing the lobby of a Fortune 500 company. I walked with Salvador and pointed out the work I wanted to have done. He took notes and measurements, and he snapped a few photos with his cell phone. He then shook my hand, said gracias, and left.

When the three proposals for the work came in, I had a decision to make. Joey Black's price was the highest, almost double the other two prices. So, whether he needed the work or not, he was out of the picture right off the bat. So it came down to choosing between Walt and Salvador, and their prices were within a few hundred dollars of each other. I could either have a guy who was going to call me "sir" or "Mr. Harper" every other sentence, or a guy who began every sentence with *Si*. I thought about it, and then I did what any other college educated business executive would do in a tough situation like this. I reached into my pocket and removed a quarter. It was heads for Walt, and tails for Salvador. I flipped the quarter into the air, and let it fall to the floor.

The winner of the toss was Salvador. I called him on his cell phone and asked him to bring me a contract. "Si," he said. "No problem, boss." The next day he swung by my office with his so-called contract in hand. It was handwritten on a piece of paper and signed by him at the bottom. What it said was, "I will remodel two restrooms. Fifty percent down, and fifty percent on completion." I laughed when I looked it over, and Salvador was expressionless. "Are you changing your mind?" he asked.

I said, "No, but I think I'll write a new contract. I need it to be more specific. I want to know exactly what I'm getting." Salvador said that would be fine, and he said he would come back the following day to sign. In the meantime, I had my secretary type up a detailed contract listing everything we'd talked about doing. When Salvador came back, I handed him the new contract. He didn't even bother to read it. He just glanced at it and signed his name. "I guess we're in business," I said, and Salvador said, "Si, we're in business, boss. All I need is a check, and I'll start work tomorrow night."

I wrote his check, and sure enough he and his crew showed up right on time. They had to do their work in the evenings so it wouldn't interfere with our operations. The first night, I hung around in my office to be sure that nothing went wrong. I did the same thing the second night. By the third night, I felt comfortable leaving Salvador to do his work without having me around, and of course he had my cell phone number in case anything went wrong, or in case he had questions. After a week, Salvador was about halfway done with the project, and as far as I could tell, everything was going fine. Then came day eight. I knew they were laying down the vinyl flooring that night, and I came to check it out in the morning. I couldn't believe what I saw.

Previously, I had Salvador bring in some flooring samples, and I showed them to my employees, asking them to select their colors. I thought they'd appreciate being included in the process, and they did. I took the employees a day to agree on their colors. The men picked out their room, and the women picked out theirs. The men's room was to be dark gray, and the women's was to be a shade of pink. I wrote their choices down on a piece of paper, and I gave it to Salvador. He assured me that the choices were within our original budget, and he proceeded to order the materials. On the night that the flooring was to be installed, I heard nothing from Salvador, so I assumed it all was going fine.

The next morning when I walked into the restrooms, I was quiet at first. I was trying to figure out what to say about what I saw. Salvador looked at me and asked, "What's the matter, boss? You don't like?"

I was a little angry. "No, I don't like at all," I said. "You installed the wrong colors. The men were supposed to get the gray, and the women were supposed to get pink."

There was silence, and then Salvador said, "Well, I was actually wondering about that."

I said, "You were wondering?" Salvador then removed the piece of paper I had given him with the selections, and he unfolded it. Pointing to the paper, he said, "Here's what you told us to do. Gray for the women, and pink for the men." I looked at the paper, and all it had were catalog numbers, one set of numbers for the men, and another for the women.

It turned out that I had made the mistake. I mixed up the catalog numbers while writing them down. Of course, the wrong colors in the restrooms would never do, especially since I had asked our employees pick them out. The flooring would all have to be ripped up, the subfloor would have to be prepared, and the correct flooring would have to be installed. I asked Salvador how much this was going to cost, and I told him he ought to absorb some of the price since anyone knows that you don't put pink flooring in a men's restroom. "I'll see what I can do for you," Salvador said. "But we will have to be paid something for it. I'll just charge you time and materials. I won't add any profit. It will be a lot cheaper that way."

When Salvador was done with his work, we walked through the restrooms. I have to tell you that he did a marvelous job on everything, and I had no complaints about the workmanship. He had done exactly what he said he would do, and the restrooms looked great. He handed me his invoices. I think he was expecting us to write him a check right then and there, but my bookkeeper was not in that day. I told him to come back the next day and that she would pay him what he was owed.

There were two invoices. There was one for the balance due on the original contract, and one for removing and replacing the flooring. I had no problem with paying for the balance due on the original price, but the extra charge for the flooring didn't sit right with me. First of all, I still felt he should've known that pink floors belonged in the women's restroom and not the men's, no matter what. It was a mistake on my part, but he was the professional, and he should have noticed my error and pointed it out. Second, the charge to remove and replace the flooring was ridiculous. He had all the man-hours listed, and the materials listed, and he listed the dump fees to get rid of the old flooring, but it was still way too much. I told my bookkeeper to write Salvador a check for the invoice on the original work, but I told her we weren't going to pay anything for the floors. I told her to explain why to Salvador. Sure enough, Salvador was there to get paid.

I didn't see Salvador that morning. He picked up his check and listened patiently to my bookkeeper explain why only one invoice was being paid. She said he didn't argue. He just took the check and left. Four days later, I received a letter from Salvador's attorney, demanding payment for the second invoice. The letter said that if payment wasn't received in four days, legal action would commence. I was disappointed that it had come to this. An attorney? Really? And maybe I am a little bit of a racist, but I thought it was weird that Salvador even had an attorney. What the heck is a Mexican doing with his own attorney? I sat down and wrote a letter to Salvador and his attorney explaining the reason why I felt I wasn't obligated to pay the flooring invoice. It was a great letter, and in it I firmly held my ground. I thought surely that once the attorney read this letter, he would advise Salvador against taking legal action against me. They would both see that I was going to win this battle and that all Salvador was going to get out of it was a big invoice from his attorney.

I wanted Salvador to read my letter right away, so I decided to hand-deliver it. Salvador's address was on his contract and invoice, so I drove there. He lived in Santa Ana, and I had no trouble finding his house. It was an old ranch-style house in one of Santa Ana's old and poorer neighborhoods. The place needed repairs and a paint job. There were children's toys littered all over the front yard, and the landscaping looked like it hadn't been tended to for years. On the roof was a leak that had been repaired with duct tape and plastic sheeting. In the driveway was a beaten-up Mazda sedan that looked as if it belonged in a junkyard. There was no pickup truck, so I figured Salvador wasn't home. The old Mazda was probably his wife's car. My shiny Mercedes was parked on the street, and as I was about to climb out of the car with my letter, the front door of the house opened. A heavy Mexican woman, who I assumed was Salvador's wife, stepped outside with three rambunctious kids. She said something to them in Spanish, but they ignored her and ran all over the front yard. Then there was a teenage girl in the doorway, and she shouted to Salvador's wife. She said, "Get some ice cream. We're all out of ice cream."

Salvador's wife said, "I will if I have enough money. But things are a little tight."

Jesus, I thought. *They can't even afford ice cream.* I put my car in drive, and I drove off without delivering the letter. I couldn't bring myself to do it. I drove straight to the office, and I went to my bookkeeper's office. I told her to write a check to Salvador for the floors, and I told her to call him.

"Are you sure you want to pay him?" my bookkeeper asked.

"I'm sure of it," I said, and I stepped out of her office. As I walked down the hall to my own office, I passed one of the employees. He thanked me for the new restrooms.

"You're welcome," I said.

"You hired a good contractor."

"Did I?"

"He didn't cut any corners. The guy definitely knew what he was doing."

"Yes," I said. "He was pretty thorough."

A week later I got a call from Lou Mathers. Lou was the friend who had recommended Salvador to me, and he wanted to know if I had hired him.

"I did," I said.

"How'd he do? Isn't he great?"

"He did a good job."

"He does exactly what you tell him to," Lou said. "No bullshit. He just does his job."

"Yes, I said.

"You would use him again, right?"

"Probably," I said.

"I recommend him to all my friends."

Was I being unreasonable, expecting Salvador to notice my mistake on the flooring? I still thought he should've said something about the pink floors. Would I recommend him to my own friends? I guess I would, but the recommendation would come with a warning. I would say, "Be careful what you tell him. He will do exactly what you say. When he says, 'You just tell me what to do, and I'll do it,' he means what he says."

My dad would've been proud of the way I handled Salvador. He was a true believer that the better you treated people, the better you'd eventually be treated by others. He believed in this almost absurdly, meaning he would tie events together that had absolutely nothing to do with each other. Do you know what I mean by this? He would say to me, "Do you see what I mean? It never fails. Treat the world square, and it will be square with you."

Dad used to give me examples. There was, for example, the wallet my dad found on the sidewalk while walking home from school as a boy. He would tell me the story about how he had stopped and picked up the wallet, and inside was a load of cash. He said there was at least a hundred dollars, which was a heck of lot of money when my dad was a kid. Also in the wallet was a driver's license with the address of the man who had lost the wallet. Dad said he took the wallet home that afternoon and hid it in his underwear drawer in his room. He said he then sat on his bed and stared at the drawer for over an hour. A hundred dollars could go a heck of a long way for a ten-year-old kid. It could buy an awful lot, and it could last for months. Dad said he thought about all the things he could buy with the money, and then he said the truth hit him. And the truth was that the wallet did not belong to him. The truth was that, as much as he wanted the money, he had to return the wallet to its owner. Keeping the wallet and the money was suddenly out of the question, and the next morning, my dad walked to the address printed on the driver's license. He knew where the house was, since it was just a street down from where he found the wallet. He gave the wallet to the man. The man thanked my dad and gave him a one-dollar reward.

According to my dad, it was two weeks later that his act of honesty paid off. It was show-and-tell day at school, and Dad had brought in a medal his father had won in World War I. His dad had given the medal to him and told him that he won it for "uncommon bravery." So which medal was it? I don't know. My dad showed it to me when I was a kid, but I remember very little about it. I'm assuming the medal was legitimate, but on the other hand, my grandfather also used to enjoy making things up. The story behind the medal could've been entirely bogus. That's how it was with my grandfather; you never knew if you were being told the truth or getting a tall tale.

Anyway, Dad took the medal to school, and on the way there he was tossing the medal up in the air and catching it as he walked. As he did this, the medal suddenly bounced out of his hand and into the ivy of a neighbor's house. The ivy was thick, and it mercilessly swallowed up the medal so my dad couldn't see where it went. Dad got on his hands and knees, and he searched through the ivy with his hands, but he could not find the medal. He searched through the ivy for at least fifteen minutes before he finally decided he had to leave for school. When show-and-tell time came, he had nothing to show. He didn't dare tell the teacher what had actually happened, so he just told her he had forgot to bring it, and she went on to the next student on her list. That afternoon, my dad said he took the same route home, and when he came to the house with the ivy, he got down on his hands and knees. The afternoon sun was shining into the ivy, and lo and behold, reflecting the sun was the lost medal. Dad said it was like a religious experience, the way the medal was glowing. And my dad new immediately what it was. It was his moral payback for having returned the wallet to the man the week before. It had to be. There was no question about it.

Of course, if you're rational, you know that the wallet had nothing to do with the medal. But my dad truly believed there was a connection. I can't tell you how many times I've heard my dad tell this same story to others. And every time he told it to me, it was as if it were the first time he was telling it. It was mysterious and magical. But it was also as true to life and as plain as the nose on your face.

One month after I paid Salvador, I got a call from a man named Bryce Ackerman. Bryce worked at a large mail-order shoe company in San Diego, and he said he had terrific news for me. Bryce's boss had agreed to sign a contract with our company for over half of its box needs. This was indeed great news. I had been working on Bryce for over a year, trying to sign him up as a customer.

So you tell me. Would I have gotten the call from Bryce if I hadn't paid Salvador's floor invoice? I mean, it seems crazy, but if my dad were alive today, he'd say, "See? What did I tell you? Give the world a break and a good deed, and it will return the favor."

Thinking about all of this, it occurred to me that we each had our own personal version of Arcadia. I mean, it's nice to think that all good deeds are rewarded. It's a sweet, naive, and Arcadian view of life that's impossible for many of us to resist. But it's just an illusion, isn't it? It's not based in fact, and it's not rational. Later, when I asked April what she thought of me connecting Salvador's payment with my new shoebox contract, she said, "What goes around, comes around." I laughed when she said this.

CHAPTER 28

FOOTSTEPS

—— ••• ——

There were the six of us. There was April, me, Jacob, Amy, Zach, and Janet. We were all seated around the table for our annual Christmas prime rib dinner, and we were starting off with our salads. It was great having everyone over for dinner. It was a shame that the grandparents had all passed away. They would've loved it, having the family together.

"So," April said to Amy, "we hear you have a new job."

"I do," Amy said.

"Tell them about it," Jacob said.

"I'm teaching."

"Where at?" I asked.

"At a tutoring school called Aristotle's Pupils."

"I've heard of them," April said

"I'm teaching first graders though twelfth graders. We get all ages."

"What do you teach them?" I asked.

"I help them with their school studies. Most of them need help with math and English. Sometimes other subjects."

"Like philosophy?" Zach asked.

"No philosophy."

"It's a shame that philosophy degree you got never did you much good."

"I guess it was a mistake. Well, it was and it wasn't. But I do like what I'm doing now. It beats the heck out of what I was doing. It beats making coffee, responding to emails, and updating databases all day."

"It sounds very rewarding," I said.

"Too bad you weren't around ten years ago," Zach said. "Jacob could've used your help."

"I didn't need any help," Jacob said.

"Oh, that's right. You were a straight-A student," Zach said sarcastically.

"Getting good grades didn't interest me."

"Well, that was obvious."

Jacob took a breath and then said, "It's funny how you got all those good grades while you were in high school, and how you went to UCLA, and yet you're still an idiot."

"Compared to you, I'm Albert Einstein."

"Hardly," Jacob said.

"Is everyone done with their salads?" April asked, changing the subject. Everyone nodded, and April stood up to collect the salad bowls. Amy and Janet also stood so that they could help April out.

"You boys are in your early twenties, and you still sound like you're back in high school," I said, scolding them.

"Zach started it," Jacob said.

"Really?" Zach said.

"Try to get along," I said. "If not for my sake, for your mom's sake. Seriously, enough is enough. We all came here to enjoy ourselves."

"Here's the prime rib," April said joyfully, bringing the large plate of meat into the room. I could tell she was truly happy. The girls were right behind her, carrying the rest of the dinner.

"Jesus," Zach said. "That looks great."

"It does," I agreed.

"So," Jacob said. "I've got a good one. A guy is sitting in a restaurant with his date, and he ordered prime rib. The waiter shows up with the food, but his thumb is pressed on the guy's prime rib. 'Jeez,' the guy says. 'I really don't want your thumb touching my food.' The waiter looks down at him and says, 'Sir, I suppose you'd rather I let it fall on the floor again?'"

Everyone laughed, and I said, "I suppose you heard that from Hank."

"I did," Jacob said.

"Who's Hank?" Janet asked.

"He's Jacob's mentor at work."

"The guy is a joke-telling machine," I said.

"Have any of you heard of Wagyu?" Zach asked.

"Isn't that a Star Wars character?" Jacob asked.

"Very funny, but no, little brother. I thought at least you would know what it is."

"What is it?" I asked.

"It's Japanese beef."

"I hear their beef is really good," Amy said.

"It's the best in the world," Zach said. "And it's as expensive as hell. Those people took their beef very seriously. When the calves are born, they're not just numbered. They're given actual names and birth certificates."

"Birth certificates?"

"That's so every Wagyu stead can be traced back by its bloodline. They're fed special diets throughout their lives, and they're cared for like children. They're all raised in barns, and they even get warm jackets to wear when the weather is too cold."

"Too funny," I said.

"Have you ever tried a Wagyu steak?" Amy asked.

"Not yet, but I intend to. It would be worth taking a trip to Japan just to eat one—one that hasn't been frozen, I mean. You can find them in the US if you look around, but they've all been frozen."

"All of them?" Jacob asked.

"I think so," Zach said.

"Remember John's Steakhouse?" I asked

"Oh, yeah, John's," Zach said. "I used to love that place."

"Are they still in business?" I asked.

"I don't know," Zach said.

"They probably are," April said.

"You'd always order a salad," Zach said to Jacob. "A salad in a steakhouse."

"Yeah, well, those were different times," Jacob said.

"You wouldn't eat a steak if your life depended on it."

Jacob laughed and then said, "We should go there. I mean, if they're still in business."

Everyone was quiet for a moment, working on their food. Then I said, "Jacob, did you ever go to visit Mrs. Hardin?"

"I didn't," Jacob said.

"Why not?"

"I don't know."

"I think she'd really like to see you."

"Who's Mrs. Hardin?" Amy asked.

"She was one of my teachers."

"She liked Jacob a lot."

"Remember Fred the toaster?"

"Of course I do."

"Who is Fred the toaster?" Amy asked.

"He was the reason I didn't win the science fair."

"The judges were just shortsighted," I said.

"They were just doing their jobs," Jacob said. "You guys should've encouraged me to do something different. I could've won that competition."

"In my book you won," I said.

"In your book—right."

"Jacob was always good for a laugh," Zach said. "Remember when he was on TV? He was claiming that 9/11 happened because of the Vietnam War."

"That's not what I was claiming."

"That's what everyone thought."

"I didn't know you were on TV," Amy said.

"It's ancient history."

"We should change the subject," April said.

"Fine," Zach said. "Anyone know any good riddles?"

"Riddles?" I asked.

"I know one," Amy said. "What do throw out when you need to use it, and bring back in when you're done with it?"

"An anchor," Zach said.

"You've heard that one."

"I have," Zach said.

"It could be a fishing line," Jacob said.

Zach thought about this, and then said, "You're right; that works too."

"I've got another one," Amy said.

"Fire away," Zach said.

"David's father has three sons. The first son is Snap, and the second son is Crackle. What's the name of the third son?"

"Pop," Janet said.

"Nope. Guess again."

"The third son is David," Jacob said. He paused. "I've got one. How do you make the number seven even without any addition, subtraction, multiplication, or division?"

No one had an answer for this.

"How do you do it?" Zach asked.

"You drop the s," Jacob said.

"Ha, that's good," Janet said.

"Mr. Caldwell told me that one. Do you remember Mr. Caldwell?"

"The hockey coach?" Zach asked

"Yeah, the guy that made his son give me back that Gordie Howe puck. He used to give us riddles while we were putting on our hockey gear."

"Whatever happened to that puck?" I asked.

"I still have it somewhere," Jacob said.

"So many memories," I said. "I forgot all about that hockey puck."

"Those were great years," Zach said.

Jacob didn't say a word, but I knew what he was thinking. At least I thought I did. He was thinking, 'If those were such great years, why did I wind up getting my wrists sewn up, and why did they take me to a mental ward, and why was I locked up for those months, and why was everyone treating me as though I'd fall completely apart if the slightest wrong thing was said to me?'

"Jacob," April said, "you'll never guess who I ran into last week."

"Who?" Jacob asked.

"Veronica Schaffer."

"You're kidding."

"I hardly recognized her."

"Who is she?" Amy asked.

"An old girlfriend," Jacob said. "I only went with her for a few months."

"Where'd you run into her?" I asked.

"At the nail salon. She was getting her nails done."

"How'd she look?"

"She looked good. She has two kids, a boy and a girl. Can you imagine that? Two kids already? She brought them to the salon with her."

"I wonder who she married."

"An attorney," April said. "She said he's fourteen years older than her."

"Jesus," I said.

"I wonder if she's still into astrology," Jacob asked.

"I don't know. You know, I barely recognized her. I mean, she still weighs about the same, and she hasn't grown, but she looked so much older. Not like she's aging quickly, but just more mature, like a woman."

"She was an odd-looking girl," I said.

"She said she and her husband lived up Marin County and that she was down here with her kids to visit her parents. I think it's so interesting how kids grow up. She was such an interesting girl."

"She's awful young to have kids," Jacob said.

"Too young," I agreed.

"They were very well behaved."

"She probably had them under one of her magic spells," I said.

"She wasn't into witchcraft," Jacob said. "She was into astrology."

"It's all the same thing," I said.

"Actually, it isn't," Jacob said.

"Sure it is."

"You don't even know what you're talking about," April said to me.

"I knew a girl in high school who was into all that weird stuff," I said. "She threatened to turn me into a toad. I was teasing her in our English class, and she didn't like it. She said I was ignorant. But am I a toad? No. Have I ever been a toad? Hardly."

Everyone was quiet for a moment, eating. Then Jacob said, "I've got a good story for you guys."

"Let's hear it," Janet said.

"Is it about one of your old girlfriends?" Amy asked. She was still a little miffed about having learned about Veronica.

"No, no," Jacob said. "And just for the record, I didn't have that many girlfriends."

"Go on," I said. "Let's hear your story."

"Do you guys know who Carl Swenson is?"

"Never heard of him," Zach said.

"He's a big deal in the real estate business—at least he is in Orange County. If you keep your eyes open, you'll see his signs everywhere."

"I think I might've seen a few," I said.

"The guy owns a ton of property. Mostly commercial stuff. Mostly retail centers. He inherited a pile of money when his parents passed away, and he has invested it in property all over the county."

"So what about him?" Zach asked.

"I sold a shopping center to him."

"Where?" I asked.

"In Costa Mesa. It was a nice center, but the main tenant space was empty, so he got a good deal on the center. He had a tenant who was interested in the vacant space, and as soon as he bought the center, he started working on this tenant. After a couple of months, the tenant agreed to move in. But there were a few things that needed done to the space before the tenant would sign the lease. And they needed to get done right away. Carl asked me if I knew the name of a contractor who could help him out, and it just so happened that I had the perfect guy for him. In fact, it was the contractor who had built the center in the first place. This contractor's name was Dan Wolfe, and I called Dan up and introduced him to Carl. Dan convinced Carl that the cheapest way to get the improvements done would be at cost plus a profit. It wasn't a lot of work, but it needed to be done immediately. Dan's proposal seemed fair to Carl, and they began work right away. A week later, the work was done, and Dan met with Carl to get paid. And this is where the story gets good."

"What happened?" I asked.

"Carl asked Dan how much the final bill came to, and Dan said, 'Let's just make it an even twelve.' Carl opened his checkbook and said, 'That seems like a lot of money.' Then Dan said, 'It really isn't. I could've charged you a lot more.' Carl then wrote a check and handed it over. I got a call from Dan the next day, and he asked me if I thought he should deposit the check."

"Why would he ask that?" Zach asked.

"When Dan said to make it an even twelve, Carl thought he meant twelve thousand. Dan only meant twelve hundred.

"So Carl wrote him a check for twelve thousand dollars?" Zach asked, laughing.

"As God is my witness," Jacob said.

"What did you tell him to do?"

"I told him to deposit it."

"Jesus," I said.

"I told him if the work was worth twelve thousand to Carl, then that was fair."

"That's awful," Amy said.

"Carl is loaded." Jacob said. "It was no skin off his nose. And Dan needed the money."

"I think it's hilarious," Zach said.

"Just remember," April said. "What goes around, comes around."

"I know people like to say that," Jacob said. "It makes us feel like things all work out in the long run. But the truth is that what goes around often doesn't come around at all. I've seen people do all sorts of good things, only to get screwed over. And I've seen people do a lot of bad things, only to get rewarded. I hate to say it, but that's life, Mom. That's the way it works in the real world."

"Jacob's right," Zach said.

"Oh, I just thought of another one," Janet said.

"Another what?" Zach said.

"A riddle."

"Let's hear it."

"Two girls who have the same parents were born at the same hour of the same day, of the same month, but they are not twins? How can this be?"

"They have to be twins," Amy said.

"But they're not," Janet said.

"I know the answer," Jacob said.

"What is it?"

"They weren't born in the same year."

"That's the right answer," Janet said.

"I've got a good one," Jacob said. Hang on a second. I have to say this just right." Jacob thought for a moment and then continued, "I am the beginning of the end. I am the end of time and space. I am essential to creation. What am I?"

Everyone thought for a moment.

"Carbon?" Zach said.

"No, not carbon."

"God?" April said.

"No, not God either. Too funny, but you people are on the wrong track."

"This riddle doesn't even make sense," Amy said. What does it mean to be the beginning of the end?"

"It'll make sense when you hear the answer."

"So what is the answer?"

"Do you all give up?

"We give up," Zach said.

"It's the letter e."

"Oh, hell," Zach said. "One of us should've figured that out."

"Who told you that one?" I asked.

"A guy at work."

"Is that all you guys do all day?" I asked. "Sit around and tell each other jokes and riddles."

Jacob laughed. "Not exactly."

"I've got a question," Zach said to Jacob. "What did you guys ever do with that restaurant space in Orange that smelled like sewage? Did you find out where the smell was coming from?"

"We got prices from a few contractors to sawcut into the concrete floor and dig up the waste line to look for the cause of the smell. But none of them would guarantee that they could stop the smell. And their prices were outrageous. So we decided to nix the idea of ever putting a restaurant there, since that obviously would never work. We tried to think of a tenant who wouldn't mind the smell once in a while. Then one of the other guys in the office said, "How about postal boxes? You could rent them out for cheaper than the US Post Office, and no one would give a damn about the smell, especially if it only smelled bad now and then." It was a great idea, right? I ran it past Sid."

"Who's Sid?" Janet asked.

"Sid Sanchez. He's the owner of the building. At first, he wasn't crazy about the idea. Then he thought about it for a few days, and he came to his senses. He called me and said, "By God, I think your idea will work. We can fill the goddamn place with postal boxes and rent them all out. Then we'll sell the business."

"Why not keep the business?"

"Sid is in the business of owning real estate, not small businesses."

"So did the plan work?"

"It worked like a charm. The space is now being leased by a man named Charles Lang, who bought the business from Sid. All the boxes are rented. In fact, they have a waiting list a mile long. At the low rates charged for the boxes, the place could smell like the ass end of a hippopotamus and no one would care."

"Did you tell Sid about the guy in your office who gave you the idea?"

"Are you kidding?"

"Didn't he want a cut?"

"Of what?"

"Of your commission."

"It wasn't that much of a commission. It was more just the idea of doing something to help out Sid. I think he appreciated what I did."

"Which equates to more business from him?"

"Something like that."

As everyone at the table continued to talk and eat their prime rib, I fell into a kind of a daze. I was thinking about Jacob and how far he'd come. And I was thinking about what he had left behind. I should've been pleased, but I also felt a little sad.

I don't think Jacob has ever realized how close I've always felt to him. When I found him in that pool house shower on that grim afternoon, wet and naked, bleeding under the running shower water, turning cold, his heart beating a million miles a minute—it may as well have been me. Jacob's joy has always been my joy, and his despair has always been my despair. And there we were, throbbing, aching, bent over in pain, with the piss-warm shower water running down our faces and shoulders, our blood mingling and staining the white tile floor and running to the drain. There was nothing to hear but the rush of water and the sound of two lives slowly pulling away. No, I'll never forget that afternoon—the sorrow, regret, and pain. It wasn't just Jacob. It was me. It was both of us, the two of us, father and son, son and father, saying hello and goodbye in the very same breath. We were falling together. For that moment in time we were inconsolably one.

And now we were eating prime rib with the family, telling jokes and riddles. I think Jacob was truly happy. I think Amy made him happy, and I think life made him happy. He was taking his ride until the end of the line, wherever that turned out to be. And on the way there, he would celebrate Christmas with his family, close some more real estate deals, make some new friends, wash his cars on the weekend, work in his yard, replace the burned-out bulbs in his house, exercise, diet when he gained weight, watch American Idol, heat up Pop-Tarts for breakfast in the morning, buy April flowers on Mother's Day, make love to Amy, and maybe have a couple kids of his own.

I should be happy for my son, and I am. But I also miss him. Do you know Jacob hasn't written a single poem, short story, play, or anything else since that awful afternoon in the pool house shower? Well, not that I know of. There's been nothing new to add to the box I keep hidden away in my study closet. The last thing I added to the box was the poem written by Dr. Trill, and Jacob didn't even write it. He was just told to read it over and over. "Read it over and over," the doctor said, "until the message sinks in—until you can see life for what it is and not for what you wish it could be. Until you realize Arcadia is not a place on a map but a place that never was, and isn't, and never will be."

I'd like to end this story with a haiku written by the famous Japanese poet and philosopher Akihiro Kobayashi. This poem was written in the late 1800s but could easily have been written a week ago. It goes as follows:

> We laugh at the foal
> Balancing on unsure legs
> Then it runs away

"Stan?" April said. I looked at her, and she was smiling and staring at me. In fact, everyone at the table was looking at me. There was a piece of medium-rare prime rib stuck to the end of my fork.

"Yes?" I said.

"Are you with us?"

"I'm here."

"Where did you go?"

"I was just thinking."

"About what?" Jacob asked.

"Just some things," I said.

"You should've seen the look on your face," April said. "Your brow was furrowed."

"My brow?"

"I thought he was choking on a piece of fat," Zach said. "Does anyone know how to do that thing?"

"The Heimlich maneuver?"

"Yeah, that."

"I know how it's done," Jacob said.

"So do you know the answer?" Zach asked me.

"The answer to what?"

"The riddle I just told."

"What was it again? Tell me again. I'm afraid I wasn't paying attention."

"The more of me you take, the more you leave behind," Zach said. "What am I?"

I'd heard this one before. Of course, the correct answer was footsteps.

Footsteps. They were always taking me forward, one stride after the other. And it now seemed that forward steps were the answer to everything, anything, and all that ever mattered. I would not look back.

Made in the
USA
Middletown, DE